Tay leaned in close.

*L*izzie was starting to panic, as his face seemed awfully close to hers, his eyes even more intense than usual. "You have to tell me what you want," Lizzie repeated.

"Is that ever even possible? Especially, Lizzie, for people like us who either don't know what we want, or know that what we want is impossible?"

"Nothing's impossible," she insisted.

He leaned in closer.

Or maybe she had leaned closer.

It was impossible to know, impossible to breathe.

Their lips touched.

A light kiss. Still, it set Lizzie on fire. She was too shocked to move. It was more a touching than a kiss. A connection. And yet, she'd never felt anything quite so intense as this man's lips on hers. She let her eyes flutter closed and her thoughts fell away and she felt him, his intensity a physical vibration through her just like she knew it would be . . .

HOW *Sweet* IT IS

SOPHIE GUNN

FOREVER

NEW YORK   BOSTON

Copyright © 2011 by Diana Holquist
Excerpt from *Teaser Title TK* copyright © 2011 by Diana Holquist
All rights reserved. Except as permitted under the U.S. Copyright Act of 1976, no part of this publication may be reproduced, distributed, or transmitted in any form or by any means, or stored in a database or retrieval system, without the prior written permission of the publisher.

Book design by Giorgetta Bell McRee

Forever
Hachette Book Group
237 Park Avenue
New York, NY 10017
Visit our website at www.HachetteBookGroup.com.

Forever is an imprint of Grand Central Publishing. The Forever name and logo is a trademark of Hachette Book Group, Inc.

Printed in the United States of America

First Printing: January 2011

10 9 8 7 6 5 4 3 2 1

*To all my good friends, the original Enemy Club,
who swear to tell the truth, the whole truth, and
nothing but the truth. And then, naturally,
break out the wine . . .*

Acknowledgments

Thank you endlessly to my first readers, Ellen Hartman and Leslie Daniels; to the unbelievably patient and supportive folks at Grand Central Publishing, especially Michele, who is, as usual, right again (darn it!); to my agent, Natasha; and especially, to my family for eating so much cold pizza while I worked on this manuscript. I owe you all my undying gratitude.

HOW
Sweet
IT IS

CHAPTER

1

$\mathcal{F}$or over a week the envelope sat on the dining room table unnoticed, buried under a stack of birdseed catalogues and household bills like a bomb waiting to go off.

Life went on around it. Work, grocery shopping, and housework for Lizzie Bea Carpenter. School, babysitting, and friends for her fourteen-year-old daughter, Paige.

Tick tick tick.

Normal life. A good life. Maybe not great, but fine. Galton, New York, *centrally isolated,* the locals liked to say, wasn't exactly the kind of town where momentous things happened.

Until Saturday, September 8, 8:22 in the evening, when Lizzie's world turned upside down.

"Who do we know in Geneva?" Paige asked, coming into the kitchen, holding up an envelope covered in foreign stamps. It had been Paige's turn to clean the dining room after dinner. She'd swept the crumbs under the threadbare Turkish rug, pushed around the ragtag assortment of antique chairs until they looked more or less orderly, and tossed most of the pile of mail, including an ominous-looking letter from her middle school, into the overflowing recycling bin with a quick, guilty second glance.

Lizzie turned off the faucet, put down the mac-and-cheese pan she was scrubbing in the sink, saw the handwriting, and said, "Ratbastard." She backtracked quickly, her throat constricting. "I mean, Geneva? Ha! No one. Let me see that." She grabbed for the letter, but Paige was too quick. Lizzie's heart was pounding. Her throat was dry with dread.

"Who?" Paige tore the letter open while dodging around the counter.

"Don't," Lizzie said, but the word came out listlessly because she knew it was too late. Everything was about to change, and there was nothing she could do to stop it.

"It's addressed to both of us," Paige said, unfolding the single sheet.

Lizzie didn't know that she knew anyone in all of Europe, much less Geneva, but apparently she did, because she recognized that handwriting at a glance, even after fourteen years. Her traitorous body knew it, too, and was responding as if it were still sixteen and stupid. This couldn't be happening. *Oh, Paige*...

Paige read the letter. She stopped, frozen, on the other side of the counter. "Oh. I see," she said, letting the letter fall to the counter. "Ratbastard." She said it as if it were an ordinary name like Steve or Joe.

Lizzie wiped her hands on the dishrag, trying to look like a mother in control. "Well. He could have changed," she said as carefully as she could. "We shouldn't jump to any conclusions."

"He wants to come here, Mom."

Lizzie cleared her throat. "That's lovely," she managed to get out.

"On Christmas Day."

"Ratbastard! Sorry. Lovely. Hell." *Nice work.* Lizzie needed a few minutes to pull herself together. She needed to sit and to breathe and definitely not to cry. She wanted to hit something but she couldn't. Not now, in front of Paige. At least, not anything that would break. Not that there was much left to break in their kitchen, which was clean, but failing. Two burners were dead on the stove. The icemaker had quit eleven months ago. The radio worked when you banged it. Hard. Couldn't do much damage in here, even if she tried.

But that letter had done damage.

Paige looked as if she'd already been pummeled. Her face was blank and pale. Her new black, chin-length Cleopatra haircut made her face seem rounder and her brown eyes even huger than usual. She looked like an eight-year-old and an eighteen-year-old simultaneously, a special effect in a bad after-school movie about girls growing up too fast.

Lizzie picked up the letter. She imagined Ratbastard walking into a store and asking for the stationery that screamed *I'm rich and arrogant* the loudest. The cream-colored paper was heavy and stamped with a fancy watermark. The handwriting was neat, the tone straightforward. He spelled realize like a Brit, even though he had been born and bred in Michigan—*I realise this is out of the blue. But I'd like to meet my daughter. I'll be in the States over the holidays, and will stop by then. Twelve o'clock Christmas day? I hope she'll be willing to see me.* There was no return address, no phone number, no e-mail contact, nothing but a breezy signature—*Ethan Pond*. Then, in parentheses, *Dad*.

Lizzie excused herself, climbed the stairs, turned on the water in the bathroom sink to muffle the noise, and threw up.

Ethan Pond, Paige's father, the boy who'd changed Lizzie's life forever in the back of his Lexus during her senior year of high school, was coming back.

This was a matter for the Enemy Club.

CHAPTER

2

$\mathcal{J}$ay Giovanni sipped his coffee, wishing he could taste it. It was 7:27 in the morning, and he was hunkered down on a stool in a chrome-and-mirrors diner in a nowhere town waiting for Candy Williams, the woman who hated him most in this vast, frozen world.

Was this bottom?

A hum of activity from four women at the end of the counter distracted him from his dark thoughts. The buzz grew until it exploded into shouts.

"Ratbastard."

"Pondscum."

"Ninnyhammer."

"Ninnyhammer?"

"What's wrong with 'ninnyhammer'?"

"Fuckface is better."

"You know I won't say that word."

"Face? Why not? We all have one. C'mon. Just once? For Lizzie? This is Ethan Pond we're talking about."

"He's a fartface, Liz."

"Oooh! She said 'face'!"

A wrinkled, gray-haired man on the stool next to Tay nodded to indicate the women. "That's the Enemy Club."

Was the man talking to him? Tay looked around, hoping someone else was nearby.

No such luck.

The old man went on. "I come in Wednesday mornings just to watch them." The man's baseball hat read *John Deere Tractors*. He was missing two fingers on his right hand. These two facts combined rocked Tay's already rocky stomach. The man lowered his voice as if telling a juicy secret. "They used to be the worst of enemies. Now they're the best of friends. But friends with a difference. They tell each other the truth, the whole truth, and nothing but the truth the way only natural-born enemies can. I could sell tickets!"

Natural-born enemies.

The words stuck in Tay's gut. If any words described his relationship to Candy—to the world in general—those about nailed it. He wondered if the Enemy Club had openings.

The old man elbowed Tay good-naturedly, then chomped into his chocolate-covered doughnut with pink sprinkles. "But now look at them. Best friends forever. Right, Lizzie Bea?"

The waitress had come down the counter to top off their coffees. "Best *enemies* forever. Leave that poor man alone, Mr. Zinelli." She poured more coffee into Tay's mug, even though he'd barely touched it. "Ignore him."

One of the women stuffed a cream-colored piece of paper into a matching envelope and held it above her head. The address was handwritten, *Elizabeth and Paige Carpenter, 47 Pine Tree Road*. "I say we burn it."

The waitress hurried back down the counter. "Put that lighter away, Jill!"

Tay tried not to watch, but he couldn't tear his eyes away. Were they really enemies? They certainly didn't look like they had anything in common, but they were completely at ease, the way they moved, touched, threatened to burn each other's possessions.

The old man leaned in close, pointing as he spoke. "The princess, the oddball, and the brainiac. Oh, and the waitress—she's the good girl gone bad. All leaders of their packs back in the day. Look close, and you'll see. They don't look like normal friends, right?"

Tay didn't need a close look; it was obvious they didn't have anything in common without a second glance.

Jill, the woman with the lighter, was a bottle blonde, her hair pulled back in a brain-pinching bun, her earlobes dripping with diamonds. She drank from a takeout coffee cup that read *Brewhaha*, the hopping, trendy coffee joint across the street that Tay had gladly passed by for the quiet neglect of the diner. *Friends don't let friends bring takeout to other friends' restaurants.*

A pixie of a woman in an orange flouncy sweater, coral beads, and short-cropped, orangish hair snatched the blonde's lighter and slipped it into her canvas bag. Her nose was covered in orange freckles.

"I have to go," a third woman in itchy-looking tweed said, obviously annoyed by the other two's jostling. She was short, her brown shoes nowhere near reaching the ground. How she'd gotten herself up on the stool, Tay couldn't imagine. The muscles in his arms twitched, jonesing to help her down.

He clenched his teeth until the urge passed.

Ever since the accident, he'd been like this, possessed by the soul of a souped-up Boy Scout, needing to jump in and save the world, or at least the part in front of him. When the urge hit him, it was like an epileptic fit, unexpected and uncontrollable.

As if a million good deeds would even out his karma.

Not that he believed in karma.

Or, in his case, in the possibility of even.

Hell, he had no idea what he believed in anymore.

"Wait, you can't go, Georgia," the waitress said. "Not yet." The other women treated the waitress with deference, as if she were the leader of the group, or maybe it just seemed that way because she was standing, moving, while they sat and watched. Tendrils of wavy brown hair had escaped her bun, softly framing her round cheeks. Her waitress uniform was simple, with no necklace or earrings or any adornment to make it appear anything more than what it was. Minimal makeup, just a bit of faded color on her lips, a touch of blush on her cheeks. *The truth, the whole truth, and nothing but the truth...*

The blonde caught him staring at the waitress, so he trained his eyes back on his coffee. The old man had taken up with his doughnut, and the Enemy Club quieted to a low murmur. Tay tried to focus on his situation. He glanced at his watch: 7:28. Candy would be here in two minutes.

Or not.

The women's conversation drifted in and out until the freckled one's calm tone silenced the others so that Tay could hear clearly, no matter how hard he tried not to. "Lizzie, if you want something, you have to face it, admit it, then wish for it with all your soul. That's how the universe works. It will hear your wish, and if it's sincere, it will answer."

The waitress crossed her arms, leaned back against the service counter, and said, "Don't get me started on the universe granting wishes. I love you, Nina, but that's nuts."

Tay tried not to smile. He liked that waitress.

"But if it could?" the freckled one persisted.

"Then I wish for the perfect man."

Despite the blackness that was numbing him, Tay stilled, hoping to hear better.

The blonde said, "No such thing," and they all exploded into an uproar over the possibility of a half-decent man ever appearing in Galton, New York.

The waitress held up her hand for silence. "The perfect man is one who'll show up once a week, fix stuff around my house, and then split. That, O great universe, is what I wish for."

And they were off again. Tay looked down at his mug, trying to clear his head of waitresses and wishes. Candy would walk through those doors any second.

...if you want something, you have to face it, admit it, then wish for it with all your soul...

He agreed with the waitress—nuts. But he couldn't help himself.

He wished he wasn't in this Podunk college town in the middle of nowhere, waiting for Candy to rip him to shreds.

But that was a coward's wish, so he tried again: He wished with the few pieces left of his soul that Candy would show up and take the money and then maybe, just maybe, he could taste his coffee again, feel the cold, sleep at night.

The old man was staring intently at him, his gray eyes narrowed. Tay wondered for a sickening second if he'd said his wish out loud.

The blonde threw her arms out and proclaimed, "I wish for the perfect man—one with good pecs!" She lowered her voice and looked right at Tay. "And beautiful green eyes." He concentrated on the pies in the case across from him. Cherry, key lime, banana cream. There was a time when he'd have been plenty interested in a beautiful blonde dripping in diamonds eyeing him as if he was dinner, a time when he'd have been completely at home shooting the shit with a friendly old man over coffee and doughnuts. But now, he just wanted to be out of here and on his way back to Queens. This small town where everyone knew a person's business wasn't his kind of place. Tay could imagine what the old man would whisper about him to some stranger the next stool over. *There's that man who was in that tragic accident. The woman in the other car died, you know. He hasn't been the same since. I come in every Wednesday just to keep an eye on him...could sell tickets...*

Seven-thirty-one. Tay watched the women joke and cajole, and despite his worry, a tiny sliver of hope snuck into his consciousness. *Enemies can be forgiven, can become friends.* There was a connection between the four women that mesmerized him. The freckled one touched the blonde lightly on the shoulder and secretly passed her the lighter under the counter. The tweedy one sloshed her coffee distractedly and the waitress wiped it up without a word. They all watched the waitress carefully, warily, concern evident in the way they licked their lips, pursed their mouths, caught and held one another's eyes. They leaned in across the counter that separated them from her as if it was all they could do to keep from leaping over it and whisking her away to safety.

Was it really possible to befriend your enemies? What did it take? Telling the truth, the whole truth, and nothing but the truth? *I am Dante Giovanni. I went through a red light and hit another car. No excuses, just a dumb accident, a distracted moment that I can never take back. A woman died. There's no way to make it right. No way to fix it. But she left behind a daughter who needs help. I will find a way to help that girl.*

For an instant, the smell of coffee, eggs, and toast hit Tay full on.

Then Candy walked in the door, and his senses went dry.

CHAPTER

3

$\mathcal{I}$t was shocking to see Candy in person after carrying around her picture clipped from the paper for so many months. Not that Tay had expected that she'd be made up of a million tiny printer's dots or still dressed in black funeral mourning. But he hadn't expected her to look so normal in her skinny jeans and layers of tight shirts, like every other college student in the town.

Only the hatred in her eyes signified otherwise.

Candy eyed Tay as if he was the devil. Hell, she had probably only seen him in his black-and-white mug shot–like picture in the paper, too. He had come to her mother's funeral, but he had stood in the back under an umbrella in the pouring rain, his hat pulled low. The etiquette of coming to the funeral of the stranger he'd killed escaped him. Emily Post wouldn't go near that one with a ten-foot pole.

Candy stiffened and marched toward him, her waist-length black hair swinging. She sat on the stool on the other side of him. The old man, fortunately, had finished up the stray crumbs of his doughnut and moved off, waving good-bye to everyone in the place.

Candy stared straight ahead at the pies in their refrigerated case behind the counter.

"What do you want?" she asked.

He felt her hatred crashing off the Formica, shaking the doughnuts under their glass dome, vibrating the chrome napkin holders. He figured he had about two minutes before the whole place came crashing down around him. He had known this would be hard, but he hadn't guessed he'd feel paralyzed. He hadn't planned to be abrupt. He had wanted to hear her story, to tell her his.

I'm sorry. So very, very sorry...

But he saw now that his fantasy of a connection was just that—fantasy. *Forgiveness. Wishes. Enemies becoming friends.* Softheaded nonsense. He nodded at the bag at his feet. "Enough to get you through school. Take it. It's yours." His grip tightened on his coffee mug until his fingers were white.

Candy glanced down at the bag, her long black hair skittering off her back like a waterfall. She shook her hair back into place. "Is that what this is all about? Money? You're such an asshole."

"I wish it had been me," he said.

"That makes two of us," Candy said. Her ice-blue eyes met his and the effect was suffocating. Tay looked down the counter at the Enemy Club disbanding, leaving behind the waitress and her letter. She looked almost as mad as Candy, scrubbing an invisible spot on the counter with gusto. Maybe it wasn't as easy as the old man made out to hang with your natural-born enemies.

"I won't take your money," Candy said. "I don't want it."

There was nothing else to say. Candy was a kid, and he didn't know a thing about kids. What he did know was that she needed the money and he had it to give. He tossed a five-dollar bill onto the counter and made for the exit.

"Hey! You forgot your bag," Candy called after him.

"It's your bag." He was five steps from the door.

"I'm going to throw it off a cliff," she called. "Into a gorge."

Four, three, two, one...

"I don't want your stupid money! I only came here to tell you to leave me alone or I'll call the cops—"

The closing door cut off the rest of her words. He was outside in the crisp fall day and he could breathe again.

A woman in a blue jacket searched her pockets for change for the meter. A fit, determined mother pushed an oversize baby carriage past. Two college students in Galton U. sweatshirts walked together, ignoring each other while they texted.

Tay's red truck waited by the curb, his sheltie, Dune, in the driver's seat. His cat, White, was curled up in the sunspot on the dash.

Well, the cat wasn't exactly his.

The beast had inexplicably taken a liking to him and Dune at a rest stop off Route 81, or was it Route 79? The roads had become a blur. Or rather, since he drove so slowly after the accident, a never-ending asphalt river of curses from angry drivers or offers of mechanical assistance from kinder, curious ones.

The cat didn't mind his slow driving.

But Tay minded the cat. He'd expected the creature to

be gone somewhere around Binghamton. Instead, it refused to leave, and to Tay's dismay, he had developed a maddening superstition around the animal—that she'd leave when his debt was paid off. It was ridiculous, he knew. Just another sign that he was losing his grip, trying to find meaning where there was just a mangy, flea-bitten cat just as he was trying to find meaning in four women at the end of a diner counter, or in a terrible, inexplicable tragedy on a dry road at four on a sunny afternoon almost a year ago to the day.

He wished he could give it a rest. Go back to his old life taking care of the two apartment buildings he used to own in Queens. But it ate at him like a cancer, from the inside out.

Anyway, what was left of his property was gone. Or rather, after the sale and paying off the mortgage and lawyers and expenses, then giving a hefty sum away to charities, causes, vagrants, and unsuspecting people who caught his eye, what was left of his livelihood was on the shiny floor of the diner in a duffel bag. He'd saved his whole life to buy those properties, had hoped soon to buy the building next door. But then the accident happened, and he lost his taste for business, for expansion, for success—for any kind of happiness. His easy success with women, with business, with life in general suddenly seemed wrong. It was impossible to enjoy anything anymore without a blackness rising in him that canceled out any pleasure.

"Go." He held the driver's door open for the cat. "I gave her the money, so scram."

Dune looked stricken.

"No, not you." He scratched Dune between the ears.

"You're stuck with me, buddy. Oh, don't look at me that way. You're the one who should have chased her off in the first place." Dune was a herding dog, and instead of chasing White, he seemed determined to keep her close. Talk about natural-born enemies behaving badly.

White stared at him, refusing to budge. So Tay cursed and climbed in, chiding himself for believing in signs, in wishes, in some kind of control, when he knew deep down that life was what was hurled at you at seventy miles an hour when you let your guard down for a split second. It was his job to deal with the consequences, to make things right.

It was his job to stop talking out loud to animals.

Especially rogue cats.

Dune hopped dutifully to the passenger side and Tay nudged White to her spot in the middle of the bench, no easy feat. He pulled out his keys, fired up the old truck, and cursed again.

He shut down the engine.

In front of him was a store window stuffed with Galton University paraphernalia. T-shirts, hats, and a bumper sticker that read, "Galton Is Gorges."

Gorges? The slogan was printed on T-shirts, hats, even maroon boxers.

I'm going to throw it off a cliff... into a gorge.

This town was famous for cliffs?

Had Candy been serious?

She wouldn't. She couldn't. She needed that money more than a kid her age could understand. The newspaper article had reported that her father was "absent" and that her mother had left behind piles of debt. But what was debt to a kid until she was kicked out of school or her car was repossessed by some stranger on a cold winter night?

Galton is gorges.

She's a kid. Doesn't know a thing about real life.

He raced back to the diner, but a quick glance through the plate-glass window told him that she and the money were gone. The waitress was still behind the counter, reading from her letter, her head down, looking so sad he had to force himself not to bust into the diner and offer whatever help she needed.

Lizzie and Paige Carpenter, 47 Pine Tree Road . . .

He drove his truck slowly up and down the steep streets of the gray town crawling with identical students like a *Where's Waldo?* picture book. *Where's Candy?* Jeans, T-shirts, long black hair . . .

It was as if she had thrown herself into a gorge.

Great, now he was getting morbid. He felt sick. He had to keep his head on straight.

He had thought giving Candy the money would make him feel at least a little better.

But it didn't. He gave her the money, and not a damn thing had changed.

How did a person know when he was forgiven?

When he could taste his coffee again?

When he could sleep through the night?

When the cat left?

He looked down at White. The light ahead changed to yellow and he rolled to a gentle stop. The car behind honked angrily, skidding to a stop behind him, just touching his rear bumper. He rolled down the window and said to the cat, "Out. For your own good."

White looked up at him, then went back to sleep.

He rolled up the window, put his truck in gear, and kept searching for Candy, stupid cat dozing as if everything were going just according to plan.

Twenty minutes later, he spotted Candy on campus, heading toward a big stone building. He jammed the truck to the curb, slammed on the emergency brake, and jumped out, the door hanging open behind him. "Candy! Please! Just one minute more. I swear."

She looked back at him and smiled. It was the first time he'd ever seen her smile and it knocked him backward.

The coldest smile he'd ever experienced.

"Done. It's fish food. At the bottom of a gorge." She held her hands out to show him the bag was gone. "Now, I never, ever want to see you again."

And with that, she walked into the building and disappeared.

CHAPTER

4

*W*hy had she made that wish?

Lizzie stroked red paint onto the roof of the bird feeder that she'd set on a bed of newspaper on the dining room table. It was almost midnight, but Lizzie couldn't sleep, thinking about what it meant that she had wished for a man to come and help her impress another man. It was infuriating that she still wished for a Prince Charming to come to her rescue. Especially after fourteen years of making it on her own, not relying on anyone. What did it mean that such a wimpy wish had popped out of her mouth at a critical time like this?

Paige's footsteps on the stairs startled her from her thoughts. She had thought Paige had been asleep for hours.

Paige came into the room, her eyes glued to her cell phone, texting as she walked. Somehow, she didn't bonk into the doorframes or trip on the edge of the rug. Paige could walk across a four-lane highway, texting the whole time with four different people, and not even feel the breeze of the cars zipping by her. "Geneva is in Switzerland," Paige said.

Lizzie had sometimes considered wearing a clown wig around the house, just to see how long it took Paige to look away from whatever screen her eyes were fixed on. But one good thing about Paige's distraction was that it let Lizzie study her daughter's face closely. She had caught herself doing this with an obsessive intensity since Ethan's letter had come, as if it were possible to soak up as much of the girl as she could now, before it was too late and Paige left for the bigger things her father and Geneva might be able to offer. Her daughter's beauty, her flawless skin, her shiny, pin-straight hair, the just-forming sophistication of her bone structure—it all took Lizzie's breath away. And yet she said, "Shouldn't you be in bed?"

Paige didn't need to know that her mother was coming undone.

"It's Friday night. No one's in bed," Paige said, glancing up, teenage exasperation flashing in her eyes. Lizzie forced her own eyes to the feeder. She didn't want to get caught staring at Paige. She was desperately afraid she'd let on how hard it was for her to think about Ethan's sweeping back into their lives. She wanted to appear in control. So she inspected the tiny house. It was a gingerbread cottage, its windows opening onto feeding trays, but its porch a clever mechanism that shut the windows tight if a heavier squirrel tried to visit.

Too bad they didn't make one of those mechanisms for shutting out would-be fathers.

"Switzerland, Mom."

"Yep."

Paige's eyes went back to her phone, and she slumped

into a chair without looking behind her. How did she do that without crashing to the ground? "The Alps are in Switzerland. Geena's been to Europe. She knows." *Tap tap tap* on the tiny keyboard.

Lizzie knew where this was heading. Her stomach was already in a knot. She concentrated on painting the roof of the little birdseed house because she could make it right, perfect even. The original fire-engine-red roof had faded from the summer sun to a pale pink, and she was fixing it. This, she could fix. Ethan, not so much. Paige, who knew?

"So I can go there with Dad and really learn to board? On real mountains? Not these pathetic New York anthills?"

It had been less than a week, and Paige had already switched from "Ratbastard" to "Dad." That word was like a knife to Lizzie's gut, the first sign of Paige's pulling away, moving on, growing up.

But Paige wasn't grown up. Not really. And that was the problem. She thought that she could ride her snowboard to fame and fortune. Lizzie had caught her just last night practicing Mountain Dew commercials into the mirror. *Do the Dew.*

Do the bachelor's degree just didn't have the same ring.

"Sure. After college." Lizzie put down her paintbrush, willing Paige to put down her phone. *Look at me and tell me that you'll stay here and not run off with Ratbastard and ruin your life. I mean, with Dad.*

No such luck. "Forget college. That'll be too late. I'll be too old. This is the chance of a lifetime, Mom. It's like it's meant to be. What are the chances my father would live near awesome mountains?"

"Fifty-fifty? Sixty-forty? At worst, maybe seventy-thirty." Lizzie hated that she sounded so glib, but it was only to cover the panic that was gathering like a storm, pressing against her skull. *Don't leave me, Paige. Don't choose him.*

"Mo-om!"

"He hasn't invited you yet, Paige," she said, sounding exactly like every awful mother in existence.

Paige, naturally, started texting, her thumbs flying over the tiny keyboard furiously.

What Lizzie wanted to say to Paige was even worse. *He might be a criminal. Or, worse, he might already have a perfect daughter. Several.* Heck, based on what little Lizzie knew of him, the guy could have hundreds. But that wasn't the kind of thing she could say to her fourteen-year-old. Lizzie hoped that Paige was smart enough to realize how many possibilities stretched out before her. But she refused to be the one to dash her daughter's dreams against the sharp edges of all those ugly scenarios by suggesting them out loud. Being the messenger would only get her blamed for the message.

"Details," Paige insisted.

Lizzie leaned across the table and snatched Paige's phone. She needed Paige's full attention on this one.

"Hey!" Paige refused to look at Lizzie. She stalked to the window to peer into the blackness outside. "You care more about those stupid birds than you do about me. At least you fix their houses. Our house is a mess. My dad's going to fly across the ocean, drive five hours from New York City, take one look at our house, know we're losers, and get out of here as fast as he can." She leaned her nose against the window as if she were watching her father's car do a U-turn in their driveway, screeching away into the night.

Was that why Lizzie had made her wish? Had she imagined the same scenario?

Paige went on. "Those birds get to have nice houses and then they get to split this town and do something with their lives. Unlike me. Or you."

Now Lizzie was glad Paige was looking elsewhere. She composed her face, erasing the pain the accusing words inflicted. She thought, *What's so wrong with here?* But she said, "Men don't fly in on magic carpets to fix things, Paige. You don't need anyone's help to make something of your life. All you need is here. Good schools. Good friends. Time and space to grow up."

Paige rolled her eyes. "Honestly, Mom. I'm going to barf." With that, Paige turned, shot Lizzie her patented preteen look of death, and dashed up the stairs.

Leaving Lizzie with her phone.

CHAPTER

5

$\mathcal{L}$izzie didn't plan to read Paige's text messages.

Not that there was anything wrong with doing that.

After all, they had an agreement that since Lizzie paid the bills, she got to monitor the phone.

It was the responsible, upright, good-parenting thing to do. She'd read that in more than one parenting book, so it must be true.

It wasn't exactly snooping. She was *keeping tabs*.

But as soon as she decoded the annoying patois of the first message, she was sorry she'd begun.

Help! Cnt go w/ D & lv M 1lone. 2sad 2live.

Lizzie bristled. She wasn't alone. She had family, friends. Okay, so not a man. But who cared? That did not qualify as too sad to live.

Geena responded: *Go! Follow heart.* (The heart was a symbol, which throbbed.)

Lizzie had never liked Geena much.

Paige typed: *& Lv M 1lone? Can't.*

Geena typed: *Find her BF.*

Paige had replied eight seconds later: *Not possible.*

Lizzie looked at the perfect little house on her table. She put down the phone.

2sad 2live? Not possible for her to find a boyfriend?

She went to where Paige had stood at the window and looked out at the nighttime street. The walk outside was softly lit by the glow of the light by the gate, and she could see the falling-down fence, the hanging gate. Was Paige right, that Ethan would be so unimpressed by their lives that he wouldn't help Paige? Would Paige stay because it was too sad to leave her mother alone?

Wait.

She could see the fence, the gate?

The light was on?

That light hadn't worked for over a year. It had gone dead the night before Paige's first day of seventh grade, something wrong with the wiring. Lizzie looked closer. She went to the switch by the front door. She flicked the light off, then on.

How strange.

It felt like a sign.

It felt like hope.

Like she was on to something.

But what?

Lizzie closed her eyes. Just this once, couldn't she believe in something besides hard work, frugal living, and saving every spare penny for Paige's college? Couldn't she for just one second believe in magic? The universe listening?

If she wished for what she truly wanted, what would it be?

Don't let Paige leave me.

Oh, hell. She was 2sad 2live. That wish was pathetic. A coward's wish.

She looked out over the yard of the house where she'd lived her entire life. It had been her childhood home. Now it was her and Paige's home. Ethan had known exactly where to send that letter. He'd known they'd still be here.

Disgust flooded her. How could she wish this small life on Paige who wanted bigger things? How could she be so selfish? What if the universe was listening, and it answered, and Paige ended up never leaving? Was that really what she wanted for her daughter? For her to live here out of a sense of duty to her mother? For Paige to give up her huge, crazy dreams just because they were huge and crazy?

Wasn't that what Lizzie had done? Given up her own huge, crazy dreams to take care of Paige? She wouldn't have had it any other way. But Paige wasn't in her situation, pregnant senior year of high school. Paige still had a future that could go anywhere. Ethan's coming might be a huge disappointment—or it might be the chance of a lifetime.

Lizzie closed her eyes again. The panic that was pushing at the back of her eyeballs became painful, but she took a deep breath and forced the words out. "Let Ethan be a good man who can give Paige what she wants," she whispered. The unjustness hit her hard, and she couldn't swallow the hurt that flooded her. The sense of betrayal almost choked her, as if it were a thing being forced down her throat. It was unfair that Ethan would get to be Paige's hero, when it was Lizzie who had done all the work. But that was life, wasn't it? It wasn't about fairness; it was about moving on. Getting somewhere. Taking advantage of the doors that opened, no matter who opened them. The only way to move forward was to quit looking back.

If Ethan was a decent man, Lizzie would do everything in her power to help Paige get whatever she wanted out of him.

Step one: Fix the house so Paige will feel worthy.

Step two: Find a temporary but suitable man, so Paige will be able to wave her happy, well-loved and cared-for mother good-bye.

Lizzie let a tear fall, but just one. Then she wiped her eyes and pulled herself together. She could do this.

Tay paced the night streets of the good town of Galton, New York, unable to sleep. Dune trotted behind him. White kept to the shadows, disappearing for blocks, then suddenly reappearing, a pair of glowing eyes in the bushes.

Tay had righted a knocked-over trash can set out on the curb for the trashmen the next morning. Dune good-naturedly tried to herd the guilty raccoon into their little band of wanderers, another friend along for a moonlit walk.

Luckily, the raccoon had other plans.

Tay had roused a drunken student from a privet hedge and pointed him in the general direction of campus.

He walked on aimlessly.

Or did he?

He knew the waitress's address from the envelope: *47 Pine Tree Road*. When he saw a street sign from afar that might read *Pine Tree Road*, his heart beat a little faster.

Peach Tree Street had made him grit his teeth.

Pine Tower Lane nearly made him scream into the empty night.

And then he saw it.

Pine Tree Road. His mouth went dry.

Now what?

He told himself again that he hadn't been looking for her street. Yes, he had been checking every street sign with his breath held. But that was only because his insomnia-addled brain needed something to focus on or it would spin into outer space.

Or worse, into the deep, inner recesses of itself.

Okay, he'd been searching for it.

He hadn't wanted anything at all since the accident. He'd been heading away from everything for a year. To head toward something, even just a darkened street in a strange town, took him by surprise. Dune seemed to sense his discomfort and trotted closer to his heels. White just blinked at him from the shadows as if she knew.

Damn cat.

Even though he thought better of it, he'd gone down the soundless, darkened, tree-lined street to check out her house, swearing to himself that he was only curious to see if she really needed help.

Lizzie's house had been dark except for two rooms, both shrouded behind closed blinds.

The place was a mess. The fence was halfway to collapse; the gutters hung loose. Even in the dark, he could see that the porch needed repair and painting.

Fixing this house could be a long, involved job. Keep him busy for ages.

As hard as he tried not to, he couldn't resist. He'd unscrewed the bulb, then silently tweaked the wiring on her path light, happy when the dusty bulb lit up.

Happy.

He wanted more of happy.

It was a simple fix, less than a minute, not long enough to make a dent in the endless night in front of him.

And the happiness didn't last long enough to make a dent in the endless blackness inside him.

He didn't have the tools to fix the gate that was hanging loose.

So he and his crew walked on.

Finally, after what seemed like days, the first rays of light started to form on the horizon. Finally, he could go back to the gorges and look again for the duffel bag that had seemingly disappeared, evaporated. Maybe, his sleepless brain thought, it had never existed at all.

No, it had existed. It still existed—but where?

He hadn't expected that finding the duffel bag would be so hard. But the gorges were deep, some of them inaccessible, some of them already closed for the winter with gates, temporary fences, and warning signs. Not that those barriers stopped Tay, but still, they slowed his progress.

Plus, there were so many gorges surrounding the campus, each one crisscrossed with bridges and overlooks, just perfect to toss a duffel bag over the side and watch it wash away in the fall currents.

But he couldn't just leave two hundred thousand dollars at the bottom of some cliff.

Hell, maybe he could. Lord knows, he didn't want the money back.

Maybe it had been swept to the lake already, or sunk to the bottom of a deep pool.

But maybe it was caught on a rock, or washed up on a pebbly shore. The streams that raged through the gorges around campus weren't that deep. There were endless rocks and crags to catch and trap a bag, turns for it to get pushed into, branches for it to dangle from.

If Candy changed her mind and wanted the money, he'd be the one who ended up stuck, caught, dangling, helpless. He hated to think about that. Refused to think about it.

And what if someone else found it? Leaving that much money lying around in a duffel with no rational explanation of where it came from was like leaving a loaded gun, a bomb ready to explode into someone's life.

Tay knew better than most how disrupting a random event like that could be. You could spend the rest of your life trying to recover from something like that. He had enough responsibility on his shoulders already without having to deal with busting into another stranger's life and blowing it wide open with another irresponsible act.

No, he had to find that money. For Candy or for whoever might find it before him.

Looking for the money gave him purpose, something to do to fill his empty days.

It was his nights he was starting to worry about.

CHAPTER

6

*L*izzie couldn't sleep. It had been a week since she'd made her decision to help Paige, and her heart was already breaking from the strain. Maybe this was a terrible idea. After all, what if Ethan wasn't a good person? What if he was downright awful?

But what if he wasn't? What if he was exactly what Paige hoped?

Her mind hopped back and forth between the two equally dangerous possibilities.

This afternoon, she'd set up a date for Friday night with a man named Scott who was a yoga student of Nina's, and she was already dreading it down to her toes. The last thing she needed now was a man to complicate her already complicated life.

She lay in bed until six in the morning, when she couldn't stand tossing and turning another moment. Paige would be up for school in another half hour, anyway. Might as well get a jump on the coffee.

Lizzie got out of bed, looked out her window.

It was still dark outside, the first pink rays of light just emerging on the horizon. Another day at the diner, work and worry and—

—and there was a person on his knees at her front gate.

She leaned forward to look closer.

A man.

A jolt of fear shook her.

Lizzie threw on her purple fuzzy robe over her faded Mickey Mouse T-shirt and flannel candy-cane pajama bottoms and snuck as silently as she could down the stairs, having no idea why she was sneaking. She knelt on the bay window seat in the dining room and peered out.

What was that guy doing?

Maybe he had dropped something. His cell phone? Maybe he had lost a contact. Was he hurt? Maybe he had been on his way down their path to rob them and his gun had rolled under the gate . . .

Was he praying?

He shifted, and she could see his profile in the early morning light. He wasn't exactly handsome. More like solid, weathered, maybe even worn. Despite the September chill, he was dressed in a light, faded T-shirt that might as well have read *Real Men Don't Get Cold*. The sole of his right workboot, resting partly upright on its toe, had cracked clear through.

The man reached into a box that Lizzie hadn't noticed before. Her nose was now touching the glass so she could see better. A radio? A lunchbox? What was that?

A toolbox.

Her skin went cold.

He brought out a screwdriver. Lizzie tried to hide her

alarm. Her throat tightened. No. It couldn't be. Wishes coming true...a handyman at her gate...

Lizzie let the lace curtain fall back into place.

The Enemy Club.

They were the only ones who had heard her wish who would even consider acting on it.

One of them had obviously sent this guy.

Jill? Georgia? Nina?

Whoever the culprit, it was not okay.

No, wait—it was okay. It was her wish come true.

No. She jumped up, paced the room, confused by her conflicting emotions.

Sure, she wanted to fix the house for Paige, but she didn't want charity. The Enemy Club had an unspoken agreement that allowed them to be friends: They didn't agree with each other's wildly different life choices, but they respected them. That was the deal that none of them had ever violated. If they started sending free handymen, then what was next? Wardrobe consultants? Job-training specialists? Psychologists? Dieticians? Soon, they'd be like any other group of regular old friends, each of them just like the other, like that book club that came into the diner Thursday afternoons. They all looked the same, talked the same, ate the same Cobb salads—and looked deadly bored with one another.

The Enemy Club had grown through the years to love and respect one another too much. They knew better than to try to change one another's lives.

Lizzie's blood was starting to heat. She went back to the window, hoping he was gone, but he was still there. She dropped the curtain and sat back, feeling betrayed and honored all at once.

It was so kind of them to do this, and yet, sending a charity handyman was a violation of their creed. Ten-yard penalty. Change of possession. Potential disqualification. Game over. This was an action that demanded a reaction. Lizzie might have wished for a free handyman, but she wasn't going to be anyone's charity case, even if this man's mysterious appearance at her gate was supposed to be a joke (if it was Jill) or a well-meant but wrongheaded favor (if it was Georgia) or an overgenerous, awkward attempt at friendship (if it was Nina).

So now what?

She could call the cops.

Or go outside and calmly ask the man to leave.

Or stay inside just long enough so that the annoying hinge on the gate was fixed, then go out and confront him.

She listened for sounds of Paige being awake, but there was only silence.

Best to just get it over with.

She took a deep breath and headed for the door.

CHAPTER

7

$\mathcal{T}$he man didn't look up.

Lizzie strode down the front walk, letting the screen door slam behind her to announce her approach.

He still didn't look up.

She avoided the holes in the walk where bricks had once been. Where did bricks go when they left her walk? To a better-maintained, happier walk down the road? She stopped in front of the man, hands on her hips. Even though she was five-foot-eight, she could tell by the expanse of blue-jean-clad folded leg that this man was much taller.

She cleared her throat.

No response.

A small dog rose from the shadows, startling her. It had a tennis ball in its mouth, which it dropped at her feet. The dog looked at her expectantly.

"Don't mind Dune," the man said. He unscrewed the last screw and caught the hinge adeptly as it dropped free. Then, slowly, no hurry, all the time in the world, he stood, looked at her, really looked, no rush. She could knit a sweater before this guy spoke, if she knew how to knit, which she didn't, but she could learn before—

"Tay Giovanni." He offered his hand. "Short for Dante."

She'd seen him before.

But where?

His gold-tinged green eyes had the look of a practiced lady-killer who knew it. A long, deep scar ran from the outside corner of his left eye, down his well-stubbled cheek, to the corner of his mouth, as if someone had started to make an X, then changed his mind. He was handsome, in a rough-and-tumble way Lizzie usually liked. A lot. But something about him gave her pause.

It was his eyes. They had a stillness to them that was eerie, as if he could go through a thousand emotions, but those eyes would hold steady through anything.

A chill raced up her spine.

His dog nudged its nose into her hand, and she couldn't help but scratch his head. It was hard to look tough when you were scratching a dog, but she tried. "You'd better watch your dog. My pit bulls are trained to kill. All seven of them."

He looked at the house dubiously, then went back to his work on the broken hinge. "No worries. Almost done. Then you can set them loose. Dune will herd them. He's a sheltie, it's his nature."

I'm independent, it's my nature. "Did Georgia put you up to this? Georgia Phillips? Thirtyish? Short? Lots of tweed?" she asked. Georgia was a psychiatrist so she made the most money, so she was the most likely to have sent this man.

Tay stopped working long enough to envelop Lizzie with his calm stare. He bathed her in it. Looked her up and down thoroughly. Finally he said, "No one puts me up to anything."

"Okay, if it wasn't Georgia, did Jill send you? Blonde? Expensive clothes? Beautiful?"

"I told you, no one sends me anywhere." His voice was rough and low with a slight New York edge. He looked entirely straightforward, a man who told it like it was.

When he was good and ready.

And he obviously wasn't ready.

The dog lay down, the ball at his feet.

Lizzie hoped her tongue wasn't lolling out like the dog's. The man was exceptionally handsome, the way dark-skinned Italians with green eyes and longish, thick black hair could be. But she was going to ignore that, because this was not okay.

Dante Giovanni knelt by a green metal toolbox that was as scuffed as he was. After a bit of shuffling around, he said, "Amazing house—1920s?"

"Thank you. It's 1918. But compliments will get you nowhere."

"Original slate?" He motioned to the roof.

"From the local quarry," she said, trying hard to hold to her resolve. He had to go before Paige woke up. Lizzie didn't want Paige to see her chase him away. Or to see her struggling not to ogle him. *What shoulders on this man.*

"Shoulders?" he asked.

"Shoulders?" she repeated, shocked and alarmed to blushing.

He scratched his cheek. "Shutters. Your shutters. They look original."

Right. Shutters. "Antique. Listen, you really have to go," she said.

"Early 1900s I'm guessing," he said.

"Nineteen-oh-four," she said, trying not to let her guard down. "Got them at a local salvage place. Well, my father did, anyway. When he was still around to do that sort of thing." Great. Tell the strange man that you're orphaned and no one will miss you after he chops you to bits. Nice work. She glanced back to the house, but still no sign of Paige rousing. The dog stared at her, so she tossed his ball into the yard. He bounded after it, then was back in an instant, panting for more. It was impossible not to scratch his head. It was a cute dog, like a mini Lassie, but black and white instead of orange.

Tay shuffled some more in the toolbox. He compared screws as if they were pieces to a puzzle. "You served me coffee last week. At the Last Chance diner on Buckman Street." He said it as if that explained anything. Just another fact. Just the way it was. Like his deep, still eyes. *Fact.* Broad, rounded shoulders. *Fact.* Nicely tanned hands. *Fact.*

"I must have served a hundred coffees last week. A thousand." All at once, she remembered him—the man Mr. Zinelli had been yapping at. "Wait—dry toast. Black coffee."

"You've got a good memory," he said.

"I never forget an order. I knew I recognized you. Are you feeling better?"

"Me?" He fell back a little, narrowed his eyes.

"You didn't touch the toast and hardly touched the coffee. Or maybe it wasn't good enough? The coffee's not gourmet, like the place across the street. You don't look like you're from around here. Next time, try the Brew-haha," Lizzie said, aware that she was rambling, but not sure exactly how to handle this beautiful man who really had to leave.

"Wouldn't know about the coffee." He seemed to have overcome his surprise that she recognized him, because he was back to his work. He pulled a fresh screw out of the box, went back to the gate, knelt, and began to re-attach the hinge. "From the looks of your clientele, I'd assume it gets the job done."

Lizzie watched him, mystified. "So I served you crappy coffee and you thought that was a reason to show up on my property and touch my latch?" Why did that sound sala-cious? She tried to think pure thoughts, but none came.

Tay Giovanni was that kind of man.

She threw the dog the ball again, feeling acutely aware of not being that kind of woman. Her goofy flannel plaid pajamas stuck out from under her threadbare robe. Her slippers were a Christmas present from Paige when she had been eleven. The left one had an ancient Florida-shaped cranberry-juice stain that wouldn't come out no matter how many times she scrubbed it. She hoped he couldn't see it in the early morning light.

He tested the gate latch, dropping it in and out of its slot with soft, rhythmic clicks. Tested the hinge. It swung level and free.

"Mr. Giovanni—"

"Ms. Carpenter?"

"How do you know my name?"

He ignored her question. "I heard you tell your friends at the diner that you wished a man would show up once a week, fix things that needed fixing, then disappear."

"I didn't wish," she began, then stumbled, then started again. "I did. But I didn't mean—and they're not exactly my friends."

"Right, your enemies."

"Mr. Zinelli told you," she said.

"Yep. He explained the whole thing. Anyway, it sounded like a real wish to me."

Lizzie could hear her own breathing. "Did you fix the light?"

"I have trouble sleeping."

So do I. She had to be careful around this too-observant, slow-moving, slow-talking man.

"It just needed some wires jiggled. Took a minute."

She didn't know what to say so she said, "Thank you."

"You're welcome."

They stood on the path, looking at each other. Lizzie felt as if she was being pulled in two. On the one hand, he was everything she had wished for. On the other, he was possibly a serial killer. What kind of man shows up out of nowhere to lend a hand?

Then, there was something else. Something even more disturbing. A nagging discomfort starting as an itching at her palms, then blooming into a heat on her cheeks. She knew that feeling so well, even if she hadn't felt it in a long, long time.

It was shame.

He—or whoever sent him—felt sorry for her.

He was here out of charity.

She said, "You have to go. I don't accept charity, even if in a moment of weakness, I wished for it."

He nodded. "I get that. And I know this sounds strange, but this isn't about you. I happen to have some free time.

I happen to be stuck in this town for a little while. And I happen to be pretty decent with a screwdriver." He wiped his hands on his jeans. "Plus, not that it matters to either of us, believe me on this one, but coincidentally, I happen to be a man."

Like she could have missed that little detail. Was this guy for real? Why was her mouth so dry? "How did you know where I live?"

"Destiny?" he suggested, just the slightest flash of humor in his eyes. He looked around at her house and yard, his eyes lingering on points of particular decay.

Oh.

The wooden picket fence had gone gray and flaky, slanting in the middle like a row of dominoes that had frozen halfway to falling. What bricks remained in the walk seemed held against their will by the world's healthiest dandelions. The porch was riddled with wood-bee holes, its paint peeling. The driveway was overrun with weeds and potholes. The gutters were hanging loose. Worst of all, every other house on the shady, suburban street was pristine in the early morning light.

It wasn't that Lizzie didn't care. Her house was worth more than she liked to contemplate. But after years of trying to keep up with the constant repairs, she had started to slip. First little things cropped up, like a brick coming loose here and there. But soon, they added up until they seemed insurmountable and she didn't know where to begin.

She hadn't meant it to be this way. Her parents had bought the house for a pittance when she was three and the market had been in a slump. Her father had fixed it up; it had suffered years of neglect at the hands of the alcohol-addled previous tenant, Georgie Lutz. Then, when her parents died ten years ago, they left the house to Lizzie and Paige, the mortgage long ago paid off. After all, she had Paige to look after alone with only her diner job to support her.

Owning the house straight-out made her and Paige's precarious life possible. Lizzie made just enough to cover their bills and taxes, and to put something away for Paige's college account. So maybe her house was gradually falling apart around her. Small price to pay for a life that was otherwise working out just fine.

At least, she had thought it was fine, until that letter...

The sun had almost cleared the purple-pink clouds, and Lizzie could see Tay better in the pale, tinted light. He didn't look quite as ominous with the sky opening up behind him, but where were the birds? She looked to her silent feeders.

Odd.

Dante Giovanni gathered his tools. He picked up the toolbox and started down the sidewalk toward a broken-down red pickup truck parked at the curb. The dog picked up his tennis ball and trotted after him. A white cat stood on the passenger seat watching them approach through the lowered passenger-side window, its front paws on the door, its huge, yellow, glowing eyes tracking them with a steady stare identical to Tay's.

Lizzie looked back to her bird feeders. No wonder it was so silent. Usually this early, predawn hour was the time the birds were most active. But even the bossy blue jays had gone into hiding. At least the birds were smart enough to understand when a predator was near.

"Wait. Come back here, Mr. Giovanni." She marched

after him to the truck. Out of the corner of her eye, she saw the curtains part across the street, the shadow of Judy Roth silhouetted behind them.

One problem with buying on the cheap, then holding on for dear life, was that Lizzie and Paige fit into this proper, maple-lined, college-town street like a pair of pink plastic flamingos. All she needed now was old, widowed, busybody Mrs. Roth coming out here in her plaid robe and blue curlers to learn about Lizzie's freebie, wish-come-true handyman. She'd be delighted to tell the whole town about the latest disgrace at 47 Pine Tree Road.

Lizzie waved at her elderly neighbor. "Hi, Mrs. Roth! Everything's fine! Just a stalker from the diner!" Mrs. Roth was stone-cold deaf. She waved happily, the curtains fell back into place, and the shadow receded.

Thank goodness. Lizzie didn't need gossip. She didn't want to cause this guy any trouble. He seemed nice enough, and whatever the Enemy Club had put him up to, it wasn't really his fault. She just wanted him and his animals gone. She'd figure out how to fix the place herself.

He hoisted his toolbox into the back of his truck, then opened the passenger door. "Well?" he asked the cat. He waited a few moments, as if hoping the cat would leave. Then he sighed, shut the door, and walked around the truck to the driver's side. The dog hopped in with him, then moved to the passenger's window. The cat jumped into Tay's lap, nuzzled his cheek, then looked at Lizzie with curiosity, as if it was odd that she was here, not at all odd that they were.

"Mr. Giovanni." Lizzie leaned in through the dog's lowered window. The three of them watched her as if she were talking equally to them all. "If you're being honest and you're here to grant my wish, which I don't believe, by the way, then I'm sorry, but that's too creepy for words. And if Jill or Georgia or Nina sent you, you tell them it's hilarious and now back off. I don't need or accept charity from anyone. Not from you and especially not from them."

He waited patiently as the truck sputtered reluctantly to life. Once the motor had caught and had quieted to an uncertain idle, he asked, "Why do you wish for what you don't want?"

She couldn't answer. She'd wished for help when she couldn't abide it. She'd wished for Paige to leave when the last thing she could survive in this world was Paige leaving.

"Don't come back," she said as firmly as she could, more to herself than to him.

"Now, how do I know if that's what you want or just what you're saying?" he asked in a friendly casual way, as if they'd known each other forever, as if they had something deep and important in common and had come to some kind of agreement long ago. "See you around."

And then Tay Giovanni, whoever he was, drove away without waiting for an answer.

CHAPTER

8

*L*izzie watched the truck rumble slowly down her street, then come to a halt at the stop sign at the end of her block. The truck sat a long moment, as if Tay was unsure which way to go. Maybe he fell asleep at the wheel? Maybe he'd had a heart attack? Just as Lizzie was getting genuinely concerned, the turn signal blinked on. And on. And on. Finally, the truck swung left, down the steep hill that led to town. He was not a speed demon. Which boded well for him in bed...

Oh, for Lord's sake! After fourteen years of hardly a second date, Lizzie was not going to fall for the mysterious stranger who appeared at her gate no matter how handsome and, well, downright considerate he was.

He had been awfully considerate.

And he had a cute dog.

And the cat had seemed to think he was okay, even if Lizzie wasn't one for cats. She spent too much time feeding the birds to abide a cat strolling around.

And he was her wish come true.

But it felt all wrong. As he had pointed out, she had wished for something that she didn't want, which was unsettling, as if it pointed to a bigger problem, one that she was in no mood to face.

So she woke Paige and acted as if nothing at all had happened. She waited until just after Paige had left for school, and then she did what she always did when she didn't know what else to do. She called her sister, Annie and her brother-in-law, Tommy. Ever since Annie and Tommy had their baby six months ago, Lizzie could count on them to be up early. She hoped Tommy, who was one of Galton's twelve policemen, hadn't left yet for work.

Tommy answered the phone. Lizzie felt a twinge of relief that it wasn't Annie, relief that was quickly replaced with guilt for not wanting to talk to her only sister. Annie had been so depressed lately, she was getting hard to talk to. Which of course was why Lizzie should reach out and talk to Annie more. And she had tried. But Annie had started getting hostile toward Lizzie lately, her depression transforming into anger whenever Lizzie was near. It was too early in the morning for a fight.

After she'd told Tommy the whole story, he said, "I should arrest your fence, not the man who fixes it. That thing is a crime the way it's falling down."

"You're not going to do anything?" Lizzie demanded. "What kind of cop are you? What if the Enemy Club didn't send him? Then how did he get here? He might have followed me home! I'm terrified. *He knew my name.*" She could hear Annie in the background, calling Tommy to help her sweep up the Cheerios Meghan had flung to the floor.

"You? Terrified? I don't believe it. When have you ever

been scared of anything? Liz, you went out alone in the near dark and talked to him."

"Okay, I wasn't exactly terrified. But I am furious. He was trespassing. It was very presumptuous."

"Okay," Tommy admitted. "You're right. It is a little odd. But he's gone, right? You're safe? No harm, no foul."

Lizzie heard Annie ask him what was odd and who was gone and Tommy explained the whole situation and Annie said loud enough for Lizzie to hear, "Let Tommy off the phone, I need him. And let that man fix Mom and Dad's house!"

"It's my house!" Lizzie said quietly, dreading this fight. Annie had it all, great husband, beautiful baby; she even used to have a great job as a librarian at the public library downtown before she left to take care of Meghan. And yet, Lizzie felt for her sister. She was obviously struggling with the new baby, which Lizzie understood more than anyone could. Still, Lizzie wished Annie wouldn't take it out on her.

"You want me to come over? Drive you to work before my shift starts?" Tommy asked.

Annie picked up the extension. Lizzie imagined them in the same room, each holding a phone, glaring at each other. Lizzie could feel the tension from her house a mile away. "Don't leave. I still need a shower, Tommy!"

Lizzie backed off. "No. No. Forget it. It's okay. The guy's gone. I'm fine. I just wanted someone to know what happened this morning, so if I disappear, you know to start searching for my body. I shouldn't have called. I can deal with this myself if he shows up again."

Annie said, "Good. That's my Lizzie. Tommy, I'm getting in the shower." The extension clicked dead.

"I'll look out for him today around town, okay?" Tommy said. "Red Chevy, you said? What year about?"

Meghan started to shriek in the background.

"Tommy!" Annie called, her voice shrill. "Get her! Please? I'm in the bathroom!" A door slammed.

"No. Really," Lizzie said. "Forget it. I'm fine. I've gotta get to work. I'll call Joy to pick me up on her way in so I don't have to walk alone." Lizzie felt guilty for butting into her sister and brother-in-law's domestic morning chaos, but she also felt angry that Annie made her feel guilty by constantly dragging up their past.

Lizzie had dated Tommy for a few months in high school, right before Ethan came along. It was nothing. They had barely kissed, much less slept together. But the last few months, Annie kept bringing it up. Just last week, she had even said that she thought Tommy sometimes acted as if he had chosen the "wrong" sister. It made Lizzie feel two inches tall.

"We still on for Friday night?" Tommy asked. "Oooh, don't eat the phone, honey."

Lizzie could hear Meghan snuffling the receiver. "Burgers and dogs?" Lizzie asked.

"What else?" Tommy said, his voice rising to be heard over Meghan, who had started to sing, *Baaaa baaa baaaa Baaa...*

"Why don't you guys come here for a change? You sound tired." She and Paige had eaten at Tommy and Annie's every Friday night since forever.

Tommy said, "No way. I still have propane in the tank." Tommy was famous for using every last gasp of the summer's gas from the grill, even if he had to grill in the snow in his parka.

"All right. If that's really what you want," Lizzie said. She knew that Tommy insisted because he didn't want to upset Annie by changing anything without her permission, but she let it slide. He was dealing not just with a new baby, but with Annie's depression, and Lizzie knew it wasn't easy.

As if Tommy could read her mind, he said, "Thanks, Liz. Every little thing sets her off."

"I wish I could help more. I just don't know what to do. She gets angry with me all the time. I find myself running the other way when I see her coming." Guilt ate at Lizzie.

He said, "She won't talk to anyone. We just have to hope she'll get through this. And meanwhile, damage control. We eat here."

After hanging up the phone, a bad taste lingered in Lizzie's mouth. She knew her sister's moods were about the baby and not about her, but still, the coldness stung. Postpartum depression, Georgia had diagnosed. But Annie wouldn't hear any of that. She insisted everything was fine. Perfect Annie with her perfect life couldn't have a problem she'd ever admit to.

That was so not Lizzie's issue. She had plenty of problems.

With the arrival of Dante Giovanni, she suspected she'd just picked up one more.

CHAPTER

9

"Mom, there's a guy outside," Paige said.

Lizzie joined Paige on the dining room bay window seat. It was six-thirty in the morning, almost exactly twenty-four hours since Tay had first appeared, and Lizzie's stomach had been in a knot for every single one of them. She'd had trouble sleeping, her mind ricocheting between curiosity and dread about whether Tay would come back and what she would do if he dared.

"I think he's fixing stuff," Paige said. "Did you hire someone?"

"No. I didn't." Lizzie peeked out the window, her heart thumping an unwelcome welcome. Tay walked the length of her fence, wobbling the loose slats and kneeling here and there to inspect the rotted wood. He was wearing jeans and another faded T-shirt like the one he had worn yesterday, despite that the chill of fall seemed to have blown into town with a vengeance overnight. Did the man not feel the cold? At this rate, it would be winter by the month's end.

She wanted to bring him a coat, to invite him in for a coffee, *to take him into her bed*. Just ten minutes earlier, she'd woken up from a dream of Tay that was so hot, she'd need an extra-long shower to get it out of her system.

She combed her fingers through Paige's shiny hair. "We don't accept charity," she said. *Especially from men who show up in my dreams naked...*

She went to the kitchen, sank into a chair, and picked up the phone. She dialed and waited.

"Why not?" Paige asked. "We need charity."

"First, no we certainly do not. And second, because letting men show up out of the blue to solve our problems is lame," Lizzie said.

"You're talking about Dad or that guy out there?"

It sucked to have such a smart kid, "Both," Lizzie said just as Jessie Ray answered her call.

"Galton Police Department."

"Jess? It's Lizzie. Is Tommy there?"

"Mom! You're calling the cops on him!" Paige tried to grab the phone, but Lizzie pivoted away. "How could you?" Paige asked. "He's fixing stuff! If a guy can fix stuff, why not let him?"

Lizzie's stomach cramped. Why not? *Because you might not be able to count on him in the end. He could leave, not come back for fourteen years...*

"Hold on, Lizzie. I'll see if I can track him down," Jessie said, and put her on hold.

"You're not going to call the cops on Dad when he comes, are you?" Paige asked.

Lizzie ignored her.

"Liz?" Tommy asked.

Lizzie sighed with relief at the sound of her

brother-in-law's voice. She turned her back to Paige. "Tommy, listen. I need you to swing by. Now. That man is back."

"Back? He's been here before?" Paige asked.

"Er, which man?" Tommy asked.

"My mysterious fix-it man. Remember?"

"Oh. Right. Fastest screwdriver in the West."

"Tommy, he's fixing my fence now."

A pause. Then, "Sounds dangerous."

Paige leaned in close so that Tommy could hear. "He's gor-ge-ous," she sang.

"Oh, in that case, I'll be right over. I do loves me a good-lookin' man." He sounded remarkably unimpressed.

"Tommy, this is serious. He's not my fix-it man. I didn't ask him to come. We've been through this."

Tommy put on his best Clint Eastwood drawl. "Yes, ma'am. I did hear tell of a rogue fix-it man on the loose. But I never thought he'd dare set foot in my town." Tommy's best Clint Eastwood drawl sucked.

Lizzie nudged Paige's shoulder. "Go to school."

Paige plopped down at the kitchen table. She called out loud enough for Tommy to hear, "I can't go out there! He's not wearing safety goggles! He's a bad, bad man."

"Just come!" Lizzie insisted. She looked out the window. Tay was measuring the length of the fence.

Paige called over Lizzie's shoulder, "I'm so scared, Tommy! What if he retars our driveway next?"

"Okay," Tommy said. "This I gotta see."

"Oh, for heaven's sake!" Lizzie said.

Tommy had pulled up in his blue-and-white cruiser, lights flashing, looking official. But now, two minutes later, he was talking to Tay as if they were old college buddies, smiling and nodding as they kicked at the ground. All they needed were beers in their hands, a game involving balls on the tube, and some burgers on the grill. The two men were inspecting the fence together. "I think they're talking shop." Tommy loved his tools. He fixed anything that even appeared to be maybe thinking about breaking. Which was why Lizzie had forbidden him to fix anything at her place. It was too humiliating to be her sister and her brother-in-law's charity case.

Of course, now she was the charity case of either one of the Enemy Club or a total stranger.

A total beautiful stranger. She was trying very hard not to notice how good Tay looked out there. There was something about a man with a toolbox...

Lizzie turned to Paige. "Stay inside."

"Yes, ma'am." Paige saluted. But then she followed Lizzie out the door so fast, it didn't get a chance to slam. At least she stayed on the porch, riveted there by the death glare Lizzie threw back at her.

"Officer Wynne. Please tell that man to leave."

"Hi, Liz." Tommy tried to get her into one of his bear hugs, but she skirted the embrace. She wanted this to stay official. "Liz, this is Tay Giovanni."

"We met. I told him to get lost."

"That's true, Officer." Tay nodded in agreement, then kept on wiggling fence posts.

"Can I talk to you a moment, Lizzie? In private?" Tommy took her elbow and steered her clear of Tay. He whispered, "He's very knowledgeable about fences."

"Oh, no. You want him to stay. You're supposed to be kicking him out."

"But why, Lizzie? He really knows his way around a toolbox. And that fence is about to collapse. He says no one sent him. He says he doesn't want money."

Lizzie was growing exasperated. She wanted Tay to stay as badly as she wanted him to go. She wanted to make Paige happy as much as she wanted to teach her how to do the right thing and not accept men who show up out of the blue, granting wishes. *She wanted what she also didn't want,* and the confusion of that made her head hurt. "If my friends didn't send him, then don't you think it's a little creepy for a stranger to appear out of nowhere and start fixing things for nothing?"

"He corroborated your story about the wish. Said he thought, *What the hell?* He's just a nice guy, Liz."

Lizzie eyed Tommy suspiciously. "Why do you want him to stay, Tommy?"

Tommy sighed. "Lizzie, you know how Annie feels about this house. She kind of thinks it's still hers. You can't totally blame her. I mean, she grew up here. And she hates to watch it go to hell."

Lizzie put her hands on her hips. "And she's furious that Mom and Dad gave it to me. But they did because I had a kid I needed to support and no husband. She needs to get over it. It's my house. I want him gone." She was aware of the hardness in her voice, but she couldn't help it. She couldn't let this spin out of control.

"Look, all I'm saying is that the house being in bad shape puts her in a terrible mood whenever she comes by and she's already pretty prone to terrible moods since the baby. So if you just let this guy fix it up—"

"So you don't care if he's an ax murderer, just so long as your wife is happy?" Lizzie gave Tommy's shoulder a playful shove. She knew that Tommy was a good guy—the best. But she needed him to help her out on this one.

"I would care if I thought he was an ax murderer. Really, I swear I would. He's an honest guy, Liz. I meet a lot of criminals."

Lizzie raised one eyebrow. "In this town? Who? Old Mr. Tilsdale who forgets to put his quarter in the meter?"

"Okay, but still, I meet more criminals than the average guy." He lowered his voice and pulled her farther away from Tay. "This guy isn't a criminal. He's for real. A nice guy. Let him do a good deed."

"I'm not a charity case." Was she going to have to climb onto the roof and start shouting this? She'd put up a neon sign on the porch: *Please don't fix things for the single mother. She can do it herself. She's trying to set a good example.*

"Mom, I'm going to miss my bus." Paige was sitting on the porch railing, legs up, back against the post, watching her bus pull away, as unconcerned as a teenager could get, which was pretty darn unconcerned.

"Oh, heck."

"I'll take you to school, Paige," Tommy called.

"With the lights and siren?" Paige asked. "Can I sit in the back and when I get out, you take off the handcuffs and I'll go in, like it's a perfectly normal Thursday morning?" She was hopping up and down with excitement, her little-girl charm showing through her layers of form-fitting shirts. Lizzie noted that the bottom one was black. When had Paige gotten a black camisole? *Stay pink and sherbet-colored just a little longer.*

"No lights, no siren, but you can sit in the back if it'll make you feel better." Mercifully, he ignored the rest of her plan. "Don't worry, Liz. I'll get your daughter to safety." Tommy started for his cruiser, with Paige trotting happily behind as if she were all angels and rainbows.

Lizzie chased after them. "Let me get this straight. You're leaving me alone with him?"

"You really want me to arrest him for doing a good deed?"

"Yes." She looked over at Tay, who was hard at work. Was there anything more beautiful than a man working with his hands? He looked up and caught her looking so she quickly looked away. "No."

Tay strolled over from where he had been measuring the fence. "You have to watch her. She says that she wants things she doesn't want. It's very confusing."

"Why do you care what I say? You just ignore me, anyway, and do as you please," Lizzie pointed out. "Arrest him!" she said.

"Look, I'll drop off Paige and go to the station and I'll run a background check on him."

Tay said, "Sounds like a plan."

"Bye, Mom. Bye, Tay," Paige said. Then she called to the house, "Bye, Figgy!" Figgy was Paige's snowboard.

"Figgy's our lead pit bull," Lizzie said.

Paige rolled her eyes.

"I have his ID. He won't try anything," Tommy said. "Right?"

"Right," Tay agreed.

Paige pulled out her cell phone and snapped Tay's picture. "And I have his picture!" She looked inordinately pleased with her amateur police work. Lizzie knew that picture would be all over school within hours, probably tagged with something like, *Check out hot guy at my place!*

"Look! Here comes Mrs. Roth to save the day." Tommy waved to Judy Roth, who was coming down her front walk in her nightgown, robe, and slippers. No way that woman could stay in her house when there was a police car on her street. "You have my permission to take this guy out if he tries anything, Mrs. Roth!" Tommy yelled to her. "Use your Glock!"

Mrs. Roth waved back and smiled. "Okay, yes, dear! It's a lovely day for a walk."

"Great. Now I feel safe," Lizzie said.

"Then I'm off to prevent greater crimes, like Paige being late for school," Tommy said. He lowered his voice, so just Lizzie could hear. "You'll remember how to treat a decent, kind man if you try. I'm sure of it. I have his info; he won't try anything with the whole neighborhood watching. Meanwhile, think about being nice. Okay? If not for him, then for me at least. Or for Annie. Or for Paige. Let him stay."

CHAPTER

10

Lizzie watched Paige and Tommy disappear over the hill, lights flashing. God, Tommy was a pushover.

Tay was watching her.

"Why did you come back when I asked you not to?" Lizzie asked Tay.

"Like you said, I do as I please. Can't help it, just my way."

Exasperated, Lizzie turned on her heel. Why bother talking to a man who doesn't listen? She left Tay to deal with Mrs. Roth, who was almost at the curb. Tay rushed over to help her across the street and Lizzie wanted to throttle him. What was he, a Boy Scout? He could go and fix Mrs. Roth's fence.

Except, naturally, her fence was pristine.

Lizzie went back inside. The stubborn man could fix her fence. If he killed her and Mrs. Roth both, that would show Tommy.

Lizzie locked the door behind her. Put on the safety chain. Made sure all the windows were locked. Shut all the curtains. Only then did she get into the shower. But the hot water didn't do anything to relieve her agitation. *He just wants to fix your fence.*

The truth was, it bothered her that he hadn't noticed her as a woman. She was more than her broken-down fence. Not that she wanted to become the lover of a stranger who had nothing better to do than hang around where he wasn't wanted. But still, it hurt.

She stepped out of the shower and toweled off faster than usual, as if he might burst into her bathroom with his screwdriver, look at her naked body, and say, *I'm going to ground your bathroom wiring, install double-insulated safety outlets, and there's not a damn thing you or your two-bit cop can do to stop me.*

I've missed my chance at love.

The thought surprised her. Somehow, fourteen years had passed, and she hadn't noticed. She had become a mother, a house-owner, but no longer a woman.

She walked across her bedroom, which was dominated by her beautiful, brass antique bed. Her feet were cold on the hardwood floorboards, leaving misty footprints across the room that evaporated after her as if she were being followed.

But she wasn't being followed. She was alone. That was what was causing the dull ache inside her. All this work, all this pride, all this struggle—alone, without a man to love her and for her to love back.

She looked at her naked body in the maple mirror, the pale morning sun slanting across her thirty-year-old thighs. Decent face, in proportion. "Cute" was the usual word used to describe her button nose, sprinkling of pale, barely-there freckles, and cheeks that tended to

Raggedy Ann–red circles when she blushed. But cute didn't make it past her chin, when her body turned *womanly*. She sucked in her stomach. Examined her unremarkable legs. Her skin was so white as to be almost blue in spots. Great breasts, there was that. She had always been satisfied with them. Her job made her arms strong, her legs maybe not shapely, but strong.

She put her brown hair up in a practical bun and pulled on her plain cotton underwear and bra and then her server's dress. She had started at the diner at age seventeen, one year after Paige was born, in a size six, then worked her way up over the years to a ten. Now even that was getting snug.

She examined her butt in the mirror and frowned.

Dante Giovanni did not follow her home for her body. So what did he want?

She cleared a spot in the condensation and peered out the bathroom window. He was nailing a picket into place, his hammer echoing in the otherwise silent street. Mrs. Roth was letting herself back into her house, apparently satisfied with whatever Tay had told her. *I'm just doing my good deed to help this poor, single mother . . .*

It would be all over town by the time she got to work.

She watched him work his way down the fence, allowing herself a moment of appreciation for how good he looked. Broad shoulders, thin waist, strong legs, arms that could hold her just right.

Okay, moment over. Time to get back to reality.

He did seem to know what he was doing out there. But enough was enough. She had her daughter to think about. Letting strange men have their way with her fence wasn't responsible.

I'm sick and tired of being responsible.

To her surprise, she kicked her trash basket, sending it flying across the room. She watched it land and roll, shocked at her impetuous move.

As she got down on her hands and knees to clean up the spilled candy wrappers and crumpled receipts that had spilled out of the basket, she thought about Tommy's last words before he left: *Think about being nice. Okay? If not for him, then for me at least. Or for Annie. Or for Paige. Let him stay.*

She took a deep breath.

What if I let him stay for me?

She let the idea sit a few minutes, to see if it would settle into place. It almost felt right, but not quite. Something still nagged at her conscience.

What if I gave him something in return for fixing the place up? Then it would be a deal between equals.

But what could she give a man like Tay?

Hot naked sweaty sex.

Okay, despite the fact that he'd shown no interest in anything about her beyond her falling-down house, trading sex for services was just wrong. It was too icky to even think about a trade like that.

There had to be something that Tay wanted. Something else. It didn't have to be tawdry, even if part of her wished it was.

Maybe he wanted love.

The thought scared her to death. She had to sit down, breathe. *Remember, Lizzie, he didn't even notice you. Not one little bit.*

She pulled herself together. *Think.* Maybe he needed something in this town. He obviously wasn't from around here. There was hardly anyone she didn't know.

Anyway, she didn't have to guess. They were grown-ups. She'd ask him what he wanted and he would tell her.

Then, if they made a deal, he could stay and fix her place.

She thought about going out there to confront him with her plan, but she hesitated.

Best to wait for Tommy to do his background check first.

No sense in taking risks with a stranger fallen from the sky.

Plus, she really should think about this some more. Because no matter how much she told herself that she just wanted a rational exchange between equals, she knew that deep down, she wouldn't mind more.

She'd have to get another opinion.

Or three.

The next few days, Tay drove around Galton looking for a place to stay that would be better for the animals than the too-small hotel room they'd been holed up in. It was taking too long to find the money, and he was starting to think about the possibility that someone else had found it first. At least the town was tiny enough that maybe he could pick up some clues to who did find it. And the town really was small. He'd been here a week, and he was already getting the lay of the land. Despite his lifelong loyalty to New York City, the more he drove around during the day, or walked the streets at night waiting for sleep, the more he liked the place.

Galton University sat at the crest of the main hill, surrounded by a series of gorges crisscrossed with bridges, some as wide as two lanes, others so narrow only one person could cross at a time.

The closer to campus and the top of the hill, the more exclusive and fancy the houses. Lizzie's house was nine blocks up the hill—exactly halfway. But its location seemed misleading, as if somehow the house had fallen *up* the hill, coming to land in its current spot, the worse for the struggle.

The town stretched out from the base of the hill, starting with the diner that nestled at the bottom of the steepest street, to a long flat plateau that spread to the edge of an impressive lake.

One endless day, he'd been driving around the lake when he'd spotted a *For Rent* sign. On an impulse, he'd driven down the long driveway to find a tiny cabin under huge pines. He called the number on the sign. It turned out to be a month-to-month rental belonging to an old, bearded hippie who accepted Dune and White with a shrug of his shoulders. *All creatures are welcome here,* he'd said. *We don't discriminate.*

It was a nice place, a huge improvement over the hotel they'd been stuck in. The best part about it was that it was away from town, where he was always afraid he'd run into Candy. He didn't like being in the town with her. She'd made clear that she wanted him gone, and he'd honor her wishes. It wasn't fair for her to have to worry about running into him. As soon as he found the money, he'd leave. Then he'd figure out some better way to use the money to help her from afar. He had no idea how, but he had to concentrate on one step at a time.

So for now, the place worked. It was modest, built into a hillside, fully furnished in grad-student shabby. But Tay didn't mind a bit, even if it was a hundred steps down from his loft in Queens. Here, he and his broken-down truck fit in perfectly, no neighbors spying from behind their drapes, wondering what he was doing up at all hours. Here, he could sit out on the deck till dawn, when he could finally fall into bed and sleep. No more walking the town at night, scaring the locals.

He had told the old hippie he'd be gone before the month was over. Probably in a few days.

But it wasn't looking good for that scenario.

He had two problems. The first one was simple: He couldn't find the money. The second was more complicated: He was out of places to look. Which meant he had hours and hours of his day to fill and every hour he didn't do something, he thought about the accident, the hatred in Candy's eyes, the crunch of metal on metal, the sad walk to the grave while the rain fell around them.

He certainly couldn't go back to work on Lizzie's house. His inner Boy Scout sure had steered him wrong with that.

She definitely didn't want to see him again. Once her brother-in-law checked his record and learned about the accident, she would have the guy chase him off with a shotgun. Or maybe Mrs. Roth with her Glock. That was okay. He got that.

Well, it was a little okay. Because in truth, he had a third problem: He wanted to see Lizzie again. He had liked her run-down house, her bunny jammies, her insistence that she didn't need any help even though she was a little more wild-eyed every time he saw her, as if something was gaining on her, and she was a deer frozen in headlights, unable to move no matter how fast it bore down on her.

He wondered what was bearing down on her.

Stop it, Tay. She doesn't want your help.

He also liked that she didn't care what her house looked like. She seemed like the kind of person who lived her life for herself, damn the neighbors, which he admired. She'd be friends with whom she pleased even if they were her former enemies, feed whatever birds showed up on that crazy bird-feeder-store of a porch, stroll out in her jammies to threaten a stranger with nonsense, even call the cops just so she didn't have to owe him anything.

What a great life, to not owe anyone.

She seemed to know it, and clung to it with all her might.

He didn't blame her.

He used to live a life like that in New York City. He'd loved working his buildings all week, then playing pickup baseball in the parks on the weekends, having a few beers or walking around the museums with friends. Or, the last year and a half, hanging out with Emily.

But then, Emily left him. She said she couldn't be with a man stuck in the past. He didn't blame her, but he didn't know how to fix it. After Emily had left, he'd spent his time dealing with his tenants, fixing what needed fixing, and sometimes what didn't, just to keep himself busy. The older ones made him casseroles and tried to introduce him to their granddaughters and nieces. *He owns property*, he'd hear them whisper. *It's a good life.*

The younger tenants flirted, and once in a while, he'd take them up on their offers of dinner or beers on the fire escape.

But no one ever stuck. No one seemed to notice that his smile was forced and empty. No one really understood why he couldn't just forget the accident, move on, and get back to making money and having fun.

Hell, he didn't understand it either.

But he couldn't go back to his old life. The accident had taught him that life was short; but even knowing that, he couldn't get on with it. Any pleasure he found made the guilt that was a constant presence deepen. It was like a game he could play on himself.

He tried it right there on his deck. He closed his eyes and called to mind Lizzie's flashing eyes. Sure enough, like a knife in the gut, there it was. First, the lump in his throat. Then, the slicing pain as images of the crash pushed away images of Lizzie and her beautiful brown eyes.

So he tried to think of Emily and how she'd left him. Selling his buildings had been the final straw for her. That matched his black mood. But it didn't lessen the guilt. Ironically, the accident spared him the huge mistake of marrying a woman who didn't understand him. The irony wasn't lost on him that the biggest tragedy of his life had helped him avoid the tragedy of marrying the wrong woman. It was as if the world conspired against punishing him. First the police let him off with not even a ticket. Then the DA didn't press charges. Then her family—what little was left of it—let it go at that.

Get on with life, everyone said. *Not guilty. Accidents happen. How 'bout them Yankees . . .*

So why couldn't he let himself off? Why couldn't he smell the forest around him or feel the cold of the fall evening? Why couldn't he think of a woman like Lizzie without the thought's being followed by stomach cramps that doubled him over?

He sat on the porch that overlooked the lake, slung his feet up on the railing, and spread the want ads in the local paper open on his lap. He had to find something to do. A day job. Anything to keep his mind and body occupied until he could leave this town. Sitting around thinking didn't suit him.

White jumped onto the paper, cutting off his job search before it even began. He stroked her a few times before easing her to the ground. "You trying to stop me, girl? You want to go back and get another shot at those bird feeders, huh?" White rubbed against his leg. He could feel the rumblings of her purring. "Look, Lizzie wants nothing to do with me. She made that perfectly clear."

He tried to focus his mind on the lists of lousy jobs—dishwasher, sales, work-from-home scams—but White wouldn't back off, so he gave up. He sat back to stroke the cat who jumped into his lap and happily crunched the paper under her paws in ecstasy. Tay let his mind wander, which was usually a mistake. But this time, to his surprise, it didn't wander to the accident. It wandered to Lizzie.

Lizzie. He couldn't blame her for chasing him off. Ever since the accident, he'd been letting the rules of society fall away, partly out of numbness, partly out of not giving a damn. But his renegade directness made him forget how odd his actions seemed to people still playing by the rules. A stranger who does a good deed for no reason, especially in the dead of night or the fog of dawn, is definitely not playing by the rules. He got that and he wouldn't bother her again. He hadn't meant to scare her. Not that she seemed scared exactly, more like insistent. He hadn't meant to get caught fixing her gate. He thought he'd be gone before she spotted him, but the hinge was trickier than he'd expected, and it had taken longer than he'd thought. He should've known from the bird-feeder chaos on her front porch that she was a morning person and not risked it. Coming back a second time had been asking for trouble.

He wouldn't bother Lizzie again and he wouldn't bother Candy again either. He'd get the money and split and figure out some other way to get on with his life.

Maybe there was a gorge he had somehow missed.

He'd go out later to get some groceries and a map. Then he'd do a systematic search before he gave up and—

And then what?

He had no idea.

He had to find the money. That was the key.

Find the money before someone else did and get out.

CHAPTER

11

*A*nnie Wynne wasn't sure this mother thing was going to work out for her. Here she was, practically attached to another human, and she'd never felt so alone in her life.

Okay, so it was a very small human. Her six-month-old daughter, Meghan, fussed in the stroller Annie pushed up the gorge trail. No one had told Annie that being a new mother would be this dead crazy, mind-numbingly hard. Well, okay, her sister, Lizzie, had, but she hadn't believed her. After all, Lizzie had her baby alone when she was sixteen. Annie was thirty-four with a husband. A police officer husband, no less.

Which is why she thought it would be different for her.

Ha.

She loved her daughter madly. Loved her so hard it hurt.

Which was disturbing, because Annie hadn't felt this aching love for another person since meeting Tommy sixteen years ago. But after twelve years of marriage, she and Tommy didn't have the kind of love that hurt any-more. They were comfortably married, snugly in love. But the years were over when Tommy walked into the room and she thought, *Let's get naked*. Now she thought, *Babysitterman*, and lusted for a shower. *Alone*.

Annie knew she was supposed to cherish every moment with her precious daughter and that lots of women would kill for her problems, but it didn't help the fact that lately, she wanted to cry all the time. Annie and Meghan's daily morning stroll through the gorge trail that climbed its way to campus had become less a lovely walk on a beautiful fall day, and more a desperate attempt to fill the hours and hours and hours (and hours) of empty time.

And that was just the morning.

Annie's head might explode if she kept on like this. She wanted to cry and she wanted to scream and if some-thing new didn't happen soon, she just might do both right there under the Main Campus Bridge.

As if to protest Annie's dark thoughts, Meghan let out a banshee cry and flung her pacifier into the undergrowth that led down to the swirling water. It disappeared into the dense foliage and Meghan's face crumpled.

One, two, three . . .

Meghan erupted into a high-pitched, piercing scream.

Disgusted undergrads on their way to class through the gorge-trail shortcut glanced at Annie. "I guess I shouldn't have poked her with that knitting needle," Annie mum-bled. The students pulled each other past on the narrow path. *Look out, good citizens, a child-abusing, knitting-needle-wielding mama on the loose.*

Annie peered into the dense green weeds, unable to see the small, green pacifier, and thought, *I am the world's worst mother because I want to hurl myself over the edge of this cliff. I just can't bear to listen to my daughter scream another second.*

Meghan's wails got louder, if that was possible. Her face had turned fiery red. Her tiny fists clenched and shook.

"Okay, honey. Okay. Mommy will find it." *Unless it's plunged over the side, in which case Mommy might just follow it over.* Annie leaned over the simple wooden fence that signified the end of safety, but she couldn't see the pacifier. She got down on her hands and knees, crawled under the rough, single fence rail. She rummaged among the leaves and tangled roots. No luck. Meghan must have the arm of a major leaguer to have penetrated this growth.

The crying stopped abruptly. "Ru-ru!" Meghan called out.

Annie looked up.

"Ru-ru!" the baby commanded.

"Ru-ru" meant "ruff-ruff," which meant Meghan thought Annie was playing doggie. This favorite game involved Annie on her hands and knees, barking.

"Ru-ru!" Meghan repeated.

So what could Annie do? She barked.

Meghan clapped her tiny hands.

"Ruff! Ruff!" Annie kept barking as she searched the ground, trying to remember what poison ivy looked like. Three leaves? Five? Nature was never her thing. She was firmly a bookish, inside sort. She knew exactly where on the shelf the three volumes of *The Illustrated Guide to Identifying Forest Plants of New York State* was located in the library where she used to work, but she had never bothered to read the thing.

A set of jean-clad legs stopped next to her. She looked up to see a handsome undergrad eyeing her with amusement. She wondered what her thirty-four-year-old butt poking up in the air looked like to a twenty-something student. Completely disgusting, no doubt.

"No dogs off-leash on the campus gorge trails, ma'am," he said, a sly smile on his face.

She growled at him and he laughed and strode onward, his backpack slung carelessly over his shoulder.

She watched him go. *Ma'am?* Ma'am!

Great. Now she was barking and crying in the gorge.

What a day.

From Meghan's usual 5:30 A.M. wake-up call, to 5:31, to 5:32...to now. It wasn't even ten o'clock and she'd lived three lifetimes already in this one endless morning. How would she make it to dinner without slitting her wrists, at this rate? When had her heart grown so black? She had been the golden girl of Galton. Her only equal had been Lizzie, until, of course, Lizzie lost her golden girl crown and scepter. Maybe that's the way it was—having a baby lost a girl her golden status no matter what the circumstances.

Annie looked up at the narrow bridge that led to campus, then down at the stream rushing far below, and wondered how much it would hurt to jump off that bridge. She'd lived in Galton her whole life and had known some of the people who'd thrown themselves over the rail. But she'd never known their secrets. Like when they hit the long, smooth rocks lurking under the black water below, had death been instantaneous, or did they feel pain? Did the fast-flowing water carry their bodies away, or had they sunk to the bottom?

What thoughts. Where had they come from? What was happening to her?

She wished for a miracle. Nothing major. Just a quick sign that she would get through this, a two-second glimpse of, say, an angel on the rocks down below. Maybe a unicorn peeking down at her, a flash of his elegant, twisted horn catching in the light. Hell, she'd settle for a winking leprechaun. That would have been enough to get her through. Just one little sign that there was something more in the world than everyday drudgery. She could take it from there.

Annie made one last, halfhearted attempt to feel around under the foliage for the pacifier.

Her hand hit something. Something wedged into a crevice in the rock, as if it had come hurtling out of the sky, or maybe off the bridge, with considerable force. She leaned over, nervous with vertigo at the closeness of the cliff.

She pulled it out.

It was a duffel bag.

Annie looked back to the stroller. Meghan had found her foot and gotten it into her mouth. She was "ru-ruing" softly to herself, the sounds muffled into the hand-knitted pink booty the New Agey one in Lizzie's Enemy Club had given her. She seemed content for the moment.

The bells in the clock tower began to chime in the distance, hurrying the last of the students still on the trail up the last ascent to campus. By the time the bells chimed their ninth peal, the path was deserted. Except for Annie and Meghan.

And the bag.

She pulled the army-green duffel onto her lap. Annie's

first thought was that she ought to leave it. Maybe some-one had meant to hide it there. But curiosity got the best of her. She tugged it and whatever was inside shifted intriguingly.

The gorge was quiet around her except for the rushing stream far below.

Annie unzipped the bag.

It was stuffed with neatly wrapped packets of hundred-dollar bills.

It wasn't exactly a unicorn. But mythological creatures were so overrated.

CHAPTER

12

*L*izzie walked along the shore, next to Scott Halpinger, Nina's yoga student and at the moment Lizzie's first date in years, trying to explain to him her fascination with birds. The plan was to hike around the lake trail where a pair of great blue herons had been spotted nesting in an enormous dead pine, then up the road that led to The Pines, where they'd stop for a bite and, she hoped, fall in love, for a few months anyway.

Lizzie jabbered about the surprise of the herons' staying so late into September, and how they'd be gone any day now, maybe they were gone already, but they'd probably come back, because that's what that kind of bird usually does...

Scott nodded politely. He had been enthusiastic about the hike, even suggested she bring her birding binoculars so she could teach him a thing or two, but now, after an hour or so of spotting nothing more exotic than a single egret fishing by the shore, his interest in habitats and tail feathers was cooling fast. She was relieved he wasn't too engaged, because she was also having trouble keeping her mind on her flying friends.

Because she couldn't stop thinking about Tay.

Stop thinking about Tay.

But she couldn't. He hadn't been back since she'd called Tommy, and who could blame him? Calling the cops wasn't exactly the best way to make friends. But his being gone was good; it gave her time to find a suitable boyfriend so maybe then she wouldn't think so much about Tay. Or dream so much about him...

Having an affair with the mysterious charity handyman was so not all right on so many levels.

She focused on the man by her side. Scott was sweet and normal. There was nothing wrong with the way he looked, blond, healthy, athletic. So she should be happy. Cute guy sent by fate, pretending to care about birds, which they couldn't find because she was so nervous and agitated she couldn't shut up long enough to not scare them all away.

Isn't this what she wanted? A lukewarm man, so that no one would get hurt.

Or was Tay right and she had no idea what she wanted?

As they searched in vain for the heron nest, she thought about all her mixed-up wishes. She had wished for what Paige wanted because she wanted Paige to be happy. After all, wishes didn't have to be selfish. Lizzie had spent her life wishing for the best for Paige. She'd spent her life being a good mother, doing the right thing. So why would she stop now? No, at this of all times being a good mother was of utmost importance. Not a time for selfish wishes.

By the time they made it to the Pines, a locals' restaurant overlooking a cliff by the lake, Lizzie's fingers and toes were frozen solid. They got a table inside by the window overlooking the water, and Scott excused himself to go to the bathroom. He'd been slathering himself with insect repellent and bug spray nonstop since they'd set off, and now, apparently, he was afraid the toxins in his protection would kill him if ingested.

He had used the word *ingested.*

Lizzie tried to keep a positive attitude.

She could like a man who said *ingested* for three months.

That kind of man wouldn't cause any pain.

She looked out over the lake and told herself that this was lovely. She should have dated more in the past years, nothing to be afraid of, if she didn't take it too seriously.

She looked over the menu and looked and looked.

I don't have the slightest idea what I want to eat.

All at once, she felt as if she might start crying.

She looked around the restaurant with alarm. Dotted around her were people she recognized. The couple at the table behind her came into the diner every so often for lunch. The man always ordered a tuna sandwich with tomato, white bread, root beer, and a side salad. His wife sometimes ordered the Cobb salad and an unsweetened iced tea, but sometimes went with the soup of the day, if it didn't have meat. But here, they were eating huge burgers dripping with blue cheese with sides of fries and ice-cold beers.

They didn't just know exactly what they wanted, they knew where they wanted it and where they didn't and probably exactly how they wanted it cooked...

When they felt Lizzie staring at them, they waved

tentatively, unsure how they knew her. She waved back and ducked her head into her menu.

How did a person forget what she wanted? Was it because her head was stuffed with what other people wanted? She thought of Nina's words at the diner on the day Lizzie had told them about Ethan's letter: *Lizzie, if you want something, you have to face it, admit it, then wish for it with all your soul. That's how the universe works. It will hear your wish and if it's sincere, it will answer.*

But what if you weren't sure what you wanted? Or worse, what if what you wanted—like keeping your daughter close—was selfish and wrong?

Scott came back to the table. "So, you know what you want?"

She started to laugh and then before she knew it, she was fighting back tears. This was ridiculous. He was going to think she was nuts. And she was nuts. Ethan's return was disturbing the equilibrium of her life and Tay's odd presence wasn't helping. She felt as if everything she thought was settled was coming undone. She buried her face in her menu and said, "I'll have the Cobb salad."

So he ordered a burger with fries for himself and a salad for her and two Molson Goldens. When conversation died down for the third time, he asked if she could see where the heron nest was supposed to be from here.

Relieved, she got out her birding binoculars and scanned the pines. The treetops were deserted, so she lowered her sights, scanning the ground. Cabins dotted the woods. They looked so peaceful, tucked into the trees, docks reaching out into the water in front of them. The leaves were almost in full fall splendor. In two weeks, the view would be postcard perfect and tourists from as far away as New York City would fill these tables.

The cabins across from her were also picture-perfect. She was jealous of people who lived on the lake. They didn't have to worry about nosy neighbors caring about their lawns getting overgrown. Some of the cabins on the other shore were so hidden, she could only see a roof or maybe a few windows. Others were open to the shore, a view over the lake their main purpose.

A man was on a deck of one of them—

No.

The man on the deck was Tay.

Lizzie felt a surge of excitement pulse through her veins that she refused to acknowledge. Seeing Tay meant nothing, a coincidence. He was a nuisance, that was all. She had no interest in him whatsoever. But when she realized there was no way she could make herself lower the binoculars and look back at her date, she knew she was in trouble.

"See something?" Scott asked.

"I'm not sure," she said. She adjusted the focus.

Tay had the cat on his lap and he stroked it slowly while he stared out over the water. She could never date a man with a cat, so she ought to just stop staring right now.

But she couldn't stop. His face looked tense, despite the lovely scene, as if whatever he was looking at was a million miles away.

She scanned for the dog, and sure enough, he was by the door to the cottage, panting and wet, as if he'd just jumped into the lake for a swim despite the freezing water. The yellow tennis ball was between his paws.

Stupid dog.

Stupid her.

Because she was waiting for the beautiful woman she was sure would come out of his house.

And she was already jealous.

But no woman came.

She felt a rush of hope.

"What is it? You look like you spotted something interesting," Scott insisted.

It was hard, but she lowered the binoculars. "I thought it was something interesting, but it's just a common—" She paused. What was Tay? She thought of all the birds she loved and the ones she hated. She wanted to describe Tay as a pushy pest, a bird who came to other birds' nests and had to be chased away. A bluebird, maybe. That was a beautiful, but pushy, obnoxious bird. But instead she said, "He's a catbird."

"He?" Scott asked.

"A male catbird. I can tell from the coloring." She felt her face blush. "It's nothing special. They're all over the place."

But that wasn't true. She'd never met anyone quite like Tay. Someone who said so little, but said exactly what he wanted to say, did exactly what he wanted to do, even if it was so clearly unwanted. And looked so good saying and doing it...

Don't do it, don't do it...

But she did it.

She raised her binoculars again.

He'd fallen asleep in his chair, his feet still up on the rail in front of him, his arms crossed over his chest, the cat still on his lap. His chin had dropped to his chest, his hair had flopped forward. She could see the gentle rise and fall of his chest. He started to tip to the side, ever so slightly. Then a little more. Then, gravity took over and he went halfway to the deck before he caught himself, startling awake, looking around as if he had no idea where he was.

Lizzie couldn't help but smile. He was adorable.

"What are you watching?" Scott asked again.

She shoved the binoculars into her bag. "Catbirds can be ridiculous," she said, making no sense at all.

Scott bit into his burger. "Funny name for a bird."

"Yeah. It's their song. They mimic, so sometimes, their song sounds like a cat's meow."

The cat's meow . . .

She forbade herself to pick up the glasses again.

"Huh. And I always thought cats and birds were enemies," he said.

"They are," she reminded herself. "Well, when life makes sense they are." She looked down at the salad she had no intention of eating.

Nothing made sense to her. Not her wishes, not her feelings for this odd man, not anything.

What did she want from Tay and his imperturbable cat?

CHAPTER

13

$\mathcal{T}$he next morning at the diner, Lizzie watched the chrome 1950s clock over the counter count down the seconds until seven o'clock. *Ten, nine, eight, seven…*

As the red second hand swept over the twelve, Jill strode past the plate-glass door, her blonde ponytail wagging behind her. Right behind Jill came Georgia in the ugliest tweed suit Lizzie had seen yet. Before Lizzie could bring the coffee, Nina joined them, a flush of autumn colors, natural fibers, and glowing good health.

The Enemy Club was officially back in session.

"Okay, I've got a bone to pick with one of you," Lizzie began once they had gotten through the small talk of their week.

"I've got fifteen minutes till a meeting with a new professor moving in from Manhattan," Jill said as she adjusted her bottom on the cherry-red vinyl stool as if it were her throne. She pulled her ponytail even tighter.

Georgia checked her watch. "I have a new patient in twenty." She was Galton's preeminent psychiatrist. Actually, she was Galton's only psychiatrist. "An interesting case, finally. I am so sick of these overindulged, bratty children who think a problem is when Mummy takes the Mercedes away. This one might be the real deal." She checked her watch again, practically crackling with anticipation.

"So nice for you that the genuinely mentally ill are finally back in town!" Lizzie said.

Nina carefully draped herself and her flowing skirt over her stool. She looked like a fairy, her delicate features dotting her broad face. Her freckles looked backlit from inside. "I have all day. Take your time, Liz. What's wrong? You don't look yourself today. You look, well, rosy."

"Thank you." Lizzie filled everyone's coffee mugs, except for Jill, who as usual, refused the diner coffee and brought in a skinny mocha latte from across the street. Lizzie tried not to notice how good it smelled.

"You do look different," Jill said.

"Happy," Georgia pointed out.

They all stared at her expectantly. She lowered her voice and they all leaned forward as one. "Okay, which one of you sent him?"

They stared at her blankly.

Lizzie studied their faces for signs of deceit, but there was only rabid curiosity.

Then Jill's eyebrows rose and her mouth opened and she said, "Oh, my God. This is about that man who fixed your gate!"

"I knew it was you," Lizzie accused.

"No. Not me. Judy Roth told Eleanor Platz who told me all about it at the Food Emporium. She gave me a blow-by-blow last night." Jill smiled knowingly. "Eleanor said, *Lizzie is finally fixing up her house! And the man doing it is quite the looker!*" Jill paused, waiting for confirmation.

Lizzie shrugged noncommittally. "He's all-right-looking."

"I knew something was up, because you're way too cheap to hire someone to fix up your place," Jill finished.

Nina kicked Jill under the counter.

"Ouch."

"It's okay," Lizzie said. "It's true. I am too cheap because Paige's education is more important. I'm going to fix the place up myself. I've already decided. But listen, this isn't funny. It's odd. Remember that conversation we had in here? When we were talking about the perfect guy?"

"The universe hates me," Jill groused. "Mine didn't show."

"Yeah, well, mine did," Lizzie said.

That got their attention.

"The Lizzie Carpenter dream man? Wham-whirr-thanks-for-installing-my-hot-tub-sir!" Georgia downed her entire cup of coffee and held out her mug for more. "Another skinny mocha latte caramel frappe, please."

"Coming up," Lizzie said, filling her mug with plain black coffee. "Would you like a sprinkle of cinnamon on that?"

"Yes."

"Too bad."

Jill rolled her eyes. "You're all just jealous that I'm the only honest one here who refuses that battery acid she calls coffee."

Lizzie got back to business. "So, really, you swear that none of you sent him?"

"Why would we do that?" Georgia asked, confused.

"We're not that kind of friends," Jill reminded her.

"Thank God," Nina said. "I'd kill you guys if you sent me a—" She paused. She was living in her brother's house, as he was away in the army for another year. The place was in pretty decent shape.

"It would be like me sending you a personal stylist to get you out of the sixties," Jill said.

"Or me getting you a few sessions with a good therapist who could help you through your passive aggression problem," Georgia said.

"I don't have a passive aggression problem," Nina said.

"Yes you do. No one is as nice as you are." Georgia checked her watch.

Nina sighed. "It would be like me making you guys come to my yoga classes. But I won't, because I accept you all the way you are."

"See, that was passive aggression!" Georgia cried. She loved being right. Just like when they were back in school, it made her bounce up and down with excitement. "She just called us all fat and lazy."

"I did not!" Nina protested. "I offered to give you a wonderful gift and you, the cynic, turned it around."

While they goofed around about what they'd all send one another if they were going to indulge in fixing one another's lives, an uneasy weight deep in Lizzie's stomach was starting to form. None of them had sent Tay. She could see it in their faces.

Finally, they noticed her stillness, and focused back on Lizzie.

"Ask the world for what you want, and you get it," Nina proclaimed. "Positive Thinking 101. We must recognize our dreams in order to achieve them." She was smiling as if she'd created Tay with fairy dust.

"Then I should get my pec man," Jill said, her tone petulant.

"Tell us the details," Georgia insisted.

"Some guy named Dante Giovanni was in the diner when we were talking and he said he overheard us. He fixed my gate latch. And my light." She explained how Tay had refused to take no for an answer. "I told him not to come back, but he doesn't listen."

"I want a man with decent pecs!" Jill shouted, her arms opened wide. She looked around at the near-empty diner. Deaf old Mr. Ruderson smiled and waved at her from his booth, a spot of ketchup on his unshaved chin. Mr. Zinelli opened his arms wide. Jill winked at them both, then turned back to her coffee. "Shoot. You always get the guy, Lizzie."

"When have I ever gotten the guy?" Lizzie asked. "You were the biggest prude at Galton High, and still the boys followed you like you were Madonna."

Jill said, "They followed me because I didn't put out, unlike some of us."

Nina shot Jill a look, and to Lizzie's surprise, Jill blushed and looked down at her shoes.

But Lizzie didn't have time to think about it, as the conversation, as usual, was speeding ahead.

"Send your handyman my way next," Georgia said. "I have two cords of firewood coming tomorrow and I need to get it stacked."

"So if this guy just showed up to fix stuff for no reason,

how creepy is that?" Lizzie said. Her skin had gone clammy. *He had been telling the truth.*

"He's not there for no reason. He's a man. He wants sex," Georgia said. "Call the cops."

"You're awfully sex-obsessed for a woman who never gets any," Jill pointed out to Georgia. "Sometimes a screwdriver is just a screwdriver, Doctor."

Georgia rolled her eyes. "You're a walking contradiction, Jill. You dress as if you understand men, but then you talk as if you're innocent. Lizzie has to protect herself—and her daughter."

"Shhh, you two! This is about Lizzie. So what'd you do?" Nina asked breathlessly.

"I told him to leave. But he wouldn't. And then he came back the next day, so I called Tommy."

"No."

"Yes. And Tommy said he was a nice guy and I should be nice to him."

"You're holding back," Jill said. "What aren't you telling us?"

Nina cocked her head. "She is."

Georgia agreed. "Tell us everything. Enemy Club rules."

Lizzie sighed. "Okay. I'm thinking of making some kind of deal with him. If you guys didn't send him, then I need to pay him back."

Nina smiled. "I'm so glad you're going to let him stay!"

"I'm not going to let him stay. I'm going to fix the place myself with his occasional expertise."

Jill studied Lizzie closely. "How gorgeous is he?"

Lizzie shrugged. "On a scale of one to ten?"

They waited.

"Eleven and a half."

"Oh, Lizzie! How wonderful!" Georgia gushed as if she were Lizzie's mother hearing about a doctor million-aire, not a strange man who lurked around at night, fixing things. "You've been so stuck. Same house, same job, same fears. You're coming loose. Getting ready for the next step: letting go of Paige and getting a new man."

Lizzie shook her head. "No, no, no! I'm not going to date him in exchange for his handiwork. I'm going to—" To what? She had no idea how she could ever pay him back.

Nina said, "There's something else you're not tell-ing us."

"He reminds me of Ethan," Lizzie admitted.

"So what? Ethan was hot," Jill said, then she blushed.

Jill and Nina exchanged glances again. What was up with that?

Lizzie didn't want to pursue that odd blush. Jill had been acting weird ever since she'd told them Ethan was coming back. But the conversation was already going a million different directions, and she had to keep it on track. "I don't want to teach Paige that men can fix every-thing. I made a deal with myself that I'd fix the place. So if he's going to lend a hand here and there, I have to offer him something that Paige can see and understand. Some-thing noble. I can never, ever, ever date him. What would that mean to Paige?"

"That you're dating a kind, helpful man, opening your heart to him?" Nina suggested. She always saw the good side of people.

Georgia leaned down to get a notebook out of her

briefcase, almost toppling off her stool in the process. She righted herself and said, "Look, you've consciously and subconsciously linked this man to Ethan, which is very astute. Your fantasy is still alive of the knight in shining armor coming to rescue you from Galton, but you know it's wrong to act on that fantasy—especially with Paige watching at this crucial time in her life. So hold firm! You're doing the right thing by either making things even or kicking him out. Plus, you understand that you can't have a relationship with him. Good girl! I'm very proud. It's a very rational solution."

"But Lizzie did the 'wrong,' crazy, irrational thing last time she was faced with a hero," Nina pointed out. "And that turned out okay in the end, right? I mean, Ethan split, but Paige is a beautiful, sweet, brilliant girl. There was no right or wrong thing to do. In a lot of ways, she's better off than the rest of us because she acted on her love."

Lizzie wanted to hug Nina for saying that, but she only let out a tiny smile, because she didn't want to say that she did feel blessed with Paige when none of them had what she had.

Nina went on. "So she should do what feels right. That's what Lizzie does, it's who she is. She doesn't make sense—and that's fine. It's ridiculous to take such an intellectual stand on an emotional situation."

Georgia rolled her eyes and kept scribbling.

Lizzie tried to peer at Georgia's pad, but she covered it up. "Are you taking notes on me?" she asked.

"Nina's right. Forget the Georgia Phillips psychobabble," Jill said. "She doesn't make any sense at all. If Lizzie's hot for the guy, she should date him. He's cute, right? Who cares if he's also handy with the screwdriver? Get your white-knight-on-a-horse complex out of your system with this guy, hon, so when Ethan comes, you're not panting and dry-humping the couch after fourteen barren years." She pretended to be taking notes on a napkin, then held up a cartoony picture of a guy with enormous muscles surrounded by hearts. "Here's my notes."

"I've had dates," Lizzie insisted. She threw the napkin in the trash.

"Bad ones," they all said.

"Well, at least I've had some dates," Lizzie insisted. "It's not like I've been celibate."

"Bad dates," they all chorused.

"Can we forget the past, please, and focus on the future?" Lizzie begged. She didn't want to rehash her dating failures.

"Hold firm!" Georgia said. "You fix the place with his occasional help, only if he accepts equal payment."

Nina leaned forward. She was wearing long beads that fell onto the counter with a patter like rain. "You wished for this guy for a reason, Liz. And he came because the universe was listening." Nina twirled her beads around her finger. "It's fate, Lizzie. There's nothing you can do but accept it. Open your heart to him—"

"Or at least your legs," Jill said.

Mr. Zinelli, who had been listening in on the entire conversation, choked on his chocolate doughnut.

Lizzie poured him more coffee, and he nodded thankfully.

"I believe our work here is done," Jill said. "Two-to-one, date the handyman. You pick your reason."

"Or maybe two-to-two," Georgia said. "We haven't heard your decision, Liz."

"It's even," Lizzie said. "I'm with Georgia. I'm going to fix the place myself and find a less complicated man to date. Anyway, Tay hasn't shown up for two days. Maybe it's all moot and I'll never see him again."

CHAPTER

14

$\mathcal{T}$hree nights later, Jill came by the diner at dinnertime. "No time to talk love," she said. "Just wanted to make sure you saw this." She tossed a copy of the *Galton Daily* onto the service counter by the water pitchers, folded back to the third page. "Enjoy!"

Lizzie was swamped with customers. When the throng finally cleared, she picked up the paper. It was folded to the crime blotter, with one item circled in red pen:

Man Fixes Gate, the headline read. *6:32 A.M, 47 Pine Tree Road—30-year-old female reported unknown male fixing her front gate latch. Officer responded 6:38 A.M. Discovered Caucasian male, 34, brown hair, 6 foot 2, 190 pounds, armed with screwdriver.*

Jill had double-underlined Tay's stats and added a few exclamation points.

Male stated he had overheard female head of household wish for free handyman. Female corroborated story, alleging she didn't think anyone would actually grant her wish. Male claimed top hinge screw was rusted out. He replaced screw, oiled hinges, and left property in proper repair. No charges filed.

Written in Jill's handwriting in the margin was a note: *You called the cops on him?!?! Now you're going to have to fight off every single woman in Galton. Including me. Ta-ta!*

She had added a PS at the bottom of the page, next to the coupon for a half-off oil change at Pacco's Garage. *Next time, take MY advice. Get that man while the getting's good. PPS: Georgia Phillips is the ninnyhammer. Why would you ever side with her?*

CHAPTER

15

$\mathcal{T}$wo nights later, the first waves of the dinner rush ended and Joy came in to take over just as Lizzie's arches were starting to ache.

Lizzie shrugged on her purple faux-fur coat and headed for home, her head down against the chilly fall night air. She glanced up just long enough to check for cars, and stopped.

Tay Giovanni's truck was parked at the curb.

Why couldn't she live in a bigger town, with more than one main street? She glanced into the cab. The white cat was curled up on the driver's seat with the mini Lassie dog. Did these animals follow him everywhere? The cat opened one eye, regarded her, then closed it again. The dog slept soundly, his head on his paws.

Lizzie looked up just in time to see Tay Giovanni duck into Lucifer's Pub.

She checked her watch; it was barely six. She had some time before Paige expected her for dinner. Still, she ought to head home. Lately, she'd been trying to sneak in time with Paige every chance she got. She'd bought Scrabble and Parcheesi and a backgammon set. Paige, needless to say, did not appreciate the newfound attention, or the old-fashioned entertainment, which she'd dubbed "totally lame." But Lizzie was finding it hard to back off and give the girl space.

Lizzie crossed the street and slipped into Lucifer's before she could think about what she was about to do. Her heart was pounding. She hadn't been this terrified since—

Oh, hell.

Since the first time she talked to Ethan fifteen years ago.

Why did she keep equating these two men in her mind?

She spotted Tay at the bar. His back was to her, his broad shoulders—

She started to back out of the bar. Her hands were shaking. Was this really the first man she'd truly wanted since Ethan? Why? She didn't even know him.

The bartender, Chrissie, who had gone through school two years behind Lizzie and came into the diner every morning for a poppy-seed bagel with cream cheese and large coffee to go before her day job at the pharmacy, called out, "Hey, Lizzie. We never see you in here! To what do we owe the pleasure?"

It was too late to turn back.

Lizzie steeled herself. She could do this. That she hadn't been interested in a man in ages didn't mean that she couldn't act like a rational woman around Tay. She reminded herself that this wasn't about romance. It wasn't about her at all. It was about making a deal in order to make Paige happy.

She crossed the red-themed bar. Red walls, red-painted concrete floor, red shades over the lightbulbs. And on the wall behind the bar, a huge mural that Nina had painted ages ago of Lucifer himself, winking and drinking a beer.

In true Nina style, she'd painted a yin-yang pendant around his neck. Naturally, she'd made him gorgeous.

Lizzie tried to quell her nervousness by focusing on anything but Tay, or Lucifer. The muted horse races on the television played to two students lounging at a back table with a pitcher of beer. A lone woman sat at the end of the bar reading a paperback novel. Pinball games blinked and buzzed behind her like children desperate for attention. The rest of the wooden chairs sat empty, ready for the long night ahead.

Tay didn't turn. He was keeping his head low, as if he didn't want anyone to see him.

Lizzie left one stool between them.

He didn't look up. His scuffed brown leather jacket over a hooded black sweatshirt camouflaged him in the red glow of the bar. His wavy black hair fell forward, covering his profile so she couldn't see his face. He was hunched over a map of Galton, marking something on it.

More houses to fix in the dead of night? She was going to ask, but couldn't find her voice. She cleared her throat, but he was obviously engrossed. She had to get his attention somehow.

"What's new?" Chrissie asked.

"Hey, Chris. How are the kids?" Lizzie would wait for the perfect moment. Her palms itched with anticipation. Her mouth was dry. This was the craziest thing she'd done in a long time. What if he said no? What if she was making a perfect fool of herself?

"Eloise is teething. It's awful. You want something?" Chrissie asked.

"Oh, poor you. And poor her. But mostly, poor you. I'll have a club soda."

The impossible man still didn't look up.

Chrissie nodded and finished topping off Tay's beer.

Lizzie had an idea. She shouldn't, she couldn't. But she was getting exasperated that he hadn't noticed her and she didn't have time to think.

Chrissie slid the beer in front of Tay on a faded Buffalo Bills coaster. Just as he reached for it, Lizzie jumped over a stool and grabbed the mug. "You can take this back," she said to Chrissie, sliding the beer back to her. "He'll have a club soda, too."

Tay looked at Lizzie. Then at the beer just out of his reach. His eyes narrowed and it occurred to Lizzie that he might not know who she was, which made her double her resolve. No one messed with her and then forgot her.

Chrissie stared from the beer to Lizzie to Tay, not sure what to do.

Lizzie rushed on, feeling the surge of nerves that being too close to Tay gave her. "You might say it's none of my business what he drinks, since I don't know him. He's a stranger, actually. But if I want to fix him, I will, no matter what he says. So no alcohol. Club soda. Slice of lemon or lime, Tay?"

She had his full attention now, his steady eyes locked on hers. "Lemon," he said. He wasn't smiling, wasn't frowning—he was a cipher, his dark face a mask in the shadows of the bar.

She wanted to touch that mask, ease it off him carefully, see what was underneath. "Bummer. I say let's go with lime." She was trying to hold her resolve, hoping he couldn't see her shaking hands. She licked her lips, but it didn't help the dryness.

Chrissie stared at them as if Lizzie had grown a horn. "So. I'll get those club sodas. And maybe a bulletproof vest." Chrissie stepped away, backward, her lips twitching in delighted bewilderment. She left the beer on the counter between them, too confused to take it away.

Tay eyed his beer, and Lizzie wondered if he was going to make a grab for it. "Try it, buddy," she said. "Not so tough without your sidekicks, huh?"

Silence. Stillness. The pinball games blinking to no one. He still didn't smile, but she felt she was making some kind of dent in his silent exterior. "Maybe they're on their way," he said.

"Nope. I saw them in your truck. They're sound asleep."

"Guess I'm on my own, then," he said.

Me, too, she didn't say. But she thought it, and she didn't want to think it because it was too close to the truth and she wanted to keep this light, keep it business, keep it safe.

His knee shifted ever so slightly and it touched hers and they both jumped away from the contact as if it set off sparks.

Which it had. At least for her. He probably hardly noticed.

Make a deal, she reminded herself. "So, have I successfully demonstrated how inappropriate your actions at my gate were? How a normal person doesn't barge into a stranger's life, touch her things, then refuse to leave when it's clear he's not wanted?"

"I hate normal people," he said.

So do I, she thought. That rush she felt in her stomach, she told herself firmly, was not affection. The yearning wasn't need or desire. And even if it was, he certainly didn't feel it, so she might as well ignore it.

"And who said you're not wanted?" he asked.

She rushed forward. "So, I've been thinking about our impasse. If you're going to insist on being impossible and fixing my place, which is incredibly nice and all—just very inappropriate—then I get to fix something about you. I don't accept charity. It has to be even."

A slight upward turn of the right corner of his mouth, nothing near a smile. "That so?" he asked.

"Yes." She coughed. "What do you want, then?" She fixed him with as serious a stare as she could hold. She felt a humming tension between them. If she reached out and touched his shoulder, she was sure it would be vibrating.

She knew she was going to dream tonight about those shoulders.

"What do you need, er, fixed?" she asked.

He considered her, all of her, in his maddening, slow-motion way. He cocked his head to the side and ignored her question. "Maybe I don't need fixing."

"Sure you do. First, there's the going where you're not wanted," she said.

The quirk of his lip again. "It's Boy Scout Possession," he said. "Can't help helping strangers. It's like a disease. But I'm starting to doubt that there's a cure."

He was so serious, she didn't know how to respond. She was distinctly aware of how she was sitting, how she had just sucked in her stomach and sat up a little straighter. Was she flirting? Was he going to think she was flirting?

For heaven's sake, she'd followed him into a bar and stolen his beer! What else could he think? She cleared her throat. "When did this, um, affliction strike?"

"'Bout a year ago." He shifted just slightly toward her.

"So a year ago, you were a perfectly ordinary man who would leave strangers alone?"

"Yep. No matter what they wished for. I minded my own business. Didn't go out of my way to help anyone. Perfectly normal guy out for women and money and a good time. Think you can get me back to that?"

"So now, you're not out for, um, women and fun?" Lizzie asked.

"Not a chance."

"Really?"

"Really. Part of the Boy Scout thing. When I'm around, you have to fear for your peeling paint, but that's about it."

"I'm not sure I believe you."

"I tell the truth." He shrugged. "Because I, unlike you, know what I want and what I don't want."

That was hard to argue with. She didn't think she'd ever met a man who was so focused on doing exactly as he pleased. So why shouldn't she do what she pleased? She took a deep breath. "I have a problem."

His eyebrows rose.

"The father of my daughter, the man who abandoned her fourteen years ago, is coming in three months. She thinks he's going to see our run-down place and flee in terror."

He nodded. "Couldn't blame him."

"That's why I want to fix the place up. For Paige, my daughter."

He didn't say anything, but a shadow passed over his face.

She rushed on. "I want her father to help her out when he comes. But I don't want Paige to think it's okay to believe that men are the answer. I know that doesn't make sense, but I want both those things at once. For her to be independent, and for her to be able to take whatever help her father can offer."

"Makes sense to me," he said.

"Good! So you see my problem. That's why I was thinking that maybe we could make a deal. If you would help me fix my house up, then I would repay you in some way. But I'm kind of broke."

"I don't want money," he said.

"And of course, anything, um, inappropriate is off the table for both of us." Her words came out like a squeak. "I certainly don't want to teach Paige, um, that."

"Lizzie, I have to tell you something up front." His jaw clenched and unclenched. "About a year ago, I—" He paused. "I came between a mother and a daughter." His voice faltered for just a second, then resumed its slow, low pace. "I'm starting to see that I won't ever be able to make that up to them. And I'm seeing now from talking to you why. People hate help from the people who've wronged them." He paused. "Heck, they even hate to accept help from people who remind them of people who wronged them."

She wanted to ask him what happened between him and the mother and the daughter. But the tenseness of his jaw told her that he'd said all he was going to about that.

"But I owe you," he said.

"You don't owe me anything. I don't even know you."

"I do," he said. He fixed her with his intense green eyes. "You let me smell the coffee."

She looked around. There wasn't any coffee. She couldn't smell anything but stale beer and old perfume.

When she looked back, he had swiped his beer. "Hey!"

He chugged it in one long gulp, finishing the entire pint. "And you let me taste my beer. Believe me, I owe you big-time."

"Tay!"

"Look, tell your daughter that you're giving me whatever you want to tell her. I'll back you up. She doesn't have to know our deal."

"But I'll know that really we have no deal."

"So this isn't about her, really. It's about you," he pointed out. "Why not just say what you mean, Lizzie?" He leaned in close.

Lizzie was starting to panic, as his face seemed awfully close to hers, his eyes even more intense than usual. "You have to tell me what you want. This doesn't work unless we're even," she repeated.

"Even?" he asked. "Is that ever possible? Especially, Lizzie, for people like us who either don't know what we want, or know that what we want is impossible?"

"Nothing's impossible," she insisted.

He leaned in closer.

Or maybe she leaned closer.

It was impossible to know, impossible to breathe.

Their lips touched.

A light kiss. Soft. A friendly kiss, if a kiss on the lips could be friendly. Still, it set Lizzie on fire. She was too shocked to move. It was more a touching than a kiss. A connection. And yet, she'd never felt anything quite so intense as this man's lips on hers. She let her eyes flutter closed and her thoughts fell away and she felt him, his intensity a physical vibration through her just as she knew it would be. *Yes, you fix my fence and I'll meet you in bars and kiss you...It's a deal...*

He separated. Or maybe she did. It was hard to tell.

She opened her eyes.

While she was trying not to fall off her stool because her bones had melted into a puddle, he was intensely rigid, his face tight, as if he'd seen a ghost.

"Tay?"

He startled, then looked at her as if he wasn't sure why she was there. "Sorry," he said. "I'm so sorry."

Sorry? For kissing me? "Are you okay?" Had she kissed him or had he kissed her? Had she attacked him? She felt humiliated, her face already hot. She was glad for the red tint of the bar. Maybe he wouldn't notice.

"I'm sorry," he said again. "Really. I don't know what happened. I didn't mean to do that." He stood, threw a five-dollar bill on the bar. He looked as if he didn't know where he was or what he was doing. He stepped away, stopped, looked back.

"Are you leaving?" she said. "What about our deal? You can't fix my place unless I can give you something—not that!—something else in return."

"I have to go." He was already halfway across the bar.

"Hey!" she called. "No! That's not okay! Wait!"

But he didn't wait.

She considered chasing him out, but Chrissie was watching. Lizzie didn't want to start the town talking any more than that kiss or her neighbor Mrs. Roth already had. *So then, Lizzie snatched this hot guy's beer, and started kissing him like she was on fire...*

"He's cute!" Chrissie said when the door had shut behind him. "New friend of yours? Don't think I've ever seen him around here."

"No. More like a new enemy," Lizzie said. What had just happened?

She looked at the bar, where his map of Galton still lay. He had circled all the bridges over all the gorges between the diner and campus. She stuck the map into her bag, hoping Chrissie wouldn't notice. "Well, I better go. Um, Chrissie, can you, you know, not mention this to anyone?"

"Wouldn't dream of it," Chrissie said.

But Lizzie knew that was a lie. It would be all over town by the next day.

Tay sat in his truck, his head on the steering wheel while he tried to breathe. Dune and White kept their distance.

He had drunk that beer and he had tasted it, smelled it, had even felt its coolness as it trickled down his throat into his empty stomach, and he was so grateful that he had kissed her. And then he tasted her and he had been so turned on by the softness of her lips—

Until his body slammed shut, all systems misfiring. The attack that followed had been as intense as if the accident had happened yesterday. Not that he couldn't take the sudden cramps, the panic, the slicing pain through his gut. That was all becoming a part of his life that he accepted, even welcomed, as pain was better than numbness.

But he couldn't go around starting something with

Lizzie that he couldn't follow through on. That he could smell his coffee, taste his beer, taste her, didn't mean that he could act like a fully functioning human again. He had just proven that, needing to pull away from her kiss to stop the blackness from rushing in.

It was like being with Emily all over again. He couldn't bring another woman into his mangled life. *Let's make love, and then I'll go outside and sit in my truck and fight the waves of regret. You just make yourself at home...*

He had tried to hide the pain when he had been with Emily, but it had turned him into a liar, which he despised almost as much as the guilt. He had been a person acting as if he cared what he ate and what movie he saw and what color the new bedspread would be when inside, he couldn't muster the effort to care about any of that because all he thought about was the accident and what he'd done and how he could never turn it back.

So he had hurt Emily. Badly. The second innocent victim of the crash, of him. They had plans to get married, kids, the works.

Until his life had narrowed to wanting only two things: to make it right with Candy and to get through the never-ending minutes of his days.

So he'd stopped pretending. Stopped trying to hide anything. And she'd, rightfully, left him.

Had he actually kissed Lizzie? Brought her into his narrow, starved world?

Of course he had, he could still feel her lips against his.

But Lizzie didn't deserve halfway to normal. She deserved a normal man—one who could kiss her without pulling back, without feeling crippling pain. One who could love her without hating himself. One who didn't roam the streets at night, or wade the freezing water of the gorges all day. She didn't deserve a man who couldn't show his face in Galton. A man who had to leave as quickly as possible as soon as he got that money because Candy didn't deserve worrying about running into him.

Dune leaned against him and moaned softly, as if protesting Tay's thoughts, as if saying, *So what's so bad about forgetting the past and moving on? I do it all the time. Forgot yesterday, even forgot this morning. Is it time to eat again… ?*

He kneaded the back of the dog's neck. "I know, boy. I know. Let's get out of here before I go back in there and—"

Dune rotated one ear his way.

Yeah, and kiss her again, he thought. *Kiss her until neither one of us can see straight and the world falls away and nothing matters. Not the past, not the future, just her lips on mine…*

Great, now he could even taste and smell her when she wasn't anywhere near.

He waited for the guilt to crush him.

It came; it crushed.

And he wanted to imagine Lizzie all over again.

But this wasn't a healthy cycle.

He had to fix things before he got involved with anyone, especially someone who lived in the town that Candy lived in, so he pushed her out of his mind.

Find the money and go! Leave these innocent women alone.

He drove off into the night, swearing he'd never bother Lizzie again.

CHAPTER

16

*L*ater that night, Lizzie heard someone banging on her front door.

Despite the embarrassment that still lingered over what had happened in the bar—what had happened in the bar?—Lizzie hoped that it was Tay. Maybe his super-fixit powers had been alerted that the oven light had just exploded. She had flicked it on two seconds ago to check the frozen pizza she was passing off as dinner tonight. The hollow pop and subsequent darkness seemed about as much fanfare as her dinner deserved, but she was dead-tired from the first full weeks of serving students back from their summer break. The Galton U. undergrads were ravenous, like migrating birds that hadn't eaten since they'd left Galton last spring. Whenever the students came back to town, Galton became a different place and it took some adjusting. When Lizzie was younger, she'd preferred the summer emptiness. Now, she preferred the school-year tips, even if she was worn to a frazzle by five o'clock.

The banging on the door grew louder. Paige wasn't going to move from the couch in front of the blaring TV unless she knew it was the pizza man.

At the door, Lizzie whispered an ardent prayer: Please don't let it be Judy Roth complaining about the raking again. The sugar maples out front had begun to drop their leaves in earnest. Judy, Lizzie's across-the-street neighbor, couldn't stand that Lizzie didn't hover all day on the front lawn waiting for them with a net to fall one by one. They had the same "talk" every year about how Lizzie's leaves blew onto the neighbors' lawns, which according to Judy wasn't fair. The neighbors all had lawn services that blasted loud, exhaust-spewing leaf blowers that frightened all the birds off Lizzie's feeders. As far as Lizzie was concerned, she and her neighbors were even.

She looked out reluctantly.

Annie was at the front door with Meghan on one hip, an enormous brown bag on the other, and—

Lizzie checked again just to be sure, then threw open the door. "Annie? Is that you? I hardly recognize you. Are you—" She almost didn't dare say the word. "Smiling?"

"Beautiful evening, isn't it?" Annie waltzed in the door. She practically tossed a cooing Meghan to Lizzie and went straight for the kitchen. "I brought Chinese. Trade you the baby for your fortune cookie."

"I get a fortune cookie," Paige said, zooming into the kitchen from her spot in front of the TV, freed from her trance by the smell of chicken and broccoli. Paige was still in her school clothes—tight jeans and layered multi-colored camisoles. "Hi, Aunt Annie. Did I ever tell you you're the world's best aunt? And you're the world's best baby, aren't you aren't you aren't you?" Paige cooed at Meghan, who rewarded her with an enormous one-toothed grin. A brief scuffle for possession of Meghan ensued. Lizzie won with her patented elbow-and-spin.

"Penalty!" Paige complained.

"All's fair in love and babies," Lizzie said, bouncing Meghan.

"I could bring a million bucks in here, and you guys would only care about the baby," Annie groused. But Lizzie could tell her heart wasn't in it. Her sister gazed in wonder at Meghan as if she were a brand-new baby, nothing at all to do with that other baby who'd depressed the hell out of her sister for the last six months.

Paige pulled the half-frozen pizza out of the oven and dumped it into the trash. "What happened to the light?"

"Dead."

Paige shrugged. "Another soldier down. Soon we're going to be living by candlelight."

"I can replace a lightbulb," Lizzie insisted.

"Yeah," Paige said. "But you won't. Because you'll have to get some special bulb, which means a special trip to a special store, and you'll be too tired and you'll never do it."

"You could replace it," Lizzie suggested.

"Fat chance," Paige said.

"So, to what do we owe this honor?" Lizzie asked, turning her attention to Annie.

"It's not so weird, me coming by," Annie protested.

"No. Not weird at all, er, what's your name again?" Lizzie asked. Meghan grinned and giggled in her arms. Lizzie tickled her stomach to elicit a squeal. "What did you do to your mommy to make her happy again?

Hmmm? Diaper-train yourself? Or maybe you got into Galton U. Very, very, very early admission you smart, smart baby…"

Paige pulled the high chair they kept for Meghan out of the corner while Annie got to work unloading the food from the grease-stained brown bag. The kitchen smelled divine.

"Oh, let's just say I came into a little extra cash," Annie said.

They plopped around the table and dug into the food straight from the cartons, passing them from hand to hand. Poor Meghan had to settle for mashed banana and grains of plain rice. She didn't seem to mind.

Lizzie said, "So, spill. Where'd you get the money for our feast?"

"I found it," Annie said. "On the ground. Just lying there."

"Oh, thank heavens. I thought it was something much worse. Prostitution is so sad amongst the middle-aged–mommy set," Lizzie said. She snagged an eggroll from the bag. "Cover your ears, Paige, dear."

"I thought she was dealing drugs," Paige said. "Using Meghan as a cover, like in that *Goodfellas* movie where they stuff the drugs in the diaper bag. What do you have in your diaper bag, Aunt Annie? I think I hear police helicopters."

Annie choked on her rice.

Lizzie whacked her on the back. "You okay?"

After a sip of water, Annie coughed out, "Fine. I think there was a stone in my rice."

"You really found money, Aunt Annie? How much? Like, forty bucks? A hundred?" Paige asked. "Can I borrow some? I so need a new snowboard for Geneva and Mom says no."

Lizzie and Annie met eyes over the cartons. They hadn't talked in so long, Lizzie hadn't told her about Paige's constantly escalating plans.

Lizzie shrugged apologetically.

"Suppose you found some money just lying around, Paige. What would you do about it?" Annie pointed her eggroll at Paige.

Lizzie was grateful to her sister for steering the subject away from Geneva and Paige's father. She wanted this to be a happy meal. It had been so long since she'd seen Annie smile.

"Keep it," Paige said without missing a beat. "Buy a snowboard. Dumbass drops money, they don't deserve it."

"Your uncle Tommy wouldn't agree," Annie said, peering into the carton of lo mein as if it were the most fascinating thing in the world. Something was still off with Annie, but Lizzie couldn't put her finger on exactly what. She was manic, too hyped-up. Something was on her mind.

"He wants you to turn it in?" Lizzie asked. "How much did you say you found?"

"I haven't told him about it. But don't change the subject. What do you think I should do?"

"Tommy would insist you give it up to the authorities. His policeman's code of honor is in his DNA," Lizzie said. It felt like Christmas to see Annie smiling after months of depression. She wanted to know what had changed her. Could it really be something as simple as some cash she found on the ground? It seemed unlikely.

"But would he be right?" Annie asked.

Lizzie thought about saying that Tommy was too trusting. Anyone could see you pick up the money, then say it was theirs, and then what? Would you believe them and give it back? And Paige had a point, too. You had to be responsible for your things. She searched for the right words. "Of course, Tommy'd be right. You shouldn't keep what isn't yours. You have a responsibility to at least try to return it. Good people drop money by mistake, too. Maybe it belonged to a mother who now can't buy dinner for her twelve sick, starving children." Lizzie put down the last bite of the eggroll she was about to stuff into her mouth. "I don't think I'm hungry anymore."

Annie pushed the duck sauce at Lizzie. "Eat. No one is starving. Trust me."

"Okay, so say a mom dropped it. She would still be an idiot for doing that," Paige said. "Her kids would be better off learning early on not to depend on a mother who was careless like that. They'd learn to fight for themselves and be independent. So we get to keep it. Pass the rice."

Lizzie tried to keep her mouth shut, tried to let it pass. But her mouth opened and she said, "Is that wisdom from your life? You learned to fight for yourself because your mother let you down?"

Paige let her head fall back and she moaned like a small animal dying a painful, bloody death. "God, Aunt Annie. She's been so touchy ever since she told me about my dad coming to get me."

Lizzie said, "He's coming to meet you. Not get you."

"You don't know that," Paige insisted to Lizzie, then turned to Annie. "See? She's totally defensive. She thinks I'm going to split on her and go live with my dad. And so what if I do? Is that so bad? This town sucks. He's in Europe! Near the Alps! I can make my dreams come true!"

Lizzie and Paige's discussion about Ethan spiraled into an argument about wishes and trusting strangers and what language did they speak in Geneva, anyway...

Annie's attention returned to the two hundred thousand dollars stuffed in Meghan's diaper bag. She had imagined telling Tommy about the money, but Lizzie was right. His policeman's code of honor was in his DNA. He'd want her to turn it in to the authorities, no doubt about it.

Because he was the authority.

She had spent the last weeks counting the money, smelling it. She'd even given a pack to Meghan, who tried to eat it. *"No, honey. You can't eat hundred-dollar bills until after you show me you can handle ones and twenties. Don't want to upset the tummy!"* She had piled it in a stack that reached to her waist until it had toppled over, to Meghan's delight. She'd even given in to her urge to roll in it. Just for a second or two, before she'd blushed and jumped up and straightened the small packets back into neat little piles.

She'd tried to keep the money at home, but it was starting to eat at her. Tommy was the kind of guy who noticed everything. It was what made him excellent at police work, but made Annie jumpy when she did anything not 100 percent aboveboard. Last April, she'd tried to throw him a surprise birthday party, but he'd discovered the party plates and streamers in the garage. He said he had noticed that the spiderwebs were broken in the top left-hand cabinet, and it had struck him as odd.

Who notices things like that?

So Annie had stashed the cash in the far back of the hall closet, careful to check for webs. But after a few days, she knew the money had to go. She felt as if she had a man in the closet and he was wearing leather undies. On his head. And was dancing the rumba.

Tommy was way too uptight and honest for a ménage-a-two-hundred-thousand-dollars.

She spent days agonizing over what to do with it. She considered taking the money to the bank. But she and Tommy knew every teller at the credit union. She could go to the new Citizen's Bank downtown, but she wasn't sure what kind of alerts went off if you suddenly opened a new account with that much cash, and she wasn't about to find out.

So she had finally decided to hide it at Lizzie's until she knew what to do with it. Once the decision was made, her elation at finding the money returned. It was perfect. This house had been her childhood home, a warren of unused rooms that she knew every crevice of like the back of her hand.

Lizzie and Paige were still at it, arguing over what language they spoke in Geneva and whether Paige could add German to her schedule this late in the year or if her French was enough.

Annie jumped up from the table. "Meghan needs a diaper. I'll be right back." She grabbed a protesting Meghan and the diaper bag and raced up the stairs.

She rushed into the spare bedroom and put Meghan on her back in the middle of the rag rug, handed her a rattle, and opened the closet.

The ancient laundry chute was still in the back, just the way she remembered it. Tommy had propped a flimsy sheet of plywood over it when he had moved her parents' laundry out of the basement years ago. But her parents had gotten sick so quickly afterward, Tommy had never gotten the chance to properly close it up. Then her parents had died, Lizzie inherited the house, and her stubborn sister forbade Tommy to work on anything anymore. No charity for Lizzie Bea Carpenter, no matter how badly she needed it.

She was letting her house—their house!—go to hell.

Which for this one moment was good. Annie pushed aside three paper grocery bags filled with Paige's old jeans and T-shirts, shoved aside the plywood board, and jammed the bag into the chute. It stuck firm, just as she knew it would. Good enough for now. She'd come back when no one was home and figure out a better spot. She quickly rearranged the bags, grabbed Meghan, and rushed back to their guilty feast, feeling somehow vindicated.

As if she finally had something that was all her own.

CHAPTER

17

*P*aige put the bag of chips she'd been munching aside, got down on her knees, and pushed the plywood panel off the laundry chute.

She felt slightly sick at the sight of the diaper bag stuffed inside. She hadn't wanted to be right, but she didn't realize it until just then.

She had known something was wrong last week when Aunt Annie had practically dropped her lo mein and grabbed Meghan to rush her upstairs as if she was on fire. Later that night, Paige had done some investigating, and there hadn't been a dirty diaper in the bathroom trash. Why would Aunt Annie run upstairs like a wild woman to change Meghan and then not change her? She wouldn't exactly take a gross diaper home with her; they had a special trash can upstairs in the bathroom just for Meghan.

The lie bothered Paige the next few days at school. That and the weird look Aunt Annie got on her face when they were talking about *Goodfellas* and the drugs in the diaper bag, the police helicopters circling.

And then, in science today, when Mr. Denning was droning on and on about forming hypotheses, Paige tried to form her own hypothesis. That was when she realized that Aunt Annie had come back downstairs without the diaper bag. Paige had run the scene over and over in her head.

She didn't know what was going on, but she could hypothesize—something. But what? She needed more facts.

Paige couldn't wait to get home. She had run all the way, grabbed some chips from the kitchen, and headed right upstairs to look around.

She had searched the entire upstairs before she remembered the old laundry chute in the spare bedroom that used to be her grandparents' room. She had used that chute to hide stuff when she was a kid. There was a little catch just inside that you could hook things on if you wanted and sometimes, when her stuffed animals had been bad, she'd hang them there in "time-out" till they learned their lessons. When she was ten, after she had started suspecting her mother of reading her journal, she had tied a string around the small book and hung it in there. She had marked the plywood with a tiny X that she made sure was always in the lower-left corner to see if anyone had disturbed it.

Someone had propped the board upside down.

Aunt Annie. Her breath had caught in her throat.

Hypothesis: Aunt Annie was sneaking upstairs to read her fifth-grade diary. Was the diary even still there? Paige hadn't thought about it in years.

She had moved the plywood with shaking hands.

The diary was still hanging from its hook—

—Under a humongous bag of cash!

No way.

No, no, no, no, NO WAY.

Now, ten minutes later, Paige was still sitting on the hardwood floor, staring at the humongous pile of cash in the bag, trying to figure out something, anything that would explain this.

She picked up one of the bundles of money and counted it. A thousand bucks. She eyeballed the stacks.

There might be a million bucks in there.

She stared at it for another long time, unable to move. She was thinking about leaving behind her fingerprints and being arrested and holding out as long as she could to protect her aunt, but finally having to give in and tell Tommy that it was his wife who had done it.

Done what?

Paige ate a few chips to steady herself.

Aunt Annie has a superrich boyfriend and they're hoarding cash so they can run away to Mexico. Yeah, right. Not in this town. Who'd be stupid enough to date a woman whose husband walked around all day with a gun?

Aunt Annie won the lottery. Could be. But then, her aunt wasn't the kind to keep a secret. As soon as she was preggers, she was running around town, waving that disgusting pee-soaked stick as if it were a flag. Privacy wasn't something Aunt Annie was good at.

Aunt Annie robbed a bank. But then, wouldn't Paige have heard about a bank robbery? Everyone would be talking about it at school and Tommy would have told her all the top secret details. Plus, Aunt Annie was a goody-goody wuss married to the Prince of Boring. She'd never do anything like that.

Paige got up and paced, trying to piece it all together.

Hypothesize; think outside the box, Mr. Denning had said.

Maybe the money wasn't Aunt Annie's.

Maybe it was her mother's.

Maybe this was the money her mother had been saving all her life.

But then, why would it be in a bag in the closet? Wouldn't it be in the bank? No, it didn't make sense.

My father sent the money. It was a random thought that jumped into Paige's head, and it stuck fast. *He is smart and rich and wants to see me.* Maybe he was helping her and her mom out already. Maybe he thought the same thought Paige couldn't stop thinking, especially late at night, when she couldn't sleep: It wasn't fair to leave her mother with nothing when Paige left for Switzerland with him. So her dad had given her mother a bunch of money and it was in the closet because—

Okay, so that one didn't make any sense either.

She looked out the window to see if her mom was coming. Sometimes she'd stay to talk to her friends at the diner. Or sometimes, the diner was superbusy, and it was hard for her to get away.

Paige went back to her money. She was already starting to feel as if it were her money. She lay back on the hardwood floor and stared up at the ceiling. She was so sick of grown-ups telling her how her life was going to be and how she had to do the right thing. Yeah, right. The right thing.

Then there's a stash of cash in the laundry chute?

The more Paige thought about it, the angrier she got.

She dumped the money onto the floor and counted it. It was one thousand shy of two hundred thousand dollars.

One thousand shy . . .

Paige sat up.

Aunt Annie wasn't hiding it; she was stealing it. She must have snatched a stack of bills.

But it was in *her* diaper bag.

Paige's thoughts jumbled around in her head. She had made so many guesses, she couldn't sort them all out. Each one felt simultaneously true.

She looked at the clock on the bed stand: 6:15. Where was her mother? She tried not to feel angry that her mother wasn't there. It was too babyish to be angry about something like that. She was old enough to be home alone, to fend for herself. She wasn't a stupid kid anymore. She deserved to be treated like a grown-up. She deserved to be trusted to go with her dad, away from Galton. To follow her dreams.

She put the money back into the diaper bag. She'd stick it back into the chute while she thought about what to do next.

But just as she put back the plywood, she stopped.

Her life was so not fair. Her life was always in the hands of grown-ups and you couldn't trust them. Just look at this money. It wasn't cool, somehow, even if she didn't know how or why.

She took out one bundle. Just one. Her heart pounded. She wiped her sweaty hands on her jeans.

She felt like a millionaire.

She could buy the snowboard she needed to get her jumps to the next level. Get the right gear, not so she'd look cool—although that would be a bonus—but so she could stay out longer, work harder before her toes went numb. Maybe she could even buy some lessons from Paulie Jones, the best boarder on Meeks Peak. Then, when her father came to take her back to Geneva with him, she'd have the gear and the moves and she could show her mother how good she really was, how she could make boarding her life, how she didn't need stupid school, which she stank at anyway but she did need Geneva, where the mountains were huge, not puny like the anthills in New York.

You had to make a wish, and if you did, the universe made it come true.

She stuffed the bills down the front of her shirt, shoved the bag back into its hiding spot, put the plywood back with her X in the right place, and straightened up the row of bags so that her mother, or her aunt, or whoever had stuffed that money there wouldn't suspect a thing.

CHAPTER

18

$\mathcal{T}$wo days later, Jill and Lizzie stood on the sidewalk, facing Lizzie's house. Jill had a clipboard in her hand.

"You sure you want to hear all this?" Jill asked. She wore four-inch heels, and Lizzie feared for her on the uneven brick path. The leaves were coming down with a vengeance today, making the walk slippery and covering the holes where bricks had been. "You're not going to like it."

"Enemy Club rules, babe. The truth, the whole truth, and nothing but the truth," Lizzie said, trying to hold her optimistic tone. She had no idea how she was going to fix up her house before Ethan Pond arrived on Christmas Day. But damned if she wasn't going to try.

Jill sighed. "Okay. Let's start at the curb. The fence is a mess. Five thousand at least. Maybe just tear it down."

Jill pushed through the gate. She scribbled notes on her clipboard. "Oh, I like what you did with that bluestone. Much better than that sinkhole of bricks that I always used to trip over."

Lizzie looked to her feet. For the past twenty years the walk had begun with an unfortunate dip in the bricks, like a warning. Now, she stood on a brand-new slab of bluestone, perfectly square, perfectly level with the sidewalk. The single, pristine blue stone glowed next to the ancient bricks that wobbled and dipped their way to her front steps. "I didn't do that," she said. "Damn it, I bet Tay came in the middle of the night and put this in!"

"I've been tripping in that hole for years. That stone's a beauty." Jill walked up the path. "And so's that man, or so I hear from Chrissie. This walk is a mess, hon. The bricks aren't the right kind for walking, that's why they're crumbling. Two thousand to lay a new brick path at the least. It's important. Paths are key. You can scare off a buyer with a lousy path before he even opens the door. It's psychological."

"Ethan's not moving in, he's just visiting for a few hours, giving Paige everything she wants, then leaving."

"Good." Jill turned her back and walked to the porch.

"Good? Jill, I'm joking. I'm doing this to show Paige that we can fix things ourselves. That we can take limited help from men, *if we make it even.*"

But Jill had moved on. She wobbled the rail post with enough intensity to break it free. "Sorry. Shoot. That needs fixing." She noted it on her pad.

Lizzie sat down on the top step and watched her friend. "You're mad at me, aren't you? Something's wrong."

Jill continued scanning the porch. "Scrape down the whole thing, repair the rotted wood and the bee holes, repaint. It's a mess." She sat down next to Lizzie. "Yes, I'm mad. Okay, I wasn't going to say anything, because you've been kind of wired lately. But Ethan doesn't deserve Paige. Why would you throw an innocent child into the jaws of the beast? Some people don't deserve forgiveness, Lizzie. You need to chase him off, not encourage Paige to ally with the enemy. I think this is stupid."

"He was a kid. I was a kid. We were dumb, but we weren't beasts and we weren't enemies. And yes, he should have called or something in the last fourteen years." Lizzie leaned on the broken post, but then thought better of it. "But if he's grown into a kind, thoughtful man then this could be Paige's big chance to get out of Galton and be someone. I'm going to help her."

Jill harrumphed. "You have to get rid of all these bird feeders."

"No! Why? They're pretty."

"They're eccentric. Sorry, dear, but pretty is feeding the birds with a lovely feeder or two. Eccentric is putting up a twenty-four-hour, all-you-can-eat buffet for every kind of bird on the planet. Look at them all! This porch is like the diner." Jill peered into the conical container hanging nearest her. "A million things on the menu. To impress Ethan, you need to run a class establishment, with just a few choice items to offer. Ethan will not be impressed by a crazy bird lady. Talk about making him turn and run for the hills."

Lizzie scowled. "The feeders stay."

"Then, baby, so does Paige. Ethan Pond is a blueblood. You think he wants to take some nature child with him back to Europe?"

"She's not—" Lizzie began.

Jill interrupted. "I'm in the business of first impressions, honey. Folks decide everything in the first five seconds of seeing a house, or a woman, or a kid. Especially people like Ethan Pond. Believe me, I've seen enough houses sit on the market for ages to know all about how people make decisions. You want Ethan to help Paige— God only knows why—you'll take down all of the feeders but one. Two max."

Jill continued her ferocious house appraisal, but Lizzie had lost her fervor for the project. What if Jill was right, and she was making a terrible mistake? She looked out over her lawn, the grass splotchy, marred by brown patches. The new bluestone caught her eye. She was sure Tay had replaced it in the middle of the night.

She smiled.

It was sweet.

Really sweet.

Like his kiss.

Still, she had to tell him to stop. She was taking over this fix-it project until he came up with something that they could trade besides kisses and vague notions of smelling the coffee, whatever that had meant.

Jill was still talking and noting things on her pad, but Lizzie was getting overwhelmed. She pleaded exhaustion and coaxed Jill inside with an offer of Diet Coke and popcorn, two of the only foods Jill would eat outside her Lean Cuisine regimen. "Don't start with what needs to be fixed in here," she said as they went inside. "Ethan won't get past the living room." Lizzie sprinkled the popcorn with sea salt.

"I wouldn't take anything from Ethan," Jill said when they were settled around the popcorn bowl.

"You would if you had a kid to worry about," Lizzie said, trying to tamp down her irritation at her friend.

Jill's face went to stone.

"Look at us, Jill," Lizzie went on. "We all wanted out of Galton and none of us made it. I'm going to do everything I can to help Paige. And if it means forgiving Ethan, then that's what I'm going to do."

"What happened to do good in school and go to college and make something of yourself? Why do you have to depend on a stupid, irresponsible, immature man?" Jill asked.

Lizzie was surprised by the vehemence in her tone. "Let's face it, in the real world, we all need a little help." She thought of the bluestone set into her walk. "And Ethan owes us."

"So tell him that. Tell him what a shit he is and that he owes you. Don't try to impress him, Lizzie."

"What if he's not a shit? What if he's sorry?"

"Then he should have been here fourteen years ago. It's too late," Jill said.

Lizzie raised her eyebrows at Jill's vehemence. "Look, I appreciate the solidarity, but Paige needs this. I can't blow it. And by the way, I still need a man. You haven't set me up with anyone."

"And I won't. I don't want to see you fake a happy life for a jerk."

"I already have a happy life. I'm faking the kind of happy life that a person like Ethan will understand." Lizzie took a deep breath.

Jill shook her head. "I wish you'd just tell him not to come."

"It's not up to me, hon," Lizzie said. "It's up to Paige."

"Did you tell her?" Nina whispered to Jill later that day.

They were in Nina's two o'clock yoga class, Jill in downward-facing dog, Nina walking the room, correcting her four students gently. Jill insisted on keeping her cell phone next to the mat, and it kept vibrating, much to Nina's irritation. Jill was supposed to be one with the universe, ignoring worldly distractions, giving her self a break. But Jill still pushed all Nina's buttons. Nina suspected that Jill did it on purpose.

"Nope," Jill whispered back. "Tried. Couldn't." Jill hated yoga, but she hated not fitting into her clothes more, so she was trying it. This was her third class, and every part of her ached.

"Right leg up," Nina said to the class. Then she pretended to correct Jill's form and whispered, "You need to tell her. The whole truth and nothing but—"

Jill kicked Nina in the leg. "Oh, so sorry! My bad."

"And bring the right leg between your hands," Nina said to the class, scowling at Jill, "and rise into warrior one."

"It's not right," Nina whispered, adjusting Jill's hand. "Just tell her. She needs to know."

"I know. I will. When I'm ready."

"It's been fourteen years."

"Yeah, exactly. So what's another few days?"

CHAPTER

19

The next few days, Tay didn't show.

Lizzie told herself that she didn't care. This was good. If he didn't show up, then she didn't have to think anymore about those ridiculous dreams she'd been having all week. They involved her and Tay kissing just the way they'd kissed in the bar, only in her dreams, they didn't stop there...

Lizzie was slipping on her shoes to leave for work when someone knocked on the front door. She carefully went to the living room, not making a sound, hoping against all her better judgment that it was Tay.

Also hoping it wasn't.

She wasn't sure what she'd say to him, how she'd tell him she was done telling him to leave.

She peered out the front window. Tay was sitting on the porch swing, gently rocking, the heel of his boot not leaving the ground.

She should answer the door. But she didn't. She was mad at him for pulling away from that kiss even though the last thing she had wanted was a kiss.

But still.

She opened the door, but didn't come out. Before he could speak, she held up a hand to stop him. "I don't want to be your charity case. I can't handle that right now. It makes me feel like a loser." *Your kissing me and then pulling away like I'm a leper makes me feel like a loser.* "I think that you should find someone else to help. It was nice meeting you, Tay." She picked up his map from the table by the door and tossed it into his chest, then shut the door.

She leaned her back against it. She could hear her own breathing, feel her blood pumping, her heart pounding.

She had done it. She had told him to leave and this time, she didn't let him get a word in.

Or a kiss.

They were done playing games.

She had started to walk away when she heard his boots clump across the wooden porch toward the door. She froze. The mail slot opened and a piece of folded yellow paper floated to the floor, landing in front of her bare toes. She considered it, but didn't move to pick it up. She heard him settle back on the porch swing. She stared at the paper and listened to the creak of the rusted chains.

This impossible man!

She picked up the slip of paper and unfolded it carefully. It had a phone number written on it in a careful, slanted hand. She sat on the couch, watching him through the living room window.

She had never seen anyone so completely, absolutely alone.

Her house hummed around her. The grandfather clock in the corner ticked, echoing through the big, empty rooms.

Tick, tick, tick...

This was ridiculous.

She dialed the number.

She heard the faint sound of his ring tone, muffled through the windows, something classical. Mozart? After a few bars of violins, he answered. "Hello. Tay Giovanni here. May I ask who's calling?"

"What do you want from me, Tay?" she asked.

"I need to know what color paint you were thinking for the fence. I'll finish it, since I started it, and then I'll go. I hate to leave a job half done."

She took a deep breath. Of course that was all he wanted. Why would she think he wanted more? "White, I guess. But then you need to go. For good."

He looked right at her through the window. Could he see her in the darkened living room?

"I will. But first, you deserve the whole story, Lizzie. If you want to hear it."

"Yes." *No. I don't know...*

He got up from the swing and walked to the window. He leaned against the frame. He felt as close as if he was standing right next to her. "It's not going to make you feel any better about me. In fact, it'll probably make you call your brother-in-law again."

"Great." She said it sarcastically, but she liked his straightforward manner. She settled deeper into the couch. Surely, he couldn't see her.

"You want to ask questions, or do you want me just to talk?"

"Talk." She wanted to hear his story, his way.

He walked away from the window, and she exhaled in relief. He leaned against the porch railing facing the lawn, his back to her, and now she wished she could see his face. "My name is Dante Giovanni and I'm from Queens. I've lived and worked there my whole life. I used to own a few buildings. Nothing fancy, just apartment rentals. But they paid the bills. I managed them, too. Which is why I know how to fix stuff."

She crept to the window.

He didn't turn.

She willed him to turn. She wanted to see his face, to read it.

He turned, and she ducked under the sill, not wanting to see his face, her back rigid against the wall, her breath coming quickly. Was she five years old playing hide-and-seek? She did feel like a little kid listening to a good bed-time story; she was hooked, dying to know what was with this guy.

"Eleven months ago, I ran a red light. I killed a woman named Linda Goodnight. It was the worst moment of my life, which is stupid because of course it was much worse for Linda."

"Oh."

They both observed an unofficial moment of silence, holding their phones tightly. His story hit her like a punch in the gut. She thought about peeking out the window again, but she was riveted to her spot on the floor.

He went on. "It was entirely my fault. I was thinking of other things, preoccupied. It was just dumbass stupid." His voice lowered. "I can never take back that moment, that day. It was a mistake. There are no excuses. Sometimes I think it could have happened to anyone. Other times, I think it happened to me—and to Linda—for a reason. Afterward, I didn't know what to do, but I knew I couldn't keep living my life the way I was living it. I was crushed by the guilt. I couldn't sleep, couldn't eat. The DA didn't press charges—called it an accident without aggravating circumstances. Linda didn't have much of a family, so no one filed a civil suit. So that was it: I was off scot-free."

"I didn't realize that could happen," Lizzie said. She had never thought about traffic accidents, lawyers, any of it. What did happen when you screwed up for a split second?

In her case, she got pregnant.

By comparison, her case sounded pretty good.

"The law allows for accidents," he said with deep sadness, as if it were a shame, a terrible weakness. "I was told by the EMTs on the scene that the people in charge of this sort of thing take pity on people like me who accept blame, show remorse, don't usually screw up. So I wasn't punished. Thing was, I wanted to be punished. Begged for it, even. But if no one presses charges, well, that's it as far as the law's concerned. I went back to my life like nothing had happened. But something had happened."

Lizzie tried to imagine herself in his position. What would she have done? How would she have faced Paige? What if it had happened to Paige? She'd learn to drive in a few years. Those beginning years were the hardest. Anything could happen. Did it have to ruin your life?

"I think about Linda Goodnight every minute of every day. It's like a huge ocean that I can't cross no matter how hard I swim. It was like it happened for nothing, or never happened at all. Like Linda never existed. No one cared. The DA told me to get psychological help. My friends told me to get over it, go on with my life and I'd get back to normal. I tried that for a while, but it didn't work. I wanted the accident to matter. It's hard to explain, but I knew that if I didn't do something, I'd never get over it. But I didn't have a clue what to do. My girlfriend left me. My friends grew sick of me. I don't have much of a family, so at least I couldn't piss them off."

Lizzie could hear his breath. Hear her own breath. She was riveted, entranced. Lizzie imagined her car sailing through a red light. It was the kind of mistake she'd made once or twice in her life. She'd even gone through a red light once downtown right after she'd given birth to Paige, when she was overwhelmed with hormones and grief over Ethan's splitting on them. Luckily, no one had been coming the other way when she ran that light. It was the kind of thing that could happen to anyone, that did happen to anyone, and yet most people got lucky and it came to nothing. Maybe a fender bender. An irate driver leaning on his horn and giving the finger.

But what if she hadn't been so lucky? What if it had changed her life?

She knew a thing or two about single moments that changed a person's life forever.

At least Tay was being honest. At least he seemed up front. At least he cared that he had done a terrible thing and was trying to figure out how to make it right. How did you make something like that right? Was it even possible?

He went on. "I spent a few months serving slop at soup kitchens, helping little old ladies with their groceries, doing whatever I could think of. But even if it made me feel better for a moment, after, it made me feel even worse."

"You don't have any family?" Lizzie asked. She was holding her breath.

"Not really. I was dating someone. I thought we were

going to get married. But she left me when I stopped being fun. She thought I should just get over it. I have a sister in California, but we were never close. My parents are both gone. The less fun I got, the more my friends melted away."

Lizzie wondered if he couldn't kiss his ex-girlfriend either. The possibility made her feel better—which of course made *her* feel guilty.

But her guilt was nothing compared to his.

"Then, a month ago, I saw an article in the paper about Linda's daughter, Candy Williams."

"You just happened to see it?" Lizzie asked.

"I was following her story. I couldn't help it. I needed to know what happened to her. She was the only link left. The only other person on this earth who gave a shit."

"I give a shit."

He didn't say anything.

Lizzie wondered if she'd gone too far. Why had she said that? Did she care about this man?

Was he even still there?

She peeked. "Go on."

"Right." His voice was calm, steady. "Candy was about to get kicked out of school because she couldn't afford it anymore and she was too in debt from her mother's bad financial planning to take out any school loans."

"Her mother didn't have any insurance?" Lizzie asked.

"A little, but her piles of debt ate it up. At least, that's what the paper said. Linda Goodnight lived beyond her means in a big way. I think Candy still does, too. Anyway, the girl goes to Galton."

That explained his presence in town, which relieved her. He wasn't just a wanderer. "There's no dad?"

"No. At least, that's what the paper said," he said. "I

saw this as my chance to repay at least a little for what I'd done. Give her money to stay in school. Buy her some time to get over her loss."

Lizzie pressed the phone closer to her cheek. She didn't want to miss a word. She was aware that Tay's story was paralleling her own—a daughter without a father, a man come to repay a debt, to ask forgiveness for the unforgivable.

She didn't like it. Jill had struck a chord with her dissent to Lizzie's plan: She didn't want to forgive Ethan completely.

And yet, she liked Tay. There was an honor in his caring about a girl he didn't even know, in his trying to make it right.

Did that mean Ethan's visit held a certain kind of honor?

No, it wasn't the same. She *had* to stop comparing the two men.

"I cut out that article. Carried it around for days. Looking at that picture of Candy was like looking into my own personal war zone. I couldn't eat. Couldn't sleep. It was as if the accident had happened all over again. On the fourth day, I sold my buildings for cash to the first buyer I could find. I tried to contact Candy, but she wouldn't take my calls. I sent her a check, but she never cashed it. Sent her another and she sent it back ripped to shreds. So finally, I bought this old truck, put some money in a duffel bag, and drove here to try to fix things in person."

Lizzie thought about how slowly he had driven away from her house that first morning. How he had stopped at the end of her street, his blinker going on and on and on. How slowly he did everything. He was dragging the weight of that girl, of her mother, of his guilt. But what did it have to do with her? "Driving sounds like the last thing you should be doing," Lizzie said.

His voice was cold and steady. "You want to know what people think is really rotten? You want to piss off every red-blooded American no matter if they're liberal or conservative, black or white, Christian or Buddhist? It's easy: Drive slow. I've never been so despised. Even sitting on the curb, watching the EMT guys take Linda Goodnight away, people felt sorry for me. They were kind. It was like something horrible had happened to me, which of course made everything worse. But drive slow, well, I'll take you for a ride sometime and you'll see what folks think of me. I just can't bear to speed up. Something happens to me. I panic. It took me three days to drive here from New York City. Should have taken me three hours."

"Maybe you like the abuse," she suggested. "After all, you came here to meet the daughter of the woman who you..." Lizzie couldn't say it. "To meet Candy."

"Yeah. When I told her I was coming to town, she flipped out. Said no way would she see me. Finally, though, she gave in. She agreed to a meeting at the diner. But it didn't go so well."

Lizzie waited, her heart pounding. She wanted to stand up, to look at him, but she didn't dare move lest she startle him away. "Did she take your money?"

"She said she didn't want it, but I left it with her anyway, right in your diner, actually."

"The day with the toast."

"Yep, the day I couldn't eat the toast. I hoped she wouldn't have a choice. She told me she'd throw it off a bridge."

Lizzie thought of the money Annie found. Was it part of Tay's money? But Annie hadn't found enough money to keep a girl in school. Or had she? Annie had never said how much money she'd found. But surely, she'd have said if it was enough money to keep a girl at Galton. Lizzie peeked over the windowsill. Tay was sitting on the top step, his back to her, his head low. His torso formed a perfect V. "Did she do it?"

"Yep. I had lost her for a while that morning that I gave her the money, but when I saw her later, she said the money was with the fishes. So then, I was really stuck. I had come all this way and I hadn't achieved a thing but lose everything I had. Which, in a way, helped a little. Felt good for a while. Really good. But it didn't last. I pretended that I was her uncle and called the school. They told me she'll be kicked out next semester if she doesn't pay. But there's nothing I can do about that now. I don't have that kind of money anymore."

"So why are you sticking around?"

"I thought I'd leave town, just keep driving, figure out something else. But first I need to get that money back, in case Candy changes her mind." He paused.

"The map is of the gorges to search?"

"Yep."

"Okay."

"I'm a simple guy, Lizzie. I need two things: a way to make this right for Candy, and a way to get through the days until I do. That's why I'm fixing your fence. It's not because I feel sorry for you. I don't. I think you're amazing. If I had half of what you have, I'd be a happy man."

She thought about the worst day of her life: Ethan walking off the porch and never coming back.

And yet, Tay was right. She was happy most of the time.

Her bad day didn't even come close to his.

Tay was still talking. "Look, Elizabeth, I'm not nuts. I don't believe hearing your wish was a message from God or fate or the universe. I'm not a stalker; I just saw your name and address on that envelope that must have been from Paige's father and it stuck in my head. I don't think of this as charity. I'm just trying to figure out what to do next and I'm kinda stuck in this town for a while and there you were, wishing for someone to fix your place. So I thought, *Hey, why not stick around and fix whatever that lady needs fixing?* Not like I've got anything better to do. The work eases my mind. It helps me get to the next day. That's all I'm trying to do. Get to the next day." He paused. "I'm sorry if I hurt you. It's not about you. It's me."

Was he referring to their kiss or to fixing her house? She wasn't sure.

She asked, "So how do you support yourself now that all your money is gone?" She tried to imagine how much money a person got for a couple of buildings in Queens, but she didn't have a clue.

"I got a job on campus. Mowing lawns. Landscaping, they call it. At first, I was afraid that Candy would see me. But actually, it's the perfect disguise. No one notices the workmen. We just planted a thousand mums for Parents' Day."

They were both silent. Lizzie imagined Candy on Parents' Day, without any parents. She guessed he was doing the same.

"It's not full-time, but it's something. I suspect that pretty soon, it'll be shoveling snow. I got a place down by the lake for a few weeks. Just until I figure out what to do about the money."

"I know about your house."

"You do?"

"I was birding and I saw you there. I was looking for a herons' nest."

"I know where it is. I've seen them."

"I thought they were gone for the season."

"I imagine they will be soon."

He knows what a heron is. Their conversation paused as she thought about him alone in the woods, watching the pair of birds tend to their nest, encouraging their young to fly so they could set off for the South before it was too late.

She wasn't the one who was alone, wandering, needing charity. He was.

No, not charity. Human kindness.

There was a difference.

Maybe this was her opportunity to fix him. So they'd be equal. But what could she do to ease his guilt? She'd have to think about it.

"What if you can't find the money?" she asked.

"I have no idea," he said.

"I'm sorry," she said. She meant it.

"Yeah, so am I."

She took a deep breath, then opened the front door. "Tay."

He looked up. *God, those eyes.* He was the perfect man. Or at least, at some point in his life, he had been. The scar on his cheek would never go away. What about the other scars she couldn't see?

"You want some coffee?"

He looked at her, then clicked his phone closed. "I'm

sorry I kissed you, Lizzie. In that bar. It was a mistake. I'm not ready for anything like that—"

"Neither am I," she said. But she was lying. She wanted him to come in, and to take her in his arms—and he'd said no. She pretended not to be hurt. Good thing she was pretty good at that.

"I came back today because I want to make sure we're straight," he said. "I wanted to tie up everything here."

"We're straight."

"So can I finish fixing your fence? Then I'll go."

"Then you'll go." His rejection of her offer to come in stung her, but she held her head up, her eyes and voice steady.

"I'll try to finish while you're gone. I might have to come back tomorrow, though, for a second coat."

She picked up her purse off the table. She was going to be late now and really had to leave. "Thanks, Tay, for telling me your story."

"I wanted you to know it wasn't you. It's me. I'm not normal. I have to leave here as soon as I can. For Candy's sake. It's not right for her to have to worry about running into me."

"Right." *But I thought we don't like normal.* "See you around," she said, locking the door behind her, leaving him on the porch.

She had to use all her energy not to look back.

CHAPTER

20

Annie planned to let herself and Meghan into Lizzie's house to rehide the money in a better spot. She had been trying to get back to the house all week. But every time she had come by, Lizzie or Paige had been there. Or Judy Roth, that nosy neighbor, had been out front in her rose garden or sweeping the front walk and had made a beeline for her, or rather, for Meghan.

Now, Judy was nowhere in sight, but Annie had forgotten about Lizzie's mysterious morning fix-it man.

Holy cow, he really was gorgeous. More than gorgeous—stunning. The way he bent over that fence. Narrow waist, broad shoulders, strong, tanned hands . . .

Now what? If Meghan would start crying, she could claim she needed to go in to get her a snack.

Meghan cooed and smiled, kicking her adorable chubby legs in the crisp fall air.

"Hello. You must be the frightening fix-it man." Annie stopped by Tay's side at the base of the steps.

He looked up, put down his scraper, shook his head

as if clearing it of fog, and said, "*Handsome* fix-it man, I believe is the term of choice."

She smiled. "I'm Lizzie's big sister."

"It's nice to meet you, Lizzie's big sister." He didn't hold out a hand.

"Annie."

"Annie."

"Is Lizzie here?" Annie asked as innocently as she could.

"Nope. She just left for work."

The guy wasn't a talker. That was good. "Well, I gotta run inside and get Meghan's sweater. I left it here. Silly me! Fall is really here." She shivered unconvincingly and pushed Meghan to the porch stairs. She unstrapped her, scooped her out of the stroller, and hurried up the stairs. She could feel his eyes on her back. For the first time, she understood why Lizzie was so anxious to get rid of this guy. She really shouldn't have tried to encourage Liz to keep him around.

Once inside, she worked as quickly as she could. She got the money out of the chute, took it to the basement, moved aside the boxes of their parents' old stuff that Lizzie had stowed down there, looking for the old record player that was set in a filigreed maple cabinet. When she finally uncovered it under bags of her mother's old sewing supplies, she opened the cabinet and stuffed the money inside. She used to hide her stashes of pennies and other treasures in this record player cabinet when she was a kid. No one would ever look in there. She put everything back the way it had been, glad that the baby couldn't talk. *Mommy played with her money bag today at Auntie Lizzie's...*

She hardly felt a moment of nostalgia.

Well, okay, maybe a moment when she opened the cabinet and saw a stash of pennies she'd left years ago, still wrapped in a square of her mother's flowered quilting fabric.

She let herself out the front door, settled Meghan in her stroller, and made her way past Tay, who was nailing in a post on the fence. "Nice to have met you."

"Likewise," he said.

Annie went a few more steps, then stopped. She turned the stroller and went back to Tay. "So, what's really up with this?" Annie asked, motioning to the fence.

"Nothing. What's really up with you sneaking into your sister's house?"

A flash of guilt, then anger, then an emotion she knew even better, especially when Lizzie was involved: jealousy. She gets the house and Tommy still loves her and now she gets this gorgeous, dream-come-true fix-it man to watch over her. The blackness rose inside Annie like a stain. She had thought it was gone, with the money making her feel lighter, but it was still there, ready to come out at the slightest provocation.

She hated herself for it, but she couldn't control it.

She glanced back at the house, at the porch swing, where Lizzie and Tommy had sat years ago when they were kids, swinging softly while Annie watched from the darkness inside. That was before Lizzie took over the house and the chains had started squeaking from neglect. Back when they were kids, Annie had wanted Tommy so badly, she might have done anything to get him. But she hadn't had to do anything. Lizzie had done it for her by dumping him for Ethan. And Annie had been there to scoop him up.

Making her forever the rebound girl.

She hated being the rebound girl. Lizzie screwed up so much, and she still got the house and Mom and Dad's help with Paige and even that little piece of Tommy's heart that Annie could never touch. Tommy went running to her whenever she called. She went running to him whenever she needed a man's help.

At least the money in the basement was all hers.

She tried to shake the ugly feelings that were building inside her. She knew they were ugly. She hated them as much as she hated Lizzie—no. She didn't hate Lizzie. Not exactly. She just needed some sleep, some time away from Meghan, something to give her the strength to stop giving in to the blackness. She thought that the money had been the thing that was all hers, but the euphoria over finding it hadn't lasted.

Tay was watching her closely. He didn't say anything.

Her own nastiness repulsed her. How could she ever raise a child when she was so black inside? She felt sick, but the last thing she wanted was to seem weak. "I wasn't sneaking," she said as forcefully as she could.

He tilted his head to the side. "Okay."

"My husband is a cop, so don't mess with Lizzie." She was aware that she was trying to get everyone, including herself, clear about whose side she was on.

I am on Lizzie's side. She really was, deep down. If only she could remember that. Why was it so hard to remember that?

"Officer Wynne. Met him awhile back. Met his gun. Suitably impressed."

"Good."

"Good."

Hell, she wanted the best for Lizzie. She wasn't pure evil. She just had been having a hard time lately and she couldn't fight the black thoughts away. If only Meghan could sleep through the night just once, Annie wouldn't feel so ragged all the time. If only her two teeth weren't coming in at once, making her so sour and fussy. Annie wanted to do something nice for Lizzie to make up for her bad thoughts, but who had the time or energy?

Tay had gone back to wrestling with some rusty nails in the fence.

If she could get Lizzie and him together, maybe Lizzie would stop calling Tommy every time she stubbed her toe. Maybe Tommy would stop running to her every time she had a hangnail.

Maybe, this could be the nice thing she'd do for Lizzie: help her get this man.

Judy Roth's curtains parted across the way.

Annie waved and called, "Hi, Mrs. Roth, just threatening Lizzie's stalker!"

He smiled and waved, too.

She turned back to Tay. "My husband will check you out, you know."

He shrugged. "I have no secrets." He looked at her more closely, then said, "How about you? Do you have any secrets?"

Annie's body went cold. Tay was looking at her as if he knew about the money. He glanced at the house, then back at her.

How could he know? She was losing it. She really had to figure out what to do with the money and then do it. She had an insane desire to tell him about the money, to come clean. This guy, of all people, could understand making a mistake. His life obviously wasn't going all that well for him to end up here, fixing Lizzie's fence.

But just as she was about to tell him, Judy Roth came out of her house and headed straight for them. She walked slowly and uncertainly.

"So you're for real?" she asked Tay. "Just a free fix-it guy."

"Aren't we all for real?" he asked.

"No. Not all of us. Some of us are fakes. Liars. Criminals." She pulled Meghan's stroller closer.

"Which one of us would that be?" he asked.

Despite herself, Annie laughed. Laughed like she hadn't in a long, long time. Meghan started laughing, too, a baby chuckle from deep down in her belly. *Heh, heh, heh*… Her eyes shone up at her mother. *Heh, heh, heh*… Her stroller shook.

Tay looked at the baby with a man's confusion, as if he was wondering who was working the remote.

"I like you, Tay," Annie said, keeping an eye on Judy's slow progress. "You have an edge. You're a little odd, but it's refreshing. We don't get many out-of-the-ordinary people in Galton. Everyone here just walks the straight and narrow."

"I doubt that," he said. "I don't think that you do, anyway."

She hesitated, then raced forward with her idea before she could think too much about it. Judy Roth was almost at Lizzie's gate, and she had to hurry. Maybe this wasn't the right thing to do—just like taking the money—but she was going to do it anyway. Because she felt like being reckless. Because she wanted her husband back—all of him. Because she wanted her childhood home to look nice again. Because getting Lizzie and this beautiful man together might be the best thing that ever happened to Lizzie, and she did want good things to happen for her sister, despite her out-of-control emotions. "What are you doing for dinner tomorrow night?"

Surprise was clear on his face. "Avoiding husbands with guns?"

Judy stepped uncertainly onto the sidewalk.

"Oh, for heaven's sakes. I don't mean it like that. Come by. Lizzie and Paige will be there. They always come for Friday night dinner. Tommy's a master with the grill. The season's over, but he won't stop till the tank is done. You'd be doing us a favor if he could grill one more burger. He could be out there in the snow if we don't empty that tank." She got a scrap of paper from her purse and scribbled her address. "Just so we can check you out properly."

"I don't know if that's such a good idea," he said. He looked at the paper she'd handed him, then looked at her again as if it had confirmed something that he already suspected. He chewed his lower lip thoughtfully.

What? Did he see that she lived in the wrong part of town?

Judy had finally reached them. "Hello, Mrs. Roth," they both said.

"Hello, dear! Hello, Tay!" Judy sang. "Can't miss a chance to see the baby."

Annie smiled, but hurried on with their conversation in a soft voice. "Why isn't it a good idea?"

Judy Roth bent over Meghan's stroller. She started cooing and making faces at her. Meghan kept her eyes on her mother, as if uncertain whether this woman meant harm.

"I don't think Lizzie wants me around," he said. "I'm just finishing up here, then leaving."

"Lizzie doesn't always know what she wants," Annie said. She turned to Mrs. Roth and said, "We have to go."

"Good-bye, little love," Mrs. Roth cooed to Meghan.

"Guess you forgot that sweater," Tay said as Annie walked away.

She ignored him and hurried down the street and down the hill toward home as if she hadn't heard. She was going to do this for Lizzie, to prove to herself that she wasn't a bad sister.

Wasn't a bad person.

Despite what she felt inside.

CHAPTER

21

*L*izzie asked the receptionist at 25th Century Realty to please tell Jill Kennedy she had a delivery of a mochaccino latte skinny caramel from the Last Chance diner.

The receptionist looked at Lizzie's empty hands with skepticism, but she called back to Jill.

While she waited, Lizzie poked around the reception area. Jill's office was even gaudier than Lizzie remembered, with shiny wooden floors covered in second-rate Oriental rugs, fresh lilies everywhere, gassing up the place with their fumes. The upholstered chairs huddled together in exclusive cliques. It gave Lizzie a certain amount of pleasure to note that they were modern fakes, nowhere close to the quality of the chairs in her own living room that she and Annie and her mother had assembled over years of eagle-eyed thrift-shop antiquing.

A surprised Jill Kennedy appeared from the back in a black pencil skirt, shimmery silk top, and three-inch heels. "Hey, where's my coffee?"

"Drank it. It was delicious. Thanks."

Jill said, "C'mon back." She yanked her down the hallway.

The receptionist glared after them.

"She doesn't like it when anyone has any fun," Jill said.

"As usual, you look perfect," Lizzie said to Jill. They made their way down the long corridor, portraits of gray-haired white men staring down at them from gilded frames. Lizzie adjusted her server's uniform. Her soft-soled white sneakers squished on the plush hall runner. Perfectly coiffed heads popped up from desks, then went back down with snarky smiles. Guess she looked like the client from hell to these folks. "So, what do you think we can find me and my six kids in a double-wide?" she asked as loudly as she could. "Don't you have some waste dump sites that are contaminated enough for us to afford something nice?" Galton was a college town composed of two kinds of people—those who worked at a professional level for Galton University and those who served them: that is, the townies.

Jill Kennedy and 25th Century Realty specialized in the former. "Shhhh!" Jill urged.

They got to Jill's office, not much more than a glorified cubicle. "Okay, you never come and see me at work. You must have slept with him," Jill said, sounding hopeful. She sat behind her desk and sucked on a straw stuck into one of her expensive iced coffees.

"No. Now listen. I need good advice this time. I don't want to have hiked up that damn hill for nothing."

"Well, it'll help you reduce that ass." Jill smiled.

Lizzie picked up a crystal paperweight in the shape of a house. "Tay told me his story." She recounted the story of the accident to Jill. She left out the part about the money. She felt like that was between the two of them. "And I felt this incredible connection to him. Like I had something to offer him, and not sex—just, you know, connection. A warm kitchen. So I invited him in for coffee." She paused. "And he said no."

Jill sat forward. "He said no? Maybe he thought it was going to be the same coffee you serve at the diner."

"Don't joke. This isn't funny. He couldn't get away from me fast enough. He just wanted me to know how screwed up he was and why it wasn't me it was him and blah blah blah. Oh, God, I'll never, ever find a decent man, will I?"

Jill clicked her pencil against her desk, ignoring her furiously blinking phone. "He's damaged goods. It's not your fault," Jill said. "Men are like that."

"I know, I know. But I felt like we had a connection, but he won't connect."

"Okay, okay, let's think this through. You want to connect? You're sure?"

"Yes. No. I don't know. We sort of kissed, also. Before. In Lucifer's."

"Sort of? Chrissie said it was totally hot."

"Oh, God. Chrissie told everyone! Why didn't you say something?"

"I was waiting for you to fess up," Jill admitted. "Took you long enough."

"It *was* hot," Lizzie admitted. "At first. But then he stopped. And I was a puddle of jelly and he was gone—just vacant, as if he wasn't even there. And that's what happened again with our conversation. He let it all out and told me everything and I wanted to reach out to him, and invite him in, and he pulled back like I was a leper."

"He's a man," Jill said. "That's what they do." Jill sipped some more of her coffee concoction.

She looked as if she was going to say more, but she didn't.

"Or it's me," Lizzie went on.

"You know, I take that back. Maybe it *is* your fault."

Lizzie's eyes went wide. "Why? What do you know? Help me out here."

"Because you did to him exactly what he did to you. You opened your soul and wished for a handyman, and when he responded, you pushed him away. Then he told you his deepest, darkest secrets, and when you invited him in, he ran. Maybe he's just like you—can't abide kindness."

"So what do I do?"

"You tell him your deepest, darkest secrets, but then, don't push him away. Break the cycle. Accept the offer."

"I don't have any deep, dark secrets."

"Sure you do. We all do. In fact, I've been meaning to tell you something," Jill said.

Lizzie's mind was contemplating what Jill had said about charity. Were she and Tay so similar that they couldn't get close? Lizzie cut Jill off. "I already told him about getting pregnant with Paige and about Ethan coming."

Jill looked irritated. She sucked from her coffee drink, her lips tight. Lizzie had missed something, but she couldn't figure it out now. She had to figure Tay out.

"Tell him about us," Jill said.

"Us?"

"The Enemy Club."

"Why?"

"I don't know. Because then, he'll see you're not so

perfect. I know I used to hate you for being so damn perfect."

"But I was never perfect."

"I know that now. But c'mon, when we were kids, it was all about trying to pretend to be the best, to show no fear or flaw or difference. I think you're still clinging a little to that."

"Me? What about you?"

"Well, okay, me, maybe. But I'm not trying to lure in a man right now. Look, Liz, he can't forgive himself and there you are with your house and your kid looking all strong and righteous. You were wronged, and you made the best of it. Maybe that pisses him off, keeps him away."

"I don't think he's pissed off exactly," Lizzie pointed out.

"Oh, yeah, right. That was me," Jill said.

"You?" What was Jill talking about?

The receptionist's voice came through on the line. "Jill, your ten o'clock is here."

Lizzie stood.

"Tell him that you're not perfect," Jill said as she walked Lizzie out. "Show a little weakness. Give him space to get in."

"I don't know," Lizzie said.

"Ask Georgia, then. And Nina. I promise. This will be the only time in our existence that all three of us agree on anything."

Georgia had a discreet office off the side of her enormous Tudor house. Lizzie walked past the *Guarded by Brinks* sign and carefully up the middle of the long driveway that turned a circle at the top. She didn't want to set off any alarms. The yard was perfectly tended, not a leaf out of place. Georgia's formidable stone house matched the stone campus buildings across the street, making the line between the campus and the town blurry.

Just as she neared the front door, a black BMW SUV pulled into the drive, sped past the front door, and stopped by the office side of the house.

One of Georgia's patients?

Lizzie realized that she was intruding. She ducked behind a bush by the front door, holding her breath, waiting for the sirens to start wailing. Georgia was famous for her hair-trigger security system. For fun, Galton students sometimes threw beer bottles just to set it off.

Mercifully, no siren sounded.

A woman got out of the car, a girl really, a Galton U. bumper sticker on the back of her car. She had glossy, pin-straight black hair that reached all the way to her butt. She strode to the office door at the side of the house without so much as a glance around, her hair swinging behind her, and disappeared inside.

Now what?

Lizzie stepped clear of the bush. She didn't want to intrude on something as private as a therapy appointment with Galton's number one shrink. She was already wondering what was wrong with the girl in the BMW. What could be wrong when you owned a car like that and went to one of the country's best schools? That girl had no idea how lucky she was.

Change of plans. Lizzie had started to scribble a note for Georgia to call her on the back of a Wegmans receipt she found at the bottom of her purse, when she heard the siren of a police car.

Oh, hell.

She considered ducking back behind the bush, but that was obviously what had tripped the silent alarm in the first place. She finished the note and dropped it through the mail slot, then calmly walked down the driveway just as Tommy's cruiser pulled up.

He stopped and rolled down the window. "You?"

Georgia's front door opened. Lizzie waved. "Hi, neighbor. Just leaving you a note. Call me!" She turned back to Tommy. "I didn't hear an alarm."

"She switched to silent. All those beer bottles." Tommy got out of the cruiser. "You okay?" he called to Georgia.

"Fine," she answered sheepishly. "I'll call you," she called to Lizzie.

"I still have to report this," Tommy said.

"Bill me. I have a patient," Georgia said, shutting her door behind her.

"Hey, you think I can have a ride?" Lizzie asked. "I need to get to work."

Tommy sighed. "Aiding and abetting," he said. "It's going to get us both in trouble someday, Lizzie. I'm not exactly a taxi service."

Lizzie shrugged and climbed in. "Who's afraid of trouble? You've got a gun, Tommy." She settled into the warm car. "Siren?"

"You know, you're just like your daughter."

"Please?"

"Liz."

"Okay, okay." They rode down the hill. "How's Meghan?"

"Perfect."

"Annie?"

"Weirdly happy."

"Yeah, I noticed that, too. She actually wanted to have lunch with me. I don't think she's invited me to lunch in months. What do you think?"

"I have no idea. Tell you the truth, she's been kind of mysterious lately. But I'm going with it, no questions asked."

"Good idea." They got to the diner. "Hey, Tommy, about my mysterious handyman. Did you ever look up his record like you said you would?"

"Oh, no. Never did. I can if you want."

"Yeah, can you?" If she was going to open up to Tay, she wanted to be sure that he was telling her the truth.

"You got it." They pulled up in front of the diner.

Lizzie opened the door to the cruiser. "Fight crime!"

"Fight hunger!" he called back. And then he drove away.

Tay was furious at himself. He had really messed up with Lizzie. What the hell was wrong with him, talking to her sister like that? But he felt that Annie was up to no good. He felt as if he had to protect Lizzie from something.

But what?

Things were getting complicated. More complicated than was good.

Candy.

The money.

Lizzie.

It was all coming together in ways that he didn't like.

It was one thing to want to fix things with Candy. That had been an accident, after all. But kissing Lizzie in that bar was no accident. He had headed straight for her, collided with her on purpose.

And left another wreck.

A hit-and-run.

And now he wanted to get even more involved? Have dinner with her family?

He had no business trying for a human connection when he felt so hollow inside. He had seen her face when he'd said no to her offer of coffee. And now he was contemplating busting into her life again.

But Annie was up to something. He was sure of it. And while it was none of his business what it was, he couldn't help himself.

That damned Boy Scout complex.

CHAPTER

22

*L*ater that day, Tommy, in full uniform, pushed through the doors of the diner. Lizzie was taking an order and tried to go back to it, even though the grave look on Tommy's face had spooked her to distraction.

Tommy took off his police hat, shook hands with the regulars, and nodded at Freddie the grill cook behind the pass.

Lizzie finished up, then came to the counter. It was always shocking to see the gun on Tommy's hip, as if it were proof that the world was more dangerous now than it had been when they were kids, back in high school.

He stared at Lizzie with a look of consternation.

"You look like you saw a ghost," she said.

"Lizzie. I finally got around to running that check on Tay Giovanni. Can you take a break?"

Lizzie's stomach sank. She knew what Tommy was going to tell her. At least, she hoped she knew. What if there was more? "I've got three tables. Just talk."

Tommy looked around at the regulars. "It's public

record," Tommy said. "But still, it's not an ethical use of my position to spread rumors around town."

All the regulars nodded agreement.

Freddie said, "Nothing I don't know in this town,"

"They're not rumors if they're true," Mr. Campos said from his seat at the counter.

"Go away, Freddie. Mr. Campos, back to your cross-word," Lizzie commanded.

Everyone continued to stare at Tommy. A small crowd had formed around him.

"Is this about the man Lizzie's been kissing at Luci-fer's?" Joy asked.

Gertrude said, "I heard that he's been wandering Gal-ton at night, doing good deeds. He stacked Lucille's fire-wood last night. At least, she figures it must be him. Who else could it be?"

"Rayanne, can you take my tables for a minute?" Lizzie asked.

"Sure, hon," Rayanne said on her way by with a platter of fries and burgers. She looked back with curiosity at the gathered crowd.

"C'mon." Lizzie pulled Tommy into a window booth. She sat down opposite him. "Spill."

"Your fence man. Dante Giovanni." Tommy leaned in close and lowered his voice. "Lizzie. He killed someone. The mother of a student at Galton U. It was an accident. But still—"

Lizzie shook her head. "I know."

"You do?"

"Yeah. But tell me anyway. I want a second source."

Tommy pulled out the thick black book he carried in his back pocket. He flicked it open and started to read.

"*Dante E. Giovanni, thirty-four years old, legal resident Queens, New York. Police record as follows: November 22, 1:24 P.M., ran red light at Forty-third and Evergreen, traveling east. Head-on collision with Linda Goodnight, forty-two, traveling south. Goodnight pronounced dead on scene. Hospital report: fatal internal organ failure from impact. Dante Giovanni, minor scrapes, contusions.*"

Lizzie thought about the scar that marked his cheek. His slow driving. His aborted kiss. It was all true. It all made sense.

Tommy went on. "*Charged with vehicular homicide. Fined and ticketed, six points for failure to stop.*" Tommy flipped the page. "*November 24, ticket and fine withdrawn. Jan 24, DA brought charges to grand jury. Grand jury no-billed it.*" Tommy paused. "That means they decided no crime took place and dismissed it as a criminal matter." He closed the book with a snap. "End of story. No other records. No civil suit was brought that I could find. The guy never did anything else wrong. Not even a parking ticket." He put his hands over hers. "Lizzie? Hello? You hearing this?"

She was. It wasn't anything more than Tay had said, but it threw her thoughts back to his predicament. A woman had died, and it was his fault. No wonder he had a Boy Scout complex. How did a person get past something like that? But she didn't want him to be a Boy Scout. She had wanted him to be a man and come in and have coffee with her. She felt for him. She really did. But she also had to protect herself.

Tommy squeezed her hands. "Liz? It's not so bad. You can't judge a man by one little unfortunate accident. That's why they call them accidents. Life happens. I just thought you should know. Before, you know, before whatever."

She felt light, as if she was floating over the table. Tommy thought she was feeling bad for Tay, but she was feeling bad for herself. She tried to fight down her selfishness. What did it do to a person to kill another person, even if it was an accident? Could that person ever be whole again? Was that why Tay was a wanderer, why he couldn't kiss her? What could she do to fix him? It didn't matter. Wasn't her business. She had her own problems to deal with. And right now, with Ethan coming back, the last thing she needed was to look out her window every morning and to feel like a woman who looked like she needed handouts from the local martyr.

"Lizzie?" Tommy leaned in so close, Lizzie could see every pore on his face. She tried not to imagine the accident. One minute, driving calmly, the next minute...

Slam!

Lizzie startled from her thoughts. Someone was pounding on the plate-glass window.

Slam! Slam! Slam!

Annie.

Her sister's lips were a thin line, her eyes were blazing. She was going to break the window if she didn't cool it.

What was Annie's problem?

Tommy yanked his hands away from Lizzie's, as if he'd been doing something wrong. He jumped up, flustered.

Lizzie let him go. Thoughts of Tay, sirens whirling, and mangled metal swirled in her head as she tried to ignore her sister. She could help him.

No, she didn't want to help him. The rush of shame at his withdrawn kiss, his refusal of coffee, came back. She had to be responsible for herself, now. Tay Giovanni wasn't a fixer-upper, he was a teardown. She didn't need a man like that in her life.

I can help him.

I'm done doing things for other people. It's time I helped myself. It was like her wishes, ambiguous, confused, both for and against her best interests. Why was that always the case? Couldn't it ever be simple?

Tommy had gone to the other end of the diner to help Annie through the door with the bulky stroller. Lizzie got up slowly, still in a daze from thinking about all the contradictions that swirled around her and Tay, helping and being helped, charity and kindness, forgiving the unforgivable...

Tommy and Annie were deep in angry conversation. Lizzie wanted to rescue Meghan, who was looking at her parents as if she was about to burst into tears. "Where's my pretty niece?" She bent to the baby in the stroller, whose face metamorphosed from worry to a happy, goofy grin.

"Leave her!" Annie screeched.

Lizzie backed off, stood up. "What's your problem?"

"I don't know," Annie said. She looked lost, confused.

"I was explaining to Annie that we were talking about Tay. And what happened to him," Tommy said.

"Holding hands?" Annie asked. "Staring into each other's eyes?" She looked as if she was going to cry. She swatted at her eyes with the back of her mittens.

"What?" Lizzie said. "No. It wasn't like that." She felt woozy and sick with shame, as if she had done something wrong. Which she hadn't. How could Annie even think that? Mr. Campos was watching closely, shaking his head sadly. This was going to be all over town by the end of the day.

Lizzie hoped that Paige wouldn't hear about it.

She had to make Annie see that she was wrong.

"That's what I'm trying to tell her," Tommy said. He turned to his wife. "Lizzie was upset. She had sort of gone into a trance. I was just trying for contact, to bring her down to earth. Honestly, Anne. I was telling her kind of shocking news."

"Tay killed someone," Lizzie said. She hated the way that had come out, and started to backtrack. "It was a car accident. Not his fault. I mean—it was just shocking, that was all. I was upset because he was on my property, and he was so—damaged." She was trying to stop the gossip mill, but instead she was adding fuel. "And Tommy was trying to keep me from flipping out. That's all."

"That's all," Tommy agreed.

Annie didn't seem satisfied. The hurt in her eyes seemed a mile deep.

"Annie?" Tommy said. "You want to go home? C'mon."

"I'm sorry," Annie said. She looked around her, as if just noticing where she was. "I just got, I don't know—"

"It's okay. Forget it," Tommy said, putting his arm around her.

She looked at Lizzie. "I'm so tired. Meghan got up at five this morning."

"I know," Lizzie said. "It's okay." But it wasn't. Not really. Lizzie was almost as shaken by Annie's outburst as she was by hearing Tay's story confirmed. Why did Lizzie always have to be the one forgiving everyone? When did she get a break?

CHAPTER

23

The next day, the grill fired up with a whoosh that always made Tommy feel good. He was going to do simple burgers tonight. Maybe a few dogs. The evening already felt too complicated with Annie's crazy suspicions about him and Lizzie without adding his new grilled Chicken Tikka recipe to the mix.

Annie came into the yard with Meghan bundled up as if there was a snowstorm. She spread out the big blue blanket and put Meghan on it to look up at the falling leaves. Meghan would be crawling any minute. She rolled over and pushed her tiny, diaper-clad butt into the air like a yogi. He was pretty sure she'd be the world's best crawler. Then the world's best walker. Then, well, the sky was the limit.

God, he loved that tiny thing.

"So, there's something I've been meaning to tell you," Annie said. She was wrapped tight in her black wool coat, her arms shoved into the pockets. "I invited Tay to dinner." She looked into the grill's flames through the glass of the hood.

Tommy looked away from his daughter to his wife. "Sorry, what? I didn't quite get that."

"I invited Tay to dinner. You know, Lizzie's fix-it man."

Tommy looked to Meghan. "I know who he is. But why, Annie? To our house?" Annie's explosion in the diner was still fresh in his mind.

"I was walking Meghan yesterday and he was in front of Lizzie's house and we got into a little chat, so I invited him. I don't know if he'll come or not. Probably not. But I think maybe we should check him out. I didn't know then about his—issues. But now, I'm really glad he's coming."

Tommy looked to his daughter. She was once again on her back, waving her arms at the falling leaves. If she got one, she'd try to eat it. They had to watch her every second. "Does Lizzie know?"

"Why do you always think of Lizzie first?" Annie asked. Then she quickly backed down. "I'm sorry. I didn't mean that. She doesn't know."

Tommy watched the temperature gauge on his grill go past the yellow and into the red. "Maybe you're right. It's good to get another look at him. That kind of accident can change a person."

"That's exactly why I invited him by tonight. So we can talk to him. Check him out."

They watched the flames for a while. The chilly wind was picking up. Tommy might even have to get his gloves.

Then Annie said, "Okay. So that's not the only reason. I think Lizzie needs a man. And even though this guy had a bad experience, I think deep down he's a good guy. Tommy, I want her to have a man so she's happy. But I also want her to have a man so that she'll leave you alone."

Tommy didn't look away from the grill. He couldn't help feeling a flicker of hope: Annie still loved him enough to be jealous. Maybe there was still a chance for them. "I need a beer." Tommy put down the grill brush and went toward the back porch for a celebratory Bud.

She followed. "I think that maybe she's still a little in love with you, Tommy. I know we've been through this, and I know I was wrong to freak out at the diner, but I can't help thinking it and I think we should talk about it."

Tommy got his beer and came back outside. Celebration over. "Annie, I don't love your sister except in a sisterly-in-law sort of way." He turned to her. "I don't love Lizzie Carpenter. I love Annie Carpenter Wynne. Annie, I'm sorry for not dating you first, but I can't change that. And I'm sorry for helping Lizzie out when I can. She's my sister-in-law. It's my job. All I can do is tell you that I love you now. You. Not Lizzie. In fact, I didn't ever really love Lizzie."

Annie watched him. "Really?"

"Really. Annie, I love you. You better try to get used to that, because honestly, I'm getting pretty sick of this. I don't know how much more I can take."

"You really never loved her."

"Tell you the truth, she kind of scared me to death."

"She was kinda—independent," Annie agreed.

"Kind of? She beat up Jill Kennedy for telling everyone her secret about being pregnant. She set poor Georgia Phillips on fire!"

"That second one was an accident. And Jill deserved it."

"True, but still. I was a kid. Not the tough, manly man I am today."

Annie smiled and it felt like a gift.

She sat down on the back steps. "Why is she always turning to you? I wish you'd say no to her sometimes. Just once in a while. I know she's all alone. It's just that, I don't know, she's gotten in the habit, that's all. She treats you like—"

"Like I'm her husband?" Tommy asked.

"Exactly. And—"

Meghan squealed as Paige came bounding around the house. "Where's my baby?"

"She's my baby," Lizzie said, coming behind Paige. She hip-checked Paige aside and made a grab for Meghan.

When the scuffle was over, Lizzie had won again. She held Meghan on her hip. "Hey, honeys, we're home." She kissed Annie's cheek, then Tommy's. "What's for dinner?"

Lizzie and Annie sat in Annie's front room, Coronas in hand, while Tommy grilled out back. Meghan was propped against couch pillows they had arranged in a semicircle on the floor. Poor thing kept tipping over like Uncle Louie at Thanksgiving. And just as with Uncle Louie, they'd straighten her without a comment, as if nothing had happened.

The aroma of Tommy's burgers wafting from the backyard was beginning to make Lizzie's stomach growl in anticipation. Paige was watching TV in the back room, which Lizzie was glad about because she had been waiting for this chance to talk to Annie about her. "Paige started showing up with new clothes. I haven't given her an allowance since she hit twelve." She lowered her voice to a whisper. "I'm afraid she's shoplifting."

Annie shook her head. "No way. She's not a bad kid." Annie handed a rattle back to Meghan, who promptly threw it across her blanket and out of reach. "Now there's a bad kid." She kissed Meghan on her way to retrieving the rattle. Meghan threw it again. "Stinker."

Lizzie said, "You know, Annie, when we were talking about that money you had found, Paige sounded so entitled. I think that's why kids steal. They think they deserve stuff, so it's somehow fair, and somehow it doesn't hurt anyone if they take it."

Annie stiffened. "Are we talking about Paige or about the money I found?"

"How much money did you find, Annie? You never told me."

"Not much. Just enough for dinner plus a little more. I think it was, I don't remember, like eighty bucks. Why?"

"Nothing." Lizzie didn't want to tell Annie Tay's story. She felt as if he'd told her in confidence. She was relieved, though, that Annie's money had nothing to do with Tay. She gave Meghan back her rattle. Meghan tossed it again.

"I have another possibility for Paige's new wardrobe," Annie said. "Maybe a boy is buying her things."

"She's fourteen!" Lizzie protested.

"They say kids grow up faster now. Paige is just two years younger than you were when you—"

"Okay!" Lizzie cut her off. "We all know what I did when I was sixteen. Let's not rehash it in front of the baby."

"Don't do like your aunt Lizzie. She was a bad, bad girl," Annie said very seriously to Meghan. "Anyway, I have no idea. I'm just saying maybe. Did you ask her?"

"Of course. She says that she saves her babysitting money or borrows stuff from friends. But I just talked to

Linda yesterday at the diner, and Paige hasn't babysat for her twins in weeks."

"Or for me. Tommy and I are too tired to go out."

Lizzie waited for more information, but Annie didn't seem inclined to elaborate on her and Tommy's troubles. Lizzie was a little relieved. She didn't want to fight. "I don't buy what Paige is telling me, but I can't just out and out call her a liar."

Annie nodded. "Do you think this is about her father coming? Her own little self-improvement project for Dad?"

"Don't call him that. Call him Ethan Pond, sperm donor. He's no more her dad than Mr. Williams at the carpet store. Hell, Tommy is more a father to her than this guy. In fact, I was kind of thinking of asking Tommy to keep an eye on her. If she's stealing, I don't want her to get caught by anyone else, if you know what I mean. Do you think he could, you know, go to the mall sometime? See what she's up to? Who she's hanging around with."

Annie got a funny look on her face.

"What?" Lizzie asked.

"Nothing. It's just that you're always asking Tommy for help."

"Is this about what happened in the diner? Because it was nothing."

"I know. And I'm sorry for flipping out there. I just still think that you treat Tommy sometimes like he's your husband."

Lizzie was as shocked by the fact of Annie's frank accusation as she was by the content of it. She felt the urge to defend herself, but a stronger urge overtook it. She smiled.

"What?"

"You know, I don't know what's changed about you these past few weeks, but I like the new Annie. I'm glad you told me that. You're right. I depend on him."

Annie shrugged, as if embarrassed for being right. "How's your quest for getting a new man before Ethan's arrival?" Annie asked.

"Lousy. I've been on three dates, and they've all been busts."

Annie stopped and sat up straight, as if she had just remembered something important. Her eyes met Lizzie's, then skittered away. Lizzie braced herself for whatever Annie didn't want to look her in the eye with.

"Speaking of men," Annie said, "let's talk about a fence-man." She looked out the window as if expecting someone. Lizzie followed her gaze. Mrs. Griffin from the post office walked by outside. Her dachshund peed on Annie's sugar maple.

Lizzie admitted, "I asked him in for coffee last week and he said no." Lizzie felt a tug of wanting something more, but she ignored it.

"Great. So you won't mind that he's coming for dinner."

"Annie!" Lizzie sat up. She had thought Tommy had been avoiding her gaze all night. "You invited him? Why?"

"If a strange guy is going to be on your property, we're going to check him out in person. Oh, and looky. Here he is now!"

Sure enough, Tay's red pickup rounded the corner, inched down the street, then pulled smoothly, albeit slowly, to the curb. The engine cut, not entirely smoothly, the door opened after hitching a bit, and out he stepped.

Lizzie looked after him for his animals, but for once, he'd left them behind.

Jeans. Button-down white shirt with collar. Brown boots. Bottle of red wine in hand. His truck might be glitchy, but Tay was one hundred percent smooth.

CHAPTER

24

Jay knew Lizzie would be here, but he hadn't antici-
pated that she'd look so good. No raggedy pajamas, no
waitress uniform. On her sister's couch, feet curled under
her, wavy brown hair loose, red skirt and tank top under a
heavy fall sweater, she looked unharried and relaxed.
Until she caught sight of him, that is. Her sweater had
slipped off her right shoulder, revealing the spaghetti strap
of the shirt underneath and her tanned, rounded, muscled
shoulders. When she saw him, she yanked it back into
place and crossed her arms over her chest.

Annie let him in, and as he stepped into the room, the
baby on the floor started to tip forward. Annie was looking
at him and Lizzie was studiously looking away, as if com-
posing herself for a difficult ordeal. Neither of them saw the
baby tipping. He jumped and caught her before her nose
bonked the floor. Her warm, soft head was shocking in its
vulnerability. Whoever decided it was a good idea to put
something so soft and fragile on top of a baby? He tipped
the baby back to sitting but didn't want to take his hand away.

"Good catch!" Annie said.

"She can't be trusted with that thing," he said.

"What thing?" Annie asked, looking alarmed.

He caught Lizzie's eye and she looked away. He shouldn't have come. This was starting to get much too complicated.

"That soft head. Shouldn't she wear a helmet or something?"

The baby batted her enormous blue eyes at him. He reluctantly pulled his hand away. "Well, you're welcome," he said.

"Not all the Carpenter women are that easy," Annie said, but she smiled at him, obviously one of the easy ones.

Lizzie turned bright red.

He scrambled to cover her embarrassment. "Believe me, I know. That's why I brought really, really good wine." He handed Annie the bottle.

Lizzie still hadn't spoken.

Annie studied the label. "Oh, very nice! French! You're welcome in my house any time." Then she jumped up and scurried to the kitchen, crying, "Just off to get the corkscrew!"

"Traitor," Lizzie muttered under her breath.

"Hi," he said.

"Hi yourself," she said. "How are you?"

"Good."

"Good."

"Good." He repeated. This was awkward. He wanted to kiss her and he couldn't possibly kiss her. Something was crackling between them that neither one of them knew what to do with. He'd move in, dart back, piss her off. He shouldn't have come.

"They're trying to set us up, you know. Just warning you," Lizzie said.

"I had that feeling," he admitted. "I wasn't going to come."

"So why did you?" she asked.

"Because I wanted to make it up to you. For not coming into your house for coffee," he said, trying to ignore how good she looked. If he kissed her again and he couldn't follow through, he'd have to jump into a gorge himself. *Hold steady, big guy. You came to warn her about her sister. That's all.*

She looked him right in the eyes. "You know what I realized just now?"

"What?" He wasn't sure he wanted to hear.

"Everyone's trying to push me into some role that they need me to play for them. I'm supermom to Paige and little sis who needs protecting to Annie."

"What role are you playing for me?" he asked. He was curious what she thought. His thoughts lately rarely jibed with other people's.

"My role is to make you feel better about your accident. But Tay, I'm sick of playing roles. It's making me feel worse."

He tried to interrupt, but she stopped him.

"Wait. Just let me finish. I've been thinking a lot about this since our last conversation. I want to help you, Tay. Heck, I get that accidents happen. I'm not horrid, you know. But I can't help you because I won't ever be her."

"Her name is Linda Goodnight." He felt the chill that always gripped him when he mentioned her name. He hoped if he said it enough, the nausea would lessen. *I lost my concentration and I killed a woman named Linda Goodnight.*

Not in this lifetime.

"Okay. I'm not Linda and I won't ever be. I can't make you feel better, no matter how much you fix my place. That's why I need you to stop coming around. Because maybe it makes you feel better, but it makes me feel bad."

Sounds of Annie moving around in the kitchen drifted out to them. The back door slammed. Tommy's and Annie's low voices from the kitchen were buried under a burst from the laugh track of Paige's television show. The calm domesticity felt alien to him, and he suspected, from the look on Lizzie's face, that it was alien to her, too.

He looked around him at the sedate perfection and compared it with Lizzie's mess of a house. He should back off, but this neat, tidy house was pissing him off because it seemed like an affront to Lizzie, although he had no idea why. What was her sister trying to do? What had she been doing at Lizzie's house? He felt as if he was stepping into the middle of something, but he also felt as if being in the middle might help Lizzie somehow. He owed her.

Heat filled his body. Not sexual heat, but the familiar heat of desperate longing for the impossible—turning back time, being understood, human connection, the usual. He leaned in as close as he could. "You don't need to tell me that I could turn your place into the Taj Mahal and I'd still feel a black hole of guilt sucking out my guts for the rest of my life. You're not doing me any favors by letting me hang around, believe me. I came because I liked you and I fixed your fence because I liked you. I liked you when you said that freckled friend of yours was nuts for thinking the universe granted wishes and I liked you when you said that everything had to be equal. And when you were around, I could smell and taste and feel in ways I couldn't when you weren't around. You made me come alive in ways I haven't in a long, long time. I haven't told anyone my story in a long, long time except for you, Lizzie." He looked around again, unable to contain himself. "Christ, Lizzie, look at this place."

"Look at what?"

"Annie's house. This place is practically shining it's so clean and spiffy. Are these things even real?" He touched a begonia on the side table. "It's real," he reported. He sat across from her on the couch. He was too big for it, and it shifted under him, every fiber creaking.

The baby cooed and wobbled on her pillows on the floor between them. Lizzie handed her a toy, which the baby stuffed into her mouth.

"Tell you the truth, a place like this makes me want to break something, just so it's not so damn perfect." He glanced guiltily at Meghan. "Sorry, kid. So darn perfect."

Lizzie gazed out over the lawn at leaves dropping from the fiery maple tree in the yard as if they were the most interesting things around. He wasn't getting through to her.

"Dare me?" he asked.

"Dare you to what?" she asked.

"Mar the perfection?"

She sat up. "I don't! What are you talking about?"

"Yes you do." He looked around, then reached out and tipped a tiny potted plant right off the table. It thudded to the rug below, spilling dirt.

A crazy little laugh escaped from Lizzie's throat. She covered her mouth.

"See, I knew you'd like that. 'Cause you're a woman who can't be trusted. You say what you don't mean." He felt a little easier as he knelt to pick up the plant. He pushed the stray dirt back in, then put the pot back in its place. "Why'd you wish for a freebie handyman, Elizabeth? Don't think, just say it. Now. Fast. The first thing that comes to mind. Mar the perfection."

"I already told you. I want to make Paige happy, to make her feel confident for when her father comes."

"Bullshit. You don't want that. You want her to stay. Try again."

"You don't know what I want."

"Neither do you, obviously. But I have a feeling it has something to do with this place."

"Here? Why?"

"I don't know, but I think you do. Isn't it kind of obvious, Liz? You do the opposite of what you want because you think it's right. But I don't give a shit about right or wrong. I don't even believe in right or wrong. Just in the truth and being honest. Come on, talk to me, Lizzie."

She uncrossed her arms. Then crossed them again.

"Your sister was sneaking into your house."

"What?"

"Get pissed, Lizzie. What do you want? Stop thinking of anyone else. She was in there for a while."

"When?"

"She has a key on a yarn string and she lets herself in. What's going on with that?" He wondered how far he could push her. "Look at your house, Elizabeth. Look at your life. Now look at this." He motioned to Annie's perfect house around them. "Is this what you want? This perfection? Why? Why would you want Annie's life?"

"I don't."

"No? Well, she wants yours. Or at least, something of

yours. So what do you want? Don't tell me you want Paige to be happy. Don't tell me you want what's right. Dig deeper, Lizzie."

"I want my place to look nice for Ethan, to show him that we don't need him and his stinking help." The words rolled out of her so quickly, she looked shocked that she had said them.

"Paige's father?"

"Yes. I can't believe I just said that. It's so childish to want revenge."

He could tell that she had meant her voice to be defiant, but it came out barely a whisper. Her limbs betrayed her, too, shaking slightly. He was getting to her and she was getting to something honest—finally!—and he liked it. Maybe this was how he could pay her back for his inability to have coffee with her, for kissing her, then pulling away. He could challenge her to be honest with herself.

"I can give it to you. Fix your place up so it looks so good, Ethan Lake will think you're a goddamned librarian married to a cop."

"Ethan Pond."

"Whatever."

"How'd you know Annie was a librarian?"

"Lucky guess. It was that or a schoolteacher."

Lizzie drew back. "That's not what I want. That's stupid. I don't want Annie's life. I don't want revenge."

"Why not?"

Lizzie opened her mouth, then closed it. "I'm sure Annie's going into my house was nothing."

He lowered his voice. "Lizzie, I'm sure it's something. I think she's toxic. Stop thinking about trying to please other people, especially toxic people."

"She's my sister."

"I'm sorry. I just don't feel good around her. And I think you don't either, Lizzie." He watched the baby, feeling odd to be talking about her mother this way. Good thing she couldn't speak English.

"What happened? Exactly?" Lizzie asked.

"Said she wanted a sweater for the baby. She didn't come out with a sweater. She was in there for a while. Just ask Mrs. Roth. She was watching the whole thing, too."

Lizzie thought about that. What could Annie possibly have been doing in her house? She felt incredibly grateful to Tay. "Crap. I don't need a handyman. I need a security guard." *I need you.*

I want you.

She thought about his words—*Stop thinking about trying to please other people.*

Annie in her house. Paige getting ready to leave her. Ethan showing up out of nowhere and Lizzie wanting to make the world look perfect for him. "I just realized something," Lizzie said. She stood up and came to Tay, her palms sweating just a tiny bit. She leaned down so their faces were almost touching. She could see him squirm, and she didn't care. All her nervousness had vanished.

"Close your eyes, Meg," she said to the baby.

Then she leaned down and kissed him ever so gently on the corner of his lips.

He didn't move. His eyes were on hers, intense and unreadable.

So she kissed the middle of his lips, softly, lingering on the warmth. She felt the presence of his body under hers, totally still, as if venom from her kiss had paralyzed him.

She stood up again and went back to her chair.

They looked at each other across the room.

"Wow," he said. "That was a surprise."

"I did it because I wanted to do it," she said. "And because I don't give a crap what you want. I'm going to fix you, Tay, whatever the hell you say. Because I want you. And I've decided to get what I want, no matter what it means to anyone else."

For once he was speechless. "I'm not so sure that's a good idea."

"I'm not so sure I care what you think."

And then, to her utter relief, he smiled.

Tay stayed for dinner.

It turned out both Tommy and Tay were mad for the Yankees and the Rangers, plus they both adored fly-fishing and old cars. When they had finished dessert and the men were doing the dishes, Paige was back in front of the TV, and Annie was upstairs putting Meghan down, Lizzie found herself alone in the living room.

She hesitated by the begonia.

She looked both ways. She could hear Annie moving around upstairs, talking quietly, the men laughing in the kitchen.

She tipped the plant right off the table.

She looked down at the spilled plant, its soil dashed across the carpet like an ominous shadow.

It felt good.

And she didn't even pick it up.

CHAPTER

25

Tommy offered to drive Lizzie and Paige home.

"I'll drive," Tay said. "If you don't mind going a little slow."

"A little?" Lizzie asked. "I've never seen you drive faster than I could walk."

"Yeah, well, that's probably true," he said.

"I promised Julie I'd sleep over," Paige said. "Tonight," she said pointedly. "I brought all my stuff. And I *don't* have all night to get there."

"I'll drop Paige. You guys go up the hill," Tommy said.

So Lizzie and Tay set off in his red truck up the hill.

"Holy cow, you really are slow. Let me drive this thing," Lizzie said.

"Gladly. You drive a clutch?" he asked.

"No." She settled back in the seat for the long ride. "We should have brought snacks."

They stopped at a stop sign. And sat. And sat. A car approached from the right. It stopped, waiting for Tay. Tay waved it through.

"We should have brought sleeping bags," she said.

"We'll get there," he said, pulling carefully into the intersection. "How come you don't have your own car?"

"I do. It's in my driveway, rusting and undrivable. Something or other expensive is wrong with it. I forget what. Anyway, I can walk to work and to town. I can borrow Annie and Tommy's car when I need to. It's no big deal."

Lizzie looked back at the long line of cars forming behind them. "Think we'll get there this week?"

"What's your hurry?"

"No hurry." She meant it. She liked being with Tay. She liked his easy way of not caring what anyone thought now that she was trying it, too.

He pulled to the side to let the line of cars pass.

One by one, they drove by, trying to stare into the truck. A few drivers shouted insults that Tay ignored. He waved back.

After an eternity, he pulled back into the traffic lane.

"I never met anyone with problems as weird as yours," Lizzie said. "I hope fixing you isn't going to be too much work."

"Yeah, well, I've never met anyone with problems as weird as yours," he said.

Cars were getting stuck behind them again, beeping and tailgating.

"My problems are not weird," she insisted.

"Sure they are. Nothing weirder than not knowing what you really want."

"It's because I want lousy, selfish things."

"We can't control what we want," Tay said, and the look he shot her made her sure he was talking about wanting her. Her toes started to tingle and the delicious feeling spread through her. He pulled over again. More cars streamed past. "Lizzie, can I fix your house now that we'll be even?"

"Nope. No charity."

"But you fix me. We're even," he insisted.

"Sorry, fixing you is what I want, Tay. You never told me what you want. So you're still out of luck there."

"I don't want anything, Liz. I already told you that."

"Yeah, well, you refused to take that lame answer from me, so I refuse to take it from you."

He was waiting to pull back into the traffic, but the car directly behind them refused to get off his bumper. "Uh-oh."

"What?"

"There's always someone like this."

She looked back. "Like what?"

"Someone who's too pissed at my driving to just move on by. Remember I told you that no one can abide a person who drives slowly?"

The man in the car behind them got out of his car. "Shit. Sit back, Lizzie. This might get ugly."

"Ugly?" She sat up.

"Hey! What the hell! Who do you think you are, asshole?" The man was at Tay's side of the truck. "Speed limit's thirty-five, not ten!"

Tay rolled down the window calmly. "Sorry about that."

"Your truck broken?" the man asked. His breath fogged in the cold night air.

"Nope."

"She sick?" He peered into the cab at Lizzie.

"Nope," Tay said.

"Hey, is that Lizzie Carpenter?" the man asked.

Lizzie peered out the window to look closer. "Why, hello, Billy. Haven't seen you in years. Tay, Billy Reddy. Bill, this is Tay Giovanni."

"Sorry, Lizzie," Billy said. "I didn't know you were in there."

"No problem. See you tomorrow, right? Fries and a chocolate shake and grilled American with tomato, sliced thin."

Bill smiled. "Be careful out here," he said. "College students drive like crazy people. I just thought something was wrong." Billy got back in his car. He kept behind them at a respectable distance, his blinkers on, waving other cars around their slow convoy until he turned off down a side road.

"Wow, do you know everyone's order in town?" Tay asked.

"Pretty much. If they come into the diner, I know."

"What about him?" Tay asked, motioning to the car that was passing on the left. An elderly man was driving.

Lizzie cracked her knuckles as if warming up for a challenge. "That's Evan Pikes. He likes a baked potato and turkey platter with gravy on the side. Black coffee."

"That's amazing," Tay said. "You're making that up."

"Never."

"Him?"

A few cars passed that Lizzie didn't recognize. Then the Bradford family passed them, and Lizzie rattled off everyone's orders—all six of them—down to dessert.

"Do people always order the same thing?" Tay asked.

"Almost always. Some people have a few favorites, but I'll know them all if they come in a few times. Those people, I can usually tell what they'll want just by the look on their faces. Like Mr. Zinelli, that old guy who wouldn't leave you alone that first day in the diner. He likes a plain glazed doughnut and coffee. But then, when he stops shaving, I know he's thinking about his wife, who died last year. So then, I give him chocolate covered with pink sprinkles, because that's what his wife, Betty, used to order before she passed. And since I notice and I remember, it makes Mr. Zinelli happy."

"I think you might be one of the most remarkable people I've ever met, Liz," Tay said. They pulled up outside her house. It had taken almost fifteen minutes to go the mile up the hill.

"That's not true," Lizzie said. "I'm a mess."

"Maybe on the outside—"

"Hey!"

"On the outside of your house," he added. "But deep down, you have a solid life."

They sat a few moments in silence.

"Good night?" Tay asked.

"Not good night," Lizzie said.

"No?"

"No. You need to kiss me first."

"I do?"

"Yes. It's what I want."

"So if I kiss you, I can come back tomorrow and finish the fence?"

"This isn't a trade. Just a kiss—"

But he didn't let her finish. His lips were already on hers, his hand behind her head, pulling her toward him.

His kiss was hungry, rough, parting her lips, opening her mouth under his.

Yes. She wanted this.

He started to pull away, but she put her hands on his face and pulled him closer. "Don't you dare pull away," she murmured.

He buried his face in her neck, biting. "Wouldn't dare," he managed.

She let her head fall back as he ravaged her neck, nibbled across her collarbone. His hands were hot on her back, pinning her arms. The warmth of him felt divine, his hunger melted her. She tasted him right back and she wanted more, but she didn't want to push him too far. Not yet.

She pulled away from him, then watched his face change from hunger and desire to blankness.

"So what happens to make you look like that after we kiss?"

"Like what?"

"Like you've seen a ghost."

"I have."

"The accident?"

"Something comes over me." He licked his lips. "It's like something is always watching me, judging me, and I'm never worthy. Like every pleasure has to be punished."

"Are you okay now?"

"No. Not really. I mean, I'm okay, but I'm shaky. It's hard to describe. Like I'm empty. Frozen."

"You know, Tay, it's okay not to be okay. It's okay to be sorry."

"What worries me is that it'll never end. I'll never be normal."

"Who wants normal?" She got out of the car and didn't look back as she let herself into the house.

She felt as if it was Christmas and her birthday and summer vacation all rolled into one when she found another bluestone in her path the next morning, perfectly placed, the broken-down bricks it had replaced stacked neatly by her front door.

Some men left flowers. Some men sent cards. But only Tay would do this.

It meant that he hadn't slept again.

And for a selfish moment, she hoped that part of his not being able to sleep had to do with her, because her sleep had been rocky, thinking about him.

Then she was sorry, because she knew what it was not to sleep.

And she hoped that maybe, somehow, she'd be able to help him figure out the cure.

CHAPTER

26

Tommy sat at the kitchen table, still wearing his blue uniform. He stared at the stack of hundred-dollar bills in front of him. His police instincts kept him from breaking the purple seal around the money, as if it were evidence. But what was the crime? Not having a clue how to make his wife happy? Failing to be the husband she expected?

He looked at the money, feeling sick, as if he'd found another man's watch on his bedstand.

Just when he thought he and Annie were getting somewhere with their relationship, he had to find this under the couch.

All he wished for was to be able to figure out how to make the old Annie come back. Ever since Meghan's birth, she had been depressed and bitter and he had no idea what to do about it. Then, lately, she'd been suddenly happy. In truth, he'd been too scared to ask her why. She was so fragile lately, he didn't dare ruin it.

But today, when he was searching for Meghan's blue bootie, he'd found this stack of cash under the couch.

He had assumed Annie had been miserable these past few months because she was bored and frustrated with taking care of Meghan. After all, she had quit her job that she loved at the library, and most of her old friends didn't come by anymore. But now that this money had mysteriously appeared under his couch, he couldn't help wondering if Annie had something going on that he didn't know about. How had he missed something so important?

He jumped up when he heard Annie outside talking to Mrs. Wendell and her schnauzer, Witzell. Tommy joined them outside, freeing Meghan from her stroller and swinging her up in the air. He gave Annie a kiss on the cheek. They all smiled as Mrs. Wendell chatted about her Witzell's hurt paw and about Meghan's new tooth and Tommy thought, *This is what unhappy families do, isn't it? Pretend?* He had the sense that Annie didn't want to come inside. That she was avoiding him.

But eventually, Mrs. Wendell let herself be pulled away by Witzell, and his small family moved toward the house. The moment the door clicked behind them, the mood shifted ominously.

Was he right? Was something awful going on with his wife?

Annie danced Meghan into the kitchen. "Time for dinner, honey-pie?" She was talking to the baby, not him.

He followed, helping to settle Meghan into her high chair. He went in search of Cheerios to keep her busy. The thousand dollars sat in the middle of the table. Ben Franklin smiled up at them.

Annie froze when she spotted the money. She looked as if she wanted to say something but didn't know what to say. Her mood shifted, as if from a fault far below the surface.

"So, I found a thousand dollars under the love seat today. How was your day, dear?" he asked.

"Tommy." She took a deep breath. "I was going to tell you. I found it and I want to keep it. I think we should. I think it was meant to be."

Tommy caught her happiness and held on to it because he loved her and wanted her happiness to be his. But he couldn't keep his grip; it was too slippery. "Okay. Great. Except no way. You found it? Where? And then you shoved it under the couch? I don't get it, Annie. That's not right. To keep it is stealing. We need to turn it in right away."

"Tommy, it's mine."

This was such an unexpected, flatly wrong statement that he had the sinking feeling he didn't know the first thing about his wife, and she surely didn't know anything about him. "You found it? Then it's not yours. It's lost property that needs to be turned in to the proper authorities, which happen to be me, so how easy is that? Where did you find it?"

"In the Galton Street gorge. While I was walking with Meghan. I found it awhile ago and I've been trying to figure out what to do with it. What kind of person has that kind of money to toss off a bridge?"

"Did it hit you?" He tried to envision the money flying off the bridge, bonking her on the head.

"If it did, do I get to keep it? A fine for endangering a mother and baby?"

After a moment of silence, he said, "You have to turn it in."

"No."

Meghan pounded her table, sending the Cheerios flying. "No!" she shouted, delighted with herself.

"Annie, it's a crime to take things that aren't yours." An indistinct pain began to form in his gut.

"Remember when we used to have fun?" she said. "Do crazy things? Remember the time we broke into the Wilsons' vacation cabin at the lake and—"

"And now we're grown-ups with responsibilities. We can't risk stuff like that anymore. I'm up for captain next month when Viller retires, Annie. You know that. I can't believe I'm having this conversation with the mother of my daughter."

Shit. Bad description. Her blue eyes darkened.

"I can't believe that I'm having this conversation with the most beautiful, sexiest woman in the world," he back-pedaled. He tried to take her in his arms, but she wouldn't let him. "I love you, Annie. But I don't get what's going on in your head anymore. You're always sad. We haven't had sex in two hundred and thirteen days—and that's only if you count a hand job as sex."

"I don't," she said flatly.

"Two hundred and thirty-six days, then. And now this."

Mercifully, she smiled. "It's not like it's two hundred thousand dollars. It's just a grand." She fixed him with a look he couldn't read.

He'd get to hold his wife tonight—maybe even break their sexless streak—if he just shut the hell up. He knew it as surely as he knew most of Meghan's cereal would end up on the floor and she needed a new diaper and he was tired and didn't want to fight or clean the cereal or change the diaper. But some demon force took over and he said, "It doesn't matter if it's five dollars. We can't keep it."

Her eyes narrowed and his hope slipped away. Meghan

sent an avalanche of Cheerios onto the floor, and Tommy stifled a grunt of pain.

"Look, let's wait," Annie said. "You poke around, see if anyone filed a missing money report or whatever it is someone would do if they lost a little money."

"A little?"

"If someone is looking for it, we give it back. If not, we keep it. I mean, what if it belongs to a drug dealer?"

"It doesn't matter if it belongs to Hitler, Annie. The law will decide, not us. That's why there are laws." He was starting to feel a kind of panic that he hadn't felt since they were in high school. Had he done something to drive her to a life of crime? Was that why Annie was so depressed lately?

Annie spoke. "I thought we could do good with the money. Not keep it for ourselves. Maybe we could fix up Lizzie's house." She said it as if the thought had just popped into her head, but he had the feeling she'd been thinking about it for a while.

"She won't let us. You know that. She's too proud. She won't even let me replace the washers in her dripping faucets."

"We'd do it secretly somehow. I don't know. I'll figure it out. Maybe we could pay Tay. Or maybe we could put half of it into a college fund. It'll pay for Meghan's education."

"Half of a thousand dollars? It'll pay for two textbooks if we're lucky."

Annie looked confused, then relieved, then he didn't know what. Jolly, almost. "It'll grow if we invest it," she said, a mysterious smile playing around her lips.

"Annie, is there something you're not telling me?"

She fixed him with a look so pained, it took his breath away. "No. Of course not. Why?"

"No reason." *Only that maybe our marriage depends on it.*

CHAPTER

27

$\mathcal{I}$t was Tuesday night, Lizzie's favorite night of the week, since she had the Enemy Club to look forward to the next morning. She couldn't wait to tell them about her dinner with Tay at Annie's and her new vow to get what she wanted and to get their opinions on Tay and on Annie and why she'd been sneaking around her house. Tay had been back twice since their kiss in his truck, and he'd still not finished up her fence. She was starting to get the idea that he was stalling, which made her smile.

Two more bluestones had appeared in her path, one each night.

"Mom, I think we should get me a passport," Paige said.

Lizzie looked at her daughter, curled on the couch, eating popcorn from the microwave bag, the blue flicker of the TV stealing all the color from her face. Nothing like a teenager to bring her mood back down to earth. "Why?" she asked, knowing the question was dumb, but not knowing what else to say.

Paige rolled her eyes. "'Cause I want to stay here my whole damn life. Duh, Mom," Paige said.

Lizzie waited out the sarcasm.

"I'm not saying I'd go to Geneva forever. I'm just saying, I should be ready just in case. Just to visit."

"The problem is, honey, wherever you go, there you are."

Paige groaned. "Here comes the lecture."

Lizzie clicked off the television and sat at Paige's feet.

"Hey! I was watching that."

She put Paige's feet on her lap, then her own feet up on the coffee table. The room was dark around them, with only a single lamp on in the far corner. "It means that running away doesn't solve anything. The world is big, but wherever you go in it, you still have the same problems, because you're still you, or I'm still me, or whoever. Whomever," she corrected herself and Paige groaned as if in serious pain.

Lizzie's mind drifted to Tay. Whenever she thought of Tay, a twitter of excitement ran through her. Not just physical excitement either, but something stronger. "That's why your dad's coming back. He can traipse all over the world buying fancy stationery and pretending to be European for fourteen years, but he still has to face his past." Lizzie reached over to steal a handful of popcorn. It was still warm, but the salty crunch didn't satisfy her the way it usually did.

"So can I get the passport? It takes like eight weeks, so we have to get on it now," Paige said, ignoring Lizzie's motherly wisdom. "You should get yours, too."

"Me? Where am I going?"

"Don't you wonder even a little bit if maybe Dad still loves you?"

The word *still* hung in the air over Lizzie's head like a black cloud. The word *dad* bumped up against it, then *love*. Lizzie waited for the thunder in her head to clear before she spoke. She was glad it was too dark for Paige to see her face clearly. *Dad. Still. Love.*

Ever?

Of course not. "We're not going to be one big happy family, hon. This isn't exactly a family reunion coming up."

"It's exactly a family reunion," Paige said, interrupting Lizzie's thoughts. "The Christmas tree will even be up. What do you think Dad'll bring me?" Before she could answer, Paige said, "I think he'll bring a snowboard. I bet he's been following me online and he knows what I love. It'll probably be a Ricco. They sell those in Europe. You can't even get them here."

"Please don't tell me about strangers following you on the Internet," Lizzie begged.

Paige rolled her eyes. "Everyone does it."

"Are you trying to kill me?"

"Well what do *you* think he'll bring me?" Paige asked.

What does a missing father bring the daughter he's never met? Probably something lame, like a teddy bear wearing a Swiss flag sweater that he picked up at the airport. Lizzie rubbed Paige's toes. When had her child's feet become so gigantic? "What do you want for Christmas?"

"A father."

"Done. What else."

"And a passport."

Lizzie faked painful death throes.

Paige relented and patted Lizzie's limp hand. "What do you want, Mom?" Paige asked.

Lizzie opened one eye. "I want you to be happy." She put her hand on Paige's knee. "That's plenty for me."

"Now it's my turn to die," Paige said, fake gagging. "I'm choking on those rainbows you're shoving down my throat! Stop! Stop!"

I want Tay. But she wasn't about to say that out loud. Lizzie patted her daughter's knee. "One day, you'll be a mother and you'll understand."

Paige recovered from her near expiration. "I'd rather be a father and be able to run around and have an exciting life."

"I don't think you would. Ethan Pond lost out big-time on this deal. I got the good end of things."

Paige looked at her mother doubtfully. "You are so lost, Mom."

"You think that Ethan Pond, a man who's never met his own daughter, is happy?"

"Are you happy? All you do is work and hoard money and work and feed those dumb birds on the porch that poop all over the place. Oh, and work."

"That sounds like a lot to me. I like my birds. I like my regulars at the diner. I like my life."

"But it's not exciting. It's not Geneva. It's just feeding people—and birds!"

But Lizzie realized that she really did like it. If she said "caring for people and other assorted creatures is all that matters" out loud, Paige would start gagging again. So she just shrugged and said, "Your father isn't the answer, Paige. Life isn't that easy or simple."

"But, Mom, what if it is? What if it's as easy as knowing what you want and then going for it, no matter what?"

Lizzie rolled her eyes, finally understanding. "You've been talking to Nina again."

"So what if I have? I like her," Paige said. "Of all your enemies, she's the one who gets me. She's going to let me into her Thursday yoga class for free to help with my flexibility. She says if I learn to breathe properly, I can do anything."

"I don't believe in wishful thinking, Paige," Lizzie said. "Look where it got Nina. She steals the creamers from the diner when she thinks I'm not looking, hon. She lives in a house that's not hers and scrapes by teaching yoga and doing little art jobs. She can let you into the class because it's not full! We all breathe just fine without her. Listen, Paige, the hardest thing in life is knowing what you want. It's much, much harder than it sounds."

"So what do you believe in if you don't believe in Nina?" Paige asked, stuffing the last of the popcorn into her mouth.

"Hard work and sacrifice." The words sounded lame, even to her ears.

Lizzie looked at her beautiful daughter. She had put a pink streak into her black Cleopatra hair. Her athletic, perfect teenage body looked powerful, as if it could do anything. She had no fear. She had huge dreams.

"What if I already sacrificed enough?" Paige asked.

Lizzie relented. How to reason with a teenager who thought she'd seen the worst life had to offer at fourteen? "Okay, tell you what. We'll go to the post office this week to apply for a passport. Just in case."

"And one for you!" Paige pulled out a folder of papers from under the coffee table. "I got a list of everything we need to bring. I printed it all out."

"No. Just for you."

"You're a coward, Mom. Just get one. It costs like eighty bucks. Will you? Please? Your Christmas present to me? Because I know you think that you won't want Dad, but what if you do? Huh? You need to be ready."

CHAPTER

28

Jay came back, promising that this was the day he'd finish Lizzie's fence, even though he had no intention of doing so. When the fence was done, he'd have to stop, unless he came up with some kind of trade that would satisfy her, and he didn't have a clue what that could be.

He couldn't stop thinking about the way her hair escaped from her bun and spiraled down around her red, full cheeks. How she'd kissed him so passionately, and then asked if he was okay.

He replaced a rotted-out slat near the corner.

Another by the gate.

When all the wood was finally in decent shape, he started to scrape the ancient paint off the slats, trying to keep his mind on his work.

White jumped out of the truck and settled herself in a sunny spot on the path. She watched him work, perfectly content to laze next to Dune, who was chewing what was left of his tennis ball, which wasn't much.

Tay worked his way down the fence while the animals watched, picket by picket. White dozed off, her head on her paws. "Go catch yourself some breakfast, you lazy beast," he muttered.

White slept on. Dune climbed onto Lizzie's porch and dozed off, too. Tay scraped some more.

"I'm not going to feed you. You know that," he muttered as he passed the cat again. He tried to keep her home at the lake house, but if he didn't let her into the cab with him and Dune, she jumped into the back of the truck, a tiny stowaway. And if he kept her in the house, she destroyed what was left of the shabby furniture. Plus, if he locked her in, how would she leave? "Might as well go. Shoo. Go on. Bet that old lady watching us across the street likes cats. Bet she's got a hundred of them."

White looked up at him, blinked, set her head back on her paws. She knew he'd feed her. And the good stuff, too. It was hard not to buy organic when her small, scarred body seemed as if it had been through too much hardship already. He wondered how long she'd been begging at that rest stop before she'd joined his crew.

He turned back to the fence.

"Since you're becoming a permanent fixture here, we're going to have to do something about that cat."

Tay's scraper slipped. A splinter jabbed into his thumb and he cursed, then he looked up and cursed again, this time silently.

Lizzie looked good, as always. She wore a purple faux-fur jacket over her uniform to fight off the morning chill. He hadn't felt the cold at all until he saw her. He rubbed his arms with his hands, feeling the goose bumps under his fingers.

How did she do that to him?

"If she eats one of my birds, I'm never going to forgive her," she said. "We need to put her in the truck. Or if you want, I can put her inside."

He looked at what could be mistaken for a bird-feeder store on Lizzie's front porch, at the two empty birdbaths in various states of disrepair on her lawn. White would surely be curled up asleep in the sunniest of them soon, because he'd be damned if he'd try to pick that beast up. She'd shred him for sure. "White's not my cat. Remember? She does exactly as she pleases."

"The feline version of you," Lizzie pointed out.

"Believe me, I'd love nothing more than to get rid of her." He thought of his superstition. "She won't leave my side."

Lizzie held out her hand and the cat came to her. She patted her back, then scooped her up.

"Hey, you traitor!" Tay said. "She hates it when I pick her up. If I tried to do that, I'd have no eyes left."

"If she's not yours, then now she's mine," Lizzie said. She walked with White up onto the porch, unlocked her front door, and dumped the cat inside. Before the door was relocked, White appeared in the dining room window, sniffed around a bit, then settled down to look out at them. She definitely looked pissed off. "There's a key under the third flowerpot. Let her out when you leave."

"No way. Finders, keepers."

"Tay, there's no litterbox in there. You have to take her home."

"You trust me to go into your house?" he asked.

Lizzie said, "Remember, Tommy has your info. Anyway, if you want to steal anything, you'll be terribly disappointed. It's not like I keep a stash of cash under the mattress."

His eyes lingered on her. He liked the way Lizzie stood, with her hands on her hips, completely at ease, in control.

"Well," she said. "I better get to work."

"Me, too," he said. As much as he knew it was ridiculous, he felt like White's agreeing to hang out in Lizzie's house marked some kind of triumph. He examined his finger. He tried to pull the splinter out with his teeth. Damn thing went in deeper.

She considered him for a moment. "What?"

"Splinter."

"Give me that hand."

"It's fine. It'll come out on its own."

She rolled her eyes, messed around in her bag, then pulled out a tiny matchbook.

She was going to set it on fire?

She opened the matchbox, which turned out to be a tiny sewing kit. He hadn't been with a woman in so long, he had forgotten how practical they could be. She took out a pin. "You're a coward. Give it here." She held out her hand for his hand.

"Forget it. It's fine."

"Stop protesting and give me your hand. You have no choice in this until you come up with something better that you want. For now, you fix my fence, I fix your finger. I still want us to be at least a tiny bit even." She took his hand and scraped around above the splinter with her pin.

"That's not sterile," he said stupidly. He was getting delirious from the flower aroma of her shampoo. *I can smell her shampoo*. He couldn't remember the last time he'd smelled flowers.

"Tough cookies." She handed him the pin to hold while she squeezed his finger. "Boy, Tay, I gotta tell you. I really like this doing-whatever-I-please stuff." The tip of the splinter popped up, but not enough to grab. "Shoot, I don't have a tweezers."

"Are you sure?" He nodded at her enormous purse. "I'd put money on you having at least three pair."

She took the pin back and scraped some more. Then said, "I'll squeeze. You yank."

He smelled her hair some more as she leaned in again. His lips brushed against her hair and she pinched his finger. Hard. He winced and pulled back and she smiled. The tip of the splinter cleared his calloused fingertip and he pinched it easily between his thumb and forefinger.

She moved away. He felt the distance between them snap a connection that he now had no choice but to acknowledge had been there and had been strong and that he wanted back.

"Thank you," he said.

"What?" she asked. "Why are you staring at me like that?"

"Every time I get near you, I want to kiss you, even though I know it's a terrible idea. Because I'll start out kissing you—" He paused. "Like this."

Before he could think about it, he pulled her to him.

Their lips crashed together and she opened her mouth under his. She tasted good. She'd gone soft and limp in his arms. She moaned softly and then it hit him—

The images.

He tried to hold on. Pulled her closer. Kissed her harder.

Then stopped.

"And then, I'd have to stop because I'd feel awful."

"So, feel awful. Maybe that's what's supposed to happen. You have to keep feeling awful until all the awful is gone."

"I'm not so sure there's not an unlimited supply of awful. It's like my brain short-circuits."

"So, we just have to circumvent your brain," she said. Her hand teasingly brushed his side, producing a whole different kind of ache.

Oh, hell, he wanted to kiss her all over again. "I'm an awful companion," he said.

"Well, no one here is perfect," she said, raising her arms to take in her falling-down house. "Except maybe Mrs. Roth." She waved at her neighbor peering out from behind her drapes. "I better get to work," she said.

She started down the sidewalk.

He watched her go and it killed him. He couldn't stand this anymore. He wanted to be normal. He was sick of feeling bad. "Lizzie!" he called after her.

She turned.

"I have an idea."

She waited.

"Can you tell me about the Enemy Club? Every detail. I need to understand how you guys did it."

"Did what?" She walked back toward him.

"How you guys forgave each other. I want to know what you did to become enemies, then how you made up. I want to hear every story. That would be payback for the fence."

"Just stories? It wouldn't, Tay."

"I swear, it would." He took her hands. "I can't find that money, Lizzie. I can't make it right for Candy. But you guys made it right somehow for each other. I want to know how. I want to know if I stand a chance."

CHAPTER

29

*B*edtime stories?

She'd asked him what he wanted and he'd asked her for stories?

Or had he? Maybe what he was really asking for was her. He wanted to understand her.

Lizzie had agreed to come out to his lake house after lunch the next day even if his deal was, as she put it, completely nuts. He was surprisingly nervous, not just because he'd asked her for such an odd thing, but also because despite all the time they'd spent together and all the kisses—and aborted kisses—they'd shared, this felt like a first date.

He hoped he could go through with it.

He'd changed twice, from one pair of jeans to the other. From one T-shirt, to another, to another. The only other clothing he had was the button-down shirt he'd bought to wear to dinner at Annie's house last Friday night, and that felt too fancy for now.

"This is weird, isn't it?" he asked when she got there.

She had borrowed Annie's car, a red Toyota, and had left it at the top of the driveway. "I'm not so good at these conventional things."

"No. I like it," she said. "It reminds me of another date. I almost feel as if I've been here before." She had a sneaky smile on her face, but he had butterflies in his stomach and was too nervous to ask what she meant.

"Do you want to go out somewhere to eat?" he asked.

"No. This is nice, Tay."

"Good. Because I made you lunch," he said, leading her into the cabin.

They went inside. He fixed turkey sandwiches and tall glasses of iced tea with fresh mint. They carried the meal to the living room and ate side by side on his couch, while White and Dune watched with intense interest.

He was too nervous to taste his sandwich. But he didn't think that it was the numbness of his guilt, but nervousness at having Lizzie so close.

Finally, when they were done and had run out of little things to chat about, he took her plate and put it on the coffee table. He leaned back on the couch. "So, tell me a story."

She offered a stray flake of turkey that had fallen on the table to White, who turned up her nose. "I don't know where to start." Dune wolfed down the chunk, then jumped onto her lap, hoping for more.

"How did the Enemy Club start?" he asked, pushing Dune back to the floor.

She made herself comfortable, tucking her legs under her. "You sure you want to hear this?"

"Positive."

She sighed. "Okay. Jill and I were the founders. See,

we'd always been enemies. All through grade school we fought, threw sand, pulled each other's pigtails, that sort of thing. When we got older, she single-handedly kicked me out of the cool clique. All the girls feared her. All the boys loved her. I still got a little attention, but you know how it is. There was the alpha group and then there was everyone else. Jill controlled the alphas. Always."

"Always?" he asked.

"Well, except once." Lizzie couldn't help slip a little smile.

"Ethan," he said.

"Yep. A fraternity from Galton was going to come to the high school to tutor once a week. I was never great at school, so I jumped at the chance to get some extra help for free."

"And you ended up with more than help."

"The next day, it got out how cute the Galton tutor boys were. Sure enough, the next week, there's Jill and her cheerleader friends. But Ethan was already tutoring me. She tried to pry him away. Tried *everything*."

"Everything?"

"She even sat on his lap at one point. He was clearly the cutest boy in the room. But he wouldn't budge. She ended up doing math for two hours with a greasy boy in broken glasses with horrible breath. I dressed up like that poor boy last Halloween and everyone knew exactly who I was."

Tay smiled. "That's cruel."

"Just a little. It was all in good fun. Anyway, Jill threatened to dress up like Ethan this Halloween before his letter came. But I don't think even she'd dare now."

"So you two were already enemies because she'd

kicked you out of the clique, and then Ethan made it worse?" He put his feet up on the coffee table. He'd kicked off his shoes, and she studied his long, thin feet. Then his ankles. She wished she could study further.

"I probably shouldn't have teased her about it the next day. In the lunchroom. In front of everyone."

"You probably should have." He wanted to touch her, but also didn't want her to stop talking.

"Jill always won. Always. She had the money and the social status and the looks. But this one time, I had won. It wasn't like she didn't deserve a little razzing. She was the kind of girl who'd walk by my lunch table and knock my drink to the floor just for the fun of it." Lizzie watched out the window as a late gaggle of geese flew south over the lake. "She did that every day to some kids. Nina, for instance. I really hated her for that.

"But Ethan wasn't just about her. I fell for him hard. And he took advantage so fast, it makes my head spin to think about it. Next thing I knew, I was pregnant. He immediately transferred to Oxford. And was gone. That part of the story is fast."

"England? The coward!" Tay said. "I'm definitely going to have to get out of Galton before he comes, because I'm going to want to level him."

"No. It's okay. He split, but we could have stopped him, sued him for money or responsibility or whatever. But we weren't that kind of family. My parents were so ashamed of me. They just wanted to keep it as quiet as they could. They were climbers, trying to be more than they were. I had ruined everything for them."

"So you just let him go," Tay said.

"Like Candy let you go," she said, suddenly realizing

the parallel. "I didn't want any part of him. It was better with him gone."

They sat for a while in silence. She touched his arm, traced down his elbow to his fingers. She watched his face. Nothing rebelled inside him, not a single cell. He was shocked, but encouraged, and he wanted her to know. He moved closer to her. "Can he make it up to you when he comes back?" Tay asked.

Lizzie shrugged. "I moved on. He owes Paige something. But not me. I'm over it."

"Maybe that's what Candy thinks: that I owe her mother, not her." He narrowed his lips. "Maybe that's why she thinks I'm so crazy to try to get involved. She thinks I can't make it right with her."

Lizzie put her hand on his hand. Her touch was so gentle, he closed his eyes to take it all in. He waited for his mind to plunge into flashbacks, for his body to retreat into numbness. But it didn't happen.

"I think Candy needs to take time," she said.

He nodded. "Yeah, but when a fatal accident happens, you start to understand that life is short. That you don't have time."

They were holding hands and it felt completely natural, like they'd never not held hands. She went on with her story. "Anyway, we didn't think anyone would find out I was pregnant. The plan was that I'd stay in school until I started to show, then I'd go to my aunt's in Rochester, make a life for myself there."

"Banished?" he said. "That's so 1955."

"I think it was natural to want to run. I was ashamed. All I wanted was to get away." She paused. "It's what you did, in a way, Tay."

"No. I did the opposite. I wanted the shame. I chased it by coming here."

"That's so twenty-first century," she said.

"Didn't quite work out, though."

"Well, it didn't quite work out for me either. Because Jill Kennedy found out. Her father was a professor and had been Ethan's advisor at Galton. Turns out Ethan and Jill even knew each other, because the Kennedys would have dinners for their advisees at their house every once in a while. They'd also have students who lived far away over for holidays. Anyway, Jill overheard her dad talking about what had happened to Ethan, put two and two together, and told the whole school. She knew everything."

"Ouch."

"Yeah. It wasn't good. Once it was out, there was no reason to leave. So I quit school, stayed, had Paige, lived with my parents while I worked at the diner."

"But you forgave Jill? Why? It was a terrible thing she did." He was playing with her fingers, turning them this way and that, studying them.

"It was. I hated her for a long time. I'd pass her mother's real estate signs all over town, and I'd want to rip them out and throw them into the gorges."

"But you never did?"

"Never. Nina did once, though, but that's another story. Anyway, a year after school ended, I was working in the diner one night. It was the Blizzard of the Century."

"I remember that. It hit Queens, too. But not so bad."

"That night the Last Chance diner had planned to be open all night, storm or no storm. I volunteered for the hardship duty, since I was desperate for the extra money and my parents could watch Paige, since we all lived together. To tell the truth, I was pumped. I liked extreme weather those days. It made me feel at home, as if the world were finally feeling as intense as I did. By the afternoon, the sky had darkened and the weather service was warning of road closings, power outages, ice, frogs, locusts, the end of days. I didn't care. I felt like: Bring it on! I wasn't the happiest person then, with the baby and trying to figure out what had happened to my life. All the crew had gone but Freddie and me. By four o'clock even the die-hard customers had bailed. So Gertrude, who owns the diner, said it's the Storm of the Century, shut it down and go home. She lived the farthest, so she left me and Freddie to close up.

"So Freddie split as quick as he could for Lucifer's. He wrote, 'Closed Till Hell Unfreezes' in the frost on the window on his way out." Lizzie smiled, remembering. "I was closing up and Bruce Springsteen was cranked on the radio so loud, I almost didn't hear the banging on the door. It was Jill."

Tay was listening, rapt, so she went on.

"I hadn't been face-to-face with Jill since senior year."

"You didn't see her around town?" Tay asked.

"Sure. I'd see her tooling around in her shiny pink Mini Cooper. She was helping her mom in real estate right out of school. But I hadn't seen her up close."

"No college for the princess?"

"No. I never asked her why. I guess because she could already make money with her mom, so who needed it? I love Jill, but she wasn't exactly a scholar."

Tay shifted closer and without thinking much about it, she stretched her legs across his lap. "I told her we were closed, but—" Lizzie paused. She tried not to smile.

"What?"

"Well, I shouldn't smile since we're friends now, and I really do love her. But at the time, it had been like Christmas. She was wearing strappy high heels a mile high and a see-through red teddy under her parka. And that was it."

"Oh, my," Tay said. "I like this story."

She kicked him playfully in the ribs and he caught her foot and held it and stroked it.

"She was going to spend the storm with her boyfriend, Jake, who lived in an apartment over the vacuum store two blocks down. You know, Cole's Vac and Sew? Her plan was to surprise him with champagne and, well, herself. But since her Mini did lousy in the snow, she had called a cab to deliver her to Jake's. Unfortunately, when she got there, Jake was otherwise occupied with another woman and her cab had already split." Lizzie paused. "She was too pissed to go back for decent clothes. So we tried to call another cab for her, but the dispatcher said they had called in all their cars. So there she was, stuck. With me— her worst enemy in Galton. We were the only place open except for Lucifer's. And she wasn't about to go in there dressed like that."

"You must have been having fun," Tay said. "Payback."

"You know, the Last Chance is at the bottom of the two steepest hills in Galton. Freddie always said that makes it the place everything in town ends up eventually, by sheer force of gravity and human nature. It just seemed inevitable that we'd have to hash it out one day. I swear, that day in the diner, I could still hear her taunting me." Lizzie mimicked a high-pitched singsong. *"But Ethan Pond isn't here anymore. His mummy transferred him to Oxford to get him away from Galton trash."* She scrunched up her lips. "That was how I learned that Ethan had left town. He didn't even say good-bye."

CHAPTER

30

*J*ay spun her around and put his arm around her and she snuggled into him, fitting perfectly. "Jill couldn't go anywhere in the storm without real shoes. I was wearing my sneakers, but my boots were in the back because I had planned on walking home. I could have lent her the boots, probably even scrounged up a pair of chef whites and sent her on her way. But I didn't want to."

"Revenge?"

"Not so much." She paused. "Okay, maybe a tinge." She smiled up at him. "Mostly, I was lonely. And I could tell she was lonely. I remember thinking, *Someone would have picked me up if I was stuck. Someone would have come and gotten me.* And there was no one to pick her up."

He played with her hair, stroking it, smelling it, dying to kiss it.

"So we ate pie and drank coffee for hours, watching the snow fall. She told me about Jake, every raunchy detail. And I tried to tell her about Paige, but it wasn't nearly as interesting. She kept cutting me off, changing the subject. It was weird, Tay. Nothing had changed. Not really. Jill was still a rich bitch, so sure she'd get her way she'd pranced out half-naked in a blizzard. I was still me, playing catch-up, working and struggling and trying to hold on to what I had. We were exactly the same as we were in high school. Still stuck in this town. Still hating each other for no good reason. We didn't decide to do something about it. We didn't decide to forgive each other. It just happened. She said she was really sorry and I said I was sorry for baiting her, and then Jill started coming in on Wednesday mornings after that night. I liked talking to her. I had friends, don't get me wrong, but they were all predictable, homogeneous, loyal. Jill meant more because we had a past that mattered. And she was fascinating in a way only someone who sees the world from a completely different vantage point could be."

"So just like that, she said she was sorry and you forgave her?" Tay asked.

"I did. And you know, it felt good."

He kissed the top of her head. Then he stretched out, so he was lying on the couch, and she spooned in front of him.

"It sucks to be alone," she said.

He was glad she couldn't see his face, because he felt as if she was talking about him.

"Forgiving let us be together." She rolled around to face him and pressed her body along the length of him and he pushed his leg between her legs and she let him and even pulled him closer. "Neither one of us wanted to be alone."

He wrapped his arms around her, pressed his body into her. He couldn't get close enough.

They lay like that for a while, not talking.

"I wish I could get to that place with Candy," he said, nuzzling the top of her head with his lips. "There can't be a person more alone in this world than her."

"Sure there is," Lizzie said. "You." She looked up at him, her huge brown eyes so close, he could see each eyelash.

"Not me. I have a beautiful woman beside me."

"Hmmm, you do, don't you?"

"And I'm hoping she'll even kiss me."

She did.

They both waited to see how he'd react. He waited for the pain and guilt and numbness, but they didn't come.

"And maybe, she'll even let me kiss her."

She did.

And then she slid her hand down his chest and into the waistband of his jeans and he knew that there was no turning back.

No matter how painful the consequences, he couldn't have cared less.

Lizzie couldn't get enough of Tay's warmth as he pressed against her. She wanted more. She slid her hand under his shirt, feeling that expanse of his skin for the first time. "Mmm…"

He whipped the shirt off and finally, finally, she got to see the full width of his chest, to touch it, to kiss it. She bit and he moaned and she raised above him and took off her shirt and he moaned again. "Lizzie."

So she dropped back down to him and he unhooked her bra and then a flurry of discarding clothes and he was on top of her, his hands stroking, soothing, pulling. He splayed a hand over her breast and her nipple responded, leading the rest of her body into an explosion of need and heat. "Tay. God."

"I've wanted you for so long," he said, taking her mouth into his. "You want to go to the bedroom?"

"No. I don't know. Don't care." She pushed her hips against him and felt his hardness react. "Protection?"

"Hmmm?" He was nuzzling her neck, kissing, biting, licking down her neck to her breasts. He took his time with each of them, then moved downward, downward, her hips held firmly in his hands.

"Tay. Wait."

He came back up. "Only a woman would say wait at a time like this."

"Make love to me. It's what I want."

"Oh, hell, no. I know all about you and what you want. If you say you want to make love, you probably really want to play Scrabble." He jumped off the couch, went to the bookcase, leaving her on the couch, splayed, panting, hot, completely naked, and oh so bothered.

"Tay!"

He was back in an instant. "Just kidding." He held up a condom. "I hate Scrabble." He tore open the condom and she helped him put it on and then he was back on top of her, spreading her legs with his. "Are you sure, Lizzie?"

"Tay."

He moaned something she couldn't understand as he pushed inside her.

She gasped with the sensation of it. It had been too long. She grabbed at his shoulders, his back, his ass, pulling him as close as she could. "Why did we wait so long for this?"

"I have no idea," he practically growled. "God, Lizzie. You're so soft, so perfect." He moved inside her and she arched up to meet him and with every thrust, she felt one more piece of her come undone until there was nothing left of her but spinning molecules that all exploded at once, coming back together to land in the same shape, but forever changed.

She felt him shudder, and moan, and hold her tight until he had also exploded, and landed, and settled.

She wondered if he was okay.

He rolled her so that she lay on him and he closed his eyes and neither one spoke for a while.

"Are you okay?" she asked.

"I'm amazing," he said.

She kissed his chin. Bit his shoulder. "That's amazing. Are you fixed, then? Just like that?"

"I don't know. Maybe it'll hit me later."

"Maybe."

"How about another story?" he asked.

"I don't think I can handle another story." She didn't want to let him go. She felt herself drifting off into sleep, but it was almost two in the afternoon and she had to get back to work at three. "You tell me a story."

"Once upon a time, there was this beautiful woman, and she had this broken-down house, and this messed-up guy came to fix it, not knowing that she was magic—"

"A true story!" she protested.

"It's true," he said.

"Okay, so what happened?"

"I have no idea. It didn't make a lick of sense. But it was awesome. And they lived happily ever after."

"Your stories suck," she said.

"That's why it's your job to tell the stories. C'mon. One more. Tell me about Georgia."

"Next time."

"When's next time?" he asked. "Tomorrow? Can I see you tomorrow?"

"It's the weekend tomorrow. I was going to build a new path with Paige." ·

He rose on one elbow. "You and Paige are going to build a path?"

She hit his shoulder. "Don't be a jerk. We can do it."

"I'll help," he said.

"You won't. You've done enough. We're going to do it. A mother-daughter project. You're awfully cute, but you're not invited."

He sighed. "Okay. Monday, then. Can I see you Monday?"

"I'll come here."

"You'll finish telling me about the Enemy Club? How Georgia and Nina joined? I can't wait to hear what Georgia did to make you her enemy." He stroked her side, her belly, her cheek.

She could stay here for eternity. Except that she couldn't. She pulled away from him and started to get dressed. "I have to go, Tay."

"Did Georgia try to steal Ethan, too? C'mon, a little teaser."

"It wasn't so much what she did to me. It was what I

did to her," Lizzie said. She straightened her hair in the small mirror by the door.

"Give me a hint. I can't wait till Monday," he begged.

Lizzie smiled. "Okay, one little hint. But that's it." She kissed him, taking in all she could before she had to get back to the real world. "I set her on fire."

CHAPTER

31

$\mathcal{T}$he truck pulled onto Lizzie's street at dawn and backed up to Lizzie's driveway with an annoying high-pitched beep.

It took four beeps for Paige to throw open her bedroom window. "Mom? What time is it? What are you doing?" Paige looked to the neighbors' houses, concern knitting her brow, and Lizzie fought her urge to look, too. She failed. Judy Roth was already at her curtain post across the street.

Lizzie waved at her daughter from where she stood on the driveway, then waved to Judy Roth. "Come on down to help. You, too, Judy. It's do-the-walk day!"

Paige's window slammed shut.

Judy let the curtain fall back into place.

The driver maneuvered a forklift to lift the pallet of bluestone from the truck bed. He deposited it in the middle of the driveway along with eight enormous bags of sand. Lizzie wondered how she'd ever lift the bags. How she'd move all that stone...

Lizzie tipped the driver.

"Good luck, little lady." He smirked. "Don't hurt yourself."

The old walk with its missing bricks and haphazard leveling was dangerous, so Lizzie was bewildered why she felt such a sense of loss pulling the old bricks from their weed-bed, sending earthworms and spiders scurrying. She tried not to flinch at the wildlife, or at the beauty of the old bricks that she tossed behind her. Their edges were worn, and a few of them had split. They were crumbling, woefully inadequate. But they were pinkish-yellow, multicolored. How had she never noticed how lovely they looked? Some of them had grown a lovely coat of moss, which of course was what made them treacherous by mid-November, deadly by December. But it was lovely the way the moss contrasted with the pink.

By the time Paige came outside in her bathrobe and slippers, her hair a rat's nest, Lizzie had half the old bricks in a pile behind her, and she was wondering if she could put them back when the ground was leveled. There wouldn't be enough, especially since she had read in her copy of *The Perfect Path Home* that a pleasing walk should be at least three feet wide, and hers was currently only two and a half.

"What are you doing?" Paige asked.

"You told me that you want the place to look nice for your dad. Well, I decided that's a noble goal. So we're starting here. We're going to make the place look nice, you and me. Get dressed and come out and help me."

"You scared away Tay, didn't you?" Paige asked. She picked up a brick as if it were made of radioactive waste. "Yuck. It's slimy. Oh, my God, there's a slug stuck to the bottom." She tossed it into the grass. "And it's freezing out here."

"It's only going to get colder as the weeks go by. C'mon. It'll be fun. Working warms you up."

"It's Saturday morning! Blankets warm me up!"

"Help. I'm not asking, Paige."

"If I don't, will I have to play Monopoly again?"

"Yes."

"Oh, God, not that!" Paige stomped back into the house. "I want my old mother back. The one who let everything go to hell and left me alone."

By noon, Lizzie had pulled up all the old bricks and laid string tied to stakes to indicate the boundaries of the new, improved walk. She studied the copy of *The Perfect Path* that she'd checked out of the library to make sure she hadn't skipped any steps. She knelt to check her stakes. Her line was straight, wide enough to be "more inviting, drawing people to your front door."

What if she didn't want people to come to her front door? What if she veered the walk around the house and into Mr. Newell's hedges next door, would that keep Ethan away?

"Hi, ma'am."

Lizzie looked up past the work boots, the ripped jeans, to the Iron Maiden T-shirt. She stood, wiping sweat from her forehead with the back of her hand. She wondered if she had streaked her face with dirt. *Hi?* Was the walk leading people to her front door already?

The kid was blond and handsome. "I'm Aidan Treaman. A friend of Paige's. She said you needed help."

Lizzie looked to the silent house. Paige had better be well hidden, because Lizzie intended to kill her. "Did she?"

The boy picked up the shovel that was leaning against the porch. He inspected it like a pro, then went to work jamming its pointed end into the sod, digging out clods of grass along her string lines. He was like a machine, strong and efficient. "How deep you gonna lay the bed?" he asked.

She looked again to the house for Paige. *Don't you talk about beds around my daughter, Mr. Treaman.* "I'll be right back, um—"

"Aidan."

"Right. Aidan." Lizzie sprinted up the porch steps two at a time, knocked most of the dirt off her boots, and went inside. "Paige!"

Paige, still in her pajamas, looked up from the couch. "Problem?"

Was it necessary to wash her hands before she strangled her daughter? *Perfect Path* left out all the essential details. "Aidan? Excuse me? Get your butt out there."

"Aidan is totally strong. He can do it twice as fast as we can."

"That's not the point. The point is that we're going to do it together."

"Your idea. Not mine. Anyway, he wants to help."

"Why?"

"Because he's a nice guy."

"No. Because he likes you! He thinks he's going to, to—" Lizzie faltered. "You don't just invite boys to help you lay your bed."

"We're just friends, Mom. Jeesh." She flopped back on the couch and focused her attention on SpongeBob. "Tay helps you."

Lizzie flicked off the TV. She refused to be baited by

the Tay comment. "Aren't you even going to say hello to him?"

"I'm going to wait until he gets all hot and sweaty. He'll like that better, believe me."

Oh, my God.

"I'm kidding, Mom. God. You turned completely white. I'll be out in a minute. I didn't think he'd show up so early."

Lizzie tried to recover. "You'll be out there ready to work?"

Paige leveled a doubtful stare. "To supervise."

"Paige. We are not helpless little ole things who manipulate men to do our bidding. We can do the front walk, just us."

"But why? Life's so much more fun with friends. Right? You're not exactly avoiding your new fix-it-man friend."

"What did you hear about me and Tay?" Lizzie asked.

"Joy told Susie's mom that you took a two-hour lunch break with him," Paige said. "At his house. And came back grinning."

"Get your butt out there or I'm sending him home." Lizzie felt her blood pulsing. She tried to breathe. This was just exactly what she hadn't wanted to happen: Paige to see men as saviors.

Paige didn't even sit up. "Did Ben show yet? His dad's a contractor. He knows all about this stuff."

"How many boys did you call?" Lizzie went to the window to look outside. Two more boys had appeared. They had brought their own shovels. One hooked up a sound system and a bass beat began pulsating from the porch, vibrating the windows.

"If you're not out there in five minutes, I'm sending them all home," Lizzie said. Then she stomped outside to meet her adolescent crew.

Paige tried to hide her smile as Ben put in the last stone. The walk looked amazing, and with the five of them, they'd done it in less than three hours. She never even had to break a sweat and she hadn't ruined a single nail. Plus, Paige had never noticed just how cute Aidan was until she saw him all sweaty in his loose T-shirt and jeans. He was flirting with her by the end, she was pretty sure. As soon as her mother went inside to get them something to drink, the boys collapsed on the porch steps around her.

"Done deal," Ben said.

"Done deal," Paige said. She handed him forty bucks. Then handed the same amount to Aidan and Paul. "Don't tell my mother. She'll freak. She thinks you're all doing this 'cause you want to make out with me."

Ben and Paul laughed, but Aidan went a little red around the ears.

"Why are grown-ups so sex-crazed?" Ben asked. "Especially the moms. My mom gives me the Condom Talk like every time I leave the house."

"No clue," Paul said. He kissed his forty bucks. "I love you madly, mmmm..."

"Gross," Paige said.

"So, what's on for next week?" Aidan asked. "That porch? It totally needs painting." He turned red again. "And I totally need the gas money."

"I don't know," Paige said, watching her mother come out with a pitcher of lemonade and paper cups. She hoped her mother didn't notice the boys stuffing their money into their front jeans pockets in unison. She probably just figured they were adjusting themselves. "I'll call you," she told them. "Now, smile and drink lemonade and flirt with me."

"Lemonade?" Lizzie asked.

God, this was humiliating. It was as if her mother thought they were all adorable five-year-olds and horny, out-of-control thirty-five-year-olds simultaneously.

Aidan accepted the lemonade with a polite, "Thank you, ma'am," but when Lizzie turned her back, he leaned over and pecked Paige on the cheek. He whispered, "Just for show," in her ear and it was her turn to go red.

Maybe she would call them back next week for the porch. After all, it wasn't like she didn't have the money.

CHAPTER

32

*L*izzie had her binoculars trained on the shore of the small pond, near the forest's edge. Tay sat beside her on the bench, his legs stretched out, his head leaning back. Since they had finished the path in one day, Lizzie had relented and agreed to see Tay before Monday. But she didn't want to go to his house again and have Paige hear about it. Instead, she'd suggested this wholesome expedition to the bird pond.

She looked at her companion. "Tay? Are you sleeping?"

He mumbled something and she nudged him with her elbow. "You have to keep alert if you want to see the green heron."

"It's six o'clock on Sunday morning. I don't care if I see it. I just came out here because I wanted to be with you."

His words warmed her more than her coat and gloves and hat ever could. "You said you wanted to try birding. C'mon, get with the program, mister. We can't be naked all the time."

"Why not? You know, I had to practically tie myself to the deck yesterday to keep from coming out there to help you guys."

"We didn't need you. We had three big strapping men."

"Are you cheating on me with other handymen?"

She glanced up at him. "What are you going to do if I am? Maybe you weren't the only one who overheard my wish."

His eyes flashed. "I'll rip out that damn walk stone by stone and rebuild it myself, with the three of them buried underneath."

Lizzie relented, thrilled at his reaction. That sure woke him up. "They were Paige's friends. I told her she had to work, and she called in her admirers." Talking about Paige subdued her mood. She didn't want to talk about Paige and how she knew about their relationship. She watched the beautiful man dozing beside her. "Did you sleep last night?" she asked.

"Not so much," Tay admitted. "Fell asleep around four."

"What'd you fix?" Lizzie asked.

Tay shrugged. "The lady in the next cabin had a load of wood delivered in a heap on her driveway. So I stacked it."

"Oh, Tay." Lizzie thought about the woman's surprise when she woke up to find her wood neatly stacked, as if by elves in the night.

"I can't remember what it's like to sleep through the night," Tay said. "I can't remember what it feels like to not be tired when it's light. Or to not be wired when it's dark."

"Oh, hey. There it is!" A small green heron hopped to

the pond's edge. Green herons were nothing like the huge blue herons that had been spotted nesting nearby. They were less than half the size, and they were also shyer, and much rarer. Mr. Petray had come into the diner last week to tell Lizzie that it had been spotted all week in this pond, but she didn't think she'd actually see it. "You want to see, Tay? It's amazing that it's here so late in the fall. I wonder if there's something wrong with it."

"You know what I want?" He leaned into her. "I want to know more things wrong about you."

The heron stood perfectly still, watching the pond for prey. Two cardinals landed nearby in a lilac bush and hopped from branch to branch. "What? Me?"

"You're always talking about things being even. So after I tell you that I can't sleep and I wander the woods at night performing mindless tasks for strangers, then it's your turn to tell me your weakness."

"You're my weakness."

Tay rolled his eyes. "I'm not that dumb. I'm going to ask Jill," Tay said. "I bet she knows."

Lizzie put down the binoculars. She hadn't been kidding him, but now she was embarrassed and didn't want to admit it. "Your weakness isn't so big, Tay. You feel and so you want to make things right. What's wrong with that?"

"Oh, God. You're killing me. I'm a man. I'm not supposed to feel. I'm supposed to be a rock. I'm supposed to know exactly how to make things right." He took the binoculars from her and looked at the bird standing in the water. "We got up early and came out here in the freezing cold to see that? It's not even green."

"Its head is."

Tay looked around the marsh through the binoculars. "I wish I had these when I was looking for the money. They would have helped."

"You can borrow them."

"Nah. I've stopped looking."

Lizzie watched Tay. "Really? Why?"

"Because I've looked and relooked and then looked again. I've given up. The money's gone. Either someone's got it or it's rotting at the bottom of a creek—green heron food. I need a new plan." He handed her the binoculars.

"You're not leaving, are you?" she asked. He had said he was here to find the money. If he was giving up, then—she didn't want to think about it.

"No. Because you're here and I'm getting stuck on you, despite this awful bird-watching habit." He lowered his voice. "But I've got to tell you, Lizzie, it's hard staying. I worry about running into Candy. I assume she thinks I'm gone. But this town is so small, everyone seems to know everyone."

Lizzie said, "What's it like, Tay?"

"What?"

"Feeling like you can't make up for what you did."

He shrugged. "It's like everything is in color, but when I reach out and touch something, it turns to black-and-white. The opposite of Midas turning everything to gold. It started the instant after the accident. It was like the whole world had gone gray. I got home late that night and stood at my sink and ate some noodles that Emily had heated up for me, and I couldn't taste them. I couldn't smell them. Emily forced me to the doctor after a while to see if there was something wrong with my taste buds, with my nose. But there wasn't. It's in my head. I can feel life going on around me, I can see it, but I can't get a piece of it. Like it's a dream and I can only watch. Something inside of me shut down."

"I've had bad colds where I couldn't taste or smell."

"Yeah, it's like that. But it's worse. It never stops. A constant dullness, interspersed with wicked knife-slicing painful stabbing."

The green heron took off with a sudden flutter of flapping wings. Something brown swooped out of the sky. A wave of birds and other creatures skittered for cover. Cardinals and titmice and jays arced and darted in every direction.

Lizzie pointed. "A hawk!" She raised her binoculars. "Oh, Tay, a Cooper's hawk. Isn't it beautiful? It almost got the heron." She handed the binoculars to Tay.

"It looks like a killer."

"It is. Gets birds mostly. It was definitely after the heron. Did you see how it dove?"

The hawk landed in a pine tree near their bench.

Tay handed the binoculars back to Lizzie, picked up a rock, and tossed it at the hawk.

"Tay!" Lizzie grabbed his arm. "What are you doing?"

He tossed another rock, this one hitting the tree, but too low to disturb the hawk. The big bird didn't move a feather. "I don't want it to get your heron," Tay said.

Lizzie looked around for other birders. An old couple had set up an elaborate telescope across the pond. "Tay, trying to stone the birds is frowned upon."

"Look at that thing. It's vicious."

"It needs its breakfast, too, Tay."

He flung another stone, and then another. Finally, one landed close. The hawk rose into the air with a few powerful beats of its wings, then glided off to perch in another tree on the other side of the pond.

Tay sat back down on the bench, but Lizzie stayed standing. "You can't try to help everything all the time, Tay."

"I thought you liked the heron."

"It might be stuck so far north this late because it's sick or dying or somehow weak. It might have been a mercy for it to be eaten by a hawk, because soon, it's going to freeze to death. Nature works, Tay. You can't take sides."

Tay shook his head. They watched the heron come timidly out of the brush. It waded into the water, keeping an uneasy watch on the sky.

"It's still there." He started tossing rocks again, this time to drive the heron back into the bush.

"Tay!" She grabbed his arm. "You can't control everything. Let it go."

"It's not safe for it to come out yet," he said.

"Life's not safe. The heron has to hunt. It can't hide all day. Leave it alone. You're scaring its prey."

The heron had retreated to the scrub along the shore.

"Tay?" Lizzie turned him to her. He looked ashen, as if he'd turn to black-and-white himself before long. "Are you okay?"

He put his arms around her. "Sorry. I'm a city boy." He pulled her closer. "Nature isn't natural to me."

She held him, feeling his warmth through his too-thin coat. She let her head rest on his chest. "I'm terrified of birds," she said.

"What?" He pulled back.

"You wanted to trade weaknesses, there's a good one. They make me nervous as hell, those beady little eyes and sharp beaks. When I fill the feeders, I bang on the door first to warn them I'm coming out so they'll fly away."

"Wait—what? If you're scared of them, why do you feed them?"

"I like them. I think they're beautiful. I love to watch them through the windows and through the binoculars, but they make me nervous when they get too close. Especially the robins. They flock together in the winter and sometimes I don't want to leave the house when they're out there. They can get a little spooky, you know."

"That's why you like the hawk," he said. "You're on its side."

"I'm not on sides. I'm afraid of the hawk, too."

"It's like your Enemy Club," Tay said. "You keep your enemies close."

"Maybe I do. But only because I admire them. They're interesting, fascinating, beautiful. I like to study them. Watch them. Life's more interesting with them around."

"But what if a friend gets close?" Tay asked. "Is that even scarier?"

"A little," Lizzie admitted. "I've been burned, Tay."

"It's hard sometimes to know your friends from your enemies."

"It's true." She was thinking about Ethan, sure. But also about Annie, who wouldn't admit to doing anything in her house but looking for a sweater that never existed even when Lizzie had confronted her. Lizzie watched the hawk circle. "All my friends start out as enemies," she pointed out.

"Like me. You wanted me gone."

"That's true."

"Then you feed them and they get tame."

She smiled. "Most of them do."

They watched the hawk fly off, circling in the sky.

"I feel the opposite of tame when I'm around you," Tay said. "The longer I spend with you, the more feral I feel."

"Feeling feral right now?"

"I am."

She smiled. "Hmm... what are we going to do about that? I have an idea. Let's get out of here," she said. "Go back to your place."

"What about the green what's-it-called? What about the hawk?" he asked.

"I think they can fend for themselves. We can't control the world, Tay."

He smiled. "I can't even control my own body when I'm around you."

"That's what I'm counting on, big boy," she teased.

CHAPTER

33

*E*ven after spending Sunday morning with Tay, Monday still couldn't come fast enough. Lizzie got to Tay's house just after one, and by one-ten they were naked. Tay had Lizzie's back up against the wall by the front door and her legs were wrapped around his waist and they were making love like animals, furious, desperate, groping sex that was nothing like the soft lovemaking they'd had the day before.

When her fingernails dug into his back and she threw her head back and howled, he finally let himself go and then, slowly, she untangled her legs from around him and they staggered together to the couch and fell onto it.

"I made us turkey sandwiches," he said after a while.

"God, Tay. That was amazing," she said. "You okay?"

"I'm wonderful." He had his arm around her and he pulled her to him and she swung around so that she was sitting on his lap, naked, straddling him, and he thought he was going to die of happiness and lust, not necessarily in that order.

"Me, too," she said.

"I don't get this," he said. "For an entire year, I was miserable. I ate a half-decent plate of spaghetti and all I could think about was how Linda would never eat spaghetti again. And now, I'm thinking, how can I get more of that spaghetti? I want to eat spaghetti day and night until I'm too fat to move. I love the damn spaghetti."

"I've never been compared to spaghetti after making love before," she said. But she heard what he was saying and had no answer for the mystery, so she stroked his shoulder, his arm, took his hand.

"What is it about you?" He leaned forward and wrapped his arms around her. "This is too perfect."

"Maybe it is," Lizzie said. She felt a chill.

"What?" Tay asked.

She slid off him and padded to the door to get her clothes. It felt delicious to walk around naked after making love in a cabin by the lake to a beautiful, kind man. But then there was reality. She pulled on her underwear, her uniform. "Paige knows about us, Tay. I was going to tell you yesterday, but then I didn't because I wanted to not care. But I realized last night, after I went home, that I cared. She heard through the Galton grapevine. When we were building the path, and her boy-crew showed up, she said that if I can have a man do my dirty work, so can she."

He didn't move from the couch. "Does it matter that she knows? She's a big girl. And so are you."

Lizzie picked up his boxers and his jeans and tossed them to him. "I was going to call to tell you that I wasn't coming today. That we had to cool it. Then I changed my mind and decided that I was going to come here to tell you that this is all over. I can't have Paige thinking that men are the easy way to solve problems. Or that if a man does a favor, he gets—"

"Naked?" Tay suggested.

She fell next to him on the couch. "Exactly." She traced a finger down his thigh. "When I heard Ethan was coming, I was so afraid that she'd look to him as a savior. So I didn't want to set a bad example by letting her see me depend on anyone. That's what I was going to say when I came out here today. That we need to go slow, to cool it, at least until her father comes and goes. But then, well, I guess I jumped on you and the rest is history."

"You can tell me now," he said. "The last thing I want is to mess up things with Paige." He hadn't pulled on his clothes.

She closed her eyes and leaned against him. "I'm not sure I can get by anymore without my turkey sandwiches."

He kissed her hair. "I do make a mean turkey sandwich." He jumped up and pulled on his pants and went to the kitchen to make lunch. She stayed behind on the couch, enjoying that someone was making her food for a change.

"Paige is no dummy," he said from the kitchen. "I think she knows exactly how to play you."

"You're just saying that because you like to make me sandwiches," she said.

"Well, that's true, I do." He stood in the doorway of the kitchen, wiping his hands on a dishrag. Was there anything more delicious than a shirtless man cooking? Especially when the man had a chest like Tay's. "But I think Paige knows that you're not easy. I think she knows that you're not using me and I'm not using you. Because we're not that kind of people. I think a lifetime of being a good person makes a difference, and I think you put in the time. Liz, I think you don't give the kid enough credit. She's old enough to recognize the difference between lust and love. And old enough to play you for everything she can."

He went back into the kitchen before she could answer.

Love?

What?

He had stood there, said that word? She replayed it over and over in her mind. He was making her lunch, without his shirt, after mind-blowing sex, and *he loved her*?

Lizzie followed him into the kitchen. "Hi."

He didn't turn. "Hi."

Maybe he hadn't said it.

"Looks good." She didn't mean the lunch.

"Should be. My usual." He was spreading mustard on bread.

Okay, maybe he hadn't said anything. She picked up where their previous conversation left off. "Paige only knows what she hears in town."

Tay's back was to her. "She knows what she sees."

"But what does she see, Tay? Nothing. She's at school all day and she hears about me taking long lunch breaks."

"Let's change that."

"Okay," she said carefully. What exactly was he offering? "Tay, if we get Paige involved, then we have to be careful. What you said a minute ago—"

He put down his knife and turned to her. "About me loving you?"

"Yes." She gulped. Her knees felt wobbly.

"How else can I explain being able to taste again?" He was across the kitchen in an instant, his arms around her, his lips on hers, sending waves of warmth through her. He took her hands and whispered in her ear, "I don't know, Liz. Maybe I'm wrong. Maybe I'm crazy. But I think we have something that's worth taking seriously. So, yes, let's get Paige involved."

"I think so, too, Tay." She was thinking about saying the word, forming it in her mind, aware of what it meant and wondering if it meant the same to him. But how do you say that word if you haven't said it to a man in fourteen years and the last time you said it—the last time you heard it—everything went wrong?

He interrupted her thoughts. "Don't sweat it, Lizzie. Let's eat."

She sat and he brought her food. She watched him carefully as he ate, imagining him and Paige at her kitchen table together eating breakfast, eating lunch, eating dinner. Paige doing her homework while he watched sports in the living room. "Do you like sports?" she asked.

"Sports?"

"I'm trying to imagine a life together," she said. "Would you be watching baseball while Paige did her homework?"

"How about the three of us do something together?" he suggested.

"Okay. Like what?" She hoped it wouldn't be sports.

"I dunno. We'll think of something. How about we go bird-watching?"

"Paige hates bird-watching. She thinks it's lame."

"Oh, thank God. It was an awful suggestion."

"But maybe those blue herons are still there. They're definitely not lame."

"I haven't checked their nest lately. I'll check it today. If they're not there, I'll track them down and drag them back," he said.

"Just don't throw anything at them," Lizzie warned.

"Those blue guys are huge. They'd have me for lunch," Tay said.

They finished eating and made love again, this time more slowly and carefully, his words echoing around in Lizzie's head, *He loves me he loves me*, and before she knew it, she had to leave. "I didn't even get to tell you about setting Georgia on fire," she said as they stood at the door.

"Then you'll have to come back tomorrow."

"I can't keep borrowing Annie's car to get out here. You know how she is. She told me today I can have it whenever I want just so long as you keep fixing *our* house."

"I kind of like being your boy-toy handyman. Makes me feel virile."

"Tay!"

"Take my truck," he said.

"How will you get around? Plus, it'a a stick. No. You come and pick me up at the diner tomorrow."

"Are you sure? People will talk."

"People are already talking. I don't care. My break's at two tomorrow."

"And then, I'll drop you back at work and I'll get started on your porch."

"In the afternoon?"

"In the afternoon. Because you're going to invite me in for dinner with you and your lovely daughter."

"Am I?"

"Yes."

"I guess I owe you."

"Not because you owe me. No deals. Just doing what's right and what we want. Because you love me, Lizzie."

"I do?"

"You do."

"I do," she said.

He kissed her to seal the deal.

CHAPTER

34

$\mathcal{T}$ommy waited for Joe Pendergrast, the head of campus security, to come to the phone. The last few days had been torture. He had promised Annie he wouldn't call Joe, but the mystery of the money was killing him and he couldn't wait another second.

"Joe, here."

"Joe. It's Tommy."

"Mr. Wynne! How is Galton's finest man in blue?"

"Hey, Joe. Terrible, actually. This is a business call." He inhaled, hoping that he'd be better at lying over the phone than he was in person. "Meghan and Annie were in the campus gorge awhile back, and Meghan lost her blue bunny, Bun-bun. I hate to bug you with stuff like this, but I was wondering if anything had been reported missing in the Campus Road gorge? I mean, found. Anything out of the ordinary down there?"

"Bun-bun, huh? That's serious stuff, Wynne. Hold on." Tommy could hear Joe shouting to his secretary.

"Okay. Julie's on it. She's checking the lost and found for you. How's the family?"

"Great." *Terrible. My wife is a thief and it's been so many days since we've had sex I've stopped counting.* "How's things on campus?"

"Oh, you know, the usual. Drunken kids. High kids. Kids who can't handle the stress of being Mummy and Daddy's little lawyers-in-training. Oh, hey! We did have an interesting day a few weeks back in that gorge, now that you got me thinking about it."

"Yeah?" Tommy held his breath. His hands went clammy and he gripped the phone tighter. This was what he was hoping for. Joe was a famous talker, you just had to get him started.

"Yeah—wait. Here's Julie. Huh? No Bun-bun? Hear that? Sorry, Toms. We haven't found her yet. But we'll put out an all-points bulletin."

"Hey, great. Thanks. Meghan just goes a little nuts without her bunny."

"Been there. Done that. It's good to be old. Pull coins out of my grandkids' ears and they think I'm so corny, they don't want to come near me."

"Well, I have something to look forward to," Tommy said. "So, um, what happened a few weeks back in the gorge?" He tried to sound casual.

"Oh, Right. A jumper. At least, some kids thought it was a jumper. Got a call that a kid climbed over the rail. Six of them called it in on their cells. Six! Two of 'em even said they saw a body go down." Galton University was famous for students' diving into its deadly gorges when the going got tough.

"You found a body?" If the person who owned the

money was dead, of course there would be no report of missing money. Tommy's whole body had gone cold. Was that good or bad for his marriage? How could he think of his marriage when they were talking about a dead kid? "How come we didn't hear about this downtown?"

"Aww, you know we'd call you boys in for a jumper. It was nothing. False alarm. My boys searched, and believe me, if a person went over that rail, they weren't getting far. I've cleaned up four jumpers from that bridge since I started twenty-six years ago. None of 'em got far."

Tommy felt sick. He'd had his share of gorge "incidents" under the bridges and off the vertigo-inducing cliffs. The worst were the drunken kids who were out swimming and cliff diving, just trying to perfect their swan dives to impress their friends. An inch misjudgment, and they hit the sides, the bottom, their necks broken in an instant. "What did he look like?"

"Who?"

"The nonjumper. The kid who climbed the rail?"

"Dunno. We got there too late to see anyone and our eyewitnesses were obviously MOCP."

"MOCP?"

"Our new campus code for Morons on Cell Phones. Jimmy made it up. Funny, huh? The law enforcement community is gonna have to address that cell phone problem soon, Wynne. Anyway, all I can tell you is that most of them agree that he was a she with long black hair and she had parked her huge black BMW SUV on the bridge, backing up traffic something awful before she disappeared into thin air. Manny forgot to get the license plates, he was so focused on the invisible jumper. Who knows, maybe she could fly. Students. Think they own the world."

When they're not tossing themselves into gorges.

Joe kept on talking about his men climbing around in the gorge, Bill Twosome getting a nasty case of poison ivy—imagine that, this time of year!—the uselessness of teenage eyewitnesses, all on their cell phones and texting, only half in reality. "One even turned in a blurry cell phone movie of nothing but Bill slipping around like an idiot down there. Like maybe that was evidence or something. I'm sure it's already up on YouTube called something like, *Dumb, Fat Cop Slips: Funny!!!*" He sighed. "So you tell your Annie to come up and visit us with that beautiful baby of yours. You hear? We never see her anymore. And tell Meghan we'll find her Bun-bun. Joseph Pendergrast always gets his man."

Or woman. With long black hair in a black BMW SUV. Tommy hung up the phone. He still felt queasy. What did it mean? Did the witnesses see the bundle of cash going down? But even if they were idiots, as Joe had complained, how could they mistake a tiny wad of bills for a body?

CHAPTER

35

Wednesday morning, and the Enemy Club was assembled by ten minutes before seven, a minor miracle that didn't escape Lizzie's notice.

"So, spill," Jill demanded once they'd all settled. "I heard you're taking long lunch breaks to be with your handyman at the lake house. Betsy Coffit saw you guys from the deck of a house she's selling across the way." Jill was practically squirming with excitement. Lizzie wondered just exactly how much she'd seen. She felt her face go hot.

"Tracy Luge, in my Tuesday four o'clock yoga, told me that he's always at your house, fixing stuff, no matter when she goes by."

"Tracy Luge is stalking me?" Lizzie asked.

Nina sighed. "She said she couldn't help but go by after that crime blotter report and that now she jogs that way every day just to watch him. She thinks it's so romantic. She says she cries a little bit every time she passes."

"It is romantic," Georgia said with very little conviction.

"But dangerous. Are you sure you know what you're doing?"

"Of course she does," Nina said before Lizzie had a chance to speak. "Look at her. She's glowing. You can't deny the glow."

When they all finally settled down, Lizzie leaned forward and whispered, "I'm not telling you guys a thing."

"It's serious!" Jill said, slapping the counter. "We've lost her."

"Oh, Lizzie, I'm so, so happy for you," Nina said.

Georgia remained silent.

Lizzie grinned, then turned to Georgia and her grin faded. "What's wrong?"

"What about the accident, Liz? He hasn't worked through that." Lizzie had told them all everything about the accident over the last few days.

"He has," Lizzie insisted. "He said he realized that there's nothing he can do to turn back time." She wasn't about to tell Georgia that he said love cured him. That *she* cured him. That he'd said *love*. That she'd said *love*. In the bright glare of the diner, none of it sounded as plausible as it had in the dappled, soft light of the cabin.

"What about the girl whose mother died? The girl's in this town," Georgia said. "Wasn't that why he came here? To tell her that he's sorry? And she wouldn't accept his apology. Wasn't that what you told us?"

"So?" Lizzie crossed her arms over her chest. Sometimes, she still didn't like Georgia very much. Usually, she just had to imagine her on fire, and she'd forgive her. But she wanted desperately to ignore the nagging fact that Georgia was right: Tay had come here for a reason, and it wasn't pleasant and it wasn't worked out.

"So, I'm just saying that you need to be careful. I don't want you to rush into this just to have a man standing by when Ethan comes."

"You think I'm using him?"

"I think maybe you're ignoring some very important facts because you don't want to be alone when Ethan gets here," Georgia said. "You told us yourself that you wanted to fix the house and have a man so that Paige could have her dreams come true. It's all fallen together—maybe too perfectly?"

"I love him," Lizzie said. She startled herself with the words. But there they were, spoken before the Enemy Club under the glaring fluorescent bulbs. *The truth, the whole truth, and nothing but the truth...*

"Oh, hooray!" Nina clapped her hands.

"And he loves me," Liz said.

"He told you that?" Jill asked.

"Yes."

General mayhem ensued. Even Mr. Zinelli raised his coffee cup to her.

"We need to meet this guy," Jill said. "You need our approval. When can we meet him properly?"

"I do not need your approval," Lizzie said. *Because I love him. I love Tay Giovanni. I am in love and loved in return.* She poured herself a glass of ice water and drank the entire thing in one long gulp. She wanted to dump it over her head, just to be sure she was awake.

Georgia pursed her lips and didn't say anything.

She was the first one to leave.

Jill and Nina left the diner together.

"Get back in there," Nina whispered. "Now is the perfect time to tell her. She's in love. She won't care."

"I know," Jill said. "I will. Soon. Not now."

"Why is this so hard?" Nina asked. "We've all made mistakes and we've all forgiven each other."

"I know. But this—" Jill tightened her ponytail. They'd reached her car and she clicked the lock open. "Do you think this Tay thing is for real?"

"I sure hope so," Nina said. "Lizzie deserves it."

"You want a ride?" Jill offered, looking around for Nina's car.

"Nah. I parked in the church lot. I'm going to walk over and light a candle for Walt."

"How's he doing?"

"Good. I guess. Haven't heard from him in a while."

"His tour's done in August, right?" Jill asked.

"Yeah. You need to find me a place before he comes back. I'm going to have to move out of his house."

"C'mon, he's your brother. He might want you to stay."

"Nah. It's his place. When he comes back, he'll need his space. I imagine two years in Afghanistan makes a person need their space."

"Well, don't be so sure. He might want his sis nearby."

Nina shrugged. "I hope everything works out for Liz."

"Yeah, me, too. Especially because then, I won't ever have to hear about Ethan Pond ever again."

"Tell her," Nina said.

"I will." Jill slipped into her car. "I promise."

CHAPTER

36

Jay spent the next few weeks painting and stripping the porch. He'd changed his schedule so that he'd be there at dinnertime. Lizzie would invite him in, and he'd sometimes say yes and sometimes say no, depending on what he could sense of their moods.

After a while, she stopped having to ask and he stopped having to refuse. Paige would lean out on the porch and say, "Dinner."

The three of them—plus White and Dune, who almost always came with him—would eat.

After a while, Paige started to offer to help him. They'd work together until Lizzie came home, and then they'd keep on working until she called them in. At dinner, they'd talk about the projects that Lizzie and Paige were doing on their own—well, on their own with Paige's friends' help. He offered advice, but stayed out of their landscaping of the front yard, their work around the path. They had their project and he and Paige had their project.

And he and Lizzie had their stolen moments,

when Paige was at school, and that was the best part of all.

Tay was careful to leave right after dinner, so Paige could do her homework and Lizzie could have time to bully the poor girl with offers of board games and other unwanted attention. Sometimes he'd leave Dune and White, if Paige begged for the animals to stay. They didn't seem to mind, and it felt like a simple, meaningful gift to give the girl.

When he and Paige finally finished the porch—in the nick of time, as the nights were starting to freeze and the days weren't much better—Tay suggested a trek downtown for dinner to celebrate, his treat.

They went to the Italian joint and feasted.

By the time Paige finished her dessert, an ice-cream banana-split sundae with extra chocolate sprinkles, Tay felt as if everything in his life might be okay. He and Lizzie were getting along better than ever. The sex, naturally, was amazing. But more amazing, he had come to peace with the accident. With the fact that he'd never get the money back. That Candy would maybe one day forgive him, but until then, there was nothing he could do.

Tay watched Paige finish her sundae. "Remarkable," he said. "I never knew a girl who could eat so much."

"You think this is something, you should see her sleep," Lizzie said. "Eating and sleeping are the varsity sports of teenagers. I have no idea how they have time for anything else."

Paige stuck her tongue out at Lizzie. "She's just jealous because anything she eats makes her fat."

"You're not fat," Tay assured Lizzie.

"Oh, yuck," Paige said. "Please don't start the mushy

stuff. I'm still eating." She was cleaning the bowl with her finger. "Talk about something else."

"That's disgusting," Lizzie pointed out.

"Whatever. New topic," Paige said.

"What do *you* want to talk about, Paige?" Lizzie asked.

"How about this? Tay, are your intentions toward my mother honorable?"

"Paige!" Lizzie cried.

"No, it's okay," Tay said. "Are you asking if I'm going to marry her? Because the truth is, I'm not sure she'd want me. I'm not much of a catch. I used to be. But not anymore. I think your mother can do better."

"You were okay before you, you know, had that accident?" Paige asked, completely serious the way only an oblivious teenager could be.

"Paige Carpenter!" Lizzie could feel her face go hot. "How do you know about the accident?"

Paige traced the long history of her sources.

"So you know why I came to Galton?"

"'Cause that girl is here, the one whose mother—you know."

"What else do you know?" Tay asked.

Lizzie knew he wanted to know if anyone had heard anything about the money. So far, they'd been able to keep that part under wraps.

"Nothing else," Paige said. "Just that you came to try to help her but she won't speak to you. I think she's mean."

"You didn't hear any more details?" Tay pushed. "Like about how I was going to help her?"

"I heard that you kept trying to tell her you were sorry, but you weirded her out and she threatened to call the cops on you."

Tay's and Lizzie's eyes met across the table. So the secret of the money was still between Candy, Tay, and Lizzie. He wondered how long it would take to come out. Maybe it wouldn't.

"It's a little weird," Paige said. "You have to admit. Everyone thinks so. But then Jimmy said that in parts of Africa, there's a justice system where if you steal from someone, you, like, have to work on their farm until you pay them back. So it's personal. Not like here, where we don't do that kind of thing and you stay away from the victim."

Lizzie visibly flinched at the word *victim*. "Tay didn't do anything wrong. It was an accident."

"So, when can we start snowboarding?" Tay wanted to change the subject.

"I can't believe it hasn't snowed yet," Paige said. "But we'll get you out there soon."

"Tay? On a snowboard?" Lizzie asked.

"He's going to take lessons. From me," Paige said.

Tay shrugged. "She says she's the best."

"I am. But it doesn't mean much around here, 'cause the competition isn't great."

Lizzie met Tay's eyes.

"Boarding lessons?"

"Why not? You think I can't do it?"

"Old people board, too, Mom," Paige said. "I think my dad probably boards."

That put a damper on the conversation. "We have no idea, Paige," Lizzie said. "And Tay's not going to pay you. You're going to do it for free."

Paige rolled her eyes. "Of course he's not going to pay me. We're trading snowboard lessons for him fixing the house."

"How about that?" Tay smiled. "Like mother like daughter. We made a deal."

Tay insisted on paying the bill, and soon they were in the foyer of the restaurant, putting on hats and gloves to face the two blocks to Tay's truck. Paige dropped her glove and Tay bent to get it and the door to the restaurant opened and Candy walked in.

Tay could feel the extra chill in the room before he looked up.

Candy stared at him and the smile evaporated from his face.

Her eyes went from Lizzie to Tay to Paige.

Then she spun around and left the restaurant as quickly as she had come in.

"Tay, what's wrong?" Lizzie asked.

"Nothing," he said. "Maybe something I ate." But the numbness was back all at once as if it had never left. He felt nauseated and dizzy. He considered going after her, but what would he say? That he was deliriously happy like he'd never been happy in his life, and he had her to thank for it because she'd brought him to this town and tossed away his money, forcing him to stay, and then he'd fallen in love and even, just maybe, started to become part of a family?

He felt like the world's biggest jerk.

They walked down the street to his truck, his arm around Lizzie and Lizzie's arm around Paige, and he could still feel Candy's eyes boring into him as if she were there. He looked around, paranoid. What if she was watching? Lizzie and Paige were singing a popular song that had been on the radio lately. They sang badly and they laughed and their little group looked as if it didn't have a care in the world.

He took his arm from around Lizzie's shoulder, separating himself from them.

How did he deserve all this happiness, togetherness, boarding lessons, hot sex, and this cozy town where everything was forgiven? He thought of Lizzie's Enemy Club and their forgiveness. How they had to come together eventually, *by force of gravity and human nature.* And how they forgave each other because being alone—

Candy was always so alone.

He and Candy weren't citizens of this town.

He dropped Lizzie and Paige at home and Lizzie watched him leave, clearly worried despite his assurances that he was fine. He'd talk to Lizzie later. He had to think this through.

He had given up on finding the money. So Candy would be kicked out of Galton. Then she'd leave and he could stay—

—and he'd feel like the world's biggest putz.

He imagined learning to board with Paige. He imagined the winter turning to summer and maybe Lizzie and Paige would come out to his lake house. They'd swim, sun—

And Candy.

He'd never helped Candy. In fact, by his presence, he hurt her. How had he forgotten that?

It was so wrong, just thinking about it made him want to spit to get the taste out of his mouth.

Why was he so blessed with happiness?

He didn't want to leave Lizzie. He didn't want to leave Paige.

But he couldn't stay here. Even if Candy left because

she was kicked out of school, it was her town. He'd come to help her and he'd only helped himself. It wasn't that he'd forgotten her—

He had.

He had moved on just like that.

He drove slowly down the hill, across the town, toward the lake.

He got to the fork in the road. To the right, the road led to the highway out of town. To the left was the lake and his cabin.

He stopped his truck in the middle of the intersection, his headlights lighting up a sliver of trees in front of him. The road was deserted around him, the only sound his motor, echoing off the unseen cliffs.

If he wasn't helping Candy, then he was hurting her. He had no right to stay here. The look on her face had been one of pure distress. When he'd not been a fully functioning person, he hadn't run into her. He had been either at Lizzie's or holed up at the lake cabin. He'd been up most nights, slept in most of the days. But now that he was getting more normal, he'd surely run into her. He'd been sleeping more at night now; sometimes, he'd even fall asleep before two in the morning, which felt like a miracle.

Candy didn't deserve to have to worry about running into him.

Just as he turned his steering wheel toward the right and eased his foot off the brake, a deer poked its black nose out of the woods.

They stared at each other, and then, with a start, he remembered Dune and White.

He couldn't leave them behind.

He looked into his eyes in his rearview mirror.

Who was he kidding?

He couldn't leave Lizzie.

He steered his truck to the lake road, to home. He had to slow down. Think this through.

He'd talk to Lizzie tomorrow. Somehow, they'd figure this out.

CHAPTER

37

$\mathcal{T}$ommy saw the girl driving the black BMW SUV and he put the lights on before he could think. It was the car from the bridge. Or maybe it wasn't, but it was a black BMW SUV, and he'd already pulled it over.

The driver pulled over right away, in front of the hardware store, and it was too late to turn back. Tommy stared at her back bumper, wondering what he was doing. As if compelled by a strange force that he couldn't control, he put on his hat and his sunglasses. He never wore the sunglasses. He hated cops who wore the sunglasses.

He strode to the side of her car.

She rolled the window down. With these new higher SUVs, you couldn't stare down on drivers anymore. It took away a lot of the advantage. "License and registration."

But of course, it couldn't be that easy. "Did I do something wrong, Officer?" she asked. Her voice was defiant. She looked as if she hadn't slept in days. Probably a partier, from the look of her fancy car.

"Crossed the double yellows when you made that left,"

he lied. He took a deep breath. "Is this the BMW that was blocking the bridge awhile back?"

She was searching in her red leather bag, but he saw her flinch. When she found her wallet, she turned back to him. "God, this is the world's smallest, most boring town if you remember that. That was months ago." She handed over her papers without smiling. "I hate this town," she said.

He took her ID wordlessly back to his car. He copied down the information, staring at her picture. Candy Sue Williams. Blue eyes. Black hair. Nineteen years old. The license was from Newton, Massachusetts. A fancy town to go with her fancy car. No wonder she hated it here. Her nails were perfectly manicured. He could hear Annie's voice in the back of his head: *Now that's one whose hair hasn't been cut in this town.*

This kid was the kind of girl who might stop traffic, climb a guardrail, and scare innocent bystanders half to death by tossing a thousand dollars down into a gorge just for fun. She didn't care about the town, well, hell, why did he care so much about her and her money?

He went back to her car and gave her back her papers. "I'm just going to give you a warning this time. But next time, watch the yellow lines." His heart was beating hard. He was ruining his marriage over a snotty kid. How had he gotten it so wrong?

She rolled her window up and pulled away, her tires screeching, not at all careful about a thing. For the first time in weeks, the thought entered Tommy's head that maybe Annie was right about the money after all. Some people, maybe, deserved to lose what they were careless with.

Maybe he was the one who had to stop being so careless.

Maybe he was the one in danger of throwing his life away by insisting on being right. Tossing his marriage away like a wad of cash over the side of a bridge.

At breakfast, Tommy told Annie about meeting Candy Sue Williams. Annie reached across the table and squeezed his hand, her first purposeful physical contact in ages. "You mean, you did something against regulations? I'm so proud of you, Tommy."

Meghan cooed her agreement, banging on her tray for emphasis. He put some mashed home fries on Meghan's tiny rubber-covered spoon and offered it to her.

A jolt of gratitude swept from the hand that Annie was still holding, through his body, and he thought, *This is still wrong.* He pulled his hand away from Annie, even though he tried not to. "It wasn't exactly a proud moment. What I was trying to say is that the girl practically had money dripping out of her tailpipe." He crossed his arms across his chest and leaned back. He looked down at the hearty breakfast he had cooked—eggs, reheated home fries, two strips of no-nitrate turkey bacon, and cut-up melon. Sensible and healthy. It had all seemed so clear on the bridge. Now, it didn't seem so cut and dried.

Annie loved him when he agreed with her? Withdrew her affection when he stood his ground?

He wasn't hungry anymore.

"So you're saying it's okay to keep the money?" Annie bit into the bacon with her front teeth, like a teenager splitting a piece of gum to share with a friend.

Meghan had lost interest in eating and was busy mashing pieces of potato on her tray.

Tommy needed more from Annie. He didn't want to fall in line behind her like a meek puppy dog, starved for affection.

Even if he was that, just a little bit.

He shook his head. "It's not okay. The money might not even be hers. It's just a hunch. But I gotta tell you, I didn't like this girl. She seemed careless, uncaring. So if it'll make you happy, we won't turn in the money. But let's do something good with it. Charity."

"Oh, God, no! Let's do something reckless and irresponsible. Let's take this new Tommy all the way."

The challenge hung in the air between them. Tommy pushed back his chair and took his plate to the sink. He scraped his food into the trash. "Like what? You want to blow it in a spa? On a fancy dinner in New York City? It's all empty, Annie. It's nothing." He rinsed the plate and put it into the dishwasher, his anger rising. She wanted to challenge him? He'd challenge her. But how?

He went back with a sponge for Meghan's tray.

"No, no, no. Stop cleaning and think of something crazy, Tommy. You be the one. Make it something wild."

"Is this some kind of test?" He looked out the window over the sink at the play set he was building in the back yard. *Wild.* She wanted wild...

"Yeah, I guess it is." Now her arms were crossed.

He thought of all the important things they could do with the money. Give it to the food kitchen, the church. Or maybe a hundred hours of babysitting. Give the money to Paige so she could do two hours a week all year long and give Annie a break.

Or maybe blow it all on marriage counseling.

He wasn't ready to have that fight. Plus, it seemed like

reconciliation, and he was in no mood to reach out to Annie. So instead he said the first thought that entered his mind: "Let's throw it off the Campus Road Bridge and back into the gorge." The wave of anger that had been roiling in his gut stopped cold as if it had been flash-frozen. An odd, chilly peace descended over him. He unstrapped Meghan from her seat and took her to the sink to wash her hands and face.

Annie's mouth dropped open. "No way."

"If you don't want to, then don't. It's your money. But don't bug me about it anymore. I don't want to hear about it. I've said my part. I've done what I could. You know what I think."

"Drop a thousand bucks off the bridge?" she asked. Her voice was breathless. "Why?"

"Do it and see what happens. Watch to see where it goes. Watch to see who finds it. Watch to see what they do with it."

"Why, Tommy?" she repeated.

"Annie, if we don't get rid of this money, we're done. We can't ever agree on it. Ever. We have to get rid of it." He sat down, adjusting to the new climate in the room as if he'd opened a window. The idea had come to him blown in on the breeze, changing the air around him.

"You're saying, toss the money or toss me," Annie said.

Meghan looked up at him and flashed the sweetest baby smile. Tommy smiled back, mesmerized by Meghan's soft, wispy blonde hair, her tiny hands, her perfection. "Make a choice, Annie. The money or us. I choose us."

Annie hedged. "I don't know, Tommy. How would it work? Would we drop it as a package, or open it and let the bills float around? Would we do it when there were lots of people around? Or at midnight?"

"It doesn't matter how we do it. All that matters is that we do it." He felt remarkably calm, cleansed even. "Next time Meghan wakes up in the middle of the night and can't get back to sleep, we bundle her up, go out, and do it."

"You're crazy, Tommy. It's a waste."

"It's not. It's necessary. And then, once it's gone, we figure out what's left."

CHAPTER

38

I can't do this anymore," Tay said. They were naked on his bed, spent from their intense lovemaking.

"Rather unconvincing," Lizzie said, glancing down at him. She had been dreading this conversation ever since he'd told her about seeing Candy.

He scowled at his traitorous body. "Always the last to get the message."

Lizzie rolled onto her stomach next to him.

He lay on his back, staring up at the ceiling. He had told her the whole story about running into Candy at the restaurant. "I can't forget the look on her face when she saw me. I knew I'd run into her eventually—such a small town. But I didn't think it would be like that. I thought I was honestly getting used to the idea that we could both be in this town."

"What was it like?" Lizzie asked.

"Like me, so happy. And her, so alone. Liz, every night for the past week, I've been driving my truck a little farther out of town. But then, I always turn back."

"How far'd you make it, Speed Racer?" she teased. But she softened her words with a kiss on his forehead. The truth was, she was terrified. He really was going to leave.

"Almost to Trumanstown," he said. Trumanstown was less than five miles away. "Okay, so quick getaways aren't my thing. Liz, I turn back for you. But it's getting harder to justify, because you keep making me happier and happier, which makes me feel guiltier and guiltier. Lizzie, I don't think I have any choice but to leave."

"We can figure this out," she assured him. "Somehow."

He got up and started pacing. "I don't know. What right do I have to hang around this town? For the next few months, it's Candy's town. I could come back when she's gone—oh, hell, that isn't much better. Every student I'd see, I'd think of her getting kicked out of school and me here, with you, so happy."

"We'll find a way. Candy doesn't own this town. Just because she's right doesn't mean she gets to rule you."

"You sure? I think it means exactly that. What kind of schmuck moves into the tiny town where the girl lives who—" He shook his head, unable to finish. He sat back down on the edge of the bed and let his head hang.

"It's like everyone trying to run me out of town when I was pregnant, Tay. They don't get to set the rules just because we made the mistakes."

He thought about that. "It's not the same, though. What if Ethan had stayed?"

"I'd have hated him, but I'd have gotten over it and in the end, it would have been better for Paige. Tay, don't leave. Don't do this." She could hear the desperation in her voice and she hated it.

"Let's talk about something else. Anything else. You

never told me about setting Georgia on fire. That would cheer me up," he said. He'd been down on Georgia ever since Lizzie'd told him that Georgia had warned her to stay away from him. He traced her nipple with his thumb. "Please, just talk."

She smiled. "Actually, it's the perfect story. Because my relationship with Georgia is a little like yours and Candy's. Georgia was always right. Always. She had innocence and goodness on her side."

He lay back and closed his eyes. "I hate those people."

"Me, too. I had hated Georgia since forever. Since preschool. She was one of those kids who was a know-it-all teacher's pet. We weren't exactly enemies the way Jill and I were, with the constant fighting. Georgia and I mostly stayed away from each other. By high school she had turned into a fussy, self-righteous prude. She hadn't ever done anything to me but scorn me for not being smart enough, and I never did anything to her but maybe tease her a little for being such a geek. Never to her face, though. Deep down, I hated her a little more than even Jill, because I hated how self-righteous she was. Like she thought her way was always better than everyone else's."

"She's still a little that way," Tay pointed out.

"She is. And she's still usually right," Lizzie said.

Tay shook his head. "Not about the important things. Not about us."

"Yeah, those people never are right about the key stuff, are they?" Lizzie asked. "Anyway, when news of my pregnancy got out, Georgia was the editor of the school paper. She published a letter from the editor about the irresponsibility of teenage promiscuity that was so obviously about me, she might as well have used my name."

"Ouch."

"I didn't pay it much attention. I had more important things to deal with. But it got worse. She wouldn't leave it at that. She made it her personal mission to redeem poor little old me."

"Why?"

"She'd found God. And of course, he took her side. She'd come to my house and bang on the door and beg to talk to me. After it became clear that I wasn't going to invite her in for tea, she started to shove pamphlets and personal letters through the front-door mail slot. The pamphlets were mostly about hell and damnation, illustrated with red-tinged gory pictures of fire and demons. The letters were about the same, just without the pictures. Boy, could she write a scary story. I had sinned, you see, and I had to ask for forgiveness."

"From her?" Tay asked.

"It sure seemed that way. Anyway, I ignored her. Stuffed her propaganda in the trash. But then, one Sunday morning, I was in bed, sick as a dog with morning sickness. And I heard singing."

"Singing?"

"Yep. Outside on my porch. I came downstairs and my parents had pulled all the blinds and my mother was in the kitchen, weeping, saying we'd have to move. It was awful. Georgia had assembled a prayer vigil to save my soul on my front porch. They seemed to think that since I was unwed, as they put it, I was going to hell unless I repented. I don't know what they wanted me to do—marry one of them? Hunt down Ethan and marry him? At least I was having the baby. Can't imagine what they would have done if I'd decided not to do that."

"So what happened?"

"I was furious. And doubly hormonal. Remember I was a teenager *and* I was pregnant and my mother was wailing in the kitchen. So maybe I went a little nuts."

"I can't wait to hear this," Tay said.

"I probably shouldn't have lit that broom on fire and waved it at them, screaming that the devil had arrived and he was me and if I was going to hell, then damn it, they were coming with me." She paused. "I hadn't meant to set Georgia's jacket on fire, but she wasn't as fast as the rest of them. There wasn't any real damage. Georgia, naturally, was an expert at the drop and roll, being that kind of girl. She didn't get burned. Just ruined the jacket, which was butt ugly anyway. Tweed, if you can imagine a teenager in tweed." Lizzie shuddered. "Stop laughing, it wasn't funny. She told everyone that I'd set her on fire and it was true and my parents were beyond furious at me."

"Were you sorry?" Tay asked.

"No. It was one of the best days of my life."

They lay side by side for a while.

"Tay, you can't let anyone tell you what to do. Even if they're right. I had done bad. I knew it. But no one, *no one,* had the right to demand I apologize. No one had the right to run me out of town."

"I don't know, Liz. I don't know that the story applies. I wronged another person."

"Sure it does. They thought I'd wronged my unborn baby."

"So how did Georgia ever forgive you?"

"Jill and I were at the diner one Wednesday and we got to talking about Georgia and I decided to send her a letter, to invite her to our club. Poor Georgia had wanted to leave town after high school. She thought she'd go to Harvard or Yale, but her parents fell on hard times. Her dad was a Galton professor, but there was a scandal—"

Tay's eyebrows rose.

"I know! Her dad had messed around with a student, and he'd lost his job. But her mom worked in the library, so she had Galton benefits. Including almost free tuition if Georgia stayed and went to school here. Georgia had no choice, and the family couldn't leave and give up the cheap tuition. Georgia still had two brothers who needed to go to college, and her dad would never work at a university again. I knew she was miserable about going to Galton, because all she ever talked about was leaving here and going to Harvard, then Yale divinity school."

"So she never left Galton after that? What about Yale?"

"She was so upset about how her life had fallen apart, she had lost her faith in God. She was a teenager. It felt like the end of the world to her to have to go to this fantastic school in this beautiful place for practically free. We laugh about it now, but at the time, she was miserable. I used to see her sometimes, scurrying around town, her head down. She was getting fatter and fatter. Sometimes, it seemed as if she was also getting shorter. She was always alone."

"So one day, she's scurrying by, and Jill just runs out and grabs her. Invites her in. Tells her that we're having a reunion of sorts."

"So she joined you guys willingly?"

"Yep. And the next Wednesday, she came back."

"Just like that," Tay said.

"Just like that," Lizzie agreed. "And, Tay, if she had

run away from Galton, like you want to do, no one would have ever had the chance to forgive anyone. She's my good friend now. She has a point of view that isn't always right, but it's always thoughtful and deep and nuanced in ways I often miss."

"I don't know, Lizzie. It's not the same. I hurt Candy worse than I can imagine."

"Don't hurt me, Tay," Lizzie whispered.

"Come with me," he whispered back.

She sat up, startled at the offer. "I can't."

"Why not?"

"My life is here. Where would we go?"

"I don't know. Come to Queens with me. I'm going to start over."

"I can't run around. I have a daughter. A family. A house. A life. I can't just start over."

He held her close. "I know. It was just a Hail Mary pass."

The next day, Tay came for dinner. When Paige had gone upstairs to do homework, he took Lizzie's hands. "I haven't slept in days," he said.

She steeled herself for what she knew was coming.

"I've thought it through and thought it through again. Liz, I'm going to stay until Ethan comes, so that you'll have what you wanted—a man to be here for you so that Paige can follow her dream. But then, Lizzie, I have to leave."

"I know," she said. She wasn't going to beg again. He'd made his decision. It didn't make it hurt any less, but at least she looked brave. "I'm sorry, I can't come with you."

"I know," he said. "I'm going to beat this thing. I'm going to make it right."

"I know," she said. "I have total faith in you." He was like a bird that had to migrate to survive. "But I'm not a saint, Tay. I can't wait forever."

"You won't have to," he said.

The birds always came back, she told herself.

They were smart enough to come back.

She hoped that Tay would be, too.

But sometimes, smart wasn't enough. Sometimes, life was just too full of dangers.

CHAPTER

39

The second week of November brought a freak early blizzard that dumped a foot of snow, and Paige became a stranger. The minute school let out, Paige and her friends hitched rides from whoever would take them, piling into cars for the twenty-minute drive to Meeks Peak, the local mountain. They rode their tubes or chutes or whatever they called the death traps they raced down in an unimaginable array of dangerous variations.

Tay kept putting off the lessons he'd promised Paige he'd take. Ever since running into Candy, he'd hardly gone anywhere but their house and his cabin at the lake. He'd quit his job on campus the day after running into her at the restaurant, as that, naturally, was the most dangerous place of all. He'd taken up doing odd jobs in Trumanstown, the next town over, for various people, but he wouldn't work in Galton and Lizzie got the feeling he did it more to keep busy than for the cash. Lizzie felt as if they were hanging on by a string that was getting more and more frayed every day, but they had stopped talking about it. There was only so much to say, and she was determined to enjoy the time they still had together.

Tommy's grill tank had finally emptied, and they celebrated the end of Friday night burgers with Chinese food at Lizzie's. It was a testament to Annie's feeling better that they were able to eat there. Lizzie was still curious about Annie's mysterious visit to her house for the sweater, but after asking point-blank, and having Annie evade her, Lizzie had let it drop.

"I saw Paige had a new board," Tommy said.

"Yeah. I have no idea where she got it. It must have cost a fortune."

"She couldn't steal a snowboard," Annie said. "She might be telling the truth that she got it from friends." Paige had not only a new board, but also a new coat and snow pants, and most disturbingly, she was somehow paying for daily private lessons. Lizzie had only known about that since last week, when Geena's mother had told her. It took a lot of effort for Lizzie to pretend she wasn't shocked. When she asked Paige about it, she said she'd been making money giving informal lessons to some of the smaller kids.

"I'm worried that she's pushing herself too hard so she can impress her dad," Lizzie said.

White jumped onto the table, and Lizzie pushed her down. Now that the snow had come, the cat had refused to leave Lizzie's house. Sometimes, White, Dune, and Tay would all sleep over.

She liked having the animals around, but she worried that one day she'd wake up with White and Dune, but Tay would be gone.

• • •

Tay hoped to finish fixing the staircase before Thanksgiving. He was grateful for the worn treads, the wobbly posts, every detail he could attend to so he didn't have to think about anything else. Like leaving.

Paige had let him in this morning before she left for school. Now, she was gone and he could hear Lizzie moving around upstairs. His mouth went dry, thinking about her and about how good this all was. A little more of her appeared with each step as she came down the stairs until she reached the landing and there she was, all of her, taking his breath away.

"Morning."

"Morning."

"The newel post is wobbly," he said. "I have to remove the bottom tread and secure the joint."

She came down to him and kissed his shoulder and he felt as if everything was right in his world even if he knew it wasn't.

"Right," she said. "I didn't understand a word you just said, but it sounds like just what I'd do with a wobbly jewel post."

"Newel post."

He pulled her into his arms.

The kiss wasn't as electric as it had been in the beginning, but it was warmer, completely comforting, absolutely perfect. "Up or down?" he asked.

"Neither." She pushed him away. "I need coffee. And I've been late to work the last two days."

Tay followed her into the kitchen. "Do you have any Gorilla Glue for that post?"

"In the basement, maybe. I don't know. It sounds like

the kind of thing I'd buy with good intentions, then never use and let dry up. You want me to go get some in town?" She'd been running his errands in town for him ever since they'd run into Candy. He didn't like it, but he liked it better than the alternative, which was Candy's seeing him again. "Coffee?"

"Nah. I'll get it." The mention of going into town made his lips go thin. "What are the chances that Candy is buying nails at the hardware store this morning?"

He could read the compassion, but also the exasperation on her face. He wasn't sure which was worse. "No Candy spottings. It's been a month," Lizzie said.

"I saw her last week, but she didn't see me," he admitted. "I was driving through town and she was walking. She was alone, which depressed the hell out of me. Every time I see her, she looks thinner and thinner, even in her parka." He sat down at the kitchen table and rubbed his hands through his hair.

This was killing him.

Lizzie had an overwhelming desire to run to campus, find Candy Williams, and drag her to her kitchen so she could see that Tay was an okay guy who was suffering. She wanted to shout at the poor girl that he deserved her forgiveness. "I wish there was something I could do," Lizzie said for the hundredth time.

She went to him and sat on his lap and he put his arms around her. She felt lovely surrounded by him. "You're a good man, Tay."

He kissed her hair, her cheek, her forehead, then took her mouth in his.

She let her head fall back.

He kissed down her neck. He reached under her sweater and sighed as he cupped her breast. He let his head fall to kiss her. "God, you're beautiful. I would give anything to taste you right now." The days were slipping by too quickly. They never seemed to have enough time.

"Mmmm," she sighed. "I could call in late to work."

"That sounds like a fantastic idea."

BZZZZZZZZ.

They pulled apart.

"Who fixed my doorbell?" she demanded.

"I did," he said. "Damn it. I can break it again. Wait—don't go."

Lizzie ignored him and went to the door.

It was Jill and she was holding a pie.

CHAPTER

40

"Hi. Can I come in?" Jill asked, almost sheepishly, which was so unlike her, Lizzie let her in without another word.

"Are you okay?"

Jill looked around the foyer. "Wow. It looks great in here."

Tay came into the foyer.

"Now it looks even better." Jill tried a weak smile, her heart obviously not in it. "Hi, Tay."

"Ma'am." He nodded to Jill. "Back to work with me. I've got to find some glue."

His footsteps disappeared into the basement.

"Oh, God, you're so lucky," Jill whispered to Lizzie as they went to the kitchen. "He's a dream."

"A dream I'm about to wake up from. Coffee?" Lizzie asked.

Jill sat down, plopping the pie on the table. "He's still insisting this town isn't big enough for him and Candy?"

"Yep. And I can't exactly blame him. But still. Crap!"

"Did you ever think about going with him, Lizzie?"

"No. I like it here. I like my house, my job, my birds, my daughter, my very worstest enemies. How could I leave all this?"

"You're nuts."

"I know. But it's more than that. It's also that I don't want to wander around, following a guy who doesn't know what he's doing. He's got to figure this out, Jill. Remember how I said I didn't want a guy to save me? Well, I also don't want to give up my life for a guy who's having such a hard time saving himself. I know that sounds harsh, but I worked hard for all this. It might not be much, but it's what I've got."

"You're right," Jill said. "Always right."

"Not always," Lizzie pointed out.

"Okay, I'm just going to come out and say this and then I have to go. I'm busy. I have clients."

Lizzie sat down. "You're the one who came here." Lizzie couldn't imagine what this visit was about. It was rare of Jill to stop by out of the blue. Even rarer for her to be so fidgety.

Jill nodded. "Right. Well. Okay. Thing is—there's something I wanted to get out of the way." She inhaled deeply. "We've been enemies for a long time."

"We have."

"Good enemies."

"The best," Lizzie said, and she meant it.

"And we promised each other to tell the truth, the whole truth, and nothing but the truth."

"Right."

Jill sighed. "I haven't been telling the truth." She paused. "I also slept with Ethan."

Lizzie whistled under her breath. She tried to adjust to the news, but there was nothing to adjust. It rolled off her. "You know, I don't really care. I'm pretty over Ethan. I swear, I don't think there's a cell in my body that wants him back."

"And I also—" Jill's voice started to waver. She coughed.

"Jilly?" Lizzie had never seen her friend so pale.

"He also got me pregnant. I also got pregnant. I had a baby, too."

"Oh." Lizzie absorbed the news, her mind darting to all the possibilities. "You left school early senior year, just after I did. With mono."

"Mono!" Jill laughed and then her eyes welled up with tears. She let out a yelp like an wounded animal, which brought Tay dashing into the kitchen. He retreated just as quickly as he saw the crying woman.

"Oh, my God. Here, have some pie." Lizzie jumped up for a knife and a plate. "When were you going to tell me this?"

"Never." Jill accepted the pie. She shoved a bite into her mouth. "But with Ethan coming, I couldn't stop thinking about it and I couldn't not tell you anymore and—" She mumbled something incoherent.

"What? I didn't get that."

"I gave the baby away," Jill said, a little too loudly. She put down her pie. "God, I hated you so much. There you were, having your baby right out in the open like it was no big deal. I couldn't do that. Girls like me didn't have babies when they were teenagers. I had to go to college. Get a good husband. Make money. But you didn't care what anyone thought. I did, though. I wasn't going to ruin my life with a baby. I had big plans. I thought, thank God I wasn't like you. I didn't want to ruin my life like you did. I was—"

"Higher class?"

Jill exhaled heavily. "I was an idiot. And Ethan coming is making it all come back to me and I'm trying really, really hard not to hate you all over again because what if he's perfect and he gives Paige a chance at a great life and I don't even know where my baby is? I've never made a bigger mistake in my life."

They sat in silence for a few moments, staring at the destroyed pie while tears streamed down Jill's face.

"Your baby might already be in boarding school in Geneva, studying to be president," Lizzie pointed out.

"She might," Jill allowed.

"Paige has done pretty darn well without Ethan all these years. I bet wherever your baby went, she's doing fine."

"The only other person who knows this is Nina," Jill said. "I don't want it to get around town."

"Nina? Why Nina?"

"Yeah. She caught me barfing one day in the school bathroom and she was so nice to me. I told her everything and she swore secrecy."

"So you guys weren't true enemies?"

"We were secret friends."

Lizzie made the coffee. She had always wondered why Nina had joined the Enemy Club. She had just appeared one Wednesday and sat down at the end of the counter. Jill had noticed her and called her over. Now Lizzie understood that Jill had set the whole thing up. She handed a mug to Jill, who took it like a child. "Did Ethan know about any of this?"

"No. I never told him. Then he started dating you and I hated you both so much because he pretended I had never existed." She paused. "I had met him at one of my father's dinners for his students. He came up to my room, and we made out a little, and he invited me to meet him later."

"You little slut," Lizzie scolded.

"I know. We kinda had a thing going for a little while. We went on a few secret dates." Jill shrugged. The tears were streaming, but she didn't look as miserable. "And now, he's coming back to you to make it right. But I can never make it right for my baby. I don't know where she is."

"She?" Lizzie said. "You're the mother of Paige's half sister. We're related."

"I couldn't be more sorry. I feel like I let her down." She tried to bring her sniffles under control, then she ate the last bite of her pie. Lizzie cut her another generous piece and shoveled it onto her plate. Jill pushed it aside and took the whole pie, digging in haphazardly with her fork.

"Ethan wasn't even that good," Lizzie consoled her friend.

Jill fell into a fit of sobbing. "He stank. Like, two seconds and he was done."

"Two seconds was a second longer than I got," Lizzie said.

Jill picked her wrecked face up off the table. She hiccuped. "Really?"

"No. I'm just trying to make you feel better." Lizzie patted Jill's shoulder.

Jill smiled and wiped her nose with her sleeve. "Are we still best enemies?"

"Forever. Even better, now that we're half aunts. Is that what we are?"

"Something like that, I guess. I hate him for coming back like this."

"Maybe one day soon, your daughter will come back like this."

"You think?"

"Yeah. Galton's awesome. No one can resist. It has a pull. And Jill, when she comes, you'll be ready for her. You'll be a great birth mom. The best."

Jill smiled. "You know, I used to wish and hope for the day Paige would leave, because whenever I saw her, I felt so much loss. But now, I want her to stay. I feel like she's part mine."

"She is. You took care of us so many times." Lizzie paused. "Are you going to tell Ethan?"

"No. Definitely not. It's none of his business. I just wanted to tell you. It's been hanging over me for so many years."

"Okay. You sure?"

"No."

"Okay." They sat for a while.

Lizzie said, "Do you want to tell Paige?"

"No!" Jill said.

Lizzie was relieved. "She has a lot to deal with."

After Jill left, Tay peeked out of the living room.

"I heard the whole thing," he said.

"Good," Lizzie said.

"Good? Why?" He sat down at the table.

"Because, dummy, I always thought that she hated me because she hated me. But she hated me because of her own screwed-up life. It had nothing to do with me."

"Are you trying to make me stay again?" he asked. "I love it when you try to make me stay."

"No, if I was going to try to make you stay, I'd do this." She went to him and kissed him until he moaned, then she walked away.

"Hey, come back here."

She cleared the dishes from the table. "Not a chance. At least, not until you admit that Jill's story was a bombshell. Tay, her hating me had nothing really to do with me and what I did. It was all about her."

"You're saying that Candy doesn't hate me for what I did?"

"I'm saying that life is so complicated in ways we can't possibly imagine. So don't assume it's the way you see it, because you could be wrong."

CHAPTER

41

The day after Thanksgiving, Lizzie and Paige and Tay went to the tree farm and chopped down the biggest silver pine they could find. They trimmed it with fourteen years of mismatched decorations.

It looked pretty darn good.

In fact, everything looked pretty darn good.

For the next few weeks, they fixed and decorated the house to within an inch of its life.

By the time Annie, Tommy, Meghan, Tay, Jill, and Paige sat down for Christmas Eve dinner, it was so perfect, it almost felt like Annie's house. The table was laid with their mother's orange antique tablecloth. Pumpkin-scented candles were lit on every surface. The meal had been a weeklong marathon of shopping, chopping, baking, and roasting.

But none of them could concentrate on tonight with tomorrow looming. Especially Lizzie. Her focus, however, had shifted from what would happen with Ethan when he came to what would happen to Tay when he left.

He still held firm to his plan that he had to leave this town. Lizzie couldn't stop thinking about it.

"What kind of car do you think he'll come in?" Paige asked as she speared another piece of turkey for her plate. When Paige got nervous, she talked too much. Not getting caught up in her manic flow wasn't easy.

"Santa rides a sleigh," Lizzie said. "He doesn't drive." She poured herself more red wine. Then poured some for Tay.

Paige kicked her under the table. "Not Santa. God, Mom. *Him*."

"Jesus?" Annie asked. "He's the true meaning of Christmas, you know. I'm pretty sure he floats in a cloud surrounded by little naked cherubs." She was feeding Meghan mashed-up sweet potato, most of which was ending up on her face.

"You all know who I mean," Paige said, exasperated.

"A plain Chevy rental," Tommy said. "He'll pick it up at the airport. All his Rolls-Royces are back home at his mansion, after all, being waxed by his slaves."

Paige practically swooned. "You think?"

Lizzie shook her head. "No. I think slaves are frowned upon in Switzerland." She took another swig of red. Tay moved the wine down the table, out of her reach.

She pouted, but didn't protest. If she got too tipsy, she might say the wrong thing to Paige, and that would start everything rolling downhill.

"If he's smart, he's going to come in a bulletproof limo," Jill said.

Lizzie patted her hand. Jill had stopped crying every time they discussed Ethan. Now she mostly expressed a desire for painful revenge. She'd even offered to buy

Lizzie and Paige plane tickets to Disney World, so they wouldn't have to be here when Ethan showed up.

Lizzie said, "He's going to ride in on a magic carpet, honey. All the men who grant wishes do that." She looked across the table at Tay.

"Careful what you wish for," he said.

"Oh, I know exactly what I wish for," she said.

"Gross!" Paige said. "Cut it out, you guys. They've been gross like this for months," Paige complained. "Pass the yams so I can eat them and then vomit."

After dinner, Annie and Tommy left with Meghan, and Paige went upstairs to text-message her friends. Jill took off for her aunt's house in Albany, where she was going to spend Christmas Day with her sister, whom she fought with, her brood of nephews and nieces, and a bottle of Jack Daniel's.

Lizzie walked Tay to the porch.

"My house is perfect," she said. Tay had wrapped tiny white lights around the porch columns. The lights blinked like crystals of melting snow. "We had the first Christmas Eve dinner ever without the leaf on the dining room table collapsing."

"Easy fix," Tay said. He had on a coat and she didn't, so he pushed her up against the railing, put his hands in his pockets, and wrapped them both in his coat so they were face to face, body to body.

"And all the burners worked on the stove."

"No problem. Just a few replacement parts." He pushed against her.

"I can't believe you even fixed the squeaking of the dining room floor."

"Joist work is easier than people think."

"Why don't you stay tonight?" She pushed back against him. "Why don't you stay forever?"

"You and Paige should be together tomorrow on Christmas Day. Just the two of you," he said into her neck.

"The four of us, if you count White and Dune." The animals hadn't been back to Tay's cabin at the lake in weeks. Would he take them with him? She wasn't up for asking, the night was too perfect. "Five if you count Ethan," she added.

"Merry Christmas, Lizzie."

"Merry Christmas."

Tay held her tight and she put her head on his warm shoulder.

"So you're going to spend Christmas alone tomorrow?" Lizzie asked him.

"I like it that way."

"You want to be alone because you think Candy is alone. She might not be, you know. She might be with friends. Or grandparents. She might be off in the Caribbean, having the time of her life. Assumptions, Tay..."

"I want to be alone because it feels right. I'm not leaving until Ethan comes and goes," Tay said. He pulled a tiny package out of his pocket and handed it to her. "I almost forgot. For under the tree."

She took it with girlish excitement, happy to forget what was coming in the days ahead, if only for a moment. "Can I open it now, since you won't be here tomorrow?" she asked.

"Sure."

She ripped off the paper. It was a pocket watch. "Oh, Tay, it's beautiful."

"It doesn't work," he said.

"It doesn't have to. I have a fix-it guy. He takes care of everything."

"It's set to eleven o'clock." He pulled her closer.

"And why is that?" she murmured.

He pressed his thigh between her legs and it felt heavenly. "Because tomorrow, I'm going to leave you and Paige alone so you guys can deal with Ethan. And then, the next day, you're going to come to my place, and we'll make love."

"Am I?"

"Yes. But—"

"Always a but."

"But then, I have to go."

She pulled away from him. "That's the crappiest gift ever. I'm taking it back for a refund."

"It's not. It's a promise that I'll come back," he said. He pulled her back to him and pressed into her. She closed her eyes. This man knew exactly how to move even with all his clothes on. "And until I do, time will stop."

She let her head fall onto his chest. "But it won't really, Tay. Time doesn't stop."

He held her close. "It'll feel that way for me."

She pulled him closer. She let herself get lost in the sensation of him. "I got you something, too." Her eyes fluttered open.

He waited.

"Are you going to give it to me?"

"No. It's not Christmas yet. And since you refuse to be here on Christmas, you have to come back and get it the day after tomorrow."

"That's blackmail."

"Yep. I'm really scared you're going to take off tonight,"

she said. "It's a really, really good present. So don't you dare leave." She was trying to joke, to not let the tears out.

They stood together like teenagers. Or, rather, like the teenager that Lizzie had never gotten a chance to be. Tomorrow, Ethan would come. The next day, Tay would leave. It didn't seem like a good trade.

"God, tomorrow is going to be hard," Lizzie said finally. Her toes were starting to go numb in the cold.

"Tomorrow will be fine," Tay assured her. "And if it's not, call me. I'll come by and beat Ethan to a pulp."

"It's not about Ethan anymore, dummy. It's about you." She was trying not to cry, but it wasn't going so well. "You should be here on Christmas, not him."

He lifted her mouth to his and kissed her. "Good night, Elizabeth Carpenter. I'll see you the day after tomorrow. Is 5:00 A.M. too early? Maybe four-thirty?"

"Good night, Tay Giovanni. Merry Christmas."

Something was scratching at the window.

They turned. It was White. "Look, she doesn't want you to be alone on Christmas. Take her with you, Tay."

"I'll take Dune, too. So you don't have to worry about him."

"No way. If you take them both, I'm afraid you won't come back. I'm holding Dune hostage along with your Christmas present." She opened the door and White slid out. She scooped her up and handed her to Tay. "Merry Christmas."

"Not the present I was hoping for," he said.

"Careful, she bites," Lizzie reminded him. "Take good care of him tonight and tomorrow, White."

"I'll see you the day after Christmas," he said. "And I'm returning the cat."

CHAPTER

42

When the first rays of light woke her the next morning, the clock said 8:34. Lizzie had heard Paige up most of the night, pacing the house, but still, she hadn't expected they'd sleep so late. She crept into Paige's room. She was sound asleep.

Lizzie went downstairs and looked out the window.

The thirteen inches of snow that had come down over the past weeks had hardened into an icy crust. A soft flurry was dusting down gently on top of it. A picture-perfect tableau for a happy Christmas story.

Paige got up an hour later looking as if she'd been sleeping for years. After much grumbling, she agreed to open one present. She picked a small one, from Annie and Tommy. It was a pair of super-advanced ski gloves.

"Things don't have to be perfect for him, you know," Lizzie said when Paige had snatched up the wrapping paper, balled it up as small as possible, and walked it to the kitchen trash.

"Look who's talking," Paige said, and she flicked on

the TV. "You're the one who spent the last three months fixing up the entire house."

Lizzie spent the next hour cooking pancakes, eggs, and sausage. Squeezing fresh oranges for juice. Making the coffee. She took her time, hoping there might be a third at the table.

There wasn't.

Neither one of them ate a bite. Lizzie was starting to panic, but she knew she couldn't show it.

"I'm going back to watch TV," Paige insisted, pushing back her chair from the full table.

"Sit with me awhile. It's Christmas."

Paige crossed her arms and flung her feet onto the table. The leaf didn't fall, and Paige seemed disappointed. "Did Tay fix everything in this stupid house?" she asked.

"Not everything," Lizzie said. *Just me.* Or had she fixed him? Not yet. He still was going to leave. She glanced back out the window. Where was Ethan? Waiting for him to arrive today was going to be torture.

"You know, Mom, if you love Tay, that's cool. 'Cause I might go with Dad."

Lizzie took a calming breath. She kept her eyes on the falling snow outside, but she could feel Paige getting fidgety. Lizzie went to the tree and brought back a small package. "Open it."

It was a passport.

"It came two weeks ago, but I wanted to save it for today," Lizzie said. "Oh, and look! A present for me, too!" She pulled out an identical package and opened it. "What d'ya know? A passport for me!"

Paige's face lit up. "Awesome. Totally awesome. I

thought maybe it hadn't come. Mom, will you come with us? Just till I get settled in Geneva?"

"No. And we're not making any plans. Ethan hasn't even shown up yet. I just wanted to prove to you that I could leave if I wanted to. I'm open to whatever the future brings just like you." She said it, but she didn't really mean it. Sure, maybe she'd go and help Paige settle in Europe if that's how things ended up. But she wasn't leaving Galton. Not for Ethan and not for Tay. Too much of her was here.

"You wish for what you want, and you get it," Paige said, her voice full of triumph.

"You wish for what you want, and you might get it or you might not," Lizzie said. Her stomach was tight, wondering what was holding up Ethan. "But what's important is that you know what you want."

"Whatever."

"No, really, this is important, Paige. Sometimes, you think you want something, and you don't really."

"If you're talking about Dad, just spit it out," Paige said.

"I'm sort of talking about your dad. But I'm also talking about me. I think I wanted a lot of things for the wrong reason. And until I figured out what was standing in my way, I couldn't understand what I really wanted."

"You're totally weird, Mom," Paige said. "I know what I want and I'm going to get it. I want to be the best snowboarder in the world. And I can't do that in this stupid town, with crappy equipment, on a second-rate mountain."

Lizzie swallowed the insult. It hurt, but it hurt more to limit her. "Oh, Paige. I hope your father can help you. All I'm saying is that you need to be really, really careful what you wish for. Wishing for him to help you is okay. But you have to realize that you can do it on your own, too. We don't need men to make our dreams come true."

"I think I hear the violins," Paige said before she went back upstairs, leaving Lizzie alone to contemplate how her life was about to change.

By two, the passport didn't seem like the best idea. Paige had given up pretending that she didn't care whether Ethan showed or not, and had seated herself wrapped in a quilt in the dining room window seat, staring out over the freshly fallen snow, the passport on her lap.

Lizzie went upstairs and stared out her bedroom window. She was getting angrier and angrier with Ethan. Why had he not at least called?

By three, Paige had opened two more presents, but she might as well have been opening junk mail. She didn't even blink at the gift certificate for the ritziest snowboarding store in town that Lizzie had spent way too much money on. It ended up on the floor with the wrapping paper where Paige tossed it before scurrying back to her seat at the window.

By five, Lizzie was in full-blown panic. As much as Paige tried to hide it, her eyes were wet with tears and she was snuffling in her blankets.

Lizzie called in reinforcements. Annie and Tommy came with Meghan. But their nervous chatter and forced merrymaking didn't help.

"Damn him," Lizzie whispered to Annie in the kitchen. "Why couldn't he have given me a phone number or something?"

"Because he's a bastard?" Annie suggested.

"I don't know if Paige can handle much more of this. I don't know if I can either."

By eight, they all sat silently in the living room, the blue light of the TV overwhelming the colored, twinkling lights of the tree. Ripped wrapping paper covered the floor. Paige lay prone on the couch, shredding every piece of paper she could get her hands on. The pile of shredded paper on the floor was growing alarmingly tall. At least Lizzie had rescued the gift certificate before Paige could shred that. Lizzie had also snatched Paige's passport and shoved it into a kitchen drawer for safekeeping before it could be absentmindedly destroyed.

By ten, Annie and Tommy had left with a sleeping Meghan. "I'll have Tommy hunt him down and shoot him on sight," Annie assured Lizzie, but no one even smiled.

Tommy patted her shoulder. "Call us. We'll come running."

Eleven came and went.

"Maybe his plane was delayed," Lizzie said to Paige, stroking her head. "The snow. You know. It might be worse in New York City. Or there might be a blizzard in Switzerland. Maybe his plane never took off." The girl lay on the couch in the same position she'd been in for hours.

"He could call," Paige pointed out.

He could go to the lowest levels of hell and die a painful death over and over and over again for all eternity.

Lizzie covered Paige with quilts. The hot chocolate she'd placed in front of her hours ago was ice cold. She wanted to punch something—or better yet, someone. How could he do this to Paige?

"He's not coming, Mom," Paige said finally. "I was such a stupid little kid."

"Anything could have happened," Lizzie assured her. "Let's not give up on him yet."

"Why not?"

Because I want you to keep believing that your wishes will always come true. "Come to bed."

"I'm going to sleep here."

"Okay." Lizzie looked out the window one last time for the ratbastard. "I'm going upstairs to bed. Come up if you want." Paige hadn't climbed into Lizzie's bed in years, but tonight it seemed like the right thing to offer.

"It's not fair," Paige said before Lizzie had gotten to the stairs. "Everything is perfect. The house. The tree. I even perfected my 720 flip. I made everything perfect and wished for it with all my heart and it didn't come true."

"Maybe everything is perfect even without him here," Lizzie suggested. "Maybe you don't need him to get your wish. Maybe all your hard work by yourself and your dedication is enough."

Paige rolled her eyes. "It's like getting ready for the Olympics, then missing your event. It's not perfect. Not even close."

CHAPTER

43

*W*as it wrong for Tay to admit that he hated Christmas? All the celebration around him made his solitude, usually silent and deep, a thing that flashed and beeped in alarm. He tried to lie low most of the day. Nothing was worse than having other people notice that you were flashing and beeping. He made it through *It's a Wonderful Life* on two channels, then the *Frosty the Snowman* marathon, but by nighttime, he'd grown too restless to stay in.

He'd go for a drive. On Christmas night in a college town, the roads would be deserted and he could drive as slowly as he pleased without cars honking and drivers giving him the finger. White slipped out the door with him as he left, so he scooped her up. "C'mon, girl. We'll take a midnight ride, you and me. See if we can spot Santa on his way back to the North Pole. Catch us some reindeer."

When Tay had first come to Galton, he'd gotten into the bad habit of checking the parking lot for Candy's BMW. She parked it on the right side of the lot by her dorm, space number 465. As things developed with Lizzie, he'd stopped checking. After all, what good did it do to see her car? In the beginning, he might have hoped to catch a glimpse of her—a hope for a connection. But now, he didn't want connection.

Still, he checked.

It was there, but that didn't mean she was in the dorm alone. She could have taken a cab to the tiny local airport. She could have gotten a ride somewhere with a friend. He drove past Lizzie's diner, the one day of the year it was closed. He rode through the deserted town. He wound his way up the hill, past Lizzie's house, but there was no new car out front. Ethan better have shown up. Maybe they'd all gone out to the movies, or a late dinner. He resisted the urge to pound on the front door, or even just sit on the porch swing. This night was between Lizzie and Paige.

And a stranger named Ethan.

Annie and Tommy stood on the bridge, watching the hundred-dollar bills float away into the darkness of the gorge, one by one. Meghan was just a tiny face staring out from her snow gear, nestled in a pack against Tommy's chest, under his coat. She hadn't been able to sleep. The excitement of the holiday, and of Ethan's nonappearance, had kept Annie awake, too. So when Meghan started crying the third time, Annie decided that tonight was the night.

"This is the last one," Tommy said, holding up the last bill. "Do you want the honor?"

"I do," Annie said. She let the bill go and it floated up, then away, then it disappeared into the darkness. "I can't believe how good that felt," she said. "You were right, it was the right thing to do." She thought about the rest of the money, still hidden in Lizzie's basement. She should tell Tommy, tell him right this instant.

But he took her in his arms and said, "Annie, thank you. I can't tell you how much this means to me. Please, let's not ever let anything so stupid as money come between us."

So Annie kept her mouth shut, vowing to come back herself as soon as she could and put the money back exactly where she had found it.

Tay was finally starting to feel the effects of his midnight wandering. Maybe now he could sleep. He made his way home, swinging past the student parking lot one last time.

Candy's BMW was gone.

Tay wasn't superstitious. He didn't believe in signs. And yet, it was hard to ignore the feeling in his gut: Something was wrong. Why would Candy leave her dorm between 11:31 and 12:10 on Christmas night? Maybe she was getting a liter of Diet Coke. A pack of smokes. Did kids still get packs of smokes?

He had no reason to worry.

And yet, he worried.

There was no one else to worry.

He drove off the empty campus and into the deserted town. All the stores were closed. So much for his Diet Coke theory. He drove around in circles, since there weren't many roads to explore. The snow piled on the side of the road was black with soot and gray salt and Tay thought that he'd be gone before it melted.

After he'd passed the closed campus bookstore for the fifth time, he made his way back to campus, not sure why

or what he would do when he got there. He sat in his truck,
looking at Candy's empty parking space. A red Toyota on
one side, a white Honda on the other. He blamed them
both for letting the black BMW get away. Both had bumper stickers that read *Galton Is Gorges*, as if they were
taunting him. The freezing air was silent around him
except for the chugging of his old motor. White jumped
onto his lap and looked at him as if she had something
to say.

"Aren't you supposed to talk on Christmas?" What was
that old child's tale? Did the animals talk on Christmas
Eve? Christmas Day? He had grown up with so many rel-
atives, shuttled from one to another after his parents had
died, he'd heard every version of every Christmas story
that was out there. He stroked the cat.

"Where's Candy?" he asked White.

She wasn't talking today, that's for sure.

He wished there was someone he could call. Maybe
campus security. But what would he say? A student drove
her car away?

White was getting agitated, jumping from his lap to his
headrest to the passenger's seat to the dash. Rubbing up
against him every chance she got. She must be picking up
on his anxiety. He tried to calm her by stroking her back,
but she only jumped away, annoyed. He ought to take her
home. Animals always went a little nuts in small, confined
spaces, even humans.

He rolled down the window to see if she wanted to go.
She didn't.

He swung the truck back onto the road. One more lap,
then he'd be tired enough to sleep.

He headed back across the campus bridge, then

slammed on his brakes. Unfortunately, he was going too slowly, and the small jolt was an unsatisfying expression of his alarm.

Candy's BMW was parked crookedly on the side of the road just past the bridge.

He drove past her car, his heart in his throat, knowing before he looked that the car would be empty.

He spun his car around. No squealing rubber, no tires spinning out, just a disappointing, slow, methodical U-turn. He forced himself to look toward the bridge. It was brightly lit in Galton red and white. Or maybe it was Christmas red and white. There was someone in the shadows, by the guardrail.

Nausea overcame him, but he kept his foot on the gas, fighting off the sensation. He pulled his truck onto the bridge as fast as he could, which was maddeningly slow, slower than usual—if that was even possible.

He said a prayer as the truck crawled toward the person by the guardrail. His hands were shaking so badly, he could barely keep them on the wheel.

Please let it be her. Please let her still be alive.

CHAPTER

44

Tay climbed cautiously out of the truck, leaving the door hanging open behind him. White followed him out, but he didn't have time to worry about her. "Candy?" The frigid air turned his words to vapor.

The person turned, but it wasn't a person. It was two people, arm in arm.

"Sorry," Tay said. "I thought you were someone I knew."

The couple wished him a Merry Christmas, then hurried over the bridge and off toward campus.

Tay tried to start breathing again. It wasn't easy.

But where was Candy?

Tay vaulted the rail separating the road where he stood from the pedestrian path. Tay peered over the edge, trying to see into the blackness below.

He moved down the bridge. "Candy?" he called. The lights on the bridge made the abyss below seem even darker, blackness stretching in every direction. The creek crackled under a sheet of ice. A faint glimmer reflected off the ice that clung to the cliff walls.

If Candy's car was parked here, she had to be nearby. Tay stumbled to the end of the path, but didn't see anyone. His breath had slowed to barely an inhalation. His fingers were numb from gripping the icy metal rails. "Candy?" he shouted into the darkness.

Something fluttered against the railing, caught between the spokes. Tay picked it up.

It was a crisp, new hundred-dollar bill.

Everything inside Tay froze. He couldn't move.

He stood, staring at the money, unable to understand. Had she kept the money the whole time, and just now thrown it over the bridge? Or was this a random hundred-dollar bill, nothing to do with any of them?

Throwing yourself over the railing will not help find her faster, Tay reminded himself. Maybe he could climb over the *Trail Closed for Winter—Warning—Dangerous Conditions* sign and slide down the path . . .

Please, don't let anything happen to her. I can't do this again.

Tay tried not to be sick as he thought of the darkness below them.

And then he heard a scream.

CHAPTER

45

Tay spun around. He couldn't see anyone.

"Candy!" Tay looked around desperately. He crossed to the other side of the bridge where the cry had come from.

No one was there.

Then Tay looked down.

Candy had climbed over the railing. She sat on a thin ledge, her feet dangling into the darkness. She was wearing only jeans and a T-shirt despite the frigid cold. The wind blew her hair over her face. She was gripping the grate below her in terror.

White sat next to her, licking her paws.

"Candy?" he said softly, terrified to scare her.

"That cat—it came out of nowhere. Scared me to death. I almost fell."

Tay felt his knees buckle, but somehow he kept upright. *Stupid cat. What if?* He wanted to reach down to Candy, but he didn't dare. What if he startled her? Obviously, she didn't know who he was. If she knew, what would she do?

He pulled his hood around his face as tight as he could. "Sorry. It's my cat. I've been out looking for her." He wasn't sure why he said that, except that he wanted to say anything, anything at all to keep her talking.

He stepped back into the shadows. If she saw his face now—

No. That couldn't happen.

Candy started to cry. "I wanted to die. And then the stupid cat scared me and I almost went down. And I didn't want to go anymore. I don't want to die. Oh, God, I don't want to fall down there."

"No one's going down there," Tay said. "Let me help you. Don't move until I've got you, okay?"

Candy nodded and Tay leaned forward and lifted the terrified girl off the ledge and over the rail.

White hopped up behind her, cool as a cucumber.

Tay stood watching but with his head lowered, his hands shaking, his heart pounding. He didn't dare to move, to breathe. She was safe. That was all that mattered. Now he just had to get out of there before she noticed who he was.

"Can I call someone—the police, an ambulance? A friend?"

"I don't have a friend," she said.

"I can't just leave you here alone."

She shrugged and got out her phone. She dialed someone.

He pulled off his coat and put it around her shoulders, then quickly turned his back to her, pretending to be blocking the wind.

"Georgia?" Candy asked. Then she started to cry.

Tay watched her sob as long as he could bear, then he gently took the phone.

Was this the Enemy Club Georgia? Tay wasn't sure, but he told the person on the other end of the line what was happening, and Georgia explained that she was Candy's psychiatrist. "I'm going to call the police," he said.

"No. Wait. She's safe now?" Georgia asked. "She doesn't look like she's going to try anything?"

"That's what she said, but—"

"But now she looks okay?"

"If she tries anything, I'll stop her," he said. Tay wasn't sure how much longer he had before she noticed who he was.

Georgia said, "Let me talk to her."

Tay handed the phone back to Candy. The girl nodded, mumbled a few words he couldn't catch, then gave him back the phone.

"Okay," Georgia said to him. "Wait with her. I'll be right there. I don't think the police are best able to deal with these things. She's not in danger right now. She's okay if you stay with her. I'm sure of it. Just stay there."

Tay didn't know how to say he couldn't wait with her, that he was the last person in the world who could wait with her.

But Georgia had already hung up.

"It's you," she said as they walked to the end of the bridge. They sat on a snow-covered bench to wait for Georgia.

Tay was shocked. Had she known all along? "It's me."

"How did you find me?"

"I saw your car at the end of the bridge. I was looking for it, to tell you the truth."

"Why?"

White put her front paws on his legs, digging in her claws. He picked her up and she settled into his lap. "Because sometimes, Christmas sucks."

"It does," Candy agreed. "Sometimes."

"I've been meaning to leave town," Tay explained. "I'm sorry I didn't. I was going to find the money and go."

"There's always tomorrow," Candy said.

"There is," he said.

"I'm joking. Don't leave. Stay with that woman I saw you with at the restaurant. You looked happy. Someone should be happy."

"Not me," Tay said, and the girl didn't disagree.

They watched the headlights of a car approach.

"Did you find the money?" she asked.

"Nope."

"Well, I guess we're even now," she said.

He looked down at White. He took his hands off her and waited for her to jump away and slink off into the night.

She didn't budge.

"I'm not sure we are," he said.

The headlights grew bigger. A white Lexus screeched across the bridge. It pulled to a stop next to them. A short woman in slippers and a bathrobe jumped out and took Candy into her arms.

Tay left the two women to talk.

He walked slowly back across the bridge to his truck, White trotting behind him. They climbed in and Tay started his motor, but he couldn't make himself drive away. All the terror he had felt on the bridge washed over him in a wave and he put his head down on the steering wheel and tried to breathe.

A rap on his window startled him out of his stupor. How long had he been sitting there?

It was Georgia.

He rolled down his window.

"I could bring Candy back to my house," Georgia said. "But I'm leaving tomorrow for the Caribbean. She can't be alone in the dorms. All her friends are away. She doesn't have any family. I could take her to the campus health center, but it's not the best place on Christmas. Too depressing."

Tay couldn't follow. What could she want from him? "Look, Candy would rather jump over that railing than lay eyes on me again."

"I know. I know the whole story. I know who you are, Tay. Candy told me. I would never suggest such a thing. I want her to go to Lizzie's."

"Lizzie's?" He shook his head.

"Call Lizzie. I ran out without my cell phone and I don't have her number. I'll head over right now, but could you warn her we're on our way?"

"Ethan came today. It might not be the best night for Lizzie."

"Oh, God. You're right. How could I have forgotten?" Her hesitation only lasted a moment. "But Lizzie will understand. She'll understand like no one else. I really think it's best. Trust me. This is the right thing to do."

"I'll call Lizzie," Tay agreed. But he felt pretty rocky about the whole situation. "Hey, Georgia—you've known about the money all along."

"I have."

"Thank you for not telling anyone what you knew about me and the money. The way this town works, the news would have spread like wildfire and everyone would have been searching those gorges."

"Patient confidentiality is important, Tay. But that doesn't mean I didn't warn Lizzie about you. A man who thinks that money will make a difference! Really. How lame. I told her to stay away." She paused. "I think I might have been wrong, though."

Lizzie answered the phone on the first ring. She had been wide awake, watching the minutes flip by on her red, glowing clock as she lay in bed contemplating whether it was better for Paige if Ethan was dead or if he had a terrible disease that kept him away—leprosy, maybe.

When she heard Tay's voice, she was both disappointed and relieved. She waved off Paige, who had appeared at her door the instant the phone rang.

"Georgia is on her way to your house," Tay said. "She needs a favor."

"Georgia Phillips? What are you talking about?" Lizzie looked out her window. The night was deadly quiet. "Ethan didn't show up."

"Bastard. How's Paige?"

"Awful." Lizzie let her head fall back on the pillows.

"I think your night is about to get more awful. Georgia needs you to look after Candy tonight."

"Candy? The girl who—?" Lizzie stopped. She sat up. "Tay?"

"I'm sorry. I feel like I got you wrapped up in this. I know it's the worst night this could be happening. Especially now."

Lizzie got out of bed and went to the window, Paige right behind her. A set of headlights turned onto their road. "I don't understand this, Tay." Paige darted out of the room and down the stairs before Lizzie could stop her. "Oh, hell."

"In a nutshell, Candy was maybe going to jump off the Main Campus Bridge. She has nowhere to go. For some reason, Georgia thinks that you're the one person in Galton who should take her in."

Lizzie heard a car door open outside. "This really isn't a good night." She had to tell Paige that the car wasn't her father's, but she couldn't bear to go downstairs and deliver one more disappointment. "Georgia has to keep her."

Lizzie watched the women approach. The doorbell rang. Where was Paige?

"I'll talk to you later," Lizzie said, clicking her phone shut. She took a deep breath.

Paige was sitting halfway down the stairs, staring straight ahead at nothing. "I'm sorry it's not him," she told Paige. She put her hand on her head as she passed, but Paige didn't respond.

Lizzie opened the door. She didn't know which teenager looked more distraught.

Candy looked past Lizzie at Paige on the stairs. They stared at each other, first confused, then resigned, as if to say, *Oh, so this is the house of the miserable teenagers. Welcome, join the fun.*

Lizzie met Georgia's gaze and just like that, she guessed at the truth.

Georgia nodded slightly.

Every cell in Lizzie's body went out to Candy. "Come in," she said, opening the door wider. "We've got you."

"You look like you need coffee," Paige said, surprising Lizzie by coming down the stairs and taking Candy by the arm. She walked her to the kitchen.

"Thank you." Georgia tried to look past Lizzie. She lowered her voice to a whisper. "Where's Ethan?"

"Scum didn't show," Lizzie whispered back.

"Oh, hell. I'll call first thing tomorrow." Georgia was studying the foyer rag rug closely. She didn't seem inclined to leave. "Merry Christmas."

Lizzie looked at her watch. "Too late for that."

CHAPTER

46

*L*izzie joined the girls in the kitchen. She'd never seen anyone look more forlorn.

Well, she had once, years ago. When she'd looked at herself in the mirror, pregnant and abandoned by the boy she thought was the love of her life. Paige moved around the kitchen as if in a daze, fixing coffee and taking out all the Christmas cookies she could find.

Candy just stared at the vast assortment of cookies. She sipped at her coffee. Then, all at once, her face crumbled. "I don't know what I'm going to do," she said, bursting into tears.

"You're going to have your baby and be a great mother," Lizzie said.

Candy looked up, shocked into silence. The tears kept falling.

"Don't worry. Georgia didn't tell me. I just knew. I think that's why she brought you here. She knew I would understand. Candy, you're going to be okay. I promise. If I did it, anyone can."

"It's true," Paige said. "She's totally lame." Then her coolness melted away and she couldn't help asking Lizzie, "You could tell she was pregnant?"

Lizzie stiffened at the girl's lack of grace, but she nodded.

"How?" Paige was trying to glance at Candy's stomach, but the table hid it.

"Because that's pretty much how I looked when I found out. Here, have a Christmas Wreath butter cookie. Both of you. Me, too."

Candy took one and bit it listlessly. Paige did the same.

"See. Progress already. We'll work this out."

The next morning, Tay tapped on the back door at seven. Lizzie was in the kitchen on her second cup of coffee.

"I have bagels," he said.

Lizzie let him in as quietly as she could so as not to wake Paige or Candy. She had finally coaxed them into bed after three in the morning.

"Still no Ethan?"

"I could kill that bastard. Or, worse, I can't 'cause he's not here," she whispered.

Tay put the bagels on the table. "Merry day after Christmas." He leaned against the cabinets.

Lizzie sank her back against the cabinets next to him, hip to hip. Tay slipped his hand behind her back and ran his fingers up and down her spine.

"Paige liked her screwdriver. You really shouldn't have."

"It's guaranteed for life."

"What happened last night?" Lizzie asked. She'd heard

an incoherent story from Candy, and was curious for the real thing.

Tay told her about the strange night on the bridge. "She's okay, right?"

"Sort of." Lizzie told him about the long night of weeping teenagers. As she finished, Paige, ashen and wrapped in a quilt, appeared in the doorway. Tay let his hand slide back to his own side.

Paige asked, "Just him, huh?"

"Sorry," Tay said. Candy was going to be even sorrier to see him when she came down. "I ought to go."

He could feel Lizzie stiffen at his side. "Go, go?"

"No. I have to pack. Clean out the cabin. I'll come back to say good-bye."

Lizzie shook her head. "No. You belong here, too, Tay." She felt deeply for Candy, but she also felt for Tay. "You saved her life, doesn't that make you guys even?"

"I don't feel even," Tay said.

"Me either," Paige said. "I'm mad! Stupid men!"

Lizzie watched her daughter carefully. "It's okay to be mad. Ethan is a scumbag for not showing up."

"I'll be right back." Paige rose in her quilt cocoon. To Lizzie's surprise, she plodded down the basement steps, still wrapped in the blanket.

"What is she doing? You think I should follow her?" Lizzie asked. Would her daughter dig a hole through the foundation and tunnel to Geneva? She surely wasn't doing laundry. Lizzie's stomach was tight.

"I never gave you your Christmas present," she said to Tay. "It's still under the tree."

Tay smiled. "Maybe you could bring it by later? I don't feel right opening presents now."

"Tay, you saved her life," Lizzie insisted again. "Why doesn't that make you feel better?"

"I have no idea," he said. "I've been wondering that myself, believe me. If that wasn't the ultimate good deed to clear my conscience, what is? It's been driving me nuts, Lizzie. I wish I understood."

"Me, too," Lizzie said. She worried for him so much, but there didn't seem to be an answer. "When are you going?"

"I told you, I'll stay till Ethan comes. I'll stand by my word." He paused. "For a week."

Lizzie shook her head, but just then, Paige came up the stairs, still wrapped like a mummy in her quilt.

"You okay?" Lizzie asked.

Paige grunted and went up to her room. The door clicked shut behind her.

"Think she's going to be okay?" Lizzie asked.

"If any of us will, she's the one," Tay said. "I better go. I'm the last person Candy's going to want to see when she wakes up. I just wanted to make sure you were okay. Merry day after Christmas. I'm sorry that Santa brought you all this crap. I won't leave till we talk. And if I catch that Santa dude, I'll tell him you have a valid complaint."

Lizzie said, "Nah. Not his fault. I got what I wanted. Paige is still here. That was all I ever wanted. What I really wished for. I should be happy." She could feel herself starting to cry and she fought it. She had so many people right now who needed her to be strong.

"Let's talk later, okay, Tay? You better go."

CHAPTER

47

$\mathcal{L}$izzie brought a breakfast tray to the guest room. Oatmeal with maple syrup. Coffee. Toast. A small glass of orange juice. They had to start talking about Candy's getting enough folic acid during pregnancy. They had to talk about so many things.

She knocked lightly on the door of the room that had been Lizzie's when she was a girl, then pushed her way in cautiously. Candy's eyes were still rimmed with red. Folic acid was the least of this kid's worries.

"I'm not hungry," Candy protested as Lizzie set the tray down. "But thanks. And thanks for letting me stay here last night. I'm so embarrassed. I can totally go back to the dorm. This is humiliating."

"You can't." Lizzie kept her voice neutral. "It would be too depressing. Think of yourself as a distraction for Paige and me from our own problems."

"You know Dante Giovanni," Candy said. "You're his girlfriend. This is weird. Freakish, even."

"Georgia is an old friend of mine. That's why you're here. Not because of Tay."

"I wasn't going to kill myself on that bridge," Candy said, breaking into Lizzie's thoughts. "I was just freaked out, that's all. See, I had thrown some money off that bridge awhile back." Candy sipped her coffee, then put it back down. "A lot of money."

"I know about the money."

Candy went on. "I didn't think about the future when I tossed that money, all I could think about was the past. Also, I thought about what an ass that guy was for thinking the money would matter. Sorry, I know he's your boyfriend, but really. Paying me for what happened?"

Lizzie nodded. She thought Candy was being a little harsh, but she was a kid and she'd had one heck of a crappy year. "He didn't know any better. He doesn't have any family. He didn't know how to act. He was trying. You have to give him credit for that."

Candy nodded. "I didn't care a bit about that stupid money. Even if they were threatening to take my car and kick me out of school. I wanted to get kicked out. I wanted that stupid car gone. But then all of a sudden—" She touched her stomach. "Anyway, I wasn't going to do anything dumb on the bridge. I was just there to think. I had to get out of my dorm. I'd watched stupid *It's a Wonderful Life* like five times."

"That might make me want to jump off a bridge, too." Lizzie went to the window. Snow had started falling again and it looked very peaceful outside. Too bad inside was a different story. Lizzie felt as if events were spiraling into a perfect storm that would hit as soon as this calm cleared.

"So what's with your boyfriend hanging around in

Galton, anyway? Has he been spying on me? It totally creeped me out to see him last night. Like a ghost."

"He means well," Lizzie said. "He didn't want to leave until he found the money. He's been looking for months."

"No way."

"Way."

"He didn't find it?" Candy asked.

"Nope." Lizzie paused. "Do you know where it is?"

"I think I might," Candy said. "I was going to go down there. I forgot they closed off the trails in the winter. I was too scared to climb the fence."

"You don't think anyone else found it by now?"

Candy's face fell. "I have no idea. Probably. Maybe some animals found it and are using it to line their burrow. The world's ritziest raccoon den."

Lizzie felt awful for the girl. "Why didn't you call the police?"

"I wanted to keep it all," Candy said. "I was greedy. It's all I've got. If I called them, I'd pay taxes and probably have to give it all to my mom's creditors and I'd be right back where I started."

Lizzie had no idea what the rules about money and creditors were, but she supposed Candy might be right.

"Is he nice?" Candy asked.

Lizzie was relieved and surprised by the change of subject. "Very nice."

"I still don't want anything to do with him."

"I get that. It's okay, he's leaving."

"Leaving?"

"Yep. He had planned to leave today."

"You're in love with him?" Candy asked.

"Yes," Lizzie said. "But I don't want it to come between you and me. I won't talk about him if you don't want to."

"What do you think I should do? Forgive him? Just like that?"

"I don't know. That's up to you."

Candy considered. "It's like the one thing I control. I can't turn back the past. But I can hold on to it. You know?"

"Yeah. I guess." Lizzie thought about Jill's telling her secret about Ethan, about Ethan not coming. "You can also let the past go. You control that, too."

"I guess. But then, I don't know, if I do let the past go, what do I have left?"

"The future?" Lizzie suggested.

CHAPTER

48

The knock on the door startled Tay. He'd been staring at the ceiling, thinking about a day when he was ten, when his mother had helped him with his math homework while a pot of homemade chicken soup simmered on the stove. It was one of the last memories he had of his mother before the car accident that took her life. Now he couldn't remember what she looked like, couldn't smell the soup.

He opened the door to find Lizzie on the doorstep. "Since you're too scared to come to my house to get your Christmas present, I decided I had to bring it to you," she said.

"Merry Christmas to me," he said, trying to put his eyes back into his head. His bags were packed; he had cleaned up the place; he was sick about leaving when Lizzie's life was so up in the air and sick about staying when Candy was living in her house. There didn't seem to be any right way to handle this.

But right now, he wasn't thinking about what was right.

She teetered into the apartment, turning to and fro, showing off her red, four-inch stilettos. Her long, strong legs stuck out from under her coat.

"You could have broken your head open on all that ice outside in those heels," he said.

Lizzie ignored him. She opened her purple faux-fur coat to reveal the rest of his Christmas present.

"Oh, my my." He took her into his arms, his heart beating madly. "I'm very very angry at you for risking your neck out there."

"So punish me."

He didn't want to rush this. It could be one of the last times they were together. His mood fell. He said. "Where are Paige and Candy?"

"Outside," Lizzie said. Then she mercifully took his hands. "Kidding. Sheesh, Tay, you should have seen your face. Tommy and Annie agreed to stay at the house tonight. They're fine. Everybody's fine. Don't worry, they're all stuck at the house. I took their car."

"I love those guys," he said. He stood before her and took her hands. "I love you."

"Prove it," she said.

His heart was pounding out of his chest. He led her down the hall to his bedroom, then watched her stretch out on his futon. He looked around at the bare room, exactly as it was when he came. Nothing had changed and everything had changed and why was he leaving again? "Why do you put up with me?"

"I have no idea." She paused. "Well, one idea." She reached for him and pulled him down beside her.

He pressed his body into hers and moaned and she moaned. "This is going to take all night," he said.

"Promise?"

He propped himself up on one elbow and looked down at her. "Promise."

She traced his lips with her finger. "Tay, before we do this, I want to tell you something. I'm done with the past. I'm sick of it. I'm all about the future, now." She paused and he felt his heart skip a beat.

He lay back beside her on the bumpy mattress. He understood what she was saying, and she was right, but there wasn't anything he could do about it. "I wish I could get over this, believe me."

"What do you think it'll take? I mean, there's no rush or anything. Go. Travel the world. Fix everything in your path and save stray cats—whatever it takes. But I just wonder: At some point, do you think you'll get past this?"

"I hope so."

She looked up at him. "Candy thinks she knows where the money landed when it went off the bridge. She said it didn't go into the water. That it caught on a ledge. She was going to go down and look for it herself, but she's afraid of the closed trails after her scare on the bridge."

Tay sat up straight. "I'll get it."

"You can't get it if you leave."

"I'll stay until I get it," he said. "But Liz, I'm still leaving."

"I know."

"Lizzie?"

"Yeah?"

"Can we stop talking about me leaving?" He hooked the straps of her teddy through his index fingers and pulled them down her shoulders. He pushed the fabric down, and then bent to take her breasts in his mouth one by one.

"Hmm...I already forget what we were talking about," she said.

"We were talking about how beautiful you are." He bent to put his mouth to her nipple. He teased it, playing with it under his tongue until it hardened and puckered. He pulled her teddy all the way down. "God, you're amazing. This is the real present. The rest is just wrapping."

"Mmm..." She pulled at his shirt and he paused to rip it off over his head. He slipped out of his jeans and boxers. Then helped her out of the teddy. He lay beside her, feeling the heat of her body transfer into his, warming him. He hoped that he was warming her. He could feel himself go hard, and he rolled closer to her and she felt it, too, and murmured.

He prepared the condom, then moved over her and then into her and then moved with her while she arched and groaned and finally cried out his name. He held her while she shook gently.

He came, too, and it was as amazing as ever. Why was he leaving this woman?

He held her, wondering if that was the last time they'd ever make love. When he left, would she wait for him? How long would she wait? He imagined Candy in Lizzie's house. Candy didn't have a home. Galton was as much a home as anywhere for the girl. What if she stayed forever? Would Lizzie ever leave Galton to be with him somewhere else?

He'd find her money, give it to her, and go.

He stroked Lizzie's arm. He wanted this night to be perfect. For it to go on forever. "Liz?"

No answer.

"Lizzie?"

She had fallen asleep, exhausted from her marathon night of tending to the girls.

He kissed the top of her head and smiled.

Perfect.

He tried to close his eyes, but he knew it was hopeless, so he watched her. She deserved more. She deserved everything. In the beginning, when they first met, she had thought that she was his charity case.

Funny how the tables turned.

But there had to be hope. There had to be a way.

He'd get the money back tomorrow. But he knew it wouldn't solve what needed solving. He'd still have to leave Galton to spare Candy the pain.

And he didn't know how long Lizzie would wait for him.

Or how long he could live without her.

CHAPTER

49

The next morning, Lizzie came home with White and Dune to an almost silent house.

Annie was in the kitchen, trying to keep Meghan quiet by reading her *Green Eggs and Ham*. When the baby saw Lizzie and the animals, she screeched a welcome. "Shhhh..." Lizzie put White down and released Dune from his leash. She took Meghan into her arms and held her tight while she spun around. "How's my little one? Shhhh..."

Meghan giggled.

Annie tossed the book across the table. "I've been reading that thing over and over for hours. Candy sure can sleep."

"I vaguely remember those days," Lizzie said.

"I don't," Annie said. "So, are these your hostages?" She motioned to the animals, who were sniffing around the kitchen. Dune was licking Meghan's chair, cleaning up the fallen crumbs of whatever she'd had for breakfast. "Tay can't leave while you have his crew?"

"Yep," Lizzie said. "I'm only sort of kidding," she admitted. "Tay's going to be busy all day, so I said I'd take the dog. The cat seems to think she's a part of the deal." She knelt with Meghan so the baby could pat the dog. White disappeared upstairs to check her territory.

"Paige went boarding with her friends," Annie said. She started to straighten the kitchen. "I figured you'd say it was okay. I thought it was good for her to get out of the house. They left an hour ago." The clock read 8:33 in the morning.

"No Ethan?"

Annie shook her head.

"Maybe he'll come today." It was the first thought that flew into her consciousness when she woke up in the morning and the last worry when she closed her eyes at night. Flights got canceled. Cars broke down.

"Any number of things could have happened," Annie said.

"The ratbastard could have called."

"So, let's talk about good men. How's Tay?"

"Perfect. Except he still says he's leaving just as soon as—" She stopped herself. She still hadn't told anyone about Tay's money. "—everything settles."

"You have to stop him," Annie said. She looked at her watch. "When a man leaves, there's no guarantee he'll ever come back."

"No one knows that like me, Annie," Lizzie said. The truth of Annie's words stung.

"Shoot. We have Mommy and Me swimming at the Y in twenty minutes. You okay here?"

"Fine, go."

"Liz, I'm so sorry. I've been thinking about what I

can do. I'm going to do something to help Paige, I just haven't figured out what yet."

"Just being here helped," Lizzie said. "Helped both of us. Thank you."

Lizzie checked in on Candy, who was sound asleep in the guest room. Poor thing had the beginnings of morning sickness and was best off if she just let the mornings go by.

So she went downstairs.

Paige's board, Figgy, wasn't in its usual spot of honor, propped against the wall by the front door. That was good. Christmas break was, after all, prime snow season. Paige and her friends liked to be there for the first lift up the mountain for the freshest snow, and by now, the mountain had been open for over an hour. Lizzie tried Paige's cell phone, just to say hi, but there was no answer. The reception on the mountain was terrible. She knew that. Something about the terrain blocked the signals.

No worries. She'd back off. Let Paige have her space.

Still, she wished she were here.

Lizzie fixed more coffee.

Tay called awhile later. He had gone to the gorge, climbed the fence, looked where Candy had said, but hadn't found anything. "The snow and ice made it kind of dicey. I couldn't get anywhere near the edge. We might have to wait for spring."

"Would you wait for spring?"

"I don't know, Lizzie. I'm having a hard time leaving. And I'm having a hard time staying, too."

"If you leave, Tay, I'm afraid you'll never come back," she said, echoing Annie's words.

"So let's take advantage of today," he said. "Let me drive you out to the mountain to see Paige. I'm sure Annie could come back to sit with Candy. We could be there in twenty minutes, right? It's just the next town over."

"The way you drive, we won't be there till next week," she joked. "Anyway, I should give her some space. No need to go crazy on her." Lizzie fought off the growing sense that something was wrong. "I talked to her best friend's mom and she told me they were coming home at five. I can wait."

But it wouldn't be easy.

Lizzie vacuumed the living room. Cleaned the fridge. Candy came down and made herself a nest on the couch in front of the television. Lizzie kept waiting for Paige to call her back. Didn't she wonder if Ethan had shown up?

Finally, Paige sent a text. *Snow gr8. Fun. Text if RB comes.*

So Ethan had become Ratbastard again. It made Lizzie sad instead of glad.

Maybe she would take Tay up on his offer of a ride. Just to check in on her. Maybe even to see her board. She hadn't seen her snowboard all season, and with all her private lessons, she must be getting good.

At two o'clock, Lizzie started making chicken enchiladas, Paige's favorite meal. After a day on the slopes, she'd be starving. They'd eat and laugh and forget Ethan and things would start to get back to normal.

She assembled the enchiladas, then put them in the fridge. She'd bake them as soon as Paige came in the door.

She wandered around a bit, cleared the presents from

under the tree, put everything away. The gift certificate she had gotten Paige was still in its box. She took it out and recycled the box. Then she opened the kitchen drawer to stash the certificate somewhere safe.

"No!"

The single word echoed in the empty kitchen.

She rifled through the drawer, trying not to panic.

Then she panicked, her heart pounding, her breath too shallow to do the job.

She picked up the phone and dialed Tay.

"Paige's passport isn't where I left it. It's gone. I need to get to Meeks Peak. Now."

CHAPTER

50

$\mathcal{L}$izzie studied every car zooming past in the opposite direction as Tay slowly wound his truck toward the mountain. Paige could be inside any one of the cars, on her way home. Which was not a problem, as Annie and Meghan were in her kitchen, waiting. They'd call the minute Paige showed up. No problems. No worries. No sense in being a crazed, overwrought mother. Such lovely barns, half-fallen, red paint peeling. Silos in the snow. Tidy little houses with rockers on the front porches, Christmas decorations everywhere. The ski patrol still hadn't found Paige, but her friends swore she was there, swore they'd just seen her on the south-side slopes, or was it the north? Such a busy time of year. So many kids looking exactly alike. No rush. No worries. To prove it, she'd promised herself she'd let Tay drive her. After all, what was the rush?

Lizzie's body felt like a tightly wound cord. She had a sense something wasn't right that she just couldn't shake.

Tay clenched the wheel in a death grip. The speed

gauge held steady at twenty-five. A Jeep passed them, beeping in anger.

She should have taken Annie's car.

No. She only got behind the wheel once in a while, and she hated driving in the snow, which had started to come down in earnest. Tay going slow was much safer. Plus, she had chosen Tay to drive her on purpose. She needed him here with her. "Tommy will call us if there's any news. No rush," she reassured Tay. Another car pulled around them. The passenger gave Tay the finger.

A sheen of sweat had broken out on his skin.

"It's okay," Lizzie said. "There's no rush. Her friends say she's there, so she's there. I bet she just wanted to show her friends her passport. It is kind of cool. I'm sure Paige is fine. Sometimes, they go off and grove ski where they're not supposed to. She'll turn up."

"I'm sorry. I thought in an emergency, I'd do better," Tay said. "We're almost there."

"But this isn't an emergency." She leaned over and kissed his cheek. It was icy cold and wet with sweat. In fact, he was sweating so badly, he looked as if he had just gotten out of the shower.

She tried not to be impatient with him. Everything was fine. The sun was starting to set, and the pink and orange sky ahead of them made her acutely aware of the passing time. "I'm sure Paige is having the time of her life with her friends. A few extra minutes won't matter."

They passed the husks of dried-up cornstalks and fields filled with cows huddling by their barns, waiting to be let in for the night. A set of headlights tailed them for less than a minute before the driver pulled out. He rolled down his passenger's window. "Learn to drive!" he shouted.

"Learn not to be an asshole!" Lizzie shouted back.

Another car tailed them for a few turns, then sped past, shooting a death glare.

"Get a life!" Lizzie yelled after them. She sat back in her seat. "This is sort of fun. Takes my mind off things," she reassured Tay. But she didn't mean it. She was ready to jump out of the truck and run the rest of the way.

They entered a small town and passed an elementary school. Tay's chest tightened to bursting as he imagined all the small children inside. They passed a car wash, a McDonald's, a physical therapist. *Fix whatever ails you,* the sign read. Wouldn't that be nice? Tay tried to breathe calmly as they drove through the sleepy town. The streetlights had come on and it looked very peaceful. He came to a slow, gliding stop at a red light. Miraculously, there weren't any cars behind them to beep and protest.

The light changed, and Tay pulled slowly into the intersection. He hated intersections most of all. The snow was getting heavy, sticking to the roads in a slick slush.

After they passed through the town, the winding country roads started getting narrower and twistier. He could only see a few feet in front of his car as the flakes thickened. Now everyone was driving as slowly as he was. He could feel his tires slide out as he took the turns, even at a crawl.

"If it keeps on coming down like this, you're going to be the fastest driver on the road," Lizzie said. She called Annie's cell for the hundredth time.

No news.

She called Paige's and left another message.

Lizzie clicked her phone shut and they rounded a corner, and Tay slammed on the brakes, sending the truck into a fishtail to the edge of the road. They skidded to an uncertain stop.

"Oh, hell," Lizzie said.

Ahead was a car, upside down in a ditch, its wheels spinning in the air. Another car was stopped diagonally across the roadway, its driver standing by the open door, a boy, one of the teenagers who had passed them earlier. But now, he didn't look quite so cocky.

"Oh, hell," she repeated.

Tay couldn't speak.

Lizzie and Tay jumped out of the truck. Tay rushed to the upside-down car. Lizzie went carefully to the stunned driver of the other car, afraid of spooking him. "Are you okay?" she asked. *Don't let Paige be here, don't let it be Paige in that other car.* Lizzie couldn't help thinking of her daughter, even while she tried not to. She was glad Tay was looking, because she couldn't even turn to face the car.

The teenager in the street couldn't speak.

"I'll call 911." Lizzie fumbled for her phone.

Tay knelt by the upside-down car. He wrestled with the door, then went to his truck. He came back with a wrench, which he smashed through the window.

The snow and Lizzie's fear muffled the sound of the glass shattering. *Don't let it be Paige...*

"Hello? I need to report an accident. We need an ambulance."

The boy started to talk, and Lizzie only half heard him as she tried to describe where they were. "I didn't even see the other car," the boy said. "The snow, it was so heavy. I don't even know what happened..."

"It's okay," Lizzie said. "Just relax. Everything's okay."

But she wasn't sure it was okay. In fact, she was pretty sure nothing was okay. The car looked bad. She tried to tell herself that none of Paige's friends drove that kind of car, but she couldn't even tell what kind of car it was.

Tay had backed away from the overturned car. He stood and stared and when her eyes met his, he shook his head ever so slightly and she tried to keep her face strong for the boy standing in the road.

She mouthed, *Paige?*

He shook his head no quickly and her heart started beating again, but barely. She started to say a silent prayer for the people in the car.

Tay couldn't take his eyes off the dead girl in the driver's seat of the car. At first, his only thought was that it would be Paige.

It wasn't. It was a stranger with long black hair, her blue eyes frozen open forever. The girl wasn't Candy, he knew that. Candy was safe at Lizzie's house. She was a stranger. But still, all he could think of was Linda Goodnight and Candy until small black spots floated in front of his eyes. He blinked them away.

It wasn't his accident. It wasn't Linda. It wasn't Candy. It wasn't Paige. It was just an accident on a snowy road. No one's fault. The universe's fault.

He closed his eyes and the awful sound of metal on metal crashed through his brain.

"Tay?" Lizzie asked. She had come up beside him. "You okay?"

The sound of sirens in the distance floated over the

hills. Another few cars had stopped behind the truck, and a small crowd was starting to form.

He opened his eyes. "She's dead," he whispered. The boy was still nearby, standing stiffly, immobile. Tay tried to go on, but he couldn't. He meant that the girl in the overturned car was dead, but it felt as if Linda had died all over again. Something was wrong with this. With him. He felt light-headed. He could hear sirens, could hear other people who were trying to figure out what to do when there was nothing at all to do but stare and pray.

"Tay?" Lizzie asked again. "Are you there?"

He took a deep breath in the warm summer air. It was so hot. He was thinking of getting home to Emily, his girl-friend. He was going to marry her. He was thinking of what he'd have for dinner. Of what a crappy day he'd had at work, with the boiler of 742 going out and having to drive all the way to the Bronx for the part he needed to fix it. What a mess. But dinner and Emily and everything that made life good was waiting for him. Out of the corner of his eye, he saw the flash of Linda Goodnight's red BMW convertible hurtling toward him at full speed. Her terrified eyes locked with his. The crunch of metal echoed through his brain as their cars collided. The sweet, sickly smell of gasoline fumes filled his nose. God, it was so hot. He couldn't breathe. What had happened? He looked around him. Glass everywhere.

"Tay?"

The wind was knocked out of him. Pieces of shattered windshield covered him like tiny jewels. He looked up at the streetlight. Red. It was red. Red for stop. But he hadn't stopped. Had been thinking about dinner, about sex, about everything but driving. Had only been thinking about himself and his pleasure. His face hurt. Was bleeding.

"Sir, are you okay? Can you hear me? There's been an accident, but you're okay."

He could see Linda's blue eyes, same as her daughter's, same as the stranger's, wide with terror. He'd see them forever. His face felt wrong, as if it was inside out. He touched his cheek, then looked at his hand, and it was covered in blood. He couldn't speak. But someone was speaking to him. He opened his eyes.

"It's okay. Just step out of the truck, sir. The medics want to look at that face."

He stumbled to the curb. The medics and firemen surrounded the other car. They looked grim. No one would meet his eyes.

He could barely stand. Couldn't find his feet. Was this really happening? What was happening?

Ambulance sirens wailed in the distance. The look on the young fireman's face as he moved away from the crushed car made him swim in and out of consciousness. No, it couldn't be.

Tay vomited in the ditch by the side of the road until he gagged. Her eyes. He was the last one to see her eyes. Her scream. Her last word was a scream. No one's last word should be a scream.

"Just sit, sir. Let them look at that cheek. You're okay. It's fine. Just an accident. Try to relax, sir."

A hand on his cheek, wet with blood.

"Tay?"

He turned to the voice. It was so cold. Why was it so cold?

He looked down at his hand. Someone was holding it. He recognized that amber ring. Lizzie.

"Tay, are you okay? Something happened. You kind of blacked out."

He was on the side of the road, Lizzie kneeling beside him. The door to his truck hung open. Police and EMTs were everywhere. A car was upside down in the snow. The snow. December, not September. Galton, not Queens. The snow was falling sideways now, covering everything as if trying to erase it.

The pain in his cheek flared.

"How did I not see that the light was red?" he said. "Why didn't I stop?"

"It's okay, Tay. I think you had a flashback. That's all. You're fine. You're here, with me. You're safe," Lizzie said. "We only found this accident. Remember? It had nothing to do with us. We're fine. We're driving to get Paige and we saw the accident after it happened."

Paige. He sat up straight.

Shit. He remembered now. What had happened to him? He pulled himself together. "No. We're not fine. This isn't fine. We have to find Paige, and instead, I'm sitting on my ass having nightmares in the snow. Let's go." He tried to stand, then fell back to the curb. "Shit, my body. I feel like I'm going to pass out."

"It's okay. Don't worry. Paige is fine; I'm sure of it. Anyway, no one's getting through this road. She's boarding on the mountain with her friends. They said she was there. They wouldn't lie. Just breathe. Tommy's on his way. He'll get us answers."

"I let you down. We have to keep going." Tay shook his head as if it were filled with water. He felt as if he'd just been through a war. "I don't know what happened to me, but I'm over it."

"Tay, stop for a minute and look at me," Lizzie insisted. She took him by the shoulders. "Look at that boy—" She pointed to the boy who had been in the other car. He sat on the bumper of a police car, his head in his hands. "Is his life over? Should it be over? What could you say to that boy?"

"Nothing."

"Nothing!" Lizzie's voice rose. "Nothing? A whole year and you've got nothing? Selling everything you own? Leaving your life behind? Losing everything? And you have nothing to say to him? What happened to Linda Goodnight was an accident. You have to forgive yourself. Right now. Right here. Tell me that you understand that. That you need to get past this. For me. For that kid. Show me that you're not just a loner, a wanderer. Because you know what, Tay, I don't have time for people like that in my life. I need people who know how to say, It was an accident, I'm sorry, and then move on. I don't have time for people living in the past. Tell that boy to forgive himself. To realize that he doesn't control the world. Accidents happen and we forgive. We forgive ourselves and we forgive each other. That's what we do, because we're human. Try it, Tay: It was an accident, I'm sorry."

"Words don't matter. They're nothing. They're empty." He forced himself to stand. He forced himself to his truck. His head was still spinning. The EMTs were loading a stretcher into the ambulance and Tay looked away and he saw the boy on the bumper of the police car. He couldn't look at him. He was him. Still? Always? Some things were unforgivable. But this wasn't the boy's fault. An accident on a snowy road in the middle of nowhere. "Let's go. We have to find Paige."

"Tay, please. Stop. Look around us. No one's going anywhere."

They sat for a while, watching the police direct cars to turn around one by one on the snowy road. Lizzie had no idea if there was another route to the mountain. They ought to turn back. Go home. Wait for Paige.

Finally, after what seemed like an eternity, Tommy pushed through the crowd, showing his badge to the police on the scene.

"You guys okay?" Tommy asked. He nodded to the police from the small town. He seemed to know most of them.

"Fine. We're fine," she said. "We came on it, maybe a minute after it happened."

"Looks bad. The roads are terrible and getting worse. My car's got the lights and chains. They'll let me through now that the scene is cleaned up," Tommy said, as if apologizing to Tay. "The roads behind us are backed up for almost a mile. I had to come down the shoulder with the lights on to get here."

Tay nodded. "Go. Hurry." He kissed Lizzie's cheek. "Be careful."

"I'm sorry, Tay," she said. "Really, I am."

She gave him a backward glance as she and Tommy hurried to his cruiser. She ducked inside and he watched them wind carefully through the accident scene, then speed off, lights and siren cutting through the freezing night.

Tay lingered, not sure why he couldn't make himself leave. They had already given their statements to the police. Lizzie was on her way to the mountain.

Then he saw the boy, alone, forgotten, leaning on the hood of a police cruiser, wrapped in a police blanket, staring into space.

Tay knew that look.

Tay went toward him. *I know how you feel, man. Something like this happened to me. Worse, because there wasn't any snow and I wasn't a kid. I was just an idiot—*

Tay stopped.

He couldn't take another step toward the boy.

I have absolutely nothing to offer.

Words were nothing. Empty. Just so much hot air.

The last thing this boy needed was to see that it never got easier—to see him.

Tay turned back to his truck, feeling a new guilt eat at him. The boy's empty eyes were seared into his memory.

Tay started his engine and backed out, away from the scene. The policeman directed him into the flow of cars turning around and he began his long, slow trip back to Galton.

CHAPTER

51

*W*hen Tay got back to Lizzie's house, Annie and Candy were in the kitchen. Annie was trying to feed something green to Meghan, who was refusing with gusto. Dune sat at the baby's feet, waiting hopefully for any offering. White sat on the counter, watching the scene with half-closed eyes.

The two women jumped up when they saw him. "Don't get up," he said. "No news." He still felt woozy from the flashback, from the eyes of the boy whom he couldn't help. If he looked in the mirror now and had gray hair and was covered in wrinkles, he wouldn't have been the least surprised.

Candy turned her back and went upstairs without a word. Tay felt the air rush back into the room as soon as she was gone.

Annie said, "You okay? You look pretty spooked."

Tay sat down at the table and rubbed Dune's neck. "Any news?"

Annie looked pretty spooked herself. "Tommy just

called. No Paige at the mountain. They talked to her friends and they admitted that she hadn't been there at all today. Tommy did his police routine, and Geena broke down and told him they had picked her up at six-thirty and dropped her at the bus terminal. She planned to somehow get to JFK Airport, then get on a plane to Geneva, Tay. By herself! To make her own dreams come true, Geena said."

Tay sank into a chair. He could feel Lizzie's panic as if she were in the room with them. He wished that he was with her. He ought to be with her.

He had to fix this before it was too late.

Was it already too late?

Annie went on. Her voice was thin and strained. "A driver at the bus depot just called Tommy back. He just got back from New York City. He said that someone who looks a lot like Paige got on his 7:00 A.M. Greyhound bus for New York City." Annie's voice caught. "He doesn't know for sure if it was her, but I think we need to take it seriously. At least we have a lead. That's good, right?"

He tried to keep his face neutral, tried to block out his growing dread. He focused on scratching Dune. "We'll find her," Tay said, hoping he sounded as if he meant it. A small-town kid with no money, no friends, trying to get to the massive, tangled airport from the vast maze of New York City didn't sound good.

"Oh, God, Tay, I hope they find her. It's not like she could get on a plane, right? I mean, she's a kid. They wouldn't let a kid get on a plane to Geneva. Right?"

"I have no idea," Tay said. He thought the plane was the least of their worries. Getting to JFK from Manhattan was no easy feat, especially from the Port Authority Bus

Terminal, a place where a lost kid was prey for all kinds of predators. Paige had no experience in the city. At least on a plane, she'd be safe. "I wouldn't think so. But they did let her on the bus. Did anyone call the airlines? See who's flying to Geneva today and when? Warn them not to let her on the plane?"

"Tommy has Jennie from the department on it," Annie said. "She's calling everyone. We'll know any minute."

"Guess that's all we can do for now," Tay said. He was itching to get into his car and go to JFK. But he knew he should wait for Lizzie.

"It's my fault," Annie said in a tiny voice that he almost didn't hear.

Tay looked up in surprise. She was weeping. A new wave of dread washed through him. "You? How do you figure that?"

"I found money, Tay. A lot of money. Oh, God, I haven't told anyone this. Not even Tommy." She executed some sort of complicated maneuver to get Meghan out of her high chair. She carried the baby to the sink, her back to Tay.

"Two hundred thousand dollars in a green duffel," Tay said. Annie had the money? Had it all along? Why didn't that make him feel any better? And why was she telling him about the money now?

Annie whipped around, sending Meghan's feet flying out in front of her. "How do you—?"

"The money was mine. Well, Candy's." He tried to focus, but his mind was on Lizzie and Paige. Who cared about the money now?

Annie blinked away her tears. She turned away from him and turned on the water in the sink. "Tay, it's gone.

Paige must have found where I hid it in the basement. She'd never have left if she didn't have money. How could she have? I feel like I'm underwater. I can't breathe." She was scrubbing Meghan's hands a little too hard and the baby started to squirm and protest.

Tay tried to clear his head. Annie had found the money, and then Paige took it? His mind slowly caught up with his body, which had gone cold with dread. "You hid the money in Lizzie's basement that day, when you said you were getting the sweater?" he said.

"Yes."

Tay remembered Paige going down into the basement the day after Christmas, wrapped in her blanket. Was the duffel under the blanket that day when she came back up? Was the kid wandering around New York with all that cash? He tried to stay calm as the bad news piled up.

"It's my fault," Annie went on. "You don't know how awful I feel. I wish I could put the money back on that cliff. Take that day back that I found it." She was really crying now. Dune was even getting agitated, whining and circling. Annie put Meghan back into her high chair and handed her a complicated rattle.

Tay wondered what it felt like to cry like that. Did it help? From the looks of Annie's makeup-smeared face, it didn't help much. But what did help?

He looked to White on the counter, sleeping, oblivious. Stupid cat. What did she care about anything?

But he wasn't any more help than the cat.

He had to act. Had to do something. Had to figure this out. Now. Here.

Annie stilled to blow her nose.

All at once, words began rushing out of him. "Every

single day, I relive the day of the accident, praying the past could be undone. But it can't. You can't dwell on what's already happened. You just have to figure out a way to move on."

She sniffled. "Have you?"

Tay touched her hand. "Look, Annie, Paige would have gone without the money. Nothing would have stopped that girl. She's an independent kid. Totally fearless. Like her mother." He picked Meghan's rattle contraption off the floor where she had tossed it and Meghan responded as if he'd given her the moon.

Annie stared at him a long moment. "I wish none of this had happened."

Tay walked to the back door. He stared out over the snow-covered lawn. He could feel every bone in his body as if it were made of lead. *Can't turn back the past. Have to figure out how to move on. Can't control the world.* He was struck by how childish Annie sounded, full of regret and self-pity.

He knew how hopeless she felt, but her wishes were impotent, silly.

She wiped her nose with the back of her hand. "If something happens to her, I'll never forgive myself."

Tay took a deep breath. He was starting to see something that he couldn't see before, as if the snow was finally clearing to reveal what lay ahead. "Yes you will. You'll have to. That's the way life is. Forgiving yourself is the most important thing you have to do to make everything right again."

She blinked up at him. He felt a strange calmness descend. Even Dune quieted and stilled.

He had to think. He walked to the dining room and

looked out for Lizzie and Tommy. The street was deserted except for Judy Roth, sweeping invisible snow from her walk in the rapidly falling dusk. Who swept snow in the dark? He waved and she waved back.

He had a feeling that woman knew more than she let on.

"Why'd you hide that money in the gorge?" Annie asked. He hadn't heard her come into the room.

"I didn't." He sat down at the dining room table. "I came to Galton to pay back a debt I owed." When he talked, she seemed to calm down a bit, so he decided to talk until Lizzie and Tommy came back. Who knows, maybe it would help them both. "I had arranged to meet Candy at the Last Chance."

Annie watched him with red, swollen eyes. But the tears had slowed. Meghan was still in her arms and she bounced her absentmindedly.

"I had quit my job, sold everything I owned, driven three hundred miles, and I was about to give a nineteen-year-old orphan two hundred thousand dollars in cash so she could stay in school."

"Because—" Annie couldn't say the words, so Tay said them for her.

"Because she was the daughter of the woman I killed." He let the words settle before he could go on. "But she wouldn't take the money. She hated me. She said she would throw it off a bridge."

"She did it." Annie's eyes went wide. She had completely stopped crying now. She looked behind her, as if Candy might be there. "It's Candy's money."

"I didn't realize right away that this whole town was a maze of gorges and bridges. I thought it was just a turn of speech, and she'd really take the money, start a new life, get me feeling better for fixing what I couldn't possibly fix with a sack of cash. As soon as I did realize, I tried to follow her. But it was too late. I had lost her."

Tay closed his eyes, reliving that morning. Rushing to the diner, but Candy and the money were gone. Driving his truck up and down the steep streets, but all the students looked the same. Finding her on campus, her hands empty, the bag gone, the smile on her face. *Fish food.*

"I had wished for a miracle, Tay. And then Meghan threw her pacifier, and there was the money. I thought it was some kind of sign." Annie laughed through her tears. "Oh, God, nothing is going right. I wanted to have stolen the money from some sicko drug dealer, and instead I stole it from a saint who was donating it to a pregnant orphan."

Tay shook his head. "I'm no saint."

"Neither am I." Annie looked past him, as if looking back in time. "I shouldn't have taken it. But, Tay, I wanted it so badly. I felt entitled to it. I felt as if I never got anything. And I was always so good. But it didn't matter. Lizzie got the house and everything in it. Lizzie got Tommy—" Annie paused at Tay's objection. "I know. It's not true. But it's what I felt then. I always got second best. The leftovers."

"No," Tay said. "I've seen the two of you together. Tommy loves you."

But Annie didn't seem to hear him. "There was the money and it was mine if I just reached out and grabbed it. It felt right, even though I knew it wasn't. I spent my whole life being good and Lizzie got everything anyway. I just wanted to be the girl who did whatever she wanted just like Lizzie so that I'd have something, too. I wanted life to be fair."

Fair. Tay considered the word.

"And now look what happened. It's all my fault. I should have helped Lizzie, and instead, I was always jealous of her. I wanted things to go wrong for her. I did. I was pretending to be her best friend when really, I was her worst enemy. And now—"

Tay watched Annie fall to pieces across the table from him.

Meghan stared at her mother for a long moment, then also burst into tears. Dune licked the baby's feet to no avail.

Tay didn't know which crying female to address. Annie rearranged Meghan in her arms and left the room with her, consoling her on the way back into the kitchen. "Poor baby, poor, poor baby." Dune trotted after them.

Tay wasn't sure if she was talking about Meghan or herself.

He sat in the empty dining room.

Damn, he could clear a room.

But he didn't have time to think about it. He didn't have much time before Lizzie and Tommy got back and they had to get to New York.

Listening to Annie's confession had made him realize exactly what he had to do, and how to do it.

He didn't have much time.

CHAPTER

52

Jay went up the stairs, steeling himself, and knocked on Candy's door.

"Not here," Candy said.

"I'm sorry," he said.

No sound from the other side of the door.

"It's not a lot, but it's all I've got, Candy. No more money. No more grief. I won't bother you anymore. The money was a mistake. I just want you to know that I'm sorry. I'll carry that moment of my life always. I'll never be the same person. I'm just so so so damn sorry. I had wanted to tell you that from day one, in the diner."

No sound. Was she even in there? Did it even matter?

He waited, hoping he'd feel the weight lift. But it didn't. Damn. Maybe he still had it all wrong. Maybe he was the world's biggest fool. What had he been thinking, that words mattered? That talking, confessing, striving for human connection could make it better?

He turned down the hallway, got to the stairs, then he

heard a door click open behind him. He turned back, holding his breath.

"So why didn't you tell me?" Candy asked.

"Because I was an idiot," Tay said. He looked her in the eye. He inhaled and exhaled and then did it again and said, "I'm sorry."

"I forgive you." Candy's voice was almost silent.

Had she even said it? His heart was pounding. Somehow, he was breathing, and it felt as if he hadn't breathed in a year. He could feel the air go in and out, smell it. Something had changed inside him.

He couldn't help himself. "You do? Really? Are you sure?" He was standing rigid, as if watching the last few seconds of a crucial football game, waiting, hoping, hands clenched, all his energy straining toward what could, maybe, just maybe, be a happy ending. If . . . if . . . a few more seconds . . .

She came out of the room and leaned against the wall. Then she sank down, so that she was sitting with her back to the wall. "I forgive you. Accidents happen. I still kind of hate you, but I forgive you anyway."

It was more than he had ever hoped for. He wanted to leap up and whoop for joy. He wanted to dance around the hallway, take her by the hands, do a jig. But he didn't, because he could see they weren't done. He could feel that they weren't done. This wasn't quite the finish line. He didn't know what to say now that he had said he was sorry, but he knew he had to keep talking, keep connecting. He didn't dare move. "Okay. Well. Thanks then."

"I want to tell you something that I've never told anyone," she said.

"You don't have to tell me anything." She didn't move,

and he felt foolish looming over her, so he sank down to sit across from her, his back to the opposite wall. *Tell me,* he thought. *Just keep talking.*

But she didn't. They sat like that for a while, not looking at each other.

"I hated my mother," Candy said finally in a tiny voice. "She was awful. We fought all the time. She drank and she manipulated people and when I heard that she had died, I was really, really sad. But I was also a little relieved. It felt awful to feel that way, but I couldn't help it."

"Oh." Tay had no idea what to say. He was new at this talking thing.

"It took a long time for me to forgive myself for feeling that way. What kind of monster doesn't care about her mother? I started seeing Georgia then. She was the first person to understand what I was going through. She told me that it was okay. That I had to forgive myself for feeling that way, because it was normal. My mother really did do terrible things. Everyone does terrible things. And it's okay to hate them, and to forgive them, too. We're all so screwed up, it doesn't make any sense to hold a grudge and ruin our lives."

Tay looked at her bare feet, her pink toenails. The big toenails had white flowers. He wanted this to be simple, but at every turn, there was so much emotion, so many twisted feelings. So much to say.

Candy went on. "When I found out I was pregnant, I understood that the worst thing in the whole world would be if I was as lousy a mother as she was." Candy ran her hand through her hair. "I couldn't be a good mother if I was miserable. That was her problem; she was so miserable. She could never let go of anything. When I was four,

I nail-polished flowers on the living room rug. The day before the accident, she was telling me how much that red stain still bothered her every single time she walked past it. I asked her why she didn't get rid of the rug, and she said that she kept it to remind herself—and to remind me—how our actions ripple on and on, forever." She paused. "Forever. That was awful to think about."

Tay nodded. He'd thought a lot about forever.

"Georgia taught me that I didn't have to live that way. I forgave myself for the rug, I forgave myself for everything. See my toes? I saw you looking at them. I didn't use nail polish at all for, like, ten years. Now I do. And after I forgave myself, I forgave her as best I could. I knew that she had trouble with depression. She struggled with alcohol. She did her best and it sucked, but it was all she could do. All she was capable of. I couldn't control it and she couldn't control it. So I forgave." She put her hand on her stomach. "Now, I'm going to have a chance to be a better mother than she was. It's a circle. A gift. It all makes sense. You have to forgive yourself, too, Tay. It's not about me forgiving you. It's about you letting it go, and moving on."

He heard a siren approach. Tommy and Lizzie were on their way back.

She leaned forward and put her hand over his. "So don't you dare be a coward and leave Lizzie. If you just keep running, you leave behind a string of wrongs. Just say you're sorry and you love her and make it right."

"She's pretty pissed at me," he said.

"We all are, dummy. So get with it, okay? Now's your chance to make it right."

CHAPTER

53

*L*izzie exploded into the kitchen, Tommy right behind her. She took one look at her sister and her body went numb. "Oh, God, she's dead." Lizzie sank into a kitchen chair.

"She's fine," Tommy assured her, taking Meghan from Annie's arms.

"Then why do you look like that?" Lizzie asked Annie.

Annie opened her mouth, then closed it.

"Tell me! What have you heard?" Lizzie asked. Her heart was pounding and she wanted to shake Annie. "Something happened."

"Speak," Tommy commanded Annie.

Tay came into the room. He leaned against the door-frame. Lizzie tried not to notice him. He was still here, but maybe he'd be gone tomorrow. She didn't have time for that now. She had to find Paige.

Annie took a deep breath. "They called. She's booked on a flight in two hours out of JFK, but they won't let her board. They haven't found her, but she'll be there soon. They will."

Lizzie watched her sister. Her spine tingled with apprehension. "But?"

"But. Lizzie. There's something I need to tell you. I hid two hundred thousand dollars in your basement. It was Tay's money. I had found it in the gorge. And it's gone. I think Paige took it."

Tommy sank into the chair across from Annie. Candy came into the room, looking worried. Tay and Candy hadn't been in a room together since Candy had come to stay with them, but Lizzie couldn't think about that now. She was floating. Paige in New York with her passport and two hundred thousand dollars in cash and a ticket to Geneva?

They all looked at her, waiting for instructions.

Lizzie had read about mothers who found incredible strength to lift cars when their children were trapped underneath. She felt like one of those mothers, the adrenaline surging through her veins.

Except there was no car.

No trapped child.

At least those mothers knew what to do: Lift. Car. It was simple. It made sense.

Okay. So she had to make her situation simple. Get rid of all extraneous information. Her mind narrowed. Emotion drained out of her. The colors around her became dull. The noises muted. She had become a Mommy Machine. A force not to be crossed.

She looked from face to face at all the people in her kitchen as if they were strangers. Her head was clear. She was aware of every molecule of air in her lungs going in and out, in and out. Her voice came out remarkably calm.

To Annie: "You stashed Tay's money in my basement?"

"And it's gone."

Lizzie felt her gaze narrow.

"I didn't know Paige knew it was there. I swear," Annie said.

Lizzie's stare was a laser beam.

"I was going to tell you," Annie mumbled.

Lizzie had heard enough.

Candy looked shocked to her toes.

Lizzie felt no emotion at all. She was pure logic. She had to follow the trail to its rational conclusion, not hesitating at emotional crossroads.

She turned to Tommy. "You didn't know about the money."

"I thought Annie had found a thousand dollars. Which I thought we had thrown away to seal our relationship." His voice became hard. "I was obviously mistaken."

"Drive me to New York City. To JFK," Lizzie told Tommy.

"I'm coming with you," Annie said.

Lizzie shook her head. "You're staying here in case it's all not true and Paige didn't get on the bus. We have to consider that. I'm going upstairs to get dressed. When I come back down, Tommy, we go."

"Yes, ma'am."

Tay was invisible. She had dismissed him as useless.

He couldn't exactly blame her.

All around him, everyone buzzed with activity.

Even White seemed to have picked up on the vibe. She rubbed against his legs and mewed at him. "Get lost, girl. I'm so not in the mood."

He could hear Lizzie upstairs in her bedroom, moving around frantically. If he raced upstairs after her to plead his case, he'd be an even bigger ass than she already thought he was. She had more important problems on her plate than listening to him try to explain why he loved her and needed her and needed to make this right.

He couldn't drive her to New York. It would take a week.

White rubbed against him, more insistent than usual. "Take it easy, girl. It's okay. I didn't mean it. Stay. You're kind of all I have left." He scooped her up and rubbed her neck.

White rubbed her wet nose against his face, then pushed her paws against his chest and mewed.

"What?" He put her down.

She raced to the front door.

He followed her into the living room. "You need to go do some hunting? Sorry, birds are off-limits here. I can't let you out. You know that."

White continued to mew and paw at the door.

"Lizzie likes birds. I mean, likes them alive. I know, it's not the kind of thing you can understand. Settle down."

But White wouldn't settle, and Tay started to get agitated, too. "Are we having a Lassie moment? Is there some danger you want to show me? Is Old Man Lewis at the bottom of the well?"

Despite his better judgment, Tay opened the door. White slid out, then started off down the sidewalk like a person with a bus to catch. Tay wouldn't have been the least bit surprised if she pulled out a tiny kitty pocket watch to check the time.

Tay went out onto the porch and watched her go.

Wait. What was going on here? Did she want him to follow her to Old Man Lewis?

It was ridiculous, but he jumped down the porch steps anyway and started after the cat.

She turned and fixed him with her yellow eyes as if to say, *Do the right thing and back off, mister.* Then she swung her head around and kept walking. Tay watched her. She reached the corner, then, without hesitation, disappeared around it.

A curious feeling came over him.

He felt light.

I do not believe in signs.

He looked up to Lizzie's room. The light was out.

She and Tommy came onto the porch. Annie was behind them, looking miserable. Candy came out, too, keeping to the shadows.

Tay looked down the street where White had disappeared.

I've been forgiven. The cat has finally left the building.

Tay stepped in front of Tommy and Lizzie as they came down the walk. "I'm driving," he said.

"We're in a hurry, Tay," Lizzie said. "I don't think you'll do." She stepped past him.

He grabbed her arm. "I'm driving, Lizzie. Tommy is staying here to be with Annie. She needs him. Let's go. There's no time to talk about this. I know JFK like the back of my hand. I can get us there quicker."

"No offense, Tay, but you can't drive to save your life."

"Get in the truck, Lizzie. For your sister's sake. For Tommy's sake. And most of all, for Paige's sake. I swear to you, I'm going to drive."

CHAPTER

54

$\mathcal{F}$or the first time since she'd gotten back from the ski slope, Lizzie looked at her sister. Really looked. Annie's face was red and tear-streaked. The beautiful baby on Annie's hip played with her mommy's ear as if nothing was wrong in the world. Poor helpless kid had no idea. Tommy stood between her and Annie, frozen. He didn't know which way to go. Someone had to tell Annie's galoot of a husband which way to go. He had to stop coming with her. Especially right now, when Annie was so upset.

Lizzie had to stop counting on her brother-in-law.

Right now.

She had to start counting on Tay. But she couldn't.

Lizzie looked at Tay. "You're going to drive fast?"

"I am. I swear."

She wanted to believe him. But how could she after what she'd just seen? "Tommy, can I take your car? I can drive myself," Lizzie said.

They all looked to the police car in front of the house. "Oh, Liz. I don't know."

"I could go home and get the Toyota for you," Annie offered.

Tay stepped in front of Lizzie. "You're in no shape to drive. You're too upset and distracted. You'll kill yourself and maybe someone else, too."

"I'll drive," Annie said.

"You're in worse shape," Tay pointed out.

"Tay. I'm sorry," Lizzie said. "I need to get to New York this week."

"I can do it."

"And I believe you because—?"

"Because you love me and you trust me," Tay said.

Lizzie looked to Candy. She nodded.

"I do?"

"Yes. And I love you and I trust you. Now stop arguing with me. Let's go. We're wasting time."

Lizzie looked from face to face.

She nodded. "Both of you, look after Candy. Call me the minute you know anything. Let's go."

They ran for Tay's truck.

"You better be able to do this," she said as they climbed inside.

"Shut up, Lizzie," Tay said. "And let me drive."

They made it to JFK in just under three hours, Tay doing eighty the whole way and feeling as if he could have gone even faster. Hell, he could have flown, he felt so good.

Tommy had called ahead to airport security, and a man in a uniform met them at the curb at the International Departures terminal.

He put something official-looking on the car's windshield, then ushered them through the airport lobby, flashing his badge as they went. "We found her waiting for a flight to Geneva," the guard told them. "She had a ticket and passport and everything."

"Would they have let a kid alone on a plane?" Lizzie asked.

"Not supposed to. But sometimes things get by. Especially with a smart kid like that." He led them through a door and down endless hallways to a small room. "There she is. Take your time." The guard motioned to a door.

Lizzie looked through the glass. Paige looked up, saw her, then looked back down. Her snowboard was next to her, an enormous blue duffel bag at her feet.

"You go in," Tay said. "And Lizzie, be a little proud of her. She's not afraid of anything. She did it herself, just like you taught her."

Tay waited in the hallway while Lizzie went into the small room. It was painted industrial gray with metal folding chairs, just the way Lizzie imagined an airport holding pen for international drug dealers would look.

"Hi," Lizzie said. She sat down next to Paige.

"I wanted to go to the Alps," Paige said. "I didn't need him. I was going to do it myself. That's what you wanted, right? That's what you taught me. To do it myself. I had it all worked out."

Lizzie put her arm around Paige. "Let's go home."

Paige started to cry. "I don't want to go home. I want to go after my dream."

"I know, honey. I know. And you will. Nothing is ever, ever going to stop you because you know exactly what you want and believe me, that is so important. You just have to be patient."

"Is that what you were? Patient? Mom, I don't want to be like you." She looked up at Lizzie quickly. "Sorry."

Lizzie looked up to the fluorescent light vibrating on the ceiling and took a deep breath. "Come home and we'll talk there."

"I could have done it."

"I know. You still can. Just not now. Not with Tay's money."

"Money?" Paige looked confused.

"Maybe sometime soon, you and me can go together. Take our passports and go to Geneva and find that rat-bastard Ethan ourselves."

"Really?"

"Yeah. Sure. Why not? We're not the kind of women who sit around and wait for men. We'll find him and demand that he be a better father and give you money to snowboard at the best places in the world."

"But I thought you didn't want anyone's help."

"I was wrong. Sometimes, going it alone is just plain stupid. It can really mess a person up."

"I'd have to go to Japan if I was serious about boarding. The best boarding is there, too."

"I like sushi."

"You've never had sushi."

"I could start."

Paige stood up. "You're really going to take me to Geneva? How?"

"With the money I saved for your college. You really don't want college, then we'll use some of it—not all of it, but a little bit of it—to find your father and kick his butt." Lizzie picked up the duffel bag. "Is the money in here?"

Paige looked at her mother. "What money?"

"The money. From the basement."

"I don't know what you're talking about."

"Come on, Paige. We know you know about the money Aunt Annie hid."

"The money in the laundry chute? I knew about that money. But then someone moved it. I looked everywhere, but I couldn't ever find it again. All I took was a thousand dollars. I swear. Just enough to buy some equipment and pay Aidan and Ben and Paul for doing our walk." She looked down sheepishly. "I thought it was the money you were saving for me so I thought it was okay to take a little."

"You thought I was saving your money in the laundry chute?"

"I don't know. It made sense at the time."

"You really don't have the rest of it?"

"No. I don't. I sort of used your credit card to buy the tickets and stuff."

Lizzie felt relieved that Paige had only stolen from her—except for the thousand dollars. But then, where was the money? "Were you really going to get on that plane, Paige?"

"Yep."

That's my girl! "I would have killed you."

"You would have left Galton and gotten to see Europe."

"Paige, you are so grounded."

"I love you, Mom. I'm sorry I scared you." Paige started to cry.

"I love you, too. Or at least, I will, once we get home and I regain consciousness."

"I'm sorry."

Lizzie put her arm around Paige. "I know, honey. I know. I'm sorry, too. C'mon. Let's get home."

Tay drove them home at the speed limit, maybe just a bit below. Paige slept the entire way.

"Thank you, Tay," Lizzie said. "You did it."

"You did it," he said. "I'm just along for the ride. Lizzie—" He stared at the road ahead. "If you'll have me, I'd like to try to stay. I don't know if I can. But I want to try."

"Really?" Despite herself, her heart leaped with hope.

He snuck a look at her and she saw how doubtful he still was. "I apologized to Candy. Remember when I said words don't matter? They do. She said she forgave me, and it felt like Christmas. So, I'm thinking I'll hang around a bit. See if it sticks."

"Good," she said. "Trying is good. Even just for a little while."

When they got back to the house, a broken-down Volvo was parked outside behind Tommy's cruiser.

Annie came out on the porch, a funny look on her face.

"No," Lizzie said, ushering a sleepy Paige inside.

"Yep," Annie said.

Tay came up behind them. Lizzie felt as if they formed a solid family, the three of them standing there, together.

A man came out of the living room.

"Oh, my God." Lizzie could hardly breathe. She recognized him in an instant, even though he was almost bald

and very, very tan. He wore a pair of ripped jeans and a
faded T-shirt under an argyle button-down sweater. His
arms were covered in tattoos. His lower lip was pierced.
He was thin in a graceful, athlete's way.

"Hi. I'm Ethan Pond," he said. "Sorry I'm late."

CHAPTER

55

*D*espite how odd it had felt, Lizzie had set Ethan up in the second spare bedroom, next to Candy. They'd all been too exhausted to do much talking.

Now, the next morning, Ethan wouldn't stop talking. They were in the dining room, Ethan looking out the window at Lizzie's bird feeders, Lizzie looking at Ethan, still amazed that he was actually here.

He was telling her how he'd missed his flight in Geneva. Then, the friend of a friend who was supposed to pick him up at the airport in New York hadn't shown and he'd taken two buses and the wrong subway, but had finally gotten to the man's house in the East Village. He had planned to borrow the man's old Volvo, but it took awhile to fix the flat and then replace a few faulty spark plugs.

As he went on and on about his misadventures, Lizzie studied him. He was nothing like what she expected or remembered. He had moved on from talking about fixing cars to the excellent hamburger he'd had at an exit off Interstate 80, while she listened in amazement.

Paige was still asleep upstairs, but Lizzie wished she was awake to hear her father's excitement to be back in "the States," as he called it.

He started in on the story of his life after he'd left Galton. "So I only stayed at Oxford for a semester. I was too restless, as you probably remember. Couldn't stay put. Later I found out I had ADD, so that was what was wrong with me. But back then, I didn't know why I was so scattered. So it wasn't just me and you that didn't work out, it was me and everything. Holy cow—a flock of robins. I forgot how they flock in the winters up here. Look at them! I can't believe you still live in this house, in Galton. Anyway, I went to Europe and to India and I climbed Everest. I know, it was nuts. But I did and it changed my life. I guess you could call me a ski bum now. I just want to be one with nature, with the universe."

Something thumped on the stairs.

"Paige?" Lizzie said. "I know you're there, why don't you just come in and talk to your dad?" It still hurt to say that word, but now that she saw Ethan with all his flaws, she had to relent. She couldn't remember why she'd been so sure that he'd be perfect and she'd be ashamed of her life.

Paige came shyly into the room. She was never shy, and Lizzie tried not to smile.

Lizzie did her best to facilitate the conversation, but it kept skittering to a halt. "So, skiing, huh? Paige, you're—"

"—not a skier," she said, as if skiers were the worst humans on the planet, on par with child abusers.

"Snowboarder," Lizzie corrected.

"Awesome," Ethan said. "I board, too. But not so good."

Paige rolled her eyes. "Well," she said.

He looked puzzled.

"You don't board so *well*."

Ethan ignored her criticism. "We have got to hit the slopes together. The hills aren't high, but snow here is awesome. I loved Meeks Peak when I was in school here," Ethan said.

"It's not exactly the Alps," Paige said, turning a little red.

"No. Not exactly. But I like it here better," Ethan said. Paige's eyes lit up with pride and Lizzie felt a wave of happiness wash over her.

"I was actually kind of thinking of staying here," Ethan said.

"Staying!" Lizzie and Paige said together.

"Here?" Lizzie asked. Lizzie tried not to jump up and hug him. She could keep Paige close, even if Paige decided to be with her father.

Ethan said, "We could get to know each other better here. Don't you think?"

"And by here, you don't mean this house, obviously," Lizzie said, suddenly concerned. His clothes were ripped and the car he was driving was almost as bad as her own dead heap of junk in the driveway. Surely, the man wasn't looking for a handout?

Later, when Ethan was in the shower, Paige said to Lizzie, "We did all that work on the house for nothing."

"Not for nothing. Now our house looks great."

"And he didn't even care," Paige groused. "This all makes you happy, doesn't it?"

"A tiny bit. But only because I love you and I want you near. I'm not sorry that you're not leaving for Geneva any time soon."

"You would really have let me go?" Paige asked.

"Maybe not right away. But if Ethan was okay, maybe after a while. How could I not?" Lizzie smiled.

"You can't stop smiling, Mom. It's sickening."

"I'm smiling because you were right all along, Paige. The universe heard my wish and it listened. My wish was that you would stay."

"Well, that wasn't my wish."

"Maybe your wish comes soon," Lizzie said, hugging Paige to her until she managed to escape. "The universe has to take care of us old folks first." She studied her beautiful daughter. "What do you think of him?"

"Well, he's not what I expected," Paige allowed. "But I think we'll get along okay. Just so long as he doesn't make me ski."

CHAPTER

56

*M*om! Tay's here!" Paige called up the stairs. It was her first day back to school after the holiday break. Candy had gone back to her dorm room yesterday, and except for Ethan in a hotel room at the Galton Marriott and a missing two hundred thousand dollars, the world was feeling back to its old routines.

Lizzie looked out her bedroom window, her heart fluttering. Tay had been keeping his distance since Ethan had reappeared, so she was surprised to see the bottom half of him sticking out from under the hood of her old, dead Toyota in the driveway. Dune sat at the toolbox by his feet.

She tried to control her excitement at seeing him. They still hadn't talked about the money or what had happened to it. They hadn't talked about what had happened on the road to New York. Or on the way back.

"Bye, I'm gone!" Paige sang. "Have fun, you two."

"It's too early for the bus," Lizzie said, suddenly not wanting to be alone with Tay. What if he had come back to tell her he was leaving?

"Dad's taking me," Paige said.

A horn honked. Lizzie came downstairs and there was Ethan outside waiting in his Volvo. He honked again and she cringed. Was he trying to summon Judy Roth to witness this new wrinkle in their odd life?

Ethan waved from the driver's seat. He and Paige had spent every minute of her last days of vacation on the slopes. Paige was trying to teach him to board. He was trying to talk her into skiing. Lizzie was thrilled that they were getting along so well. Nervous, but thrilled. It was clear that Paige and Ethan shared a love of being daredevils. And a love of the cold.

Lizzie went out onto the porch to wave good-bye, and she stopped dead.

No, it couldn't be.

But it was.

A white cat was in Ethan's car, its paws on the passenger-side door.

Tay had stopped what he was doing and was staring at the Volvo, too. He dropped his oily rag. He, Dune, Paige, and Lizzie got to the Volvo at the same time. Ethan lowered White's window. "Howdy, gang."

Lizzie was speechless.

"Nice cat," Tay said. Dune was barking with joy.

Tay reached his hand out for White, but she pulled back as if she'd never seen him before in her life.

"Isn't she a beauty? I found her last night, mewing around my car. She wouldn't take no for an answer. And I don't even like cats," Ethan explained as Paige moved the cat aside and climbed into the car. "She won't stay at the hotel. She goes nuts. So I have to take her with me everywhere."

Tay nodded. "Don't worry. At the rate you're going, I bet she'll be gone pretty soon."

Ethan looked confused.

"Ignore them, Ethan. Let's go," Paige said.

Tay and Lizzie waved as they drove off.

"How about that?"

"Hope he gets rid of the beast quicker than I did," Tay said.

Lizzie followed Tay back to her broken-down car. She had come outside without a coat, and the cold air was biting through her fleece nightshirt. "What are you doing?" she asked. It was too cold to be outside, working on a car. She wrapped her arms around herself.

"I think it's about time you had your own car," he said. He took off his jacket and wrapped it around her shoulders. "Stop relying on everyone like you always do."

"I rely on no one," she began, until she realized that he was teasing her. She pulled his coat tight around her, inhaling his aroma, which warmed her even more than the coat. "So are you fixing my car because you're leaving and you feel sorry for me?"

"Nope. I'm doing this because I'm staying."

"Tay! Really? Why?"

"Because you love me." He came to her. "And I love you. So we'll forgive each other and it'll all work out if we make the effort to stick around and keep on working stuff out. That's what people who love each other do. In fact, that's what people do in general. If you don't you end up all alone, thinking that you're perfect and everyone else sucks when really, we're all just careening around, out of control, trying to do as little damage as we can. Some of us get lucky, others not. You can't take life personally. So let's get on with it." He slid his hands under the coat and pulled her to him.

His words hung in the air between them. "What happened to the shaking, sweating guy I left freezing by his truck in the middle of that accident scene on a snowy road on the way to Meeks Peak? What happened to the guy who was terrified of Candy?"

"You liked that guy?" He pulled her closer and let his lips brush her cheek.

"He was kind of cute, actually," she said, closing her eyes, enjoying the warmth of his breath as he held her close.

"Well, he split along with White. It's a long story. Took months. Wanna hear it?"

"No. It's too cold out here," she said. But she didn't move. "What? Why are you looking at me like that?"

"Nothing. You're just beautiful, that's all. I'm glad that everything worked out okay with Paige and Ethan."

"It did. And Annie and Tommy made up, too. You were right. They needed to be together, without me muddling things up with all my problems. If we found your money, things would be perfect."

"I love you, Lizzie Carpenter. Even with all your muddling problems." He nuzzled her neck, kissed her earlobe, bit her lower lip.

"Come upstairs."

He let her go. "Can't. I've got to fix this car."

"Tay Giovanni. I want you to come upstairs and make love to me. Now."

"I don't know. You always say the opposite of what you mean."

"Not anymore I don't," she said. "Now I know what I want and I know how to get it. Come upstairs and get naked, Tay, or I'm going to rip your clothes off right here. And it's much too cold for that."

Tay slammed the hood, and they waved to Judy Roth and went inside.

The moment they got into the foyer, Tay knew that there wasn't a chance they were going to make it upstairs.

He backed her against the door, his lips on hers, his body pressed against her. His hands flew everywhere on her as they sank to the floor together, entwined.

"God, Lizzie." He could smell her shampoo, the oil on his hands, the wax she used to polish the wooden floors. He could taste her skin and her hair and her belly and her breasts. He felt every molecule of her and it wasn't enough. He ripped off enough of her clothes to reach what he needed to reach and somehow managed to rip off most of his, too. The floor was cold and hard and he didn't care, and from her moans, he got the impression that she didn't care much either.

"This isn't going to be gentle," he warned her.

"Good," she said. "I want to feel it. To feel you. All of you."

She smiled and he kissed her smile and spread her legs and pushed himself inside her, savoring every single sweet inch.

"Lizzie, I owe you the world," he said. Sweet Lord, she was so hot and wet and perfect. He moved inside her, and she opened herself to him.

"Lizzie?"

"Hmmm..."

"You know I never could have left you. Even if I'd tried."

• • •

When they had recovered, they went upstairs and climbed into Lizzie's bed and made love again, this time gently, slowly, and with all the care that she deserved.

"Call in sick," he said. "For the next two weeks. In fact, quit."

"I would, but my boyfriend is awfully careless with his money."

He shrugged and lay back on the pillows. "I still don't get it. Where could it be? Do you think Annie's lying?"

"No way. It's a mystery," Lizzie said. "I honestly think everyone is telling the truth. Tommy will report it next week if the mystery isn't solved. He'll open a case, start an investigation."

Tay pulled her close. "I think I'm ready to start my own investigation." He let his hands slide down her body.

"You really don't care about that money, do you?" Lizzie asked.

"Not now," he said. "Now, all I care about is you."

CHAPTER

57

Two days later, Lizzie looked out her window to see a *For Sale* sign on Judy Roth's house across the street. The agent, listed in three-inch-high red letters, was Jill Kennedy.

Lizzie stared at the sign for a long time. Then she threw on her shoes and coat and went across the street.

She didn't have to knock. Judy saw her coming from her perch behind the curtains.

"Hello, dear." Judy led her into the dark, dusty living room. It smelled moldy and musty. Lizzie realized that she hadn't been inside Judy's house since she was a kid selling Girl Scout cookies. Maybe she had just imagined it would be this way. "Sit. Please. Would you like some tea?"

Lizzie sat. "No. Thank you. So, you're leaving?" She said each word loudly, enunciating every sound so she wouldn't have to repeat herself.

"Going to the assisted-living place by the mall. It's a dump, but I thought I better get there while I can still walk in." She smiled. "No one walks out. Anyway, you don't need me anymore. I've been waiting for years for you to get yourself independent, but now that you have, my job here is done."

Lizzie wasn't sure she'd heard her right. "Your job?"

"Dear, I'm glad you came over. I have something for you."

To Lizzie's amazement, she pulled out Annie's diaper bag.

"I found this in your basement."

"You what? Where?" Lizzie unzipped the bag. It was stuffed with cash. She was in a weird dream; that was it. She'd blink and wake up any second.

"I still have your spare key, dear. Your mother gave it to me ages ago when we used to water each other's plants."

"And you—?" It was hard to form questions when there was so much cash in her lap. She tried hard not to sniff it, then gave in.

It smelled good.

"Your mother was such a dear. We were such good friends. I do miss her terribly. Your father, too, even if he was awfully quiet. Lovely man."

"So you—" Lizzie gave up. Judy Roth had lost her marbles. It happened to old people. But still: Judy Roth lurking in her basement? Stealing Tay's cash?

"I promised your mother and father that I'd keep an eye on you. Make sure you did the right thing, you know. That's why I make sure you do your leaves. That's also why I took the money from your house." She paused to sip her tea from a dainty china cup. "I always try to keep an eye on you and Annie. Of course, I didn't know what she was up to at first. I just knew that something suspicious was going down."

Did this little old gray-haired lady just say "going down"? "I think you've been watching too many police shows on television, Mrs. Roth."

"Oh, call me Judy, dear. And maybe you're right. But when I saw Annie sneak into your house that day—"

"Which day?"

"Oh, centuries ago. I don't know exactly, dear. But after she left, and your young man left, I let myself in. I looked around a bit."

Lizzie was growing exasperated. Could you throttle a senior citizen? "A bit? In my basement?" She sat on her hands.

"Oh, your mother and I used to joke about that girl stashing stuff all over the house. She was a hoarder, that one. Had a little trouble sharing, you know. Your mother told me all her best hiding spots. She used to check them for cigarettes and other teenage hijinks. I knew that if there wasn't anything in the laundry chute, then the old stereo in the basement was the next-best place to look."

"But I don't understand. Why were you looking for anything in the first place?" Lizzie noticed that she was speaking normally, and that Judy was hearing her fine.

"Annie always was up to something sneaky. I love her dearly, but I've been so worried about her since the baby. She'd been so blue." She paused and smiled. "Oh, don't look at me like I'm an alien, dear. People think I'm feebleminded because I'm old. But I'm not. I hear and see everything."

Lizzie considered all the things she'd been shouting to Judy over the years. "Oh."

"Patience Little, the head librarian, had given Annie that beautiful diaper bag. I was there the day she showed all the girls in the reading room. Annie carried it everywhere. Then, one day, after spending the evening at your house, it's gone!"

"You notice what Annie carries into and out of my house?"

"Naturally. I try to keep out of your business, but I do notice. It's so much more entertaining than solitaire."

Lizzie let out a choked sound.

"Well, when Annie started carrying around that Wal-Mart diaper bag, I just wondered and wondered what had happened to her beautiful bag. And then, that day I was telling you about, when she just snuck right in and the basement light went on and then off and then she told your nice fence gentleman that she had gone in to get a sweater, which she never got. I just had to check it out."

"And when you found the money, you just had to steal it?"

"Oh, no. I didn't steal it. I just took it for safekeeping, dear. It's all here."

Lizzie was speechless.

"So, you make sure she gives this money right back to whom it belongs. Make sure she does the right thing, dear. I can't watch out for you or Annie anymore. You're on your own now. I think you can finally handle it now that you have a nice man to help you."

"Mrs. Roth, I've been handling myself for years."

"Of course you have, dear. Of course you have. And making a mess of it, haven't you? I always suspected that you let your parents' house fall to pieces because you felt bad about having it."

"Excuse me?"

"Because you knew it came between you and Annie and you didn't feel worthy of it. But now that you're taking care of it, I feel that you understand it's yours. And you can move on with your life. I'm very proud of you, dear. Now, I love talking to you, but I do have so much straightening to do. That Jill Kennedy thinks I need to get rid of some of my cats."

Lizzie's eyes, which had been slowly adjusting to the dim light, could finally see the room around her. Every surface was covered with porcelain cats. A huge curiosity cabinet was stuffed with them. They pounced and licked and sat and slept everywhere. "I'm getting myself a real cat when I move. I always wanted one, but I didn't want to upset your birds, Lizzie."

Lizzie got up to go. The bag was heavy in her hands. She'd give it to Candy as soon as she could. "Thank you, Judy. I think. I think I also might know of a cat who needs a good home."

"Oh, lovely! And you're welcome, dear. It was the least I could do. For your dear mother, of course. I so miss her."

"So do I, Judy. Believe me, so do I."

Lizzie went home and called Tay to tell him about the money being found, but he said that Lizzie could take care of it; it had nothing to do with him anymore. So Lizzie called Candy and they met at the diner. She handed the money to a very surprised girl and explained everything as best she could.

Candy promised not to throw the money into a gorge.

She was going to use it to stay in school and to take care of her baby.

Then Lizzie went to Jill Kennedy's office. The lobby was covered in ornate Christmas decorations, a tree trimmed with tiny houses dominating the room. When Lizzie got close, she saw each house had a tiny *For Sale* sign in front with a dollar amount written on it in ornate red calligraphy. She recognized Judy Roth's house near the top.

Lizzie smiled. Not bad money.

The perky receptionist escorted her to the back. Jill was on the phone in her tiny cubicle, her red pumps up on the desk. She motioned Lizzie into the guest chair.

When she hung up, she leaned forward. "Ready to sell?" she said. "I've got room on the tree."

"Commissions. The true meaning of Christmas?"

"Exactly."

"Never. Well sort of. Here's what I want to do. I need you to tell me how."

When she had explained it all, Jill slapped her hands together as if it were already a done deal. "No problem. I'll set you up with someone good. Come on, we'll have this done in an hour, tops."

CHAPTER

58

*L*izzie knocked on Annie's door. Annie's shirt was covered with blotches of something green. "You're just in time for lunch," she said. "Mashed peas. Come in."

Lizzie followed Annie into the kitchen. She was surprisingly nervous. Meghan was in her high chair, covered in smashed peas. "Good girl. They never do smash them enough at the factory, do they?" She picked Meghan's spoon off the floor, blew on it, and put it back on the baby's tray. "I got you a late Christmas present." She handed Annie an envelope.

"What's this?" She opened it. "No. What? Lizzie!"

"Take it. I want you to have it."

Annie pulled out the check. "Two hundred thousand dollars? Did you find Tay's money?"

Lizzie shook her head. "It's half what the house is worth. I took out a mortgage."

"Why?"

"Because it wasn't right that I got everything. I'm

sorry. We should have talked about it. Should have fixed it right away."

Annie looked Lizzie right in the eye, then tore the check in two.

"What the hell?" Lizzie said.

"Hell!" Meghan cried.

"Ann, I wanted to make it right. Why'd you do that?"

"Because, dummy, didn't you learn anything? You can't make it up with money."

"Are you saying that you won't accept my apology? Annie? That's just wrong."

"I'm saying that we're already even," Annie said.

Lizzie waited for the explanation.

"You didn't get everything. I was just too big an idiot to realize it." They looked at each other across the table. "We're even. Believe me. In fact, I think I got the better side of the deal."

"Tommy?"

"Yep."

"Yeah, I think you did," Lizzie said.

"So you quit calling my husband whenever you need someone to butter your toast and I'll stop wanting *your* house and we'll be even."

"What am I going to do with all that money you won't take?" Lizzie asked. But before she had even finished forming the question she already knew the answer for what to do with at least some of it.

CHAPTER
59

*L*izzie's three worst enemies, also her three best friends, sat across the diner counter. Jill, the princess. Nina, the oddball. And Georgia, the brain. They perched in a line on their red vinyl stools just as they did every Wednesday morning, each one more joltingly out of place in the run-down greasy spoon than the next.

The Enemy Club.

Lizzie was the cofounder and, as waitress at the Last Chance diner, the host. She had been the high school bad girl, the one voted most likely to fail. Funny how back in high school, they had all assumed they would know who had failed and who had succeeded. But fifteen years after graduation, Lizzie still wasn't sure who to put her money on.

Jill the ex-cheerleader with her teenage looks, high-powered real estate job, and freezer full of Lean Cuisine that she ate every night, alone, in front of *CSI* reruns?

Or was it Nina, the oddball, with her toxin-free body, string of beautiful free-love boyfriends, and mysterious illnesses that no amount of herbal remedies seemed able to cure?

Or maybe it was Georgia, still the brainiac, with her medical degree, weekly baroque string quartet performing on period instruments, and her town-famous Deluxe Brinks Home Security monitoring system that was so sensitive it had become a tradition for the Galton U. undergrads to set it off with beer bottles tossed into her bushes?

But maybe, just maybe, Lizzie was the success story. Sure, she'd had the same job, same house—the same enemies—for her entire life. But at least she had a beautiful daughter to show for it. Lizzie was proud of Paige, proud of what she'd sacrificed for her. When all else was low, there was Paige. There was always Paige.

Until now.

"I can't believe you bankrolled Paige and Ethan Pond-scum on the world's best ski trip for spring break," Jill said. "I'm your best friend. I so could have taken her."

"Yeah, well, I think she and her father needed some time together." Lizzie shrugged.

"I think that you and your fix-it man just want more naked time together," Georgia suggested.

Lizzie blushed and shrugged.

"So they're starting in Europe?" Nina asked.

"A week in Europe, then a week in the American West. Two weeks of bonding and skiing and boarding."

"And you're here, serving coffee while they traipse around the world," Nina said.

"This is where I want to be with exactly whom I want to be with," Lizzie explained, smiling at them all. "I hate skiing. I hate the cold."

"You are such a loser," Georgia said, blushing slightly.

"I know. But that's why you guys love me, right?"

"Best enemies forever," Nina said.

Mr. Zinelli slid onto a stool at the far end of the counter. Lizzie plated his chocolate doughnut and brought it to him.

"How's your young man?" Mr. Zinelli asked.

"He asked me to marry him," Lizzie said as casually as she could. But loudly, so everyone could hear.

They were all silent for a split second, till they all squealed at once.

Lizzie came back down the counter. She pulled the tiniest diamond ring any of them had ever seen out of her apron and slipped it on her finger. "So I expect you all to be my maids of honor."

"We'd be honored," Jill said.

And they all agreed.

Two strangers.
One powerful romance.

Please turn this page
for a preview of
the touching novel

*Sweet Kiss
of Summer*

Available July 2011.

CHAPTER
1

My Dearest Sis,

You don't recognize this handwriting because a beautiful nurse named Sally is writing this letter for me. I don't think I'm going to make it, Nins. That's okay. Hell, if I don't pull through, I died fighting the good fight and I'm damned proud. You should be, too. So no moping around and getting sad. If I don't make it home, remember I died doing what I love for the country I love.

But Nins, you know I'm going to milk this.

Here goes: There's two things you've gotta do for me.

First, remember how after Mom and Dad passed, we promised each other we'd move on and not let them being gone stop us? So, here we go again, huh? You gotta move on. Find a good guy. Start a family. And name your first son after me. Promise me that. Little Walt, NO MATTER HOW MUCH

YOU HATE THE NAME. (Ha! See, I still get to be the boss even after I'm gone.) I want a little Walter in five years. Ready—GO!

Second, I wanna do something for a buddy. His name is Mick Rivers. Listen, I want him to have my house back in Galton when he gets out of here. He says I should go *#$% myself, but Nins, can you make it happen? It's all I've got to give besides the insurance and whatever else the army gives (which is all yours, buddy—promise me you'll do something fun).

Nins, this is important. I don't want to get all mushy on you, but listen: If there's one thing I learned in this mess over here, it's that people can surprise you if you let them. Let them.

Thanks, sis. I'll see you on the other side, baby. I miss you already.

Tell Sylvie and Roe I'll see them on the other side, too.

Wish I had eight more lives like them, huh?

Private Walton Stokes, U.S. Army

CHAPTER
2

Five years later

Nina Stokes was in her garden searching her tomato cages for the perfect beefsteak when a red car roared into her driveway. No one in his right mind would drive such a low-to-the-ground sporty contraption in hilly Galton, New York, where the snow started in October and lasted until April. Now it was mid-August, the season of gorgeous tomatoes and rich Galton University students getting lost in their hopped-up city cars on their way to their dorms. The kid in the car was surely using her drive as a turnaround. Happened all the time, since her house was the first drive on the first road that was clearly marked as leading out of town.

Nina went back to her quest, ripping out the hairy galinsoga that was creeping into the cages. She was illustrating a cookbook, *The Vegetable Virgin,* and the right tomato to nestle next to the green beans for the Italian casserole was essential.

But the car didn't turn around. It pulled all the way to the top of the long drive, went an extra two feet onto the grass, and stopped.

The crazy-loud engine revved a few times, then cut.

The driver's door of the car opened.

A man unfolded from the front seat, a flash from his sunglasses blinding her.

He stretched his arms above his head as if just waking up from a truly excellent dream.

Nina put a hand on a tomato cage to steady herself. *Talk about beefsteak.*

She swallowed. Adjusted the straw sunhat on her head. When had it gotten so hot out here?

He pulled his T-shirt over his head in a swift, one-armed movement.

She dropped her trowel.

Yes. Sure. Now? Why not? In the garden? Hell, let me just pull out these pesky tomatoes to make more room…

Then he turned to lean into the open driver's window of his car and she saw the tattoo on his shoulder. A downward-pointing Bowie knife with a flowing white ribbon wrapped around it. She couldn't read the words on the ribbon from this distance, but she knew them by heart. They had been etched into her brother's arm, too.

Judge a man by the company he keeps.

Nina's body went cold with dread.

He could be anyone.

He might not be Mick Rivers. Sure, she'd seen the guy's picture a million times. But military men all looked alike from a distance. The close-cropped hair, the square jaws, the perfect bodies. He could be anyone from Walt's unit who just happened to be passing through and remembered this was Walt's hometown. It had happened before. This guy probably had stopped in at the diner and asked Lizzie if she knew whether a Nina Stokes was still living nearby because he wanted to drop off a memento of Walt he had saved all these years. A picture, a letter, a cigarette lighter. Lizzie would have given him her address in a heartbeat. She was a sucker for military men. When Nina went inside, there'd be five messages on the machine with Lizzie's hysterical warnings that a man was coming and Nina'd better put on some lipstick because *oh what a man...*

Anyway, Mick Rivers wouldn't dare drive up her driveway after five years of silence without a phone call or letter first. Not after she'd done so much to try to contact him.

The man dug around in his car, then came up with another T-shirt slightly less rumpled than the first.

If there's one thing I learned in this mess over here, it's that people can surprise you if you let them.

Surprise!

The man looked around, but his eyes glazed right over the garden. Nina had that power, to be invisible to men. It was like a superpower, Nina Stokes, *Invisible Woman.* Too bad she couldn't harness it to save the world.

Or even save herself.

Because if this guy was Mick Rivers and he had come for Walt's house, where she'd been living for the last four years, there wasn't a thing Nina would do to try to stop him.

THE DISH

Where authors give you the inside scoop!

From the desk of Vicky Dreiling

Dear Reader,

The idea for HOW TO MARRY A DUKE came about purely by chance. One fateful evening while surfing 800+ channels on TV, I happened upon a reality show featuring a hunky bachelor and twenty-five beauties competing for his heart. As I watched the antics, a story idea popped into my head: the bachelor in Regency England (minus the hot tub and camera crew). The call to this writing adventure proved too irresistible to ignore.

During the planning stages of the book, I encountered numerous obstacles. Even the language presented challenges that meant creating substitutes such as *bridal candidates* for *bachelorettes*. Obviously, I needed to concoct alternatives to steamy smooching in the hot tub and overnight dates. But regardless of the century, some things never change. I figured catfights were fair game.

Before I could plunge into the writing, I had to figure out who the hero and heroine were. I picked up my imaginary remote control and surfed until I found Miss Tessa Mansfield, a wealthy, independent young woman with a penchant for matchmaking. In the short preview, she revealed that she only made love matches for all the ignored wallflowers. She, however, had no intention of ever marrying. By now I was on the edge of my seat. "Why?" I asked.

The preview ended, leaving me desperate to find out more. So I changed the metaphorical channel and nearly swooned at my first glimpse of Tristan Gatewick, the Duke of Shelbourne. England's Most Eligible Bachelor turned out to be the yummiest man I'd ever beheld. Evidently I wasn't alone in my ardent appreciation. Every eligible belle in the Beau Monde was vying to win his heart.

To my utter astonishment, Tristan slapped a newspaper on his desk and addressed me. "Madam, I am not amused with your ridiculous plot. Duty is the only reason I seek a wife, but you have made me the subject du jour in the scandal sheets. How the devil can I find a sensible bride when every witless female in Britain is chasing me?"

I smiled at him. "Actually, I know someone who can help you."

He scoffed.

I thought better of telling him he was about to meet his match.

Cheers!

Vicky Dreiling

♥ ♥ ♥ ♥ ♥ ♥ ♥ ♥ ♥ ♥ ♥ ♥ ♥ ♥ ♥

From the desk of Carolyn Jewel

Dear Reader,

Revenge, as they say, is a dish best served cold. If you wait a bit before getting your payback, if you're calm and rational, you'll be in a better position to enjoy that sweet revenge. The downside, of course, is what can happen to you while you spend all this time plotting and planning. Some emotions shouldn't be left to fester in your soul.

Gray Spencer is a woman looking to serve up revenge while the embers are still glowing. She has reason. She does. Her normal, everyday life got derailed by a mage—a human who can do magic. Christophe dit Menart is a powerful mage with a few hundred years of living on her. Because of him, her life has been destroyed. Not just *her* life, but also the lives of her sister and parents.

After she gets her freedom at a terrible cost, the only thing Gray wants is Christophe dit Menart dead for what he did—before he does the same horrific thing to someone else that he did to her.

I know what you're thinking and you're right. A normal, nonmagical human like Gray can't hope to go up against someone like Christophe. But Gray's not normal—not anymore. She escaped because a demon gave his life for her and in the process transferred his magic to her. If she had any idea how to use that magic, she might have a chance against Christophe. Maybe.

The demon warlord Nikodemus has negotiated a

shaky peace agreement between the magekind and the demonkind. (Did I mention them? They are fiends, a kind of demon. And they don't take kindly to the mages who kill them in order to extend their miserable magic-using human lives by stealing a demon's life force.) Because of the peace, demons in Nikodemus's territory have agreed not to harm the magekind. In return, the magekind aren't supposed to kill any more demons.

Basically the problem is this: Gray intends to kill Christophe, and the demon warlord's most feared assassin has to make sure that doesn't happen.

Uh-oh.

After all that, I have what may seem like a strange confession to make about my assassin hero who is, after all, a wee bit scary at times. He's been alive for a long, long time, and for much of that time, women lived very restricted lives. Sometimes he is completely flummoxed by these modern women. It was a lot of fun writing a hero like that, and I hope you enjoy reading about how Christophe learns to deal with Gray as much as I enjoyed writing about it.

Yours Sincerely,

Carolyn Jewel

http://www.carolynjewel.com

♥ ♥ ♥ ♥ ♥ ♥ ♥ ♥ ♥ ♥ ♥ ♥ ♥ ♥

From the desk of Sophie Gunn

Dear Reader,

After years of living in upstate New York, my husband got a new job and we moved back to my small hometown outside Philadelphia. I was thrilled to be near my parents, brothers, aunts, uncles, and cousins. (Hi, Aunt Lillian!) But I didn't anticipate how close I would be to quite a few of my former high school classmates. Didn't anyone ever leave this town? My life had turned into a nonstop high school reunion.

And I was definitely still wearing the wrong dress.

One by one, I encountered my former "enemies" from high school. They were at the gym, the grocery store, and the elementary school bake sale. It didn't take long to realize two things. First, we had a blast rehashing the past. What had really happened at that eleventh-grade dance? What had become of Joey, the handsome captain of the football team? (Surprise, there he is now. Yes, he's the one walking that tiny toy poodle on a pink, blinged-up leash!) Second, we were still terrifically different people, *and it didn't matter*. We were grown-ups, and what someone wore or whom they dated didn't feel so crucial anymore.

Cups of coffee led to glasses of wine, which led to true friendship. But friendship that was different from any I'd ever known, because while we shared a past, our presents were still radically different. My husband started to jokingly call us the Enemy Club, and it stuck.

That was what we writers call an *aha moment*.

The Enemy Club would make a great book. Actually, a great series . . .

The rest, as they say, is history. Each book of the Enemy Club series is set in small-town Galton, New York. Four friends who had been the worst of enemies are now the best of friends, struggling to help one another juggle jobs, kids, love, heartbreak, and triumph as seen from their very (very!) different points of view.

HOW SWEET IT IS is the first book in the series. It focuses on Lizzie, the good girl gone bad. She made one mistake her senior year of high school that changed her life forever. Now she and her teenage daughter get by just fine, thank you very much, with a little help from the Enemy Club. But then Lizzie's first love, the father who abandoned her daughter fourteen years before, decides to come back to town on Christmas Day. Lizzie imagines her life as seen through his eyes—and she doesn't like what she sees. She has the same job, same house, same every-thing as when he left fourteen years earlier. She vows to make a change. But how much is she willing to risk? And does the mysterious stranger, who shows up in town prom-ising to grant her every wish, have the answers? Or is he just another of life's sweet, sweet mistakes?

I'm really excited about these books, because they're so close to my heart. Come visit me at www.sophiegunn.com to read an excerpt of HOW SWEET IT IS, to find out more about the Enemy Club, to see pictures of my cats, and to keep in touch. I'd love to hear from you!

Yours,

Sophie Gunn

♥ ♥ ♥ ♥ ♥ ♥ ♥ ♥ ♥ ♥ ♥ ♥ ♥ ♥ ♥

From the desk of Sue-Ellen Welfonder

Dear Reader,

Wild, heather-clad hills, empty glens, and the skirl of pipes stir the hearts of many. Female hearts beat fast at the flash of plaid. Yet I've seen grown men shed tears at the beauty of a Highland sunset. So many people love Scotland, and those of us who do know that our passion is a double-edged sword. We live with a constant ache to be there. It's a soul-deep yearning known as "the pull."

In SINS OF A HIGHLAND DEVIL, the first book in my new Highland Warriors trilogy, I wanted to explore the fierce attachment Highlanders feel for their home glen. Love that burns so hotly, they'll even lay down their lives to hold on to the hills so dear to them.

James Cameron and Catriona MacDonald, hero and heroine of SINS OF A HIGHLAND DEVIL, are bitter foes. Divided by centuries of clan feuds, strife, and rivalries, they share a fiery passion for the glen they each claim as their own. When a king's writ threatens banishment, long-held boundaries blur and forbidden desires are unleashed. James and Catriona soon discover there is much pleasure to be found in each other's embrace. But the price of their yearning must be paid in blood, and the battle facing them could shatter their world.

Fortunately, true love can prove a more powerful weapon than any warrior's sword.

There are a lot of swords in this story. And the fight

scenes are fierce. But passions flare when blood is spilled as James and Catriona showed me each day during the writing of their tale.

It was an exhilarating journey.

Catriona is a strong heroine who will brave any danger to protect her home and to win the heart of the man she never believed could be hers. James is a hardened warrior and proud clan leader, and he faces his greatest challenge when his beloved glen is threatened.

Because SINS OF A HIGHLAND DEVIL is a romance, James and Catriona are triumphant. Their ending is a happy one. Numberless Highlanders after them weren't as blessed. Later centuries saw the Clearances, while famine and other hardships did the rest. Clans were scattered, banished from their glens and hills as they were forced to sail to distant shores. Their hearts were irrevocably broken. But they kept their deep love of the land, their proud Celtic roots remaining true no matter where they settled.

Their forever yearning for home still beats in the heart of everyone with even a drop of Scottish blood. It's the reason we feel "the pull."

I hope you'll enjoy reading how James's and Catriona's passion for their glen rewards them with a love more wondrous than their wildest dreams.

With all good wishes,

Sue-Ellen Welfonder

www.welfonder.com

Want to know more about romances at Grand Central Publishing and Forever? Get the scoop online!

GRAND CENTRAL PUBLISHING'S ROMANCE HOMEPAGE

Visit us at www.hachettebookgroup.com/romance for all the latest news, reviews, and chapter excerpts!

NEW AND UPCOMING TITLES

Each month we feature our new titles and reader favorites.

CONTESTS AND GIVEAWAYS

We give away galleys, autographed copies, and all kinds of fun stuff.

AUTHOR INFO

You'll find bios, articles, and links to personal websites for all your favorite authors—and so much more!

THE BUZZ

Sign up for our monthly romance newsletter, and be the first to read all about it!